Modern Scandinavian
Literature in Translation
MSLT

Previously published:
Winter's Child
by Dea Trier Mørch
Afterword by Verne Moberg

CHILDREN'S ISLAND

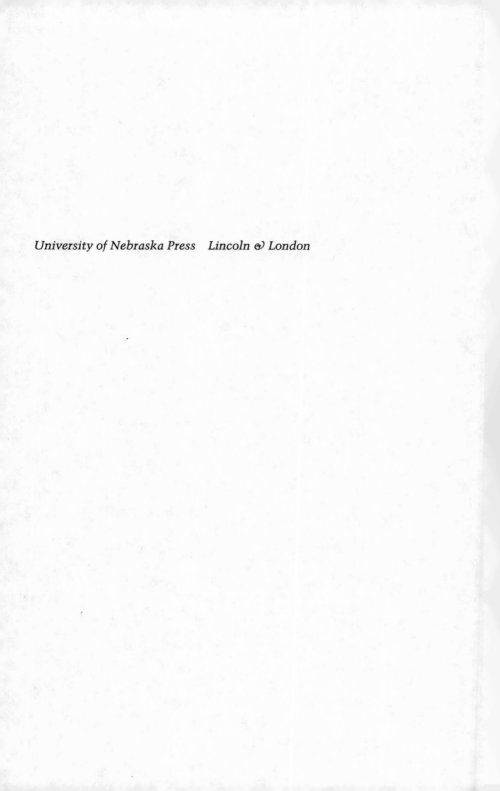

University of Nebraska Press   Lincoln & London

Barnens Ö   Translated by Joan Tate

P. C. JERSILD

Afterword by Ross Shideler

children's Island

First published by Bonniers as **Barnens Ö**,
Copyright © 1976 by P. C. Jersild
Translation copyright 1986 by Joan Tate
Afterword copyright 1986 by the University
of Nebraska Press   All rights reserved
Manufactured in the United States of America
The paper in this book meets the minimum
requirements of American National Standard
for Information Sciences – Perma-
nence of Paper for Printed Library Materials,
ANSI Z39.48-1948.
Library of Congress Cataloging-in-Publication
Data
Jersild, P. C. (Per Christian), 1935-
Children's island = (Barnens ö).
(Modern Scandinavian literature in translation
series)
"A Jersild bibliography": p.
I. Title.   II. Title: Barnens ö.   III. Series.
PT9876.2.E7B313   1986   839.7'374   86-1396
ISBN 0-8032-2569-5 (alkaline paper)

CONTENTS

CHILDREN'S ISLAND

1 The alarm started clicking at a quarter to six. After it had clicked a few times, there was a series of short rings. Reine turned it off. He had been awake for a long time, packed, dressed, fallen asleep again for brief spells, then woke up again at about half-past five. He threw off the sheet and got out of bed, fully dressed in jeans, yellow T-shirt and sneakers with their too long laces. Today he was to go to Children's Island.

He went in to Mom, who was lying snoring away in her hide-a-bed, one naked freckled leg sticking out. There were several open, half-packed suitcases in the room, and dresses and blouses on hangers here and there round the room, on the curtain-rod, on the ceiling light, on the handle of the balcony door. Mom was going away, too, though in the other direction—west to Uddevalla. But her train didn't leave until half-past ten. What if he didn't wake her? If he didn't, she would probably sleep till dusk.

He went out into the kitchen and glanced at the breakfast table he had set sometime between two and three o'clock. Hell, he felt like throwing up at the sight of the cereal box. Porridge, he thought next, his stomach turning over like a seal inside him. Porridge. That's what they gave kids at Children's Island. He had a triple pack of coconut balls in the refrigerator. He took them out onto the balcony and sat down in a deck chair. He tried to swallow the coconut balls whole, but failed. The shreds of coconut got stuck like barbs.

If he let Mom sleep on until the last minute, maybe she wouldn't suggest going with him to the Central Station to see him onto the bus to Children's Island. He wanted to cope on his own. That was the last thing he'd said the night before: if you're practically eleven, *actually* you can go by commuter train yourself. And transfer to the bus at the Central Station. He went back to the refrigerator and drank some of the apple juice he had been given for the bus trip, together with the coconut balls.

Until ten minutes to seven, he sat on the balcony reading here and there in a fine old Donald Duck, vintage 1962, to be exact. He went back in to Mom.

"Wake up!" he said, tugging at her protruding foot.

"Not now . . . ," she mumbled, rolling over toward the wall.

"It's ten to seven."

She sat up hastily and turned to look at the sun out there, as if not trusting the clock. Then she resolutely got out of bed and tottered over to the telephone.

"I'll call a cab. We still have time."

Reine hadn't reckoned with that. A cab! That had to be stopped at any price. He went over and grabbed her elbow.

"The train doesn't leave for another twenty-five minutes. I've got time. Easy."

"You?"

"You don't have to come with me."

"Hullo?" said Mom into the receiver. "Hullo?"

She put the receiver down, having clearly made no contact. In a flash, she was splashing about in the bathroom. Water always rushed out of various faucets when Mom was in the bathroom. Didn't she ever sit down and think? Reine carried his suitcase out into the hall. Everything was fastened and ready. He took a tour around the kitchen and put the kettle on for tea.

While Mom was washing, he got up on a chair and sorted through the Donald Duck comic books on the closet shelf. He closed the door again and stuck a tiny piece of scotch tape over one hinge. No creep could get in now without being exposed.

"The plants!" cried Mom from her room. "I won't have time."

He went into her room and started making her bed in order to calm her down a little.

"I can go by myself," he said.

"But I must see my little boy off at the station. We won't be seeing each other for two months!"

"I've got tea ready for you. You can have it in peace and quiet when I've gone."

Tears came into her eyes, and she gave him a hug.

"I'll go with you to the train, anyhow."

"That's good of you," he said. "That's nice."

Mom went with him to the commuter train, sleepily lugging his suitcase along. They arrived too early and had to wait, but they had nothing more to say to each other. Mom yawned, then took out her wallet and gave him a ten-*kronor* note to add to the one he had already. Reine felt enormously relieved when the train came in.

He sat in the car and looked at Mom standing a foot or so from him on the other side of the window, and he waved eagerly, nodding encouragingly to her. She said something he couldn't hear. He frowned and shook his head. As the train began to move, she quickly wrote with her finger in the dust on the windowpane:

ƎTIЯW

2 It was eight o'clock in the morning. Reine was sitting on the stone steps outside the Stockholm Concert House, writing a letter. The only luggage he had with him was a shoulder bag clamped between his backside and the step. He had put his writing pad between his feet, which meant he had to bend double with his chin between his knees as he wrote the letter. For at least the tenth time, he read:

I have to inform you that Reine Larsson has appendicitis. He cannot come to Children's Island. If any letters come for him, please forward them to Reine Larsson, Bagarby Road 44C, 191 21, Sollentuna.

> *Faithfully yours,*
> *Harriet Larsson*
> *Bagarby Road 44C*
> *191 21 Sollentuna*

The only part he was truly satisfied with was Mom's forged signature; much more stylish than the original. He also sensed that the letter was a little too short, but he couldn't think of anything else to say; everything necessary was already there.

He raised his eyes and gazed at the Orpheus fountain for inspiration, but Orpheus was wholly occupied with his stringless lyre. Reine's hunched-up position made him suddenly feel like a crap: he'd skipped that this morning, but he couldn't be bothered to look for the john, risking the pressure having gone when he eventually found one. Instead, he swallowed saliva and coughed, which usually helped. It did this time, too. A minute or so later, the pressure had risen like a great bubble into his stomach.

Reine pushed the letter into an envelope and tried licking the flap, but his tongue was much too dry after swallowing all that saliva. He tried again, this time cutting his tongue on the sharp edge of the flap. There was a disgusting salty taste in his mouth. At that moment he noticed water overflowing from one corner of the fountain. He clamped his bag between his legs and hobbled down to the edge of the pool, dipped his forefinger into the water, moistened the flap, and sealed it by pressing it against his thigh. He held up the envelope to check the address and stamp. The envelope was looking slightly crumpled. He opened his bag and put the letter inside the *Mammoth Book of World Records*, the only book he had with him.

Reine went back up the wide steps and sat at the top, using his bag as support for his back against one of the columns. He at once started on the next letter: *Hi, Mom . . .* She wanted him to call her Harriet, he knew that, but he wrote Mom. That marked out a certain distance. Calling his mom Harriet sounded false, but it was she who decided in the long run.

He looked out over the Haymarket. Most of the stands were ready, but a few had not gone up yet. There was a smell of flowers, fruit, and rubbish. Suddenly he saw a rat scuttling along the edge of the Orpheus fountain; it leaped elegantly over the zone where the water was over-flowing. The rat looked really nice, brownish rather than gray, with a short tail, a little like a thin hamster. Phwit, and it was down on the ground. Reine got up quickly and just managed to spot the rat disappearing down the grid of a drain.

Cheered by the interruption, he sat down again, took out his paper and pen, and with the Book of Records underneath, wrote: *Hi, Mom, It's really great here on Children's Island.* You could always write that on the first day before misfortunes started setting in and when the camp leaders still had their smiles on. *We go swimming and play football,* he went on, but then stopped and started chewing his ballpoint. Pencils tasted better, the wood giving way after a while; the plastic in ball-points didn't—it split if you bit hard into it. He sucked on the end of the pen for a while and then wrote: *The food is great.* But then he got no further, his attention instead drawn to an old man in bright orange coveralls hauling on a thick black hose and washing down the steps of the Concert Hall. The water surged down into the drain. Reine hoped rats were good swimmers. He looked at his watch: ten past eight. In other words, almost time for lunch.

The food is great . . . he had to find something more personal, some-thing about himself; otherwise, Mom Harriet might be disappointed. *I broke my leg this morning,* he wrote, then stopped. Maybe that was a bit much. Mom might get anxious and phone, or even come tearing back in person. He scratched it out with a dozen thick strokes and wrote instead: *A wasp stung my big toe this morning.* Good. Fine. *But Sister had some ointment.* Inspired, he went on: *We're barbecuing hot-*

dogs out in the open tonight. Then he came to a full stop, unable to think of another syllable. This depressed him profoundly. If it was so difficult to write this first letter, what would it be like with the rest? How the heck would he be able to invent a whole summer on Children's Island? Maybe it would get easier if he changed to postcards? If he wrote in capital letters, there wouldn't be room for much. Postcards! How could he get hold of postcards of Children's Island? It was going to be hell inventing a whole summer at a children's camp. But, he consoled himself, it would be a worse hell having to experience it.

Did hell exist? That was one of the questions he had thought of getting answered this summer. Grandma knew hell existed. Grandma lived in Gävle and was a member of the Maranata Church there; that was the main reason why Reine was to go to Children's Island this summer. Mom and Grandma had different views on things—among others, on hell. Grandma had no television, so she told stories in the evenings, about her memories, about her time in the pickled herring factory, but also quite a lot about God, Jesus, and Hell. She wasn't all that much into heaven, and her information on the subject was a little vague, but she certainly knew a lot about hell. There were a thousand tortures in hell: wheels, gallows, trial by water, the Iron Maiden, the Spanish Boot, molten lead down the throat. Reine had suggested electric tortures, but Grandma had rejected that as a "heathen modern idea." Grandma's descriptions of hell had both scared and attracted Reine. His nightmares had become much more detailed. But at the same time he didn't really believe Grandma, because if hell really existed, it must be much more horrible than any human being could possibly imagine. Otherwise, there would be no difference between life on earth and life in hell.

It now turned out to be seventeen minutes past eight, and hunger began seriously gnawing at his stomach. If I don't get something to eat soon, he thought, hunger will devour me from inside. He returned to his letter and read: *barbecuing hotdogs out in the open tonight.* He hurriedly scratched that out and wrote instead: *We're having our physicals tonight.* Was that good? No, supposing that got linked with the wasp sting on his big toe and Mom came tearing back? *We're having a sing tonight*, he wrote finally.

Heck, yes, of course, you have to date letters. Stockholm, Chind. 9th June, 1975, he wrote on the top righthand corner. Chind? A good abbreviation for Stockholm Area Summer Camps on Children's Island.

Haymarket looked so damned boring. A whole lot of stands, a few façades of buildings, boring people, a row of flagstaffs, an ice cream stall—no, he mustn't look at that—and a splashing statue blocking his view. Why was Sweden always so boring? If this had been France, there would have been a guillotine in place of Orpheus. A high wooden platform, masses of soldiers all around, huge crowds and little old hags knitting and howling ho-ho every time the guillotine fell and the executioner held up the decapitated head. He'd seen *The Scarlet Pimpernel* on television and knew in detail how things were done in France. *We've made a cabin*, he wrote, *though one boy wanted to make a guillotine. He wasn't allowed to join in.* That was it, then, that would have to do for this time. He felt he had gambled away a whole summer in five lines. He ended the letter: *Love, Reine. P.S. A ten would always be welcome.* He had thirty-three *kronor* sixty in his bag. God knows how long that would last if he started aching for lunch at eight o'clock in the morning.

The thought of food made his mouth water, and he managed to lick envelope number two without the aid of Orpheus overflow. So that this letter wouldn't also get crumpled, he opened the *Mammoth Book of World Records* and slipped it inside. The book happened to fall open at page 345, and he read "The Biggest Book in the World is THE LITTLE RED ELF by Will P. Wood. This sixty-four verse story in the author's own edition is eight feet high and nine feet wide." A photograph on the opposite page showed the author in a kilt on his way in between two opened pages of the book: he appeared to be entering a revolving door.

Reine put the letter inside, then curling his right fist into a telescope, he looked across Haymarket. People became as small as flies. I'm the only person in the world, he thought. Everything I can see and hear is like in a movie. Whenever I want to, I can put out my hand and switch off the film projector. Then no one can get at me.

He dropped his hand to his mouth and blew. There was no sound. He put his left hand over the opening like a mute and blew again: an irregular tooting sound. That's what it must have sounded like when God created Adam out of a lump of clay. He would ask Grandma.

3 Reine suffered endless torments before Carrol's hamburger bar opened its doors at ten o'clock. By that time, his stomach had become saturated with hydrochloric acid, only to dry up again, slide up like an old paper bag, and lie on top of his liver, or was it his kidneys? Reine was slightly uncertain of his anatomy, and unfortunately the Book of World Records had no anatomical illustrations. He had tried looking up *The Biggest Stomach in the World* and *The Longest Prick in the World*, but had instead found *The Biggest Cake in the World*, weight 11.3 tons.

Reine rushed up to Carrol's counter, where a sleepy woman took his order: one Club-burger, French fries, Pepsi-Cola, and an Apple Pie. At one blow that reduced his total capital by about a third. He gobbled all of it in under six minutes. Maybe he should check in the book . . . no, eating and drinking records were all by adults. How could he compete with them? There was really nothing children were best at, except possibly crawling in and out of small windows.

He did not feel especially full and could easily have got some more down, but he had to be careful with his money. He had to live on what he had until at least the eighteenth of August, when school started— possibly even longer, if he came to the conclusion during the summer that it was inappropriate for him to continue in school. It wouldn't work out, of course. He would either have to get a job or invest his capital in some cunning way. You could triple your money in next to no time.

Words that almost rhymed started buzzing in his head like a lingering tune: melon, lemon, cannon. Why? Because he had been sitting there staring at the fruit and vegetables in the Haymarket for so long? Pullet, bullet, gullet . . . he loaded his cannon with a pullet. The pullet hatched out a lemon. Then what? Mormon, hormone. He clapped his hands over his ears to shake out the lingering words. He had no time for such nonsense. This was his first day of freedom, almost the first day in his whole life when he was not dependent on what other people wanted.

It was no good, he could not get rid of the words. Who loaded the cannon—the Mormon or the lemon? Mormons were peace loving, of course, and weren't allowed guns. In addition, some of the Mormon's many wives might interfere. Salon? A melon and a Mormon went into a salon to play coronne? Siphon? And sprayed each other's ears with a si-phon? The Mormon he would defile, out there on Children's Isle?

Reine took out his pen and started jotting on the paper sack his food had come in. He knew from experience that those stupid words wouldn't leave him alone until he had done something about them. Half an hour later he had composed a verse he thought was so good he tore it off the paper and stuffed it into his bag. The verse ran:

> *The white Mormon*
> *loaded his cannon*
> *with a lemon*
> *and shot down*
> *an enemy melon*

It was now high time he headed for the Central Station to pick up his suitcase, which he had put in a luggage locker early that morning. The suitcase contained nearly all his clothes—trousers, underpants, T-shirts, sweaters, socks, handkerchiefs, and his only shirt—all newly washed and listed on a special equipment form. The suitcase was heavy as hell, but he was glad he had only had to lug it from the train to the lockers, instead of having to haul it all the way to the waiting bus.

Before he left Carrol's, he went out to the john and washed the thick straw that had come with his Pepsi-Cola. Such straws did not grow on trees. It was almost big enough to blow peas through. He wrapped the straw in a paper napkin and put it at the very bottom of his shoulder bag.

On his way to the station, Reine passed Wentzel's model shop. Wentzel's had had a construction kit for a helicopter in the window for a long time, and Reine had been saving for it for months. The helicopter was almost six feet long; it was powered by a combustion engine and was radio controlled. The kit cost 1,700 *kronor*, and it was not clear whether the engine and radio equipment were included in the price. But that was not that important, Reine had decided.

The helicopter, a Bell 209 Huey Cobra, was a two-seater American assault helicopter. It had played a prominent part in Reine's fantasy life that spring. When things were bad, when he couldn't sleep or for some other reason needed cheering up, he invented fantasies about the Huey Cobra—at first only that he had bought the kit and made the helicopter, and then that he had also flown it. He had gradually become more and more convinced that a helicopter with a rotor diameter of almost six feet should be able to lift about sixty pounds. And as he himself weighed about fifty-six, there was a slight margin. Besides, the radio control gadgetry could be kept in reserve if he rode in it in person. When he was bored he used to see the helicopter in his mind, parked with its rotors swirling on the school roof, waiting for him. So almost every day he flew the helicopter back home from school. But it was almost more fun when he was furious with someone—a teacher, for instance, or a school friend who preferred to hang around with someone else. Then it was tough on whoever had been nasty—not a question of peaceful air transport but of using the whole range of the assault helicopter's automatic cannons, rockets, and napalm bombs.

He stood looking at the model in Wentzel's window for quite a while. He wouldn't be able to get inside the helicopter; it was far too narrow. He would have to lie outstretched beneath it. It wouldn't be es- pecially complicated to take the frame off an old backpack and stick it to the undercarriage; then all he would have to do would be to put on the helicopter, start the engine, and jump.

The thought of flying always made him happy and excited. Unable to walk as he usually did, he went leaping and bounding along the sidewalk, his heart pounding as if trying to push its way up through his gullet. He swung around once or twice with his shoulder bag hanging from his neck like a weight. It was great to be alive sometimes, and it would become even better. Or would it? Crestfallen, he stopped at a red light; the road was far too wide to jump over, at least fifteen yards.

Before Reine got his suitcase out of the locker, he had a task to carry out. He had to get himself photographed. The photograph was for a rebate travel card valid all over Greater Stockholm. While planning this free summer, he had soon realized that he couldn't stay in Sollentuna looking for the meaning of life. This was going to demand quite a bit of traveling, and unfortunately, the helicopter was not yet complete.

There was a line outside the photomat. An officer in uniform was in front of Reine, in front of the officer a woman with shoulder-length blond hair. There was another line by the slot where the finished photographs emerged. Two plump women were standing there in knit cardigans, scarves hiding half their faces. Reine presumed they were Turks or something. The apparatus ground out a strip of photographs through the slot. One of the women extracted the photos with wrinkled red fingers that looked as if they had peeled potatoes day and night for sixty years. Though maybe Turks didn't eat potatoes? The woman showed the photographs to the other. They both burst out laughing, first giggling with embarrassment, glancing sideways, then roaring with laughter, making the spit fly and their black teeth rattle in their mouths. Reine giggled a little, too. It was nice to see people happy, once you'd got over your first fright, that is.

The blond witch was in the booth now. He could see her platform shoes fidgeting as if she wanted to go to the john. The officer had taken off his cap and was combing his hair in front of the mirror outside the booth. There was a buzzing sound inside, then a blue lamp blinked like a faulty neon light. The blond stepped out, still smiling, to be on the safe side, and the officer went in and started winding down the stool. Now he's been shot dead, thought Reine as the light flashed. Shot for a failed attempted coup.

Reine sat down in the booth and stared at his reflection in the mirror. He found it terribly difficult to look straight ahead; he kept wanting to twist around so that he would be seen more from the left. But he made himself look straight ahead—and he made himself grin. The apparatus flashed. It was really horrible; his skull seemed to be an empty ball of black air and he himself the camera receiving the picture on the inside of the back of his head.

Reine stepped out and checked the time. It wasn't true, the developing took much longer than three minutes. And when the photographs did emerge, they were so wet he could hardly handle them. He picked them up with his fingertips and went and sat down on a bench. He looked crazy, a round freckled face with fair hair and almost invisible slit eyes. There were black circles around his eyes, and his crooked front tooth looked like a sugar lump in his mouth. He felt slightly nauseated as he looked at himself—aw, heck! But this was an important photograph. This was what Reine Larsson looked like *before*. He promised himself he would take another photo in two months, in the middle of August—there was sure to be a world of difference.

4 Reine got up from his place in the commuter train; in the heat it felt as if a huge band-aid had been torn off his backside. He pushed the heavy suitcase ahead of his knees toward the doors. Eight or nine people were preparing to get off, among them a mother with a child in a baby buggy. When the doors hissed open, they all rushed out, leaving Reine and the mother behind, she with her buggy and he with his suitcase. They helped each other out under the impatient gaze of the remaining passengers.

Reine lived about five minutes from the Sollentuna station in an area of newish three-story brick apartment buildings set in regular squares around quite large yards with playgrounds and wilting greenery. To the uninitiated they all looked alike, but not to Reine. He could find his entrance in Bagarby 44C blindfolded. Anyone who had grown up in the district knew each entrance by its special smell, its special atmosphere and effect. Bagarby 44C smelt of "home."

Before going in, he stood pressed up against a half-grown birch for a moment. He would prefer not to be seen by any of the neighbors, just in case Mom had happened to mention that he was at camp. Then he plucked up courage and went in. If anyone asked him, he would say his stay at the camp had been canceled because of a power failure. He liked the word canceled, finding a lot of scope for it. Unfortunately, my homework was canceled yesterday. Brushing my teeth was canceled this morning because of a *force majeur*.

Reine drew a deep breath before opening the apartment door. What if Mom hadn't left? There were plenty of jobs in the health service in Stockholm, but Mom had longed for the sea—not the putrid little Baltic, but the real salt sea off the west coast. Reine had the greatest sympathy with her on that point. As early as March he had realized this meant a unique opportunity for canceling Children's Island.

The apartment was empty, the blinds down, and a system of thin green plastic tubes around the plants was feeding them with water from bottles. Reine had doubts about the effectiveness of the system and had suggested that the plants should be moved out onto the balcony instead and watered by the rain. But Mom Harriet hadn't wanted that, partly because the balcony had a roof over it and partly because she had no wish to tempt fate—it was going to be a stunning summer! Reine, on the other hand, was hoping for a cold wet summer, for then it would be easier to think.

It was a three-room apartment. Mom had the largest, which also functioned as a living room and was called the lounge. Reine had one of the smaller rooms. The third was called the guest room and was usually empty. Grandma used to use it quite often, but nowadays it was usually used by friends of Mom's from work. Sometimes when Reine was having breakfast on Saturday or Sunday mornings, Mom came out with a friend she had been kind enough to put up for the night in the guest room. Some of them had hangovers and were bad tempered; others left without even saying hullo; but one or two were nice and stopped for breakfast, or went with them to the amusement park at Gröna Lund, or helped Reine with his plastic models.

He put his suitcase down on Mom's sofabed. There was no point in unpacking, as he might be off again any minute. It was by no means certain the world began and ended in Sollentuna. Reine was terribly hungry, so he went out and jerked open the refrigerator. It was empty except for two cans of beer and a jar of mustard. He took out one of the cans, then found half a packet of hardbread in the oven to munch with it.

Noticing that the light was on in the guest room, he went in. No one was there. Mom must have left the light on to keep thieves away. To be on the safe side, Reine switched on the floor lamp before sitting on the bed to consume his snack. He didn't time himself this time, but he was quick about it, so quick he got hiccups from the beer. Well, where should he start? He might as well start with himself: who am I? I am Reine Agne Larsson, identity number 640909-1152. Why? Because Mom was with some man at the beginning of December 1963. Perhaps on St. Lucia Day? What matter? Harriet had never been particularly exact as to time and place. She had told him that in the autumn of 1963 she had been with a man whom she liked so much she became pregnant with Reine. But quite soon it had turned out that she and this man wanted to go their separate ways. Their love was a mistake. So Reine had no dad. That is, as long as the man had not gone and got himself run over or stabbed in the kidneys with a poisoned dagger, then of course Reine had a dad. But Reine hoped his dad was dead; otherwise, he might suddenly come back one fine day. And turn out to be a dumb jerk.

That was the greatest outrage of all, adults just making children any old how without asking them what that entailed—asking the children, that is. If he had been allowed to choose, he would certainly not have chosen to be the son of a single woman who was nearly always working, sometimes even at night. Better to be son of the director of Marabou Chocolate, Inc. Better not to be called Reine—what child didn't want to change its name, anyhow? Better to be called Roy and be son of the managing director of Toy, Inc. And the owner of a ten-geared hoy . . . oh, hell no! He thumped the back of his head against the wall to disperse the rhyming words; enough with one ding-dong verse for today.

When the neighbors had wanted to adopt a child from South Korea, there had been endless checking up. Welfare officials had been there poking their noses into everything. They'd talked to Mom, too, and she'd smiled and said lots of nice things about the neighbors. Then they hadn't been allowed that Korean child after all, probably because they were too old. But it was a good thing, all that checking, not just on foster parents. His mom, for instance, had never . . . no, now he was being unfair; Mom couldn't help not living in a fine house and not being married to a financier. So as compensation she needed a nice intelligent son like Reine. That was wrong, wasn't it? As he saw it, children were for parents and not the other way around. He drank the last of the beer and coldly established that children were for parents. Why did they otherwise have children? Not out of kindness to children. Maybe Mom had wanted revenge on Grandma? Grandma and Grandpa had had Mom without asking her, but Mom couldn't get at them. So instead she took revenge on the next generation, on Reine. But Reine in his turn was not thinking of having any children; it was unjust to take revenge on the innocent.

Reine's eyelids felt heavy from the beer, but before he fell asleep he took up an old idea: the man Mom had been with was called Dag Hammarskjöld. Hammarskjöld had died sometime at the beginning of the sixties. But before passing out, he had made Reine. There was a lot that fit; Mom had vaguely talked about the man "going away" and that he was going to be away for a long time. Either he'd gone to the United Nations, or else Mom meant he had died—people usually told children that—and so he had gone away and perhaps wouldn't come back. There were pictures of Hammarskjöld at school. He was fair with a narrow nose like Reine's and baggy cheeks like a guinea pig's. He also looked generally unreliable, just like someone who makes a woman pregnant and then goes off to America. Perhaps he should contact the family?

5 Reine did not wake up until almost seven that evening. A rhyme kept running through his head. There was a silly twerp, who couldn't even burp. But he hadn't made that up himself, so he had no difficulty in getting rid of it. He got out of the guest bed with the empty beer can under his arm and decided that he was not hungry. He was never hungry when he first got up, as if his stomach were stuffed with air. He burped, went out to the stairway garbage chute, and threw the beer can down it, counting the seconds before the can rattled into the bin. Three seconds. If you fell—was there time to relive your life in three seconds?

The beer made itself felt, and he went into the bathroom to pee. It felt so good he wanted to shout. He tried out a couple of squeaks, but they weren't up to much. If you gave a full-throated yell, you could be heard in the john in the apartment below, and they might phone the police, thinking there had been a break-in. He pulled his penis out into a long pink string and let it go; it at once wrinkled up again. Penis, prick, cock . . . or wee-wee, as Mom used to say when he was small. None of the words sounded right. Penis sounded like the name of a spice, prick sounded nuts. And cock? Cock sounded brittle in some way, like a thin pipe of brick-colored clay. Cockpot. Drop the cockpot on the floor. Ocarina. Clay cuckoo. The right word was male member. He inspected his male member, which looked like a skin ice cream cone. He pulled down his trousers and examined the base of his male member and the wrinkled pale brown scrotum. Good, no hairs, only a little white down. How long had he got? A year? Two years? The day he reached puberty, all was lost. Then he would be drawn into the world of adults and there would be no return. Imprisoned in horniness and other mucky things, your thoughts would never again be pure. All your energy would go on getting sex, and there would be nothing left to solve problems like whether God existed and if so, what had he sounded like when he created Adam. Perhaps this was his last summer, as children matured so young these days: two in his class already had hair. Every day, Reine examined his private parts with terror as if he were scared of cancer.

He pulled up his jeans, flushed the john, then unscrewed the knob on the tank and lifted the lid. He had fastened a piece of paper inside the lid with some blue tape. He pulled it free and checked that all was in order. On the paper was:

A=14, B=9, C=20, D=1, E=5, F=13, G=6, H=22, I=19, J=21, K=16, L=10, M=24, N=17, O=4, P=18, Q=7, R=2, S=3, T=11, U=8, V=25, W=12, X=15, Y=23, Z=26.

This was Reine's private and personally devised code. The great thing about it was that the letters had not been numbered in the order they were in the alphabet: A=1, B=2, C=3, etc. His code was constructed haphazardly and so was impossible to crack. He had spent a whole day on it last winter when he had had German measles, writing all the letters on small pieces of paper, which he had then put into a glass. Then he had written the numbers 1–26 on different pieces and put them into a bowl he had just emptied of raspberry jelly. By closing his eyes and taking first a letter and then a number, he had produced this brilliant code. He stuck the paper back, put the lid on again, then carefully wiped the tank top with a wet piece of toilet paper to remove all traces and fingerprints.

The color television in the lounge was covered with one of Reine's old baby sheets. It was hard work lugging the television into his own room; fortunately, the people who had built the block had equipped all three rooms with sockets leading to the central aerial. Reine's room was nine by twelve feet; the door was at one end, the window at the other with a view over the neighboring block. Just by the door was a narrow closet, with the head of Reine's bed against its wall. Opposite the bed was a narrow chipboard plank on two sawhorses: Reine's desk.

The one free surface was below the window, so Reine put the television there. He closed the venetian blind, then pulled down the roller blind so that no one would notice the flickering light of the television and think someone had broken in, perhaps someone who hadn't got a TV of his own and simply had to see some special program.

The two long walls in the room were covered with posters. Above the bed they were nearly all pictures of motorcyclists, from the old speedway hero Nygren to the motocross star Hansen of the seventies. The wall above the desk was all about terror. Boris Karloff as Frankenstein's monster was there, and Bo Svensson as Frankenstein's monster, Christopher Lee as Dracula, Charles Laughton as the Hunchback of Notre Dame, the Tiger Cages of Con Sol, Lyndon Johnson as the President of the United States, *The Mummy Awakens, Planet of the Apes, The Eye-Eating Giant Bacteria from Outer Space,* and a portrait of the lead man of *Jesus Christ Superstar.*

Hunger struck Reine a blow in the solar plexus. He abandoned television cables and fled out into the kitchen. What was there to eat? Unfortunately, almost nothing. The icebox was as empty and as defrosted as before, but there was another pack of Finnish melba toast in the oven. There were seven boxes of spaghetti in the cupboard, all opened and all practically empty. Also a few cans of soup, a plastic jar of rice, sugar, salt and other spices, jars of peeled tomatoes, another of snails, but—thank goodness—a can of corned beef and a can of pineapple. He quickly opened the last two, thrust a fork into the meat and slid a spoon carefully into the fruit. Together with the Finnish toast, he took them back to bed. A man must have some comforts.

Before he started eating, he switched on the television, and a clock against a green background said five minutes to the news. He managed to get all the food inside him except the toast before the clock reached half-past seven and faded out. Reine turned swiftly over in bed and lay on his back with his feet on the pillow. If you watched television lying upside down, it wasn't so horrible. Because it could be horrible, burning children in Vietnam, or when the police chief in Saigon shot a prisoner through the head right in front of the camera. If there must be executions, they were best watched upside down. And another thing: he had learned at school that people really see the world upside down; that was how their eyes functioned. But very early on in life you learned to turn the picture right side up in your head. It sounded a bit odd, but it was true. Reine didn't want to have anything to do with that kind of trick; he wanted to see the world as it really was, just as you'd seen it from the start when you were born, upside down.

When the news had tootled its signature tune and the news reader had stopped pretending to sort his papers, Reine closed his eyes and covered his ears. He did not wish to see or hear: Reine Larsson, nearly eleven, reported missing since early this morning. The army and dogs have been called out for a search party.

6 At seven-fifty-one the next morning, Reine boarded the commuter train into Stockholm. He didn't get a seat, but had to stand and fill in his newly purchased rebate card against a wall. He had stolen in order to buy it. That had been absolutely necessary. Mom had an old cigarette box containing an account she administered. Some of the women from Mom's previous job met once a month and put a ten each time into a special account. In December every year, they all went out for a drink together.

Reine's conscience was extremely troubled that morning; there was a nasty taste in his mouth—well, that might have something to do with his canceled toothbrushing. But he had never stolen money before. Oh, he had taken the odd coin now and again, but coins were hardly money and did not really count. Notes, on the other hand, were money. At least tens were—since fives could be coins as well as notes, theft of fives maybe didn't count. He was determined to pay it back: he could reckon on Mom putting the odd ten in her letters to Children's Island.

Reine soon had other things to think about apart from his guilty conscience. He had to sign the rebate card just below the photograph. But how do you do that when you haven't got a definite signature, when you try one out and see what comes, writing large with a flourish if you're in a good mood, but small and crabby when you think the whole world stinks and might as well be blown to smithereens? Was he in a good mood or bad? How the heck could he know that, after a partly sleepless night? As he'd slept half the day before, his night sleep had not amounted to much. He had slept through most of the news, waked up, switched over to another program, fallen asleep, waked up during the weather, fallen asleep, and then been awakened again by the buzzing and flickering of an empty television channel. He had devoted the following hours to building a plastic model of a Curtiss Helldiver on a 1:72 scale. He had finished it at about four in the morning. Then he'd made himself some tea and fallen asleep.

It would have to be one of those in-between signatures, a half-printed version, which with a little good will could be interpreted as R. A. Larsson. When he had finished the card, he stood close to the wall of the carriage and scribbled with his ballpoint: R. A. Larsson. R. A. Larsson. It went quite easily and was quite like the signature on the card. Hell! Why had he written his own name? What unforgivable idiocy! If they sent out an SOS for him from Children's Island, he would be revealed at the first turnstile. But there were seldom ticket inspectors at this hour. They usually came in the afternoons when school was over, and caught pupils traveling without tickets. Too late to change the name anyhow. Larsson was much too short; he couldn't adjust his signature so that it said Hammarskjöld instead. But how about Hansen? Reine Hansen, son of the famous motocross driver Thorleif Hansen. To hell with dads, he said to himself. Stand on your own two feet and whatever you do don't become a dad.

Reine got off at Karlberg to walk the last stretch into the city center. He was out to get a job, and that meant it would be good to walk up and down a few streets. Who knows, there might be a notice in one of the store windows? Errand boy wanted, immediate appointment for young man, work for us and get rich quick.

He walked from the station up toward the city. When he got to the triangular square in front of the church, his spirits sank; no job offers so far. What did you do, really? The answer was obvious; don't hesitate to ask. But asking about this and that was not one of Reine's strong points. Not that he had communication difficulties exactly; he could talk and mix with people as long as he didn't have to take the initiative himself. But asking strangers was exposing yourself, risking your whole existence, perhaps even losing your—what was it called—your identity. He didn't quite know what to think: if you opened up to a stranger you were left defenseless; the other person might put his fingers into your mouth and steal something off you, like a letter out of your name? He would have to go around afterward being called R ine.

He came to a fruit store and went in and bought two bananas. If you let the sugar count in your blood get too low, you couldn't think. That was why people in the underdeveloped countries had not been able to think out good ways of solving their problems. He himself was an absolute imbecile, not just at this moment but nearly all the time. How could he be so dumb as to think he could get away with a whole summer holiday on his own with an initial capital of thirty *kronor* sixty? If only he had at least had the sense to talk Mom into giving him the children's allowance she received from the government. He knew lots who got their allowance put into a special savings account, which they would then have at their disposal when they left school. But not Reine. Mom was quite adamant on that point; the official children's allowances were for food and clothing, so she saw to that and used it to eke out the housekeeping money. You simply couldn't call a mom like that Harriet.

That was why adults had children, to have something to oppress. Not children to love and hug but someone to keep down, give them a little pocket money every week and refuse to increase it without first talking to people at school or the parents of classmates. Why? What reason could there be for all children to have the same amount of pocket money when adults didn't? Why go on and on for weeks on end before handing out a raise of a few cents, when they themselves perhaps had had a huge pay raise? And the silliest of all: the last time, Mom had suggested he should start keeping accounts of what he spent his pocket money on. Very educational. Didn't adults realize that such nonsense made children money mad, thinking so much about money that their heads were like piggy banks when they shook them?

He walked dejectedly down the street and stopped for a while by the big newspaper office, watching the huge printing presses turning. People were moving around inside behind the glass, hurrying back and forth. He didn't want to work there: imagine going into one of those presses like into a mangle and coming out the other end a flattened giant frog with printing and colored pictures all over you, the Shah of Iran between your shoulder blades.

He was not going to be a printer when he grew up, but a scientist. He had hit on something very important, something no one else had yet thought of. It was all so secret he hardly dared think about it, but nevertheless it was about the mystery of cancer. People got cancer mainly from growth inhibitors . . . but no one had thought of investigating radio waves. It was as clear as crystal: you couldn't keep on polluting the air with short, long, and medium wave lengths, not to mention FM, without punishing yourself in the long run. Wherever you were, except possibly in a lead chamber, you were constantly pierced by radio programs, shortwave messages, telegrams, distress signals, television, and gale warnings. It couldn't be good for you in the long run. That was where the unsolved problem of cancer lay.

He bought an ice cream cone and licked it all the way down the street. Only five minutes left until he got to the station—and no sign of a job! Things were all going to hell. If all his inventiveness was to be taken up by unimportant details, when would he have time to think, see, and find out, to acquire the experience and material needed to learn what everything was really all about, where the world was going wrong and whether there was any point in being part of this society? If only one could dispose of hunger. Hunger and sex were the greatest scourges of mankind, hindering all sensible actions. A few years ago, Mom had been given some diet pills by her doctor because she had thought her butt was getting too big. But then it had turned out that the pills were dangerous. Cancer-causing? Anyhow, he would rummage in the bathroom cupboard to see if he could find the jar; you just couldn't go around thinking about nothing but grub all the time.

To keep well away from McDonald's and Carrol's, which were a mile or so to the left, Reine turned right, down opposite the Oscar Theater, and crossed over to have a look. It might be fun to work in a theater: always in the papers and liquor for breakfast. Pity they sang and played in some theaters so much that you couldn't hear what was being said.

Two women came past on the pavement, one in a wheelchair pushed by the other. Reine had an idea: what about applying for a job as a wheelchair pusher? Pretty heavy, maybe, but the person sitting in the chair could help by pulling on the wheels. He could see a lot that way and would be sure to be allowed to travel free on buses and trains. Perhaps go to the theater for nothing, too, and go in ahead of everyone else. People in wheelchairs were always allowed in first; he remembered that from when he had flown to Ibiza. Infants and people in wheelchairs were taken on board before all the rest. Asking a person in a wheelchair wouldn't be so bad, either—you could duck and run without the handicapped person being able to come after you.

Suddenly the two women stopped and turned into an entrance alongside the Oscar Theater and the Palladium building. He waited for a few minutes, then slipped in after them, just in time to see them going up in the elevator. He shot up the stairs but had no luck; although the elevator appeared to be old and creaky, it was too fast. He stopped on the fourth floor: of course it would take them a hell of a time to get out of the elevator, so there wasn't all that much hurry. He walked calmly up the last flight.

The elevator door rattled shut and the elevator was still swinging when Reine got to the top floor. The women were making their way through a wide metal fire door. They were finding it difficult to hold the heavy door open, so Reine plucked up courage, slid forward, and helped to prop it open. There was a beautifully lettered notice on the door in curly letters—STUDIO OLGA.

7 The heavy door with its powerful automatic closer almost shot Reine into the studio. The room was very big, at least twice the size of the lounge at home, but not as big as his classroom. It was an attic room. The outer walls sloped except where there were two windows. Long rails running along the ceiling were hung with broad ribbons in several colors—white, violet, green, blue, yellow, pale blue. The room appeared to have been decorated for a party, but they had forgotten to clear the floor, which was covered with rows of long tables, something like a school cafeteria. People were sitting at the tables, painting with brushes, all women. The woman in a wheelchair had been pushed forward and installed at one of the tables and was already taking brushes and little bottles out of a box under the table. What was this? Since it was in the same block as the Oscar Theater, could it be where they fixed the costumes, scenery, and swords with retractable blades?

An old woman turned round and, catching sight of Reine, came toward him. She had a gigantic hairdo and was wearing a full-length gray coverall. Reine recognized her at once. She must be Marie Curie, the woman with the radium; he had seen her in an encyclopedia. Not Marie Curie personally, of course, because she must have been dead and gone for at least fifty years now. But she was very like her. Reine had often thought about how few appearances there were in the world. It was a lie that every human being was unique. At a hasty glance, a lot of people were alike almost to the point of confusion. People you met for the first time nearly always looked like someone you knew or had met before. The strange thing was that you attributed the same characteristics to the new person who was like someone you'd met before. This old girl was like Madame Curie; consequently, she was a foreigner and dealt with radium. Reine made a swift estimate of the number of standard looks there were. Fifty? No, say seventy-five. No one could keep track of more.

"What can I do for you, little man?" the woman said in a foreign accent.

There you are, she couldn't even speak proper Swedish, and she talked as they had fifty years ago. Or a hundred, what difference did it make? The old girl's face looked like a mummy's; must be the radium, of course.

Reine was just about to say he had come by mistake and had simply wanted to hold the door open and would leave at once, when his conversation with the lady was interrupted by another person coming into the room. The newcomer was female and about seventeen. She had long ginger hair, freckles, and a large purple birthmark on her cheek. She was wearing an undershirt and a long blue skirt, and she was barefoot.

"So you've arrived, Birgitta," said the old woman.

"My watch was wrong," said the girl. "I thought it was seven and it was really nine."

"It's a quarter past ten now," said the lady.

"I'm hopeless at times," said the girl. "Always have been. I'll always be a quarter of an hour late. You'll have to reckon with that. Everyone does."

"We start at eight o'clock here, Birgitta dear."

"My watch says quarter past eight. I can stay on for an extra quarter of an hour this afternoon . . ."

"Well, go to your bench. Go on with what you were doing yesterday. You stopped in the middle of a word."

"Now I come to think of it," said the girl, "now I come to think of it, you're nothing but a gang of old maids, a bunch of old parchment cunts messing around with your horrible gold paint . . . go wipe your asses with your damn silk ribbons! No one can stand this."

Reine was quite prepared for the whole ceiling and all its rails and ribbons to come crashing down, and he raised his shoulder bag to protect his head. But nothing happened.

"Well, thanks for coming up to now, Birgitta," said the old girl calmly. "Come over to my desk and we'll see how much we owe you."

"Put the pittance in my account," said the girl, turning on her heel and disappearing through the heavy door.

Reine had expected some kind of reaction—a horrified cackling, or someone calling out "great," or "good thing she's gone"—but no one said a word. The studio remained quiet, the old ladies at the tables painting and fiddling around as before.

"I'm sorry," said Madame Curie. "My name is Olga. I run this studio. And what do you want, my boy? Have you come to fetch some ribbons?"

"I don't know," said Reine.

"Aren't you an errand boy, then?"

"Not exactly."

"Oh, I see. Not many people come here. Perhaps you were delivering something?"

"What would that be?"

"Perhaps you just wanted to have a look?"

"I was down there looking at the photographs outside the Oscar Theater, and I thought I might nip in and learn something."

He was slightly scared, remembering the movie scene when Frankenstein hoists the monster up into the roof where lightning can strike and bring it alive. Maybe they used radiation here instead, painting their victims with radioactive gold paint? That would be simpler than waiting around for lightning.

"Now that our apprentice has left . . ." said Madame Olga, or Aunt Curie, or however she wanted it.

Reine didn't know what an apprentice was, but presumed it had something to do with learning or getting better at it. Perhaps they did experiments on the apprentice—did they work on living people? He suddenly realized what they were all doing. They were fixing ribbons for shrouds for mummies. They were sitting there cutting up hundreds and thousands of ribbons and then painting them all over with spells. They waited for a suitable victim, a young girl, for instance, and then they all jumped on her—naturally the wheelchair was false—and tied the first ribbon over the victim's mouth as a gag, the second over the victim's eyes as a blindfold, and the third around the victim's neck as . . .

"If you were a little older, I could have offered you the job," said Aunt Olga. "The job that's just become vacant."

He dared not answer, for the more he said the more involved he became. He caught sight of a white banner hanging on one of the short walls. It was as large as a child's sheet, with two points at the bottom, and fringed all around with gold. But what worried him was not the banner itself but what was on it—right in the middle was a gold cross with a thousand rays going in all directions. What kind of trophy was it?

"Perhaps you'd like to know a little more about what we do here?"

The woman in the wheelchair suddenly looked up and smiled, a warm, genuine smile, not the kind of smile an executioner gives his victim.

"Isn't this part of the Oscar Theater?" said Reine.

"We make ribbons for wreaths," said Aunt Olga.

"Oh, really," said Reine, to be on the safe side. He was not sure what ribbons for wreaths were, but he felt calmer now. His life was in no danger.

"We get orders from florists all over Stockholm. We paint wording on ribbons for wreaths."

Reine looked up at the ceiling and with some difficulty read the peculiar spiky gold letters on several ribbons. Farewell from Otto and Renata. A Last Farewell from the Karlström Family. From Friends in the Royal Navy.

Suddenly Reine realized that the room stank, stank very strongly of

turpentine, paint, thinner, material, dust. His throat tightened as if
someone behind him had thrown . . . Stupid! But he felt he couldn't
stay another moment. It was like being in a sauna and without warning
someone throwing a scoopful on to the stove. Not a scoopful of water,
but a scoopful of turpentine.

" 'Bye and thanks a lot," he called to the smiling ladies as he hurtled
through the door.

8 Sitting in the McDonald's on King Street, Reine
found it hard to concentrate on work. Three major questions kept circling round in his head, biting each other's tails like dragonflies. How
could he get work? What should he use the summer for? How the heck
could he keep Mom in a good mood, so that she didn't suspect anything?

Dear Harriet, he wrote on the notepaper, which had a large grease
spot on it from his French fries. The grease spot didn't worry him; in
fact, it reinforced what he had thought of writing. *Today we've been out
on a trip and had sandwiches in the open. The butter melted in the
sun* . . . Uh-huh? What did a bunch of half-grown kids do next? Go
swimming? *Unfortunately we weren't allowed to go swimming because so many had colds.* Excellent. As long as he stayed ashore, Mom
wouldn't start thinking he was going to drown. Colds? Not so good.
Mom had once said that infectious diseases "rampaged" through summer camps. What did "rampage" mean? That the diseases rammed the
kids over like ninepins? He crossed out the sentence about swimming
and wrote: *We didn't go swimming because we didn't feel like it.* Hm.
Might Mom start worrying about his hygiene? *But we took a shower as
usual that night.* Great. Perfect. But what if there were no showers on
Children's Island? A pamphlet had come about all that kind of thing—
but where was it? He definitely remembered Mom getting a pamphlet
about all the arrangements for washing and bathing. But he hadn't read
it himself, only felt like throwing up at the very sight of it. It would be

back home in the apartment, which meant he couldn't mail the letter until he'd checked on the information about showers. That was only to the good, anyhow. If Mom got letters too often, she might think he was homesick.

What was he going to use the summer for? He put the carton of French fries to his mouth, threw back his head, and tipped down the last crumbs and grains of salt. Two bare-chested youths, thinking his table would now be free, came over with their trays. Reine refused to look at them, and turning the notepaper over, he wrote: *Point 1—Contact the Hammarskjöld family?* What evidence did he really have? None, to be honest. But he might reason this way: What evidence did the Hammarskjöld family have that Dag Hammarskjöld had not had sex with his mom? None, to be honest. Though of course Dag Hammarskjöld might have been on a business trip to Japan or Outer Mongolia in December 1963. But what if he had Harriet with him on the plane? As his private nurse? That really was quite an idea . . .

"You going to be sitting around scribbling much longer?" asked one of the youths.

"I'm waiting for my dad," said Reine. "He's just gone to the john."

The two young men departed to wait for a couple of older women a little farther away; one of the boys had THIS SIDE UP tattooed on his back.

That's it. In the john. In the toilet of a DC-8 on its way to Outer Mongolia. Could the Hammarskjöld family disprove it? Yes, they could. Reine was interested in flying and knew that one of Dag Hammarskjöld's nephews—or was it a third cousin?—was president of IATA, the international airline organization. In other words there wasn't a hope, because the Hammarskjöld family controlled all the air space and naturally wouldn't allow any incriminating evidence to slip out. He changed *Point 1* to *Chuck thinking about who Dad is,* adding in his mind: because if there's anything special about your dad, if he's famous or something to boast about, and he's managed to escape paying child support for almost eleven years, then that's how it's going to go on. Unless he's dumb.

What did the *Mammoth Book of World Records* have to say about dads? Reine extracted the book from his bag in the shelter of the table top and leafed through it. The best dad in the world? The biggest dad in the world? The richest dad in the world? The cleverest dad in the world? There was nothing about dads, but under predators it said:

The largest predator. The largest carnivorous animal in the world was the giant lizard *Tyrannosaurus rex*, which had lived 75 million years ago in what was now the U.S.A. It was 45 feet long and 21 feet high.

Imagine what a hullabaloo there'd be here if *Tyrannosaurus rex* suddenly came into McDonald's and ordered the largest hamburger in the world. Pronto!

It was almost eleven o'clock, and the lunch hour rush had started. What about getting a job here! Carrying trays, sweeping up, welcoming the customers. Ten *kronor* an hour plus as many hamburgers as you liked. Reine grew quite excited and jumped up. Why hadn't he thought of that before! He scooped up his belongings and went across to the counter. There were long lines at the registers. He dared not push his way ahead; a vision of rows of predatory lizards appeared before his eyes—tall ones, short ones, fat ones by the registers, some with handbags, some barefoot, some with glasses, and over there a fat old green lizard with a hearing aid. He slipped swiftly out into the street.

Three minutes later he had sprinted quite a long way away and was sitting on the steps of the Royal Library, crowds of people passing him up and down the steps. More and more came and sat down on the steps. You seemed to be able to buy food some place in the library. A large blond girl and a smaller man who might have been Javanese were sitting a foot or so from Reine, eating peach yogurt. Reine leaned over to catch a bit of the smell and see if there were any whole pieces of fruit in the yogurt or whether it was just dyed. There were whole pieces, and the Javanese kept sucking on a slice of peach that kept protruding between his pursed blue lips. Reine did a mute survey of his finances. Then the couple suddenly put down their empty yogurt cartons and started kissing. Reine turned away in disgust. People were as revolting as lizards. Even more so. At least lizards laid eggs.

Reine had been given sex education in many forms over the years and knew perfectly well how people made children. He had accepted it all in theory, much as one accepts one's own death in theory, but not in practice. He considered the description of reproduction at the same time boring and unbelievable. To think that God hadn't been able to figure out some easier way! Reproduction—what a word! Sounded like moms in rows on an assembly line.

He considered the version they'd produced at school really dumb, a typical invention of the school board. The man put his penis into the woman and left behind a few drops of seed, which then swam up to what they called the womb, where the little tadpoles of seed competed to get to the pinhead-sized egg. That was just as silly as the flowers and the bees. But true, of course. Anyone maintaining anything else got a bad mark.

Reine liked the idea of reproduction happening in lots of different ways. One Christmas he and Gran had concocted a version together: one beautiful evening, one of God's angels had come floating down below the evening clouds with little Reine in his arms. The angel had first circled round above the Mission House, then landed on the steps. The whole congregation was waiting. After they'd sung "Blessed Is the Earth," the angel had formally handed Reine over to Mom. Gran had wept with joy and embraced the angel. According to Reine, but not to Gran, Gran's handbag had got entangled in one of the angel's wing feathers, but the minister had helped to part them. Then the angel had bowed to the congregation, cried "Hallelujah," and swung up into the air, circling to gain height, and finally moving off like an arrow straight to God, who lived behind the setting sun.

But Reine had a private version of his own creation, which ran like this: one night in bright silvery moonlight, Dracula and his flying dog had come floating in like two wind-driven wisps of cloud. Dracula and the dog had pushed their way into Mom's room. While the dog lay on

Mom's body so that she couldn't move a finger, Dracula had stood astride her head with his back to the head of the bed. Then he had swiftly bent down and driven both his vampire teeth into Mom's nostrils, leaving two hard little grains of seed. When Mom emerged from her unconscious state, it was already daylight, and Dracula had for some hours been lying in agony in his silver-fitted coffin in the mountains of Transylvania. The seeds in Mom's nostrils had grown like peas, one seed dying and the other becoming Reine. One fearful night during a thunderstorm, Mom had been afflicted with a sneeze and given birth to Reine. When this had happened, Mom had been only seven years old, and after that she had hidden Reine among her dolls and teddy bears for years so that Gran wouldn't see him.

9 It was already one o'clock when Reine took the elevator up to Studio Olga. He had a long morning behind him and was in a state of almost total capitulation. The enthusiasm he had felt at the start of the morning, the world apparently lying at his feet, his winged feet, had now turned into the opposite. He often felt ninety feet tall in the mornings, cheerfully striding on stilts across streets and minor buildings, pole-vaulting over larger buildings at a pinch. But after lunch it was all over; he wondered if this effect could be due to food, whether—unlike ordinary people—he digested his lunch in his head instead of his stomach. His brain felt like a disintegrating cheeseburger.

When he got to the studio, nothing had changed. Aunt Olga was standing by her high old-fashioned desk, writing in an account book. The other women were at the tables: one in the wheelchair, the big fat one, the one with long gray braids, and the grandly dressed one with lots of gold bracelets and rings. He looked up at the rails in the ceiling and noticed that time had indeed passed. The ribbons he had seen in the morning had gone, and others hung in their place: From a Grieving Husband, Department Seventy-Two of the Company, Bertil, May-Britt, Pontus and Victoria.

Oddly enough, the smell of paint and chemicals that had frightened him away before was much milder now. Not so odd, really. Reine had noticed that when he was scared, his sense of smell suddenly became much sharper.

"Hi!" said Reine.

Aunt Olga looked up. She was wearing glasses with black cords running behind her neck. When she took off her glasses, Reine noticed she had unusually bright blue eyes. Older people didn't usually have such bright eyes; older people's eyes were usually flat and slightly boiled.

"You *are* in a hurry," said Olga. "It *was* you who came here quite recently, wasn't it?"

Recently . . . well. Reine felt he had lived through six or seven years since he had last been here.

"I suddenly thought of something," he said.

The women all looked at him. The hunched-back one was sitting so low she had to look underneath her arm. The fat lady smiled with her whole face, her cheeks flaring red like the introduction of one of Reine's favorite horror programs, World at War. The lady with the long gray braids stared in surprise, as if he were a pink lizard. The lady with the jewels smiled artificially, as if their eyes were meeting above a raised coffee cup. But the content of all those smiles was as clear as crystal: we like you, we love all little boys who haven't yet reached puberty and become thugs snatching handbags.

"Well," said Reine. "It was about that apprentice job."

Olga came even nearer and held out her hand.

"What's your name?"

"Reine Agne Larsson."

"Are you over fifteen?"

"Almost," said Reine.

"Then you've not left school yet?"

"Not quite, but I'm on vacation at the moment and I wondered, now that the other person has finished and perhaps it's hard to get someone else, whether it might be possible for me to work here. Sort of."

Aunt Olga looked embarrassed and put on her glasses, only to remove them again immediately.

"Am I too small?" said Reine.

Olga didn't reply, but went back to her high desk and stood behind it as if about to make a speech. Then she put on her glasses again. But she said nothing.

"Is it because I don't have a work permit?"

Reine knew from a boy at school that you had to have a work permit if you were a minor. You went to the school doctor and left a sample of urine. If your piss was all right, you got the permit.

"We look for qualifications more than age here," said Aunt Olga.

Reine could make neither head nor tail of it all. There was something wrong with him, but what? Had he forgotten to zip up his fly? Did he have burrs in his hair? Had someone surreptitiously stuck a label on him saying "I am an idiot"?

"On a trial basis," he said. "Couldn't I just start on a trial basis?"

"There's nothing much wrong with your interest, anyhow," said Olga.

"But?"

Olga looked to the other ladies for support, but they immediately returned to work as Olga's gaze sought theirs one after another.

"Perhaps the girls and I ought to discuss the matter . . ."

"Can I phone back at three o'clock?" said Reine.

He couldn't understand what was so funny, but the women all started cackling. All at once, not just one starting and the others following suit. They were all laughing like five outboard engines starting up at exactly the same moment.

"What do you say, girls?"

They said nothing, but they nodded and giggled, sitting idle. Reine felt he had the atmosphere with him, and yet something was still wrong. He glanced down to check his fly, but he couldn't see very well; nothing sticking out, anyhow.

"Well, you see," said Olga, coming over to him, "we've never had a man employed here before."

"What a shame."

"You can stay," said Olga firmly, "on a trial basis. Your wages will work out all right. We'll settle that later."

Typical. Adults always treated children like that when it came to money. I haven't any change at the moment. I'll give you some when you need it. Money isn't everything, is it?

"When's the lunch hour?" said Reine.

"We have lunch between half-past eleven and twelve," said Olga. "Haven't you had any?"

"Not much, actually."

"Let's all introduce ourselves," said Olga, taking him by the shoulder. Her hands were wrinkled and covered with liver spots and splashes of gold paint, like the skin of a smoked herring.

Reine was taken around to shake hands. The woman in the wheelchair stretched out an unnaturally long arm; her name was Helene. The fat woman with the red face was called Lotta; she grasped his hand with both of hers, and Reine realized he would have to watch it a bit with her or she might start lifting her skirts and shuffling him underneath and brooding over him. The woman with the braids took his hand hesitantly, smiling timidly. Her name was Kristina, and she looked very brittle.

"Kristina is very sensitive," Olga explained protectively. "But she spends the night at the hospital so there's someone to look after her."

Was she crazy? Insane? Nuts? Violent? Kristina looked more as if she lived in a world of her own, in a great soap bubble. That was why she held out her hand so hesitantly. She was afraid of puncturing the soap bubble.

The tidy lady with the rings smelled strongly of perfume, and her teeth looked as if they were made of china. Her name was Mrs. Bergman-Ritz.

After Reine had been introduced, he understood that all the smiles, winks, and little pressures on his hand meant more or less what each old girl was trying to say: Things here aren't so idyllic as you think, but there's one person you can rely on—me!

"You must have something to eat now," said Olga. "Has anyone got anything left over from lunch?"

Two of them immediately sprang into action, Helene and Lotta. Kristina looked troubled and started massaging one of her braids, and Mrs. Bergman-Ritz sorrowfully shook her head; she had clearly eaten all hers. Helene came racing up to Reine in her wheelchair with a flat aluminum lunchbox, stopped in front of him, and thrust the box under his nose with her long spidery arms. There was an egg fried on both sides in the box. Lotta loomed up alongside Helene with a cheese sandwich wrapped in wax paper. Reine accepted both gifts and bowed rather sloppily, bowing a second time to make sure. Olga showed him a place by one of the windows where he could put his lunch on the windowsill while she went to get him a glass of juice.

The view was great: down to the right there was a wide bridge over the railway tracks into the Central Station, and to the left he could see the station itself with its long covered platforms. It all looked like a model layout. If he'd had a transformer up here, he could have controlled all the trains and switches, and organized a pretty good crash between a couple of express trains.

"Just have your lunch in peace," said Olga, setting down a glass of black currant juice.

When he had finished his second lunch, Reine was shown a place at the table beside Helene in her wheelchair. Olga brought him some discarded ribbons to practice on. He was given some paint and a skimpy brush, cleaning liquid, and a template of letters. The letters were inspired by the old medieval Gothic script, Reine was told. He thought they looked more like a clumsy code than anything else.

"Don't forget to stretch it properly," said Olga.

Reine smoothed out the shiny ribbon and clipped the end firmly to the side of the table.

"What shall I write?" he said.

"Whatever you like. It's just for practice."

He tried to think of something truly sorrowful, for instance, "Farewell Reine from Mother" or "We will meet on the other side, from Dag Hammarskjöld." No—too long. The practice ribbons were only short leftover pieces. Could he do the lettering at all? Yes, he could. Reine was good at drawing—in fact, best in his class at motorcycles and airplanes. On the first ribbon he wrote KAWASAKI, on the next YAMAHA, and on the third HUSQVARNA. Aunt Olga came to inspect.

"Good. Excellent. But you must remember to practice all the vowels—not just the A."

Reine returned to the scene of mourning and again imagined himself dead. The mourners who had ordered the wreath were his classmates. He amused himself pairing them off in a way that would have gotten him into big trouble had the boys seen. PATRICK and IRENE, THOMAS and BIRGITTA, MAGNUS and CARINA, DANIEL and LOUISA, PATRICK and CAMILLA, BRUNO and KARIN, REINE and . . . no, heck, he was supposed to be dead.

Reine was exhausted by half past three, his head sinking lower and lower toward the table.

"Perhaps you need glasses?" said Olga.

Reine shook his head wearily, for there was nothing wrong with his eyesight. He was one of the few in the class who could read the letters in the bottom righthand corner of the sight-testing chart. What was wrong was that Reine was completely out of his normal daily rhythm. They had a coffee break at half past two, but Reine refused any juice. He was so tired he wasn't even hungry. He pushed the ribbons aside and put his head down on his folded arms; for his own part, he was going to use the break to rest.

He did not wake up until ten to four, and then he jerked upright.

Wherever he looked, he saw smiling women. How could he cope with so many moms all at once?

"Sorry," he said. "Must be the change of air."

He got up and walked round to stretch his limbs. The studio consisted of nothing but this large attic, plus a closet that had been made into a tiny kitchen. To get to the john, he had to go out to the stairway and in through another attic door. This had the advantage of keeping some of the smell of chemicals out of the toilet. In the attic beyond the toilet was the studio's storeroom. Reine snooped around a bit. If he got too tired on the job, he could easily lie down and snooze back here among the rolls of cloth and boxes.

Reine devoted the rest of the afternoon to ribbons that gradually acquired the wording: A LAST FAREWELL from THE STAFF OF CHILDEN'S ISLAND. Childen? It was easy to make mistakes. But at the same time, the letters were so difficult to read that perhaps it wouldn't be noticed.

10 It was two o'clock in the morning, light outside, and Reine could not sleep. As soon as he had got back from work at about five o'clock, he had gathered up all the spaghetti from the seven almost empty boxes and boiled it in a large pan. Then he had poured half a bottle of ketchup on it and eaten it all in three minutes, forty-five seconds. Ten minutes later he had been afflicted with terrible thirst, which he had tried to assuage with the last remaining can of beer. Then he had fallen asleep and slept soundly until two o'clock, when he had awakened in the middle of a vivid dream: He was standing down in the yard by the big sandpit, pissing gallons and gallons into it so that waves were washing over the edge. He rushed out to the john—what fantastic luck that he'd waked up!

After checking the alarm clock, he went back to bed but found it impossible to sleep. He got up and dug Snoopy out of the closet. He had been unable to go to sleep without this great soft bundle of cloth in his arms for several years. But that didn't work, either. He was wide awake.

He got up, made some tea, and ate a whole pack of vanilla wafers. Mom had a jar of sleeping pills in the bathroom cupboard, but he wasn't sure how long they worked; the alarm clock was set for seven.

You could think clearly when everyone else was asleep. It was like having the whole world to yourself and being able to move things without anyone protesting. He sat down at his desk, where there was a small plastic globe. Sweden was too far north. There was an unused space between Spain and Italy if you shifted Majorca and Ibiza. He measured with his thumb; if you were clever, you might be able to put Sweden so that Majorca and Ibiza came into Lake Väner and Lake Vätter. No, then you'd have to fold Norrland back so that Kiruna didn't end up in northern Belgium. What if you put Sweden crosswise between Crete and Malta? What would happen then? Well, you'd cause one great helluva flood.

The time had come for serious matters. He had got nowhere with the assignment he had set himself: to find out what was *important*. Why man existed, where he was going, how long it would take, and to what purpose. Perhaps it was all too vague. If you wanted sensible answers, you had to ask more precise questions. Answers? Maybe it'd be smarter to start with the answers and then look for questions that matched them! He couldn't be bothered to think any more, so he went into Mom's room—the lounge, that is—and pulled out an encyclopedia he used to read when he had nothing to do.

DEVELOPMENT PHASE IV
SCHOOL AGE, *"The Latent Stage"*
This differs from previous stages in that it does not bring with it a transition from inner upheaval to new control. Freud calls this the latent stage because strong urges are usually latent. But it is only a pause before the storms of puberty, when all previous urges again return in different combinations to the surface.

It sounded alarming and exact. He was at this latent stage himself, and he hoped it would last for a long time. How long? Could one do anything to extend the latent stage? . . . *when all previous urges again return in different combinations to the surface.* Reine imagined himself being thrown into a gigantic, insane, rumbling pornographic fair with such strong rotating light effects your eyes began to boil. Everywhere, on the Ferris wheel, on the rollercoaster, in the fun house, beneath the whirling chocolate wheel, in the small boats, and in heaps outside the hot dog stand—everywhere, on the roofs, in the trees, in the pools, on the railing around the dance floor, thousands of youths were all sitting blind to their surroundings, jacking off like monkeys.

In one respect, Freud was wrong: not all strong urges were latent. Had that man Freud ever stood outside Carrol's or McDonald's, as hungry as a wolf, slobbering like a dog, without a cent in his pocket? Had he never stood squashed in a commuter train after knocking back two large Cokes plus an apple juice; had he ever been really bursting?

Also, it was clear from the text that there must be something before the latent stage, that at some time—or perhaps for several years—when he was small, his urges . . . had been in a helluva muddle. But he couldn't remember. He could only remember, when he was about three or four, being scared of being alone. When Mom went off to work on Sunday mornings, nothing helped. She could pile his bed up with goodies, popcorn, soda pop, teddy bears, music boxes and Tinker Toys— but nothing helped; his urge to run after her was so strong that he stopped breathing on a couple of occasions, which had in their turn led to his fainting and having "a fit," as Mom called it. Would that urge come back, the urge for company at all costs? He hoped not. Being alone meant being in control of the situation.

What had it really been like when he was small? He had learned to walk in 1965, he could talk reasonably well by 1966, and on his birthday, the ninth of September in 1969, he had been thirty-nine inches tall. Those facts could be found in the family album, plus the information that he had looked crazy and, what's more, had a crewcut. But what had he been like inside? Inside the actual nucleus. Was there a nucleus inside human beings where they were sort of—denser? Certainly. Reine mostly felt his nucleus just behind his eyes, an inch or two straight into his skull on a level with the bridge of his nose. But the nucleus could move. When you had a headache, for instance, the nucleus expanded like a skin inside your skull, a skin that might burst at any moment. And when you'd drunk two large Cokes, the nucleus thumped away behind the base of your prick so you had to cross your legs to stop the swollen nucleus from popping out.

Did everyone have a nucleus like that? If people existed, that is? Reine hadn't yet quite dared decide whether other people existed, or whether the outside world existed at all. It was often much more comfortable to start from the fact that he was the only one who existed—or rather, only his nucleus existed. His skin, muscles, and sinews were only a tight costume, a G-suit, or a skin-diving suit with holes in it for blowing in and out. He picked up a small black notebook, an old account book his mom had given him at an earlier increase in pocket money. He wrote: 19, 3, 11, 22, 5, 2, 5, 14, 17, 23, 11, 22, 19, 17, 6, 5, 10, 3, 5, 9, 5, 3, 19, 1, 5, 3, 24, 5.

Good. Safest to keep those thoughts secret for the time being. Because if other people really did exist, and Reine had gone around thinking that wasn't so and that he was quite alone in the universe, then a whole lot of people would have good reason to be annoyed. Not just God but his classmates as well. What the hell, they would say as they chased after him, going around saying we don't exist!

Did God exist? Mom said each and everyone had to decide for him- or herself whether God and Jesus existed. As far as she was concerned, she didn't think so, because if God existed, He would have put an end to all wars. He was invincible, wasn't He? Gran said God wasn't responsible for wars, despite the fact that He was invincible. The Devil and wicked people made wars, to God's great grief. God's grief over the wickedness of man was so profound that it was doubtful whether He would ever forgive us. That was where Jesus came in, a kind of defense counsel for man. By taking on all our sins, Jesus tried to placate God. But we had to help, too; we had to confess our sins and make amends. If

Reine was allowed to state his opinion, he thought God was kind of a moaner.

Like Mom, Reine didn't think God existed. Because if God existed, you had to believe the Bible; that was all part of it. And the Bible was a pretty poor story. Take the creation of man, for instance. First God creates the earth and the animals and then on the sixth day he takes a lump of clay and makes a living ocarina called Adam. Then, out of Adam's rib, God makes Eve. And then when Adam and Eve discover they've got a prick and a vagina, the whole thing gets going like an everlasting machine of skin and flesh.

Whoever wrote the Bible, whether it was God himself or someone else, had little imagination. That Darwin had a better one. At first there had been only a few molecules of albumin that learned to contract and crawl about like minute worms on the edge of the lava. Then those white worms had started getting together, forming slipper animalcules and algae. In time they became fish, then fish that climbed on land and became land animals. Not only that, but some of the land animals climbed back into the sea and gave birth to living young. Well, the first human being was no bigger than a shepherd dog and bred in trees in the savannas of Africa. Only the strongest and most cunning had survived and moved up to Spain and settled in a deep cave, which they had then decorated with the most fantastic paintings of buffalo and deer. And so on. Of course, that story also ended with an everlasting machine of skin and flesh, but it was not so rigid as the one God had invented. In the Bible everything was provided from the start, with no possibilities of development.

Opportunities for change were what interested Reine. In two billion years, maybe human beings would have learned how to live in space. What would human beings look like then? If it was true that the innermost heart of man was a nucleus, then the rest of the body was kind of nothing but tools for fixing food and transport. But perhaps in two billion years' time, man would have got rid of all that ballast. He would consist of nothing but nucleus, a kind of big peach stone with little shoots and suckers and water wings under the shell. With the help of nothing but the power of thought, this new nucleus-man would be able to move unhindered through time and space and find himself in an ever-lasting latent stage.

11 The alarm went off at seven o'clock. Reine had fallen asleep with his head on his desk and now started up and fell off the chair. As he lay on the floor he thought: I mustn't go back to sleep although the floor is soft as an air bed, as a tepid swimming pool, as a hammock . . . he woke again at ten to eight and sat up calmly. Everything was under control. He had overslept; he had to be at work in ten minutes, and there was no hope of being on time even by helicopter, as a helicopter couldn't land directly on Olga's studio without being forced down somewhere on the railway station.

He decided to wait until five past eight and then telephone Aunt Olga. He cleared up his personal business and, grimacing horribly, made a couple of passes with the toothbrush as a punishment for oversleeping. It wasn't easy to find the telephone number, and he didn't telephone until twenty past.

"Hullo, this is Reine. I'm sick today. I've got a twisted gut."

There was a silence the other end of the wire and then Reine heard Olga chattering to the others.

"Which hospital are you in?" said Olga.

Reine realized he had made a blunder.

"Are your next of kin with you?" said Olga.

"No, I'm at home. I was in hospital last night. They *thought* it was a twisted gut. Or something like it. But it's getting better now."

Olga was very disturbed and wished to know more: which hospital he'd been in, whether the doctor was a real doctor or just some summer replacement, whether Reine had someone who would sit at his bedside, and whether he had been given orders to return immediately to the hospital if he had the slightest pain again. Which hospital was it, by the way?

"Lowenström Hospital," said Reine. "My mom works there."

Aunt Olga calmed down a lot, at the same time impressed upon Reine the importance of not getting up too soon. He was welcome to come when he could. They all appreciated him so much at the studio. They concluded their conversation. Reine went out into the kitchen to look for breakfast. There was practically nothing except a box of granola, which he stirred into a porridge with cold water. It tasted awful, but he consoled himself by reading on the package how good for him it was.

By the time it finally dawned on Reine that he would not be able to stand being shut up in the apartment all day, it was nine o'clock. He longed for Olga's studio, convinced something would happen there, a miracle, that someone would go crazy in an astonishing way, or there would be a terrible railway accident right below Olga's window. He just couldn't miss that! He telephoned again.

"Reine here. I'm feeling much much better now . . ."

But Aunt Olga protested: he was to stay in bed; that was best. Reine was lucky enough to produce the right argument.

"Well, you see, it's like this. We've talked to the doctor, and he says it's important to keep moving after an attack like this. You have to keep going so that you don't get snarled up. He actually recommended I should go to work . . ."

Olga was skeptical; she'd never heard anything like it before.

"But everyone knows how doctors all think different things. One day you have to take exercise so as not to have a heart attack, and the next day you're lying there covered from head to foot with plaster of paris. This doctor says my mom's very with it. I'm not so sure myself, but I suppose I ought to do what the doctor says, sort of."

Olga gave in, and Reine bolted off to catch the nine twenty-two train. As usual, he misjudged the time and got to Sollentuna station a quarter

of an hour too early, his enthusiasm already cooling. If there was anything he really hated, it was waiting for the commuter train with nothing to do except sit on a bench and spit gobs between your own shoes.

They were checking tickets on the train, two uniformed inspectors
appearing from nowhere just as the doors closed. They swiftly divided
up the car, one starting at the back and moving forward, the other in the
middle moving forward. There was no hope of escape. But Reine was
safe this time, since he had a genuine card. Once that spring he had
forged a card for a friend. It hadn't been difficult; all you needed was a
photograph, a piece of white cardboard, some paper, ink, a fine green
ballpoint, and an ordinary blue one. You could fix the printing of the
monthly stamp with a kid's rubber stamp. Reine hadn't dared try it out
himself, but his friend had, with Reine at his side using an ordinary
ticket. It had worked. The old boys at the turnstiles couldn't even be
bothered to look closely. But would the forgery get by an inspector? Yes,
as long as the holder of the false card was pure and clean, wore glasses,
and most of all had not yet reached puberty. Adults all hated children,
and the bigger children grew, the more they were hated. There were
some who almost crapped their eyes out just looking at a sixteen-year-
old in a denim jacket.

Reine climbed the stairs to Olga's studio. Studio? Just as he put his
hand out toward the handle of the wide metal door, he realized he had
neglected a very important matter, the daily check on his health. He
turned and opened the door to the attic office with toilet and storeroom.
The john was occupied. When he took a peep through the keyhole—for
the sake of form, mostly—he caught the acrid smell of tobacco smoke.
One of the women was smoking on the sly in there.

The elevator! Reine was in luck—the elevator had not been called
down. He stepped inside, pressed the ground floor button, let the elevator go down a short distance, then pressed the stop button. Swiftly he
whipped open his fly. There were mirrors in the elevator, as if designed
for examinations. He wiggled his prick and balls out and carefully inspected his private parts for signs of a dark strand of hair. Apart from

some minimal white down, there was not a single sign of growth. One more day, one more day to live! If one dark hair had grown, could he have postponed puberty by pulling it out?

He put his private parts back, poked the shorts flap back so that nothing would get caught in the zipper, then zipped up. Before pressing the fifth floor button, he grinned at himself in the mirror, trying to look like Marty Feldman—none too successfully, as everything was wrong: hair color, eyes, nose, chin. What had Marty looked like before he reached puberty and his eyes started bulging?

When he stepped into the studio, he was made to repeat his account of his attack of twisted gut. All the women were in their places. Who had been smoking on the sly in the john? Helene in her wheelchair could be excluded, and also Aunt Olga herself, presumably. Which of the others looked the guiltiest? Pink in the face Lotta? Mrs. Bergman-Ritz? Or Kristina, who kept glancing over her shoulder?

Today Reine was to be allowed to tackle a trial order by himself. It was quite simple: he had to print three letters, RIP, on a pale green ribbon. He was given a brand-new paintbrush. Aunt Olga kept the new paintbrushes locked in her desk. He tackled his assignment with enthusiasm—it was easy, but what did RIP mean? He asked Aunt Olga.

"Something Swedish, I suppose," she said. "I'm from Lithuania, so I don't know all your abbreviations."

Lithuania? Was old Marie Curie from Lithuania? Or was it Poland, or Paris?

"Where's Lithuania?" said Reine.

Lotta and Helene suddenly stopped working, and Reine sensed tension in the room.

"Haven't you learned that in school?" said Olga.

"No. I know where Mauretania is. In the West Indies."

"Don't you know where Estonia and Latvia are?"

"No."

"The Baltic States?"

"Maybe . . . mmm . . . no."

"Maybe you know where Finland is, anyhow?"

"Suomi," said Reine.

"Estonia, Latvia, and Lithuania were free states occupied by the Bolsheviks in 1940. On the twenty-first of July, my father and I fled to Sweden. We had to leave everything behind."

"What a pity," said Reine sympathetically.

Aunt Olga seemed very upset, and the others were all working intently.

"If only you knew how sad you make me. That Swedish children nowadays don't even know there's a place called Lithuania."

"The school curriculum is all mixed up," said Reine.

"Have you never given a thought to what lies on the other side of the Baltic, only a few hours in a boat from Sweden?"

"Soviet Russia. You can go on a cruise to Riga. My mom did that last summer with a guy—well. I got a box of green goodies she bought on the boat."

"I'm afraid I can't tell you what RIP means," said Aunt Olga, retreating to her accounts at the desk; she had a large book with a cover patterned like peacocks' tails.

Before lunch, Reine printed SIGBRIT and DAG, PSALM 103, AGNES, EVA, THE GRANDCHILDREN, and THE LITTLE ONE. He started getting into a routine, but the letters were lousy! Same old style all the time. Why couldn't they vary them a bit like they did on neon signs, for instance? Or makes of cars? How the heck could they all stand it, sitting here year after year, messing around with the same old letters?

The time before lunch went by surprisingly quickly. He hadn't given food a thought for half an hour when Olga at last said:

"Shall we have our lunch, then?"

They had all brought lunch with them except Reine. They all seemed to want to offer him some, too—except for Kristina, who washed her hands very carefully before taking out her pack of sandwiches. But Reine had other ideas.

"May I go out and eat?" he said.

"Certainly. But we start again at twelve o'clock."

"Could I have a little advance? Ten, perhaps?"

He was given a ten out of Aunt Olga's black cashbox, and he bolted out onto the street as happy as a lark and as hungry as a giant dinosaur. Carrol's was nearest.

12 On Thursday, the nineteenth of June, Reine had been working for Aunt Olga for almost a week and had received his first wages, one hundred and twenty *kronor.* He was not allowed the apprentice wages of ten kronor an hour because he was far too young. Instead, they had appointed him "internal messenger," a kind of errand boy or "gofer." There weren't many errands out in town—the florists sent their own people to fetch the wreaths—but if Reine agreed to be called messenger instead of apprentice, his wages could be taken from petty cash and taxes avoided. His weekly wage was one hundred and fifty, with an inbuilt right to go home and sleep if he got too tired, but he didn't. He hated every minute in the empty apartment.

Thursday the nineteenth of June was the day before Midsummer Eve, and Reine was anticipating his solitary three-day weekend with horror. Practically all his contemporaries were away. A few might be left, but he dared not get in touch with them for fear of possible gossip. The crush was terrific as he left the city center at about five. Cross, tired, or semi-drunk people with carriers and luggage preferred not to notice him. They had to look out for small children (trampling on two-year-olds was beyond the pale), and most adults were leery of teenagers, keeping their distance as if afraid of getting their clothes slashed with razor blades. But eleven-year-olds—well, society had allotted eleven-year-olds an assignment this hot afternoon: they were to be trampled on, pushed, crowded, squeezed, and used as handles, support, or sandwich fillings.

Reine's mood was made even worse by the sunny hot weather. He had miscalculated completely. Midsummer was usually cold, rainy, and at best also windy with a risk of hail. It was good to shut yourself indoors in bad weather, pull down the blinds, light a candle, eat, listen to records and hail rattling against the window. But if it was hot? Would he dare go out on the balcony? If Mom hadn't taken all her nylons with her, he could have pulled one over his head.

The first thing Reine did when he got home was to pay back the forty *kronor* he had borrowed from Mom's piggy bank. Then he took out an envelope, put six tens into it, and sealed it; that was food money for the next week. Twenty *kronor* remained to live on during the Midsummer holiday. That should be all right, but as a reserve he borrowed fifteen back from his mom's savings and put it into a special envelope labelled "Reserve."

The supermarket was open until eight, so he had plenty of time. Now it was a matter of shopping wisely. There was a sale on avocados and frozen salmon. He didn't like fish on principle, but he could well try an avocado. The avocado felt interesting to handle, like a leaden pear. Bread? He took a sliced loaf for toast; it was important to get some hot food into you occasionally. Something good to munch perhaps? He slipped six bags of peanuts into the cart. Saltine crackers were on the same shelf, so he took a box of those, too. He needed protein, of course; otherwise his starving body might start breaking down his brain. He dragged the impossible cart with its wobbling wheels along the counter of cold cuts and hotdogs. Hotdogs? Could be fried or eaten raw. But he distrusted hotdogs; there was something called hotdog poisoning, and naturally that should be avoided. Instead he took a pack of liverwurst.

He mustn't forget something to drink. People were seething around the beer and soft drink section more than anywhere else. Two girls of fifteen or so who were at school with Reine were loading up a shopping cart with cider. A little old woman was rushing around asking for lager but could not get at it. Reine crouched and pushed his way between two noisy men in blue overalls and landed in the middle of a great pyramid of Pripps beer cans. Wasn't there any Tuborg? There was none to be seen—they had run out of Tuborg. Would Mom remember which kind of beer? He took a chance and grabbed two cans of Heineken.

"Has your mom sent you down to buy beer?" he heard a man's voice behind him.

It was Stig, Mom's friend, who'd slept in the guest room once or twice in the spring. They had even gone on a trip to Åland, all three of them. But it had been a failure; they'd run out of those green goodies.

"Is Harriet off work over Midsummer?"

He turned toward Stig. Stig already had quite a bit under his belt; Reine could see that from his eyes and rigid face. But so far, he seemed to be in a good mood. He had also been in a good mood on the Åland boat—on the journey out. On the journey back, he had been lousy to Mom and had got up several times in the bar and said in a loud voice: "This woman's frigid." Reine didn't exactly know what that entailed, but he presumed it meant Mom couldn't have any more children. He was profoundly grateful for that. When the boat docked, they had had to put Stig into a taxi, but there'd been trouble over that, too. The driver had refused to leave until he had been paid in advance.

"Yer mom's the best in the world," Stig said, putting his hand on Reine's shoulders.

"She's not at home," Reine said.

"Working? All the weekend?"

"More or less."

Stig took over Reine's cart because he had nowhere to put his two cartons of beer in plastic bottles.

"I'll push it for ya, see. The law says kids mustn't work. Where's yer list?" he went on.

Reine realized he would have had a list with him if his mom had sent him. But he couldn't think of an excuse, so he left the question unanswered. Instead, he purposefully took a bottle of lime juice and put it on top of the beer cartons.

"Lost yer list, have ya, kid?" said Stig. "Mom won't like that now, will she? Won't like it, hear? Won't like it. Sad. Cross. D'ya see?"

"She's done the shopping already," said Reine. "These are just a few small things we forgot."

Stig leaned over and started rummaging in Reine's cart.

"Avocado? Got company coming, have ya? Anyone I know?"

Reine chose not to reply to that one, either, but snatched down a packet of spaghetti. How the heck was he going to get rid of Stig? Stig—what a bloody silly name, too. Pigstig. Supposing you had to go round with a name like Hog? Hogpog. And had a son called Piglet? Or Piggywig.

"Mom's not feeling too good," said Reine, without really knowing where he was going to get with that.

"Thought you said she was working?"

"Yeah, she is. But she's not feeling too good in between. Something to do with her bronchials."

"Smokes too much," said Stig.

Reine stopped in surprise. What the heck did he mean?

"My mom doesn't smoke."

"Yeah, of course. She smokes like a damn chimney. She stinks of smoke, too, even out of her . . . yer mom's a heavy smoker, Reine. And she knows it."

"No."

Stig stopped in front of Reine and pointed at him with his hand like a gun, forefinger the barrel, thumb up like the hammer.

"Take a bet on it?"

Reine ducked, slipped past, and went over to the magazine rack. *Technical World* number thirteen had come. There were tests on the Chevrolet Impala in it. Well, he could resist that. Who wanted a bumpy old American car? But there was an article on the Suzuki RE 5 Wankel; he couldn't miss that.

"Fifty," said Stig, who'd caught up with him, "that Harriet smokes like a refr . . . refe . . . refinery."

"She's not at home," said Reine, returning to his shopping cart. He pressed his chest against the cart's handle and pushed it over toward the shortest line—which line was shortest? The one you were not standing in.

"She leaves traces. Ashtrays, cigarette packs, the smell, boy. In the curtains. I'll give ya fifty if ya can show me a clean apartment."

Reine would not agree to any bets. He stood leaning over the cart in the line, leafing through *Technical World*, Stig behind him shoving slightly, grousing, pretending to inhale deeply and stub out a cigarette on the back of Reine's neck. As soon as Reine could get through the checkout, he'd grab his groceries and be off like a bat out of hell. If Stig came after him or rang the doorbell, he wouldn't open up.

Reine's turn came, and he slipped ahead of the cart, blocking Stig's way. Swiftly, he slung his groceries up on the counter without touching Stig's, and the cashier rang up the sum—forty-five eighty. Reine put down his own twenty first, then the fifteen in the reserve envelope. He was caught! He couldn't go and put some of the goods back now. Stig noticed the situation and pulled a bundle of crumpled notes out of the top pocket of his summer jersey.

"I'll pay for the boy! This boy's got a mom as tender as a lion."

The cashier grinned in an embarrassed way, which Stig at once took as encouragement.

"What legs! What tits! What toes! Like new potatoes. Ya don't look too bad yourself," he added to the cashier, screwing up one side of his face as if he had a fly in his eye.

Stig pushed his way past Reine and shoveled all the goods straight into two plastic bags. Reine had no means of getting away.

"If only she could give up her nicotine addiction," Stig said on the steps.

As soon as they got into the apartment, Stig went in and pissed without closing the door behind him, splashing like a horse.

"God, it stinks of smoke in here," he said when he came out, picking up his beer carton and going into the guest room to lie down on the bed.

Reine put his groceries away in the cupboard and refrigerator before going in after him.

"Mom's working," he said. "There's no point in your waiting."

"Go to hell, little whore's bastard," said Stig sleepily. "And don't forget to shut the door behind you."

13 Reine was sitting in his locked room on the afternoon of Midsummer Eve, looking through a big picture book about angels. He had been to the library the other evening to find some reading matter, but he'd already read all the airplane and automobile books they had. By chance he happened to catch sight of *Angels in Art*, a big heavy book full of color prints.

Supposing everyone suddenly sprouted wings at five o'clock one afternoon? Wings that grew out in a minute or so, something like hoisting a sail. At that time on an ordinary day he would probably be squashed in the commuter train. It'd be cramped, and the people who'd got themselves a seat would be forced to get up. You could take the opportunity to jump up on a seat then. What would it feel like? Reine put his left hand on his right shoulder, then brought his shoulder forward so that he could feel the bony edge of his shoulder blade. On ordinary birds the wings were the same as arms, but he could see from the pictures that angels had both arms *and* wings. Where exactly they were fastened wasn't visible, but the shoulder-blade was the only possible place.

How long would his wings be? The artists seemed to disagree on that point. Some of the angels looked like gliders with thirty-foot wingspans. Others had only small stunted wings like chickens, or the angels on bookmarks. But about twelve feet, roughly, would be reasonable, twelve each way. There would of course be a terrible rustling in the train when the passengers all started unfolding them. But clothes! People would have to take off jackets and shirts and blouses and—no, he hoped the women would keep on their bras so you wouldn't have to see all those horrible hanging tits.

Supposing all the passengers were suffocated by that surging mass of feathers? They could open the windows, of course, and stick their wings outside—but not too far! And not if the train was going at full speed; the train might take off and soar up into the air like a jumbo jet with hundreds of white wings. Oh, heck no, he would make sure he wasn't on a train if it was like that. He would work overtime. If wings started growing out of Aunt Olga, it wouldn't matter all that much, though they might get caught in all those hanging ribbons if you were careless, but . . . what fun for Helene in a wheelchair if she suddenly grew wings! They could open the windows facing the station, then lift Helene up and ease her on to the windowsill. Then he'd climb up beside her and hold her hand, and they could jump together. The chair was heavy, so she would weigh Reine down at first. But when they had got up speed, they would sail on stiff rigid wings, wingtip to wingtip, right across the tracks, then turn upwind and make a perfect landing—he running, she with bumping screeching rubber tires.

What had all these famous artists thought angels looked like? One called William Blake had a thing about owls; either the angels had owl's heads or else fluffy woolly owl's wings. They didn't look up to much. Another with just about the same idea was a guy called Goya. But his owl-angels clearly flew only at night. Of course, if you were a pronouncedly night angel, you ought to have owl's wings. Filippo Morghens's angels had swan's wings. Hopeless great constructions. They would never get up in the air, not to mention what would happen if the wind got up.

Most of the angels stayed on the ground, standing about in a whole lot of artificial postures, apparently wearing their wings as ornaments. One guy called da Vinci seemed to be the only one who had given a little thought to flying. He must have believed human beings might fly one day. But at the same time, his winged figures looked a bit like skinny bats or paper kites—as if their wings were something they put on, not something that grew out.

All good people would one day become angels and grow wings; Gran had told Reine that. Then there was something called fallen angels; what they were, he had never quite made out. Really wicked people never got wings. They were promptly transported downward like miners, in small wicker elevators. Fallen angels must be the kind who had bluffed their way into getting wings and then, when they were found out, had to face a bad end. In his mind, Reine saw a soot-blackened and shattered fallen angel crawling along an eighteen-inch mine shaft, dragging a rusty pick behind him.

Nearly all the angels in the book looked like fallen angels, actually—like cheats. Raphael, Michelangelo, whatever their names were—they seemed to have gone in for painting artificial angels with child faces. Faces of marzipan. You could bet your bottom dollar their wings were marzipan, too. The best was one by some old guy called Bosch. He'd painted an angel that was half human and half bullfinch. That was bound to be the only construction that could actually fly.

Reine picked up a drawing pad and a pen and did a few sketches. Eagle's wings were clearly unsuitable, and anyhow eagles were nothing but bad-tempered overgrown hawks. Swallow's wings seemed good, but you couldn't fold them. Any angel with swallow's wings would have to walk about bent forward as if he had sciatica; otherwise his wingtips would drag on the ground. The only practical thing was to equip all angels with gull's wings. The gull was a superior flier and had long slender wings that could be almost completely folded away when at rest. The gull was amphibious and could come down on water as well as land. The gull was slender and white, a suitable color. An angel shouldn't look like a capercaillie or a stuffed grouse with a great lyre on its back. Angels had to fly easily and with dignity, not blundering heavily along like a panic-stricken hen.

Angels with gull's wings—that was the answer. Gulls ignored the weather and lived just as easily in town as in the country or by the sea. And the gull was omnivorous, too, the only bird that knew its way around and had learned to love garbage dumps.

Stig was rattling the doorhandle! Reine hurriedly hid the sketches underneath the blotter on his desk and stuffed the angel book into the closet behind Snoopy.

"Open up!" said Stig.

Reine unlocked the door. Stig had slept off the booze during the night, and Reine was hoping against hope he would now leave. Without breakfast.

"Harriet's gone again, has she? Did she even see me?"

"Don't know. I was asleep."

Stig stepped inside and inspected the room all around. He was looking bad tempered and bloated, his shirt hanging out. He smelled of sweat and stale liquor. In passing, he gave Reine a shove so that he sat down on the bed. Stig stood at the end of the bed, took out a fifty note, and held it up.

"Say I'm a lousy little skunk and you can have it."

"I'm a lousy little skunk," said Reine.

"Good. Now yer fifty *kronor* richer. But ya have to say something for free. Now say Urho Kekkonen eats lemmin makkara. For free."

"Urho Kekkonen eats . . . what?"

"Urho Kekkonen eats lemmin makkara."

"Urho Kekkonen eats lemmin makkara. What does that mean?"

"No idea. Here's yer fifty."

Stig threw the note up into the air. It floated down a few feet, then altered course and sailed under the bed.

"Start work at one o'clock," said Stig.

"Are you still working at the ambulance station?"

"Am I still working at the ambulance station? Of course—why shouldn't I be?"

Stig seemed to be a bit annoyed now. He stood swaying slightly, trying his feet like a boxer who . . . no, Stig would never dare take a crack at Reine. Not here at home.

"Are you sober?" said Reine.

"Not in the slightest," said Stig. "Have I told ya how we scraped up the pieces of that pensioner who blew hisself to bits?"

Reine stopped breathing. He both wanted and didn't want to hear. He would dream about it, of course. But blood and horrors could be just as exciting as looking at a naked girl.

"Little sadist," said Stig. "D'ya think I'd tell that to a minor?"

"Do you drive an ambulance even when you're not sober?"

"Well, I damn well wouldn't dare drive my own car. Ever heard of the fuzz stopping an ambulance?"

Stig slopped out into the hall, pushing his shirt back into his trousers. Before leaving, he went into the bathroom and spat into the toilet.

"Urho Kekkonen is the president of Finland," he said before slamming the front door behind him.

14 Reine was sitting on the balcony with his little tape recorder pressed against his right ear, listening to Janne Schaffer. He was wearing his mother's pink sun hat with a heavy drooping brim. He did not wish to be recognized. The risk was not great, however, since it was dawn. Over the Sollentuna shopping center the sun was shining red, the sky behind as white as a page in a diary. It wasn't a bit cold, only a little damp; his fingertips were quite soft. Reine had *Angels in Art* on his lap as a desk. He stuck the pen behind his free left ear and leaned back in the chair. *Anyone who wanted to was allowed to stay up all night . . . one boy had beer with him*—yes, he would write that. One of the others, one of the older ones, drank beer on Midsummer Eve—that was just the kind of information that would calm Mom in the right way. First of all, it was almost certainly true; second, it wasn't Reine drinking, for if it had been, he wouldn't have been so darned stupid as to mention the word beer.

Should he thank her for the ten? Reine had still not had a letter from Mom. He presumed her letters had been addressed to Children's Island and were now on their way back to Sollentuna, probably stuck in some sorting office over Midsummer. But he had to pretend he had received a letter; otherwise she would be suspicious. *Thanks for the ten.* Supposing it was two tens? Or only a five? If he wrote the wrong amount, Mom might think someone had raided the letter, and what then? *Thanks for your letter and the contents!* Dead clever, Reine. *How are things on the west coast? Is it sunny like here? Do you go swimming every day, too? Is the food good in the hospital? Have you got a lot of friends, too?* That was just how letters should be written when you're bluffing, asking Mom what she was up to so he wouldn't have to tell a pack of lies about what he was up to. To think he'd not thought of that before!

He put down the tape recorder and started writing the letter. It came easily—he could write hundreds of letters this way, simply asking question after question. But what if Mom had asked *him* something in her letter? What? Something tricky? "Have you by any chance got the top of my blue swimsuit?" Then he'd be sunk. You could never guess what crazy mistakes Mom might make when she was packing in a hurry. He discarded the question. *Hug from Reine,* he added. Aha, this'll be good. *P.S. I've bought a pair of sunglasses for seven-fifty.* Mom would at once realize she should send a ten next time she wrote.

Reine sealed the letter and put it to press inside *Angels in Art*. He had discovered something. *Karlson on the Roof* was also about someone who could fly. He had read that book nine times. Where was it? Reine kept his library in the closet in a couple of empty beer crates. He took out Snoopy and some clothes that were in the way. There were over two hundred Donald Duck comics and a few issues of *Buster* and *Mad* in the beer crates and on the floor, and a picture magazine at the bottom of one of the crates. But where the heck was *Karlson on the Roof*?

He eventually found it under his bed, in almost the exact spot where Stig's fifty note had landed. He took the book out to the balcony, sat down, and switched on the tape recorder again—the recording was lousy because he'd taped it from the radio. Karlson flew with a propeller on his back. He'd never given that a thought when he was younger! The propeller was hellish small in relation to Karlson; he could see that from the pictures. He read a little here and there. In one place it said Karlson buzzed when he flew. Of course, propellers always buzz up to a point. But in another place it said Karlson whistled past like a jet plane. How did that connect? Did Karlson use a turbojet engine? The truth was that Karlson didn't use an engine at all. The propeller just sat there directly on his back like a bowtie. Why couldn't children's books be a little more exact? It was stupid to try to cheat kids into thinking Karlson could fly with that equipment. But of course only females wrote children's books.

Angels didn't function, and to crown everything Karlson was also a fraud. And yet naturally it was impossible for a human being to fly. But artists and authors didn't bother to read up on it and find out a single thing about flying techniques. He looked with dissatisfaction at a few more Karlson illustrations. Karlson actually had an enormous head in relation to his body. Water on the brain, of course, and dumb as well. But . . . that's it! Human beings *could* fly if they had gas in their heads. A large head containing gas as well as brain. The pressure could be regulated through the ears or nose. No wings, no propellers to get caught in telephone wires. How large? Roughly the size of a beach ball. Slow and dignified, the man-angel with a giant head would rise and gain height or sink to the ground and hover a foot or so above it without ever having to touch the surface of the earth with his feet.

Reine leaned back, put his feet up on the balcony railing, and closed his eyes. He drew a deep breath and felt his skull filling with soft gas . . . heck! He leaped out of the chair—now he knew how he would manage the task he had assigned himself for that summer. He was stupid to go around looking for a whole lot of answers, answers that would tell him what the whole thing was about, why he existed and what things had been like before he existed. People had probably been asking that for millions of years—whether other people existed, that is—but he would presume that. It was much smarter to reverse the process; he would gather up a whole lot of answers and then go out to look for questions to match them. What answers were there? Revolution, rocket warfare, Day of Reckoning? There were some answers that began with R, anyhow. Which question preceded the answer "You'll be an angel"?

Reine went into the apartment to make a list of the ten weightiest answers. As he passed through the hall, he noticed that the keys he had left below the mirror were gone. He stopped and slapped his backside and thighs. No, not in his trouser pockets. His jacket lay flung across a shelf; no keys in that, either, nor in the kitchen, nor in the bedroom, nor on the balcony. Stig had taken the keys. That bastard Stig had stolen the only apartment key Reine had.

Reine fastened the safety chain on the front door. The bastard wasn't going to come in while Reine was there, anyhow. But what about when he wasn't at home? Not then, either, because he could make a rope ladder and climb in and out by the balcony. That would have to happen at night, of course, when it was dark and no one could see him. How long was it dark these nights? Two hours? Reine would buy materials for a rope ladder with the fifty Stig had given him. Stupid! He couldn't have a rope ladder dangling from the balcony all day long. What if he had a rope ladder with some kind of arrangement, a kind of hook that meant you could jerk it free and take it with you—and then throw the hook up from the ground to attach the ladder again when you needed to get back in? Would that be possible? Mountain climbers could do it. What luck he was so inventive! It would be simplest if he got up onto the roof of the balcony instead—what luck he lived on the top floor. He could get down from the roof through some hatch or fire door. The problem was solved. He took out the last bag of peanuts, undressed, sat down on his bed, and wrote in his little notebook: 13, 19, 17, 1, 11, 5, 17, 14, 17, 3, 12, 5, 2, 3. 13, 19, 15, 3, 11, 19, 6.

15 Who was it smoking on the sly in the john? After morning coffee, which they drank without stopping work, Lotta excused herself and slipped out. Reine timed her: twelve minutes. Lotta looked flushed and uncomfortable when she came back, buttoning up a little higher at her throat and letting the smoke out. She also put a tablet into her mouth. She tried to do it without being seen but dropped the tablet on the floor, hesitated before picking it up, then decided it didn't exist and took another.

Reine stopped in the middle of ONE LAT GREETING. What? Hell and damnation, he'd left out a letter again. Lat, cat, my aunt Pat. He got up, hugging his stomach, and went across to the toilet in the attic. He got down on his knees and inspected the porcelain; not a trace of ash. He examined the basin, which wasn't really a basin but a narrow, trough-like construction of metal. Cigarette butts? Matches? There was no soap dish. A piece of soap with a string right through it hung on the tap. No flakes of tobacco in the green and white flecked soap.

Before returning, he quickly checked up on the day's state of health. Fine, no sign of puberty today. How quickly did it come when it came? Could he make do with once a week—on Sunday mornings, for instance? If he looked too often, perhaps he wouldn't notice the change? Reine knew what he would do when the first coarse dark hair appeared. He wouldn't cut it off but pull it out. Root and all.

Reine returned to the studio. They were very busy that day. The telephone kept ringing, and Miss Olga became more and more jittery. There was always the same hectic rush after a long weekend. Reine had learned that a lot of old people died during the long holiday weekends. But the silly thing was that ten or twelve or as many as fifteen days sometimes went by before the funeral. They lay that long in the mortuary, so there was plenty of time to plan the funeral—but the time wasn't used. It didn't seem to make any difference whether they were quick funerals or delayed ones; ribbons and wreaths were something you arranged at the very last minute. Sometimes a florist or a cab driver would stand impatiently in the doorway while the quickest of them, Helene, printed a ribbon from dictation. Helene—who had no legs that worked. That was why she was the quickest; she could concentrate on her arms.

At five past eleven it was Kristina's turn. She didn't go straight out to the john but took a zigzag route, first swiftly and jerkily to the window and looking out, then over to the desk where Miss Olga was on the phone. She stopped as if asking for permission, standing there for a minute or so, twisting her thick silver-gray braids. Then, without the harassed Olga even noticing her, she went to the coat rack and rummaged in her coat pocket. Aha! The cigarettes.

Kristina was away no longer than two minutes. But that didn't deceive him. A really cunning smoker could probably get in seven or eight quick drags and save the rest of the cigarette for the next visit. Just as Reine got up, Aunt Olga spoke.

"Reine, I've got an order here for a dead dog. Perhaps that'd suit you?"

Reine felt obliged to sit down again, and Aunt Olga brought a piece of paper over to him.

"Here. For a change. GREETINGS TO THE BLESSED HUNTING GROUNDS. YOUR MISTRESS MARGIT," she said.

"What color ribbon?" said Reine.

"She forgot to say. We usually take white when no particular color has been requested."

"Gold lettering? For a dog?"

Olga did not reply, but patted his head and went over to pick up Lotta's dropped tablet. Reine got up again.

"Just going down to buy some coughdrops," he said.

"Be careful when you cross the street," said Olga.

Reine examined the whole room, the toilet bowl, the metal basin, the chair. It had been such a short smoke break, the suspect would surely not have had time to eliminate all traces. Behind the pipes? No, no hidden butt. In the plastic bucket that served as a wastebasket was a tightly rolled up little white plastic bag. Reine knew he ought to open it up, but he couldn't bring himself to. It might well contain a used tampon. He looked at his watch and tried to work out how long it would take to cross the street to the tobacco and porn store on the other side, buy a box of coughdrops, and get back again. Seven minutes? He put down the lid and sat down.

"Nothing to be gained here," he said half aloud, his mouth over the edge of the basin.

Reine managed to finish the dog ribbon just in time for lunch. What did the wreath look like? Did they use greenery for dogs, too? Dogwood leaves? He tittered. He loved bad jokes. Bad jokes weren't really bad jokes at all—only adults thought they were. Bad jokes were for connoisseurs. Bad jokes were like sour pickled herring. The more you knew about pickled herring, the more ancient the pickling should be. In the end, you might just as well open a can of preserved diarrhea. He pulled a bad joke out of his card index. A little boy was going out to buy some aftershave for his father. All the way to the shop he kept practicing this peculiar word to himself so that he would remember it—aftershave, aftershave—until it gradually became have-to-shave. There was a girl behind the counter. The little boy went up to her and said, "Do you have to shave, please, Miss?"

Reine laughed out loud. All the women turned around and smiled. He arranged his features and smiled back. Better to confine thinking about bad jokes to the john, he thought. Why didn't Helene ever go to the john? Reine hadn't seen her going for a whole week—unless she took the opportunity when Reine was out for lunch. How could anyone hold out for so long? Though she had to, of course. Sitting in a wheelchair, there was nothing else to do but hold on tight, was there? Or? Reine deliberately dropped the scissors on the floor so that he could bend down. Was there a container underneath the wheelchair? It was hard to see, because Helene's skirt hung down and got in the way. But of course it was quite possible to equip a wheelchair made of tubular steel with an inbuilt john. Naturally he'd never heard of such a thing—but then people didn't talk about toilet problems all that much. Anyhow, there was no need for a special container, since the tubes themselves probably held quite a bit. But how did it work? He decided to keep a careful eye on Helene in the future and see if she pulled some lever or other under the chassis or pressed some button. Or whether she was looking strained or peculiar. Simplest of all would be to turn the wheelchair upside down and check, but she never left it.

After lunch Reine had to do lettering "for stock," as it was called. This meant leaving out the names, writing them in afterward when the order came in. Certain texts were constantly repeated throughout the day. A LAST GREETING. FROM FRIENDS. FROM A GRIEVING WIFE/HUSBAND. Then all he had to do was to add the names: August and Lotta and Pop Goes the Weasel, or the Hammarskjöld Family, or whatever the heck they liked to be called.

Reine didn't like lettering "for stock." He liked it when he himself could listen when the actual order came on the phone, preferably from a relative. He also wanted to know as much as possible about the dead person, when and where the funeral was to take place, how many wreaths had been ordered. Sometimes he could find out those things when someone from the undertaker's came with a sheaf of papers. Aunt Olga didn't hesitate to ask, and all he had to do was to keep his ears flapping. He could find out what the disease had been, which hospital, the doctor's name, whether it had been a difficult death or unexpected or a relief—he could find out almost everything. But not when he lettered "for stock"; then it seemed to be for people who weren't yet dead.

Maybe he could do lettering for his own wreath? Why not? The florists in the Sollentuna shopping center—where did they have their ribbons done? Nowhere? It struck Reine that perhaps he was occupied with a dying craft and most people nowadays put their own ribbons into some small machine and pressed a button. Nothing to it. Then the ribbon rolled out complete at the other end like a scarf coming out of a mangle. Or maybe they used decals, putting a number of letters into water until they loosened from the paper backing, then just transferring the letters to the ribbon and letting them dry. Or you could do some kind of direct photography onto the ribbon. He didn't want to ask Aunt Olga, in case he upset her again. She had been offended by what he'd said about Mauretania and Lithuania. But he might take the opportunity and check if he ever got to a cemetery. That might happen sometime. Aunt Olga had said there might be the odd errand to Skogs Cemetery or whatever. Then Reine would be first in line.

The afternoon dragged on for ever. Reine found it more and more difficult to suppress his yawns; his stomach was full of air, and he simply dared not fart in here. After the half-past-two coffee break, he felt like a barrage balloon and needed to go out, but Aunt Olga got there before him. Reine couldn't wait, so he let her go, then went out himself, continued half a flight downstairs, and let out a real corker by one of the windows. He walked up and down a couple of times to get rid of some more air, and as he stood there dispersing the smell by waving his hand, he heard Aunt Olga leaving the toilet and returning.

The afternoon culminated in a triumph; he had never considered investigating the toilet after Olga. But something told him he ought to go and have a look—and there, on the floor behind the pan, he found a mouthpiece of twisted wire. The mouthpiece consisted of a shaft and a little loop to thread the cigarette into, the whole arrangement much like the wire loops for blowing soap-bubbles, but much smaller.

16

Reine had his own reasons for not going straight home in the afternoon. He couldn't be bothered to wait for real night-fall, but he figured at least the sun should have gone down and it should be dusk. So he was forced to spend four or five hours drifting around, either downtown, or in Sollentuna, or at one of the stations in between. The day before, he had hung around the Solna shopping center for a few hours, but a repeat of that was not tempting. Now he found himself in Vasa Park instead. It was only about half-past eight and he was hungry. He had eaten two hotdogs with mashed potatoes for dinner, but the food had long since departed from his stomach, which now felt like an empty bag. He put his hand on his belly and felt the opening into it gasping for fodder.

He sat down on a bench and looked at a half-finished park theater that was being built. The stage itself was up, but the rest of the green-painted wood—for the backstage, wings, and benches—was all lying in a great heap alongside. The stage was square and as large as a boxing ring. There was a hatch in the stage floor, but he discovered it was locked when he investigated the half-finished theater more closely. What were they going to perform there? Kermit?

Reine clasped his hands round his knees, leaned forward, and pressed his forehead against one forearm, thinking feverishly. What are the most important answers? Nothing was as simple as he had thought. He had imagined, when he turned the whole shitload upside down and de-cided to take the answers first and questions later, that it would all be-come very simple. But it wasn't. A whole lot of the same old questions came pouring out instead. Who am I? Does Mom exist? Will Gran get where she thinks she will? Where was I before I was born? Was I a thinking egg in Mom's ovary? The only answer he had come up with that evening was a trifle exaggerated: blow the whole pile of shit up!

An elderly couple came walking along the path. They stopped and looked at the half-finished theater. How old were they? Fifty? Eighty? It didn't matter much. Mom was fussy about that kind of thing. Reine had once said Gran was eighty-five instead of fifty-eight; he had just happened to get the figures the wrong way round. Mom had been very upset. Okay, he'd made a mistake, but he couldn't understand what difference it made. Gran was old, wasn't she? And Mom was semi-old, thirty last March.

The elderly man went over to the stage and got up onto it, rather creakily. Then he held out both hands to his wife. It looked terribly funny, as if they were having a tug-of-war, or as if the old girl had fallen into the water. The man squatted down and hauled away until at last he got the old girl up, and they stood panting on the stage, holding hands.

Reine aimed under his arm, rat-tat-tat-tat. If he mowed them right down, would that be a crime? Their children, if they had any, would be upset, of course—but what about they themselves? A machine gun fired quite unexpectedly out of the dim light from a bench under a tree. They wouldn't have time to notice a darned thing. They'd be dead before they fell.

The two old people were still standing quite still, holding hands. Die happy! thought Reine. I'd be doing them a great service. In five minutes maybe they'll get dizzy and fall off the stage and break their hips. That was no life. Suddenly the two old people turned to each other, the man bowing slightly, holding out his left arm and putting it round his wife's waist. Slowly they began to dance a silent waltz around the stage. Not quite silent—their shoes squeaked and thumped a little on the planks.

Waltz? Tango? Hambo? Bingo? Yes, it was a waltz, because you had to stamp your feet in a hambo. Reine looked at his wristwatch and timed them. They circled round for four minutes. Then they suddenly stopped without a word, or a laugh, just nothing. Good, they were easier to shoot down when they were standing still. The *Mammoth Book of World Records*? He fished it out of his bag.

"Marathon Dancing. Marathon dancing should not be confused with dances in which a number of dancers hold hands and form a line, but is the longest time anyone has managed to go on dancing. The present record is held by two Americans who danced for 3,780 hours per individual."

Reine got up hastily. He had no wish to stay and see those two ancients trying to get down from the stage and probably breaking every bone in their bodies. What do you do with oldies who don't know what's good for them? When he came to the booth outside the park, he stopped and wrote against his thigh in his little book: 9, 10, 4, 12, 8, 18, 11, 22, 5, 12, 22, 4, 10, 5, 18, 19, 10, 5, 4, 13, 3, 22, 19, 11.

When he finally got home, it was still far from dark, but he simply couldn't wait any longer. He went in through the front entrance and up the stairs to the second floor, where there was a short iron ladder on the wall leading up to a skylight. Reine stood absolutely still for a minute or so, then quickly climbed up the ladder, pushed open the skylight, and climbed out onto the flat roof. He put the skylight back, jamming a roll of paper in the crack so that it wouldn't lock itself. Then he crept over to the edge of the roof. He got down on all fours and crawled backward for the last three feet—about nine feet below him was his balcony. He wriggled over the edge and felt the stepladder against his feet. Endlessly slowly, he shifted his weight to the ladder—and slid down.

He squatted down in a corner of the balcony and breathed out, then poked his nose over the railing. He could neither hear nor see anything special. No curtains moved. No police sirens in the distance. But the risk was probably not that great in the semidarkness.

He undressed in the bathroom before getting his evening meal. The tub was half full of water, and in it lay nine pairs of shorts, five T-shirts, innumerable socks, two pairs of jeans, and a handkerchief—all soaking so they'd be easier to wash. The garments that had been there longest had been there for ten days. Reine dropped in his red blue-bordered shorts. Then he picked up a plastic bottle of detergent and squeezed out a stream. Maybe he ought to stir it up a little? He took the toilet brush and stirred vigorously once or twice. He now had only one pair of clean shorts left in the big suitcase that had been destined for Children's Island. He'd have to do a mammoth wash tomorrow. It had been so darned hot this last week. Since he didn't much like taking a shower— and who could take a shower with the tub full of laundry?—clean shorts already started sticking in his crotch by lunchtime. Not so good. If he got too hot down there, the heat might hasten the puberty, like putting his prick into a greenhouse.

17 Something very peculiar happened on Thursday the third of July. Shortly after lunch, when Reine was half asleep with his head full of melted cheese, a youngish man came into the studio, wearing a well-pressed light-colored suit, white shirt, and white tie. Reine thought he looked peculiar, slightly gangsterlike, or as if he had stepped out of some ancient silent film, then shaken the roll of film off like wood shavings, and . . .

"Reine!" said Aunt Olga. "Would you help with a little matter?"

Reine went up to the desk where Olga was writing on a piece of paper, the light-suited man leaning over to make sure she got it right. Reine stood behind them waiting for the mass of cheese to settle in his head.

"White ribbon, FAREWELL CHRISTEN," said Olga. "Will you see to this?"

Reine took the piece of paper and read it. Christen—silly name. Boy or girl?

"Who is it to be charged to?" Olga asked the man.

"Christen Bang."

"The same name?" said Olga.

Reine went back to his place and took a white ribbon out of the box on the table. But something was not quite right over there by the desk.

The man was looking down at the floor, while Aunt Olga was looking just above his head, where his halo would have been if he'd had one.

"Is it for your father?" said Olga.

The man raised his head and looked out the window. Although Reine couldn't see his eyes, his whole stance told him the man was not looking at anything special but just needed something to do with his gaze.

"Would you like to sit down for a while?"

Olga pulled out one of the wooden chairs and patted it lightly with her hand. The chair had been around the place for many years and was spotted with gold paint. The man sat down on the chair. His ass'll get covered with gold, thought Reine. He himself had spotted the front and sides of his pants with paint. But what matter if you went around with gold all over your pants? Admirals had it on their caps.

"Is it for yourself?" said Olga. "The wreath?"

"Yes," said the man.

"Isn't that . . . what can one say, a trifle premature?"

The man leaped up from the chair and stood with his back to the window, holding the lapels of his jacket together as if someone were trying to steal his heart out of his inner pocket.

"My dear . . ." said Olga.

"Can't I even give a simple order!" shouted the man.

They were all scared now. Kristina turned right around and looked at the wall. Lotta had tears in her eyes, her face flaring like an artificial fireplace log. Helene was working, her long arms moving like crane jibs over the table. Reine slid down on his chair so that nothing but his hair, forehead, and eyes showed. Olga was holding her hand half-raised toward the man, as if trying to stroke him.

The telephone rang. Instead of picking up the receiver, Olga started walking toward the man with her hands down. The man stayed where he was, with his collar turned up, sheltering from an invisible shower. The telephone rang again, the second ring causing the man to move again and take up a kind of Japanese defense position—knees bent, head thrust forward, arms crossed in front of his face, his hands like sword blades. Madame Curie versus the Samurai of Japan!

The telephone rang for the third time. Aunt Olga cleared her throat but suddenly sounded as if she had reached adolescence and her voice had broken, or there was a hair in her throat; she closed her mouth again. The man stood there tensely, his whole body a grenade with the pin out. Then the telephone rang for the fourth time, and the man straightened up—though oddly enough he looked as if he had collapsed. A moment later, he had disappeared through the door.

Reine leaped up from his place and lifted the telephone receiver.

"Good afternoon, Three Red Roses speaking," a voice said.

Reine handed the receiver to Olga, who quickly checked her hairdo before taking over. Reine went back to his place and put the white ribbon back in the box.

When Aunt Olga had taken the orders from Three Red Roses, she said, "Shall we telephone the police?"

"That man oughtn't to be allowed out," said Helene, without looking up.

"I mean, supposing he does something to himself?" said Olga.

"No," said Reine. "Because he . . ."

"What?"

Reine did not go on. He had started to say no, he won't do anything as long as he hasn't got the wreath fixed up. But that was not necessarily so. Perhaps the Samurai was at that very moment committing hara-kiri in the elevator, leaving his descendants to arrange the funeral. Nevertheless Reine did not pursue the thought, deciding not to take the elevator at the end of the day but to use the stairs.

"I think I'll phone the police," said Olga.

Suddenly Reine realized it was serious, that the crazy guy in the light suit might really take his own life. His butt froze and his balls contracted. This was no fantasy any longer; maybe something really horrible was going to become reality. He no longer wanted to be involved. He left his place and went and stood by the farthest window, looking out over the railway lines. How could they keep track of all those signals and switches? Maybe it wasn't that strange: how could he himself keep track of his arms and legs? His stomach? Gullet? Backside?

Whereas the railways needed a colossal signal box, Reine could manage all on his own—and almost without thinking about it. One should—what was it called—rationalize? The railways should get themselves a huge human brain to look after the whole system. Supposing you took out a brain with all its nerves and connected the nerves to the electricity? Probably best to reduce the power somewhat at first, but otherwise it'd be a cinch. The nerve system worked by electricity, didn't it? The brain coupled to the signal box would then know all the tracks and signals as if they were part of its own body. Fabulous! Derailing an express train would be as easy as the drop of a hat.

It wouldn't be expensive, either. A brain without arms and legs needed hardly any more food than the average potted plant. If you took the free brain and put it in an aquarium full of glucose water—did a brain float?—and then pulled all the nerve ends into orderly bunches over the edge and connected them to clip-on plugs—the rest was already there: cables, relays, transformers, couplings, light bulbs, and fuses. What a mighty powerful person that would be, the person who became woven into the railway's largest signal box. All the men sweating away in the old signal box could go home. One man changing the water in the aquarium now and again would be enough, and maybe talking to the brain so that it didn't get too lonely, maybe reading to it out of the newspaper between trains. But supposing the brain fell asleep?

"I think I'll call the police all the same," said Olga, picking up the telephone directory.

"He'll probably go somewhere else in town and try," said Helene. "Ring Successors and Sons and warn them."

"Such a young boy," said Lotta. "Think of it, such a young boy."

Supposing the railway brain fell asleep? That wouldn't be too bad; the traffic would presumably just stop. But what if the brain started dreaming, dreaming it was someone else, another brain somewhere else? Or if the brain got paranoid and started thinking all the trains heading for Stockholm were out to kill the brain, run over the brain and slice it up? Since the brain couldn't escape from the aquarium, it would have to arrange quickly for all the trains to collide, express trains ramming commuter trains, cables collapsing, switches turned in the wrong direction, all the fuses blown and . . .

Olga was talking on the phone to the police. Reine didn't want to hear, so he sat with his hands over his ears. Back to the threatened brain: if it was an ordinary soft-hearted brain, perhaps it could make friends with one of the railway men. Some old guy with a drooping mustache who'd been oiling the switches for a hundred years. The brain and the railwayman would be friends, and one evening when they were alone, the railwayman would have a plastic bag full of water with him, and when no one was looking, he could unfasten all the clips, put the plastic bag down into the aquarium, and let the brain swim into it like a jellyfish. Then, under cover of darkness, the railwayman would carry the bag under his jacket out to his moped. After that they could escape together to the railwayman's little cottage deep in the forest, where the brain would be allowed to live out its life in a great glass jar and have its back scratched every morning.

"Are they sending a patrol car?" said Helene.

"I don't know," said Olga. "They said they'd take over now."

"Will we be questioned?" said Lotta. "That'd be nice."

"If a whole lot of police came up here?" said Helene.

"One shouldn't evade one's responsibilities," said Lotta.

"Are the police coming?" said Kristina, getting up from the table. "Are the police coming?"

"Sit down, dear," said Olga. "The police aren't coming here."

"They'll tell us what happens, won't they?" said Lotta. "They'll phone and tell us, won't they. They must keep us informed . . ."

"I don't want to know what happens," said Kristina, her voice more brittle than usual, rising into a squeak.

"Neither do I," said Reine firmly.

Then he covered his ears again, looking far away at the tall buildings in the distance and thinking: a single correctly placed brain with the right connections would be able to steer the whole world like its own body.

18 It looked like Saturday would be as hot as the other days. Reine sat dangling his feet on Riddarholm Quay, trying to spot fish in water the color of spinach soup. He was sleepy and completely zonked. He had walked all the way from Sollentuna to Riddarholm, a distance of about seven or eight miles—he wasn't quite sure—and it had taken him almost four hours. Idiotic. But he had waked up early in a radiant mood. Nothing was impossible and walking seven miles a mere bagatelle, as if his ankles had been extended into small wings and his whole chest filled to bursting with laughing gas. He would jog off into town as lightly as an astronaut on the moon, over stick and stone, streams, and minor buildings.

His shoulders were aching, his stomach burning, his back hurting; his head felt too heavy for his neck and his thighs painful. But not his calves or feet. His lower legs had gone, gone numb, gone to sleep. If he pinched the skin on the top of his foot really hard, it didn't hurt—just tingled a little as if from an electric shock. He pulled up his dead feet, shifted them to one side with his hands, and lay down flat on the quay. He must not fall asleep, because he had to meet Helene outside Riddarholm Church at eleven o'clock. He still hadn't thought out how he was going to dispose of her! He had thought of planning it as he walked from Sollentuna, but he hadn't been able to think as he walked. Someone had lied to him, some book or other, or an adult, telling him that thinking things out went especially well while walking. It was not true. All your thoughts rattled apart.

The sun was hot and Reine had no cap. He opened his bag and emptied it of its contents: the book of world records, the paper napkin and drinking straw, the secret little notebook, and Jocke his monkey. Jocke had been stuffed away on the closet shelf and hadn't been out in the world for several years. Gran had given him to Reine on his first birthday—that was before Gran joined the Maranatas. The monkey was a glove puppet, a brown glove with small arms and a nodding head as big as an egg, with brown glass eyes. Jocke had been Reine's favorite toy for a long time but had then been squeezed out by Snoopy. Reine had suddenly started longing for Jocke, longing for something to have with him, a little of the old security. Snoopy was impossible, since he would have taken up a whole suitcase, but Jocke took up no space at all—and if anyone saw Jocke, Reine need not feel embarrassed or be accused of being childish. Jocke would pass as a puppet from a puppet theater. Not a children's puppet theater but a real one. If asked, he would say that Jocke played the main part in a play about Idi Amin.

When Reine had emptied his bag, he stuck it on his head as protection from the sun. It was hot inside the case, smelling of warm plastic and old underclothes. But you get used to it, thought Reine. You always get used to smells. When you're having a crap in the can, you don't smell anything. But when Mom's been in there!

Should he kill off Helene out of sheer kindness? It couldn't be much fun sitting in a wheelchair, always in the way and being stared at, or not even noticed. Helene had once told him that people staring wasn't the worst, but that they didn't see you at all. But did Helene want to die? If she'd wanted to put an end to herself, it wouldn't have been all that difficult. All she had to do was to get up speed in the wheelchair and tip over the edge of the nearest quay. Supposing she could swim? Her legs were useless, hanging there like so much dead flesh, but she might be able to crawl with her long sinewy spider arms, rushing along like a sidewheeler. Simplest would be if she just wheeled herself down the stairs at Olga's. Richard Widmark had finished off a handicapped old woman by pushing her down some stairs. As it was obviously so easy for Helene to do away with herself, Reine had to assume she had some objection to doing so. Perhaps she didn't want to, or didn't know what was best for her. If Reine had been born with useless legs, he would have done away with himself at once by driving straight into the rush hour traffic. Did one have a little wheelchair at first? No bigger than a tricycle? Most people bound to wheelchairs presumably took their own lives. Where else did they go otherwise? There wasn't a single person in a wheelchair at Reine's school. Were they all kept in some special place, an old streetcar shed, maybe, where they stood in long rows on the tracks? So the rest didn't have to see them?

He met Helene at eleven o'clock outside Riddarholm Church. She came in a taxi, and it was all really awkward, because the driver was old and bent. He would be sure to thank me for disposing of Helene, Reine thought. But he must not upset anyone at the moment—he greeted Helene brightly. He was a little afraid of her because she could be quite snappish, but today she was looking happy. She had put on makeup and was wearing a thin dress he had never seen before, and exactly the same kind of Marimekko sun hat as Mom had, though Helene's was blue instead of pink. What right had this woman in a wheelchair to wear the same hat as Mom?

It was awfully hard work pushing the wheelchair across the bumpy ground up to the church entrance. Helene helped as best she could. Why hadn't she bought an electric chair? Reine would have gotten himself one if . . . no, hell, he wouldn't have been alive then, or would he? Maybe, if there'd been slightly jazzier wheelchairs, if Kawasaki had made wheelchairs? If Alfa Romeo had manufactured wheelchairs in their typical grayish-purple color? Or a Ferrari red? He would have one on caterpiller tracks like a tank, one that could swim, one that could mangle up all bushes and trees less than a few inches thick. Lookout, for Christ's sake!

There was a short flight of steps just inside the information booth. They got themselves a brochure and then approached the steps, which fortunately had two wide tracks down them, meant for baby buggies and wheelchairs. But how were they to get up? Reine would never manage. You could fling a rope around one of the pillars and then haul up the chair—but of course Helene didn't have a rope with her; he could see neither rope nor spare wheel on the wheelchair.

"Can you feel the wingbeats of history?" said Helene.

Reine stopped and took a deep breath. There was a smell of dust, a rather musty smell, and the smell of some kind of detergent. No, cloak-rooms. But if he felt really carefully there *was* a slight flutter in his chest—the wingbeats of history? The church was pretty dim inside, but as time went by he could see more and more.

"Let's start on the left," said Helene.

On their immediate left was an old field-marshal called Lennart Torstensson. Funny name—those old gents usually had names like Goldhelmet, Plumeshield, Silverspear and such. Torstensson—that sounded as paltry as Larsson. A steep little flight of stairs led down to a crypt full of grisly tombs. Should he push Helene down there, so she could die among her beloved field-marshals? No, if he was going to do away with Helene, she might as well disappear into a grander tomb, a royal tomb—it wouldn't cost any more.

"I suppose you still learn about the Thirty Years War at school?"

Reine pondered. The Thirty Years War? Yes, his teacher had talked about that. Someone called Gustaf Adolf who'd been murdered in Russia. But why did they call it the Thirty Years War? As long as Reine could remember there had been wars, the latest in Vietnam, and before that—now what was it?—the Korean War! And before that between Hitler and Churchill, and before that the First World War, and before that, what the heck was it—the French Revolution? And before that it was King Karl XII, that's it. In other words, there was always a war on. How could you just cut a bit of history out like that and call it the Thirty Years War? A false picture of reality, like so much else they taught you at school. Like reproduction, for instance.

Could Helene have children, even though she was stuck in a wheel-chair? Did she have the same things down there as Mom had? Of course, it must be forbidden for handicapped people to have children, even if they could. What would things be like if women staggered around on crutches having children? Or sat in wheelchairs laboring away? There was sure to be a law against it. Sweden was supposed to be a civilized country. They passed several tombs of noblemen, but no royal tomb. Were the corpses really inside those tombs? Or were they somewhere else, like underneath the floor? Then the coffins up there would be only ornamental. Reine had sometimes wondered whether corpses were really in coffins at ordinary funerals. He wasn't sure. They probably ground up dead people at the hospital and then cremated what was left. Carrying coffins around and throwing flowers—that was more of a ritual. Otherwise, it seemed pretty unhygienic. There was sure to be a law against carrying dead people around in ordinary wooden boxes.

There were some plaques on the walls, between the tombs, with coats-of-arms on them. Were they Sweden's nobility? No, they were the Knights of Seraphim. Sounded crazy—could you be a knight of a hospital? Mom had worked at the Seraphim Hospital at the beginnings of time. If you donated money to the Seraphim Hospital, you clearly became a Knight of Seraphim and were given a plaque in Riddarholm Church; no, that didn't seem right. One of the plaques was for Emperor Hirohito of Japan, and he couldn't have been so stupid as to send money to a Swedish hospital. He must have plenty of his own to look after.

Reine felt lightning strike; the name Hammarskjöld was on one of the plaques! Dad? Grandad? Uncle? Was he buried here, too, the Secretary General? Reine felt mournful. He wanted to do something, though he didn't quite know just what. Light a candle? Put a flower on the floor underneath the shield? Say a prayer? He hadn't felt so solemn for a long time. It was like when the guards paraded past. You felt proud and sad at the same time. Now, he really could feel the wingbeats of history in his breast. He wanted to go up and touch the plaque but didn't dare because of Helene, who would have known at once. Instead, he stayed where he was behind the wheelchair and made the sign of the cross.

"This is where King Karl XII is," said Helene. "I think it's the most beautiful tomb of all. You've read about Karl XII, I suppose?"

That's the tomb to bury Helene in, of course, thought Reine. She said so herself—I think it's the most beautiful of all. He would have to lure her there one dark night, then finish her off before she had time to notice anything, then stuff her into Karl XII's coffin. If heaven existed and eventually they met there, she would fall on his neck and thank him, running across the clouds toward him and falling on his neck. He felt quite weepy. It probably wouldn't work. The iron gates to the chancel looked fragile, so you could probably force them, and getting the lid of the tomb off would probably work with an ordinary car jack. There would be sure to be room for her inside, since there couldn't be much left of King Karl XII by now. He could take an ordinary black plastic garbage sack with him and stuff the king into it if necessary. But one obstacle was completely insurmountable. Reine would never ever dare go into Riddarholm Church after nightfall.

Helene chattered on. That was where Magnus Ladulås was, and King Gustav Adolf II was there, and under the floor was King Karl Gustav X who had marched across the Great Belt, and there were all the Bernadottes, except the last one who had died, King Gustav Adolf VI. He hadn't wanted to be buried here and had been put to rest out in the Royal Cemetery in Haga instead, because he really was a democratic king.

They did the other wall, and Reine started feeling terribly tired. They came to the stairs by the exit and he was struck by a thought that made him let go of the wheelchair. What would happen here on Ascension Day? What would happen after Armageddon, which Gran had described so vividly? When the angel came in here blaring away on his trumpet? How would all these poor kings, queens, and princes lying here in their stone boxes have a sporting chance? At the moment of judgment they would have to acquire superhuman strength, hurling open the lids and smashing down gates and doors. Reine wouldn't want to be in the way when all those kings were trying to get out.

At first there would be a heck of a jumble of bones and lids. Some parts would get lost in their haste, and others would probably snatch up too many pieces of skeleton. Would there be fights, or would disputes be settled through conversations? But it would have to happen quickly. When the whole bunch of them were ready in their moth-eaten mantles and tarnished silver crowns, their arms full of ribs—who would go first? Magnus Ladulås, the eldest? or Gustav V, the fittest? Or would King Gustav Adolf II and King Karl XII go first because they had been the best?

Reine rushed toward the exit and looked out over sun-drenched Birger Jarl Square, in his mind all the Swedish royal lineage slithering and dragging themselves past with rattling teeth, whining and irritable, the laurel wreath falling off Karl XII and Oscar II dropping a ring on the stairs. The great thing was not to arrive too late at the seat of judgment. The most eager were already halfway up the stairs to Svea court.

Afterward, Helene and Reine had lunch back at her apartment. It was all prepared and ready when they finally got there. Reine ate everything put before him, while Helene mostly talked on and on about Swedish history and all the kings. Reine nodded and swallowed.

"And they want to take all that away from us," said Helene. "The monarchy, traditions, all our history. But just you wait until things start threatening out in the world. Of course, you don't remember World War II, do you? I'll have you know, Riddarholm Church was chock-full of people then, although it was mostly hidden behind sandbags."

At five past two, Reine thanked Helene and set off for the Winter Palace, where they were showing the film *It's a Mad, Mad, Mad, Mad World*. He just managed to see the first few minutes before falling sound asleep. The film started with some old man driving down a steep slope in his car, falling out, and lying there dying. Reine screwed up his nose with dissatisfaction and yawned. It was badly done. You didn't die like that. He had seen several people die for real on television, so he knew what happened. Mostly executions, of course, when you didn't see much. A guy at a post with a black hood over his head, a salvo of shots, a jerk. He had also seen a program from the Japanese occupation of China. The Japanese had buried a whole lot of Chinese alive. He had seen close-ups of that, so he was quite critical when it came to death. What about insinuating some quick-working poison into Helene?

19 Later on that day, Reine was lying face down on the roof watching the sun go down—no longer round, small, and dense as before but larger, redder, and more shapeless the closer it got to the edge of the forest in the northwest. One moment it looked like an outdoor party lantern, the next like a bashed tomato. The last phase went very rapidly, as if someone had sucked down the sun. Schlurp!

The roof was covered with thick tarpaper reinforced with very fine stone chips. It was like crawling across coarse sandpaper, the small stones penetrating Reine's sore palms, and when he brushed them off they left black impressions in his skin. His feet were aching, too. The anesthetic numbness had long since gone, and his feet were throbbing. When he got down, he would go straight to the bathroom, transfer the wet clothes to the basin, fill the bath with tepid water, then sit on the edge with his feet in the water and his eyes closed.

He reached the edge of the roof and looked down over the yard. How high up was he? Three floors, each nine feet high, a little floor thickness between, the external roof . . . thirty feet seemed reasonable. From up here it looked more like a hundred and thirty. Why did it always seem to be so much higher when you were on a roof looking down than when you were standing on the ground looking up?

He had to gather strength for the most strenuous part, gliding over the edge of the roof and trying to reach the kitchen stepladder with his feet. He turned over on his back and stared straight up. That was a mistake; he felt giddy almost at once. The sky was perfectly clear, without the smallest cloud to fix his eye on—no stars, nothing. He realized he was staring straight up into space, out into *infinity*. If the earth's centrifugal force suddenly ceased, he would be flung straight up into the sky. It was enough to make anyone giddy. He scrabbled with his fingers in the fine gravel; there was nothing to hold onto. He quickly rolled over and took sight along the roof. How long was the block? A hundred and twenty feet? A hundred? Would a plane based on an aircraft carrier be able to land and take off here? A helicopter, possibly, but no conventional plane: too many obstacles—ventilators, hatches, metal edges, and the central antenna.

He fixed his eye on the top of the antenna, which was glowing in the light from a sun Reine could no longer see. Lucky it's a receiver and not a transmitter, he thought. How could any living creature on earth be quite uninfluenced by all those radio and television programs? At that particular moment, whole bunches of programs were going through his body, not just Swedish ones but a lot from powerful foreign transmitters. All those chattering squealing voices you could get by turning the knobs on an ordinary radio, all those waves were at that moment passing through his body. But you never even noticed! Perhaps it was because you got used to it. Perhaps anyone who had had hundreds of radio and television programs chattering in his body all day long since the fetal stage no longer noticed anything? What was it called—screened off? Like your own pulse and breathing—you didn't go around listening to it.

Suddenly he was aware of himself in quite a different way: instead of being alone in the world, which was the same to him as being the whole world, he now felt there was no Me at all. From all directions long waves, short waves, and medium waves were burrowing their way through his skin, blood, and muscles, all trying to reach his innermost being. But there was no innermost being, only a vacuum inside the middle of his brain where the radio waves all collided and shattered so that voices and pictures crackled like a child's sparkler. He was a radio-controlled jumping-jack that could be steered into doing anything. He was being steered by everyone simultaneously, torn and pulled in different directions. No, no . . . he thumped his forehead on the roof. Why did he keep thinking about things that made him sick and giddy?

He turned right over and approached the edge of the roof feet first. It was good that his feet were aching and the feeling had returned to them—he would never have dared try out this tricky act with numbed legs. He slid over the edge, the black metal cutting into his stomach and his bag hanging down his backside, where it weighed heavily, like a parachute. Would the chute have time to open in a fall of only thirty feet? He closed his eyes tightly and started gliding. Just as his elbows left the roof, he felt the kitchen stepladder with his toes. Home!

As usual, he squatted down in the corner of the balcony for a few minutes, getting his breath back and listening for any commotion from the neighbors, and peering over toward the next building. They were bound to catch him one day! Perhaps it was time to think up some other way of getting in and out of the locked apartment. Supposing he left the door unlocked? Or, what about . . . hadn't Gran got a key? Could he think up a good excuse? Could he write to Gran and ask her to send the key? Maybe there was a number on the key, a code? What if he could get hold of that, then go to a locksmith? What would that cost? At the moment, he stood at forty-two *kronor*, including Mom's drinking money.

It was dark enough outside now to see that a light was on in the apartment. That light was always on, so that thieves and child murderers would realize the apartment was occupied. Reine slid in through the half-open balcony door. It was incredibly hot inside; the sun had been blazing through the big lounge window all day. The blinds were not down, because if they had been, intruders wouldn't see the light was on.

There was someone in the room! Reine could hear nothing, see nothing, smell nothing. But there was someone in the room. He sank to his knees and peered along the floor. Two bare feet could be seen beyond the wing chair with its back to him. Reine got up, took one of the empty beer bottles out of the plant-watering system, pulled out the green plastic tubes, and with the bottle raised, went around the armchair.

It was Stig. He was asleep in the chair, stark naked, calm and silent, his head against one of the wings, his longish hair wet and bedraggled, face burnt scarlet from the sun, lips and eyelids swollen. He was so unshaven you could hardly see where his sideburns ended and his mustache started; his mouth was half open, and his tongue protruded like that of a hanged man. His hands lay floppily like a pair of abandoned gloves on his thighs. Between his legs was a beer can.

"What are you doing here?" said Reine, lowering the bottle.

Stig's eyes moved behind the closed lids, then he opened one eye and looked dopily at Reine.

"What the hell are you doing here?"

"Resting," said Stig.

"How the hell did you get in?"

"Bet ya'd like to know, wouldn't ya?"

He raised his head and coughed, the rolls of fat on his chest and stomach jerking. Stig was athletic as well as fat, his short calves very muscular. He coughed again.

"Harriet smokes too much. Don't you ever air this place?"

Reine had no desire to discuss Mom's smoking habits, since she had none.

"You've no right to be in our apartment."

"What sort of way is that to treat a guest?" said Stig, freeing the beer can from between his thighs and emptying it of what was left, two or three drops at the most.

"Did you swipe that beer from the icebox?"

Stig threw the can onto the sofabed and scratched at the mat of hair on his stomach with both hands. Reine examined Stig's member, which hardly had room between the fleshy thighs, only the head of it above the surface.

"Harriet isn't home today, either."

"Heard she was working in Uddevalla," said Stig, heaving himself out of the chair.

Reine scrutinized him. He did not seem to be particularly drunk; his movements were not fumbling, and his face did not have that dumb, numbed, implacable expression Reine remembered from the ferryboat trip.

"Harriet may be coming this evening. On a visit," said Reine, regretting saying it immediately.

"What time?"

"Later on this evening, maybe. If she comes."

"What's the time?"

"Twenty-five past nine."

"Then I've time for another cold shower. I put the clothes in the basin."

Stig stretched again, lifting one foot lightly and farting loudly; then he laughed, coughed, and went out to the bathroom.

How could he be so crazily dumb? He should have known Stig would come back. If Reine had had anything at all in his head besides air, he would have blocked the keyhole with chewing gum or broken matches so that no bastard could get a key in. But then he wouldn't have been able to get out himself. The only way *out* was through the door. Should he say Mom had a new man? Or that Harriet was shacked up with Ricky Bruch, the discus thrower, now? Stig hadn't a chance there. Ricky would roll Stig up into a ball, jump on him until he was as flat as a discus, and then hurl him out through the balcony door so that he landed right in the middle of next week. But what would happen then? What would Reine and Mom do with Ricky?

But! Stig was stark naked, taking a shower in the bathroom. Reine went out into the hall and listened at the bathroom door; the water was gushing down. Quickly, he went back into the lounge where he'd seen Stig's clothes lying in a heap alongside the hide-a-bed. Jacket, nothing, shirt pocket empty, pants pockets empty—but in the back pocket was Stig's large key ring with a chain fastened to his belt. Reine's door-key was on the ring. He listened again before trying to get the key off the ring with its great leather and enamel VW badge. He made it! Stig was still in the bathroom at least ten minutes after Reine had retrieved his key and hidden it in a jar of black pepper on the exhaust fan above the stove.

"No Harriet?" said Stig, coming in with a bath towel wound round his loins.

"Maybe she'll be on the night train. There's no point in your waiting."

"In a sleeper?"

Reine went into his room and lay down on the bed. The moment his head touched the heap of pillows—he had gathered up all the pillows there were—hunger hit him, pouring in like a hot wave across his stomach and aching in his gullet. His mouth watered. What had he got? A large can of baked beans? His stomach contracted at the thought of baked beans, all his innards rushing in and throwing themselves onto the can of baked beans, his intestines winding themselves round the can like octopus limbs, his digestive juices bubbling and hissing like sizzling acid.

"Up ya git," said Stig. "I'm hungry."

Reine did not reply but grabbed the crumpled sheets and turned to the wall. He was not going to share his baked beans with that flabby bastard. Go to hell, thought Reine. Go straight to the furnace of hell. The flab will burn.

Stig slapped Reine's backside, making him yell and drop the bedclothes.

"Up ya git, Reine. We'll go into town and have a bite to eat while we're waiting for Harriet."

"I'm not allowed out so late," said Reine.

"Okay, starve to death then, if ya like. I'm off for a tornydoss as big as a plate."

"What's a tornydoss?"

"Tornydoss? Shattobriand? Ontrecoat?"

"Meat?"

"Giant steaks, boy. With bernaise sauce and grilled tomatoes. Masses and masses of French fries. Some asparagus too, by all means. Giant steak and ice cream with chocolate sauce. You can have meatballs from the children's menu if ya want to."

"I've got nothing against steak."

Reine went out into the bathroom to put band-aids on his blisters. His feet were red and sore. He looked at the heap of wet clothes in the basin; he had no clean clothes, either. He'd have to do a wash tomorrow. He sat on the toilet seat and tried to put on his sneakers; they were damp with sweat and much too tight. His blue white-soled rubber boots were on the shelf in the hall, so he put them on instead. They might not be all that suitable for going out for a meal in the middle of summer, but it was better than going barefoot, anyhow. To alleviate his guilty conscience to some extent, he returned to the bathroom and brushed his teeth for the second time since Mom had left.

"Taxi's here," shouted Stig from the balcony.

As they went through the door and were about to lock it behind them, Stig said, "Hell, gotta make sure I've got the key . . ."

He pulled out the heavy bunch of keys, sorted through them, then looked at Reine and grinned. Reine didn't try to defend himself but slunk into the kitchen to fetch the key he'd hidden in the black pepper jar.

20 Ten minutes later the taxi stopped outside the Stallmästar restaurant, where gas torches were flaring in the summer night. Reine yawned and got out, thrust his hands into his back pockets and shivered. He was more sleepy than hungry now. Stig marched into the building with Reine limping behind him. It was quiet and cool inside, as quiet as a library and as cool as a church.

"Just come straight from the airport, so had no time to book a table," said Stig to the headwaiter. "But I suppose ya can fix us up with a bite all the same?"

They followed the headwaiter into the restaurant itself, which was almost empty, and were shown a booth just to the left of the entrance. Two Japanese were sitting at the next table, both looking at maps. A few tables away were some senior citizens in fancy clothes, the men in dark suits and the women in long dresses. They were clearly on their way out, because they were handing around a plate with a piece of paper on it—the check? They said nothing, appearing totally preoccupied with mental arithmetic. A buzz and clatter could be heard from inside the restaurant proper.

Reine got a menu of his own, but he hadn't the energy to read it. Stig would have to decide, since he was going to pay. Or was he? Would Reine have to pay for himself, or was Stig expecting Reine to pay for both of them? No.

"Want a seafood cocktail?" said Stig. "As a starter, I mean."

"Yes, please."

"Then we'll have two shrimp cocktails, two Tornedos Rossini, one Pripps Blue, one schnapps, and a Coca-Cola. Thanks. Wait . . . one rare and one medium."

Bread and butter were brought at once. *Pain riche!* Reine helped himself. He had hardly eaten any soft bread recently, and had stuck to French fries. He took three large pieces of bread and started spreading butter on them. Before he had finished, the beer and Coca-Cola arrived.

"Poor silly old Harriet, bouncing around in a sleeper—she should see us now!" said Stig, all but emptying his beer glass.

God, I'm sleepy, thought Reine. Perhaps if I knock off the whole Coke before I start eating, I'll wake up. That was no hardship, since they'd brought the smallest size. How much did the bottle hold? Not much. He always bought the biggest he could. There were liter bottles, of course, but you had to pay on the bottles. Best was drinking out of a can, but they were the most expensive. The worst Cokes you got were the ones where you pressed a glass against a mouthpiece; if you were unlucky, what you got was practically brown water.

"Are you off duty?" said Reine.

"What d'ya think?" said Stig. "I'm off duty half the week sometimes. I work at a snack bar, too, but not this weekend. A man has to have some time off, for Christ's sake, so I can see old Harriet now and again."

"I thought you weren't together any longer," said Reine.

Stig had no time to reply because at that moment the waitress arrived with the shrimp cocktails and Stig's schnapps. Toast, too. Marvelous!

"Another Pripps Blue and another Coke, please," said Stig.

Reine got rid of the slice of lemon and sprigs of dill, but unfortunately the shrimp were all messed up with some kind of pink sauce, and he couldn't do much about that. The glass container was on a bed of ice. Reine pressed a couple of fingerprints in the mist.

"Maybe we should drink to those two Japs," said Stig, grimacing to one side at their nearest neighbors.

Reine was scared stiff. True, Stig was stronger and heavier than both the Japanese, but supposing they were Samurai? Or had black belts in karate? A Japanese would never tolerate an insult. If Stig grinned the wrong way at either of them, he was as good as dead . . .

"Here's to Harriet!" said Stig formally, raising the schnapps glass to his lips.

Reine bowed slightly and went on eating his sauce-covered shrimp. Or weren't they shrimp? Some of the pieces were quite big. Stig only poked around in his glass, then pushed it aside and drank his second beer.

"Do you want it?"

Reine took over Stig's appetizer and ate that up, too. The sauce was really good. They must have poured a little ketchup into some yogurt and stirred it up. Though McDonald's was probably better at sauces. The Big Mac had a fabulous dressing—pity so much of it got wasted getting the lettuce and tomato out of it. Suddenly Reine felt he simply had to go for a crap. The last time must have been several days ago. Now his entire insides seemed to be filled with seafood sauce.

"Where's the john?"

"Go ask the old guy out in the cloakroom."

Reine slipped out, his backside glowing. There was no one in the cloakroom, but what great luck: at that moment one of the Japanese came out of a door marked MEN. Reine rushed in, snatched open one of the booths, hauled down his jeans and pants, spat in the bowl—he always did that—and sat down. God, it was good to crap. Then he fell asleep.

Reine didn't wake up until Stig was carrying him up the stairs back at home.

"Did I fall asleep?"

"Ya sure did, ya wretch," said Stig, dumping Reine down outside the apartment door. "You were sleeping like a hog inside the john. I thought you'd skedaddled."

"It was those shrimp," said Reine.

Stig fumbled for the key and found it eventually; swaying, he aimed it at the keyhole. How much had he drunk while Reine had been asleep? What would Stig do now? Would he reel around the apartment, or would he just let Reine in and then go home?

"You never know when Mom'll come," said Reine.

Stig jerked the door open and shoved Reine inside. Was Stig going to kill him? Stig didn't touch him but went straight into the bathroom and peed into the basin, ignoring the clothes lying in it.

"Go to bed, kid!" said Stig. "I'm going to sit on the balcony and wait for Harriet."

21 Reine was sitting right up in the prow of the sailing boat, where the tubular rail formed a seat. The sun was shining, but the wind was quite high, and the boat leaning to starboard. The whole bay was full of sails, most of them white, some pale blue, some—called spinnakers—brilliantly colored like candy wrappers. A large mahogany motorboat passed fifty yards from Reine. He had time to count to thirty-four before the wash reached them. The boat started heaving up and down, the sail whipping and cracking, the mast and stays rattling, Reine squealing as if on a rollercoaster. He had never been sailing before. It was fantastic.

Stig had brutally waked Reine at about eight that Sunday morning. Stig was going out sailing with a buddy, and the boat was leaving at nine o'clock.

"Come on with us for a sail, Reine," Stig had said. "Your mom forgot to get off the train. She's probably up in Lapland by now."

At first Reine had been reluctant, but then he realized he had forgotten to buy food for Sunday. He wouldn't dare go out when it was light, and it would be deadly boring to stay at home half starved behind drawn blinds for a whole summer Sunday.

"As long as we're back by this evening," Reine had said in the end, "because early tomorrow morning . . ."

"What about early tomorrow morning?"

To tell Stig about Olga's studio would have been utter catastrophe, so he had let the conversation ebb away. They had got up, made coffee, and eaten the last packet of spaghetti for breakfast. Stig had smothered his spaghetti with melted butter and sloshed it around so that it splashed over half the balcony. Reine had lost his appetite and dropped most of his helping down into the yard. Then they had hurried down to Stig's old car and zoomed off to Hässelby Quay.

The man with the boat was named Esbjörn, the silliest name Reine had heard for a long time. If only he'd been Assbjörn, there would have been some sense in it. But Es? What did that mean?

"Where's your chick?" Esbjörn had asked as they came on board.

"Stuck on the train," said Stig. "This is her kid, Reine."

Esbjörn had brought a dame with him; her name was Nora, and by Reine's reckoning she was nearer twenty than forty. Nora spent nearly all the time lying face down on deck with nothing on but a pair of panties and a scarf around her head. You couldn't see whether she was asleep or awake. Esbjörn sat holding the tiller at the back of the boat's seat well. When he wasn't relieving himself, Stig helped pull ropes and halyards. Both Stig and Esbjörn drank one can of beer after another, so they often needed to take a leak. When they did that, they stood astride Nora, holding on to a stay with the left hand and spraying a great bow of drops that glittered like champagne in the sunlight.

The boat was a medium-sized sailboat made of plastic that Esbjörn had rented. The hull was orange-colored, but the deck white. There were four bunks inside and hatches in the floor you could lift when you wanted more beer. There was nothing else but beer. Reine was horribly thirsty; he was counting on the two men soon being drunk enough not to notice if he swiped a beer—probably Nora wouldn't, either.

His life jacket was much too large and rubbed the back of his neck. It was also hot and the plastic stuck to his back, but otherwise everything was just great, the best thing that had happened all summer. The most wonderful thing of all was that tricky questions and answers no longer meant anything. If he had had his little code book around, he would gladly have sacrificed it to the gulls.

Reine screwed up his eyes against the sun and wind and mentally composed a letter to his mom: *They've got a sailboat here. It's really fast but we always wear life jackets, and when we climb the mast, we wear crash helmets as well* . . . he turned his head and tried to look up at the mast, but the foresail was in the way. But when he turned in the other direction, he could see it. The mast was gilded, a long narrow tube of aluminum. Only monkeys could climb those. That was an idea: if you used sufficiently well-trained monkeys, naturally you would win any sailing race. He had noticed how clumsily Esbjörn and Stig moved in the boat, but what about a few two-foot monkeys? Another thing: monkeys could hold on and pull with their feet as well as their hands. And you could be as sure as hell that there was nothing about monkeys in the sailing regulations, nothing about not being allowed to use monkeys.

"Lunch!" yelled Esbjörn from the back of the boat; he was standing up holding the tiller between his legs.

At the word lunch Reine forgot about monkeys, left the prow, and started crawling backward on all fours, but when he reached the seat well, there was no lunch to be seen. False alarm?

"Damn cow!" Esbjörn shouted at Nora.

"Where the hell's the cold cuts, waitress?" said Stig, opening another can of beer and flinging the tab into the water.

A gull immediately dived and flew back up with the aluminum ring in its beak. Other gulls hurled themselves at the first one and forced it down into the wake of the boat. Released from its trailer of gulls, the sailboat put on speed, dipping to starboard close to the wind.

Nora did not move until, at Esbjörn's mute request, Stig took a half-step up on deck and splashed some cold beer onto the small of her back. Then she turned over slowly, without hiding her breasts. Reine looked with interest. They looked nothing like Mom's. Nora's were much higher up.

Why couldn't Nora get a move on and fix the grub? The men were doing the sailing, weren't they—and she should do something. Reine crept back to his place in the prow and decided not to turn around until lunch was guaranteed ready.

One of the leaders here has a monkey that climbs up the mast. He was probably on thin ice there. But what the heck, he couldn't go on and on about roasting hotdogs out of doors. *The monkey loves peanuts, so if you could send a little* . . . no, you shouldn't mention money until the end of the letter, in a P.S. Otherwise it sounded too pressing. You should mention it so that it seemed as if you'd almost forgotten it. *The monkey has learned to steer, too, and has a little sailing cap* . . . no.

The next moment the boat was caught in the wash from a tanker Reine hadn't noticed, because he'd been looking down watching the stem meeting the water. Everything swirled around and he just managed to grab the metal rail and cling to it. Darn lucky he had a life jacket on, in case he had flown up into the air. The swell calmed, and a red buoy came racing past only a few yards to starboard; it looked as if it were twirling around in the water.

At last they had lunch. Reine was summoned and offered three kinds of pickled herring, anchovies, sardines, spicy cheese, smoked reindeer meat, and hardbread. The smoked reindeer tasted disgusting, and he also got a piece of thin plastic from between the slices in his mouth. He had a tin of sardines and hardbread with butter on it instead. The adults drank more beer and a couple of chasers. Excellent, now he could sneak down into the cabin and rip off a can of beer.

After lunch Nora wanted to take a leak, which caused great amusement. Stig proffered an empty beer can, while Esbjörn assumed she could hold out until they went ashore.

"Women have much bigger bladders than us," said Esbjörn, spitting into the lee.

But Nora was annoyed, and to Reine's surprise both Esbjörn and Stig gave in. On her orders, they went down into the cabin. Reine was allowed to hold the tiller instead, while Nora sat over the rail. Reine hoped sincerely that she had a bladder as big as a beach ball so that he would be able to steer for a really long time. It was fantastic feeling the water press against the rudder as the wind rose, the same peculiar feeling of triumph as when he was fishing and got a bite. Unfortunately, Nora had a perfectly normal bladder, and Reine had to hand the tiller over to Stig only two minutes and twenty-five seconds later.

Esbjörn and Stig had changed down in the cabin, Stig into bathing trunks and Esbjörn into revolting flowered shorts that stuck to his prick and made it look as if he'd wet his pants. Old men in underpants were really quite disgusting. Reine got terribly sleepy shortly after lunch. He slipped down to the cabin, moved right up into the prow, and lay down on the triangular bunk. He did not dare take off his life jacket but fell asleep in it as if in a cut-off sleeping bag. When he woke up, the sun was low and pouring through the portholes. He was soaked through with sweat, and there was a smell of plastic everywhere; the beer was burning in his stomach. He stumbled confusedly up through the hatch fore of the mast. It was early evening. The wind had dropped, and the mainsail was swinging slackly from starboard to port and back. Both Stig and Esbjörn were sleeping like seals, while Nora was at the tiller in panties and Esbjörn's shirt.

It was Sunday evening and early the next morning he had to be at work as usual.

"When'll we be back at Hässelby?" Reine asked.

"I think Esbjörn has to get the boat back tomorrow before six," said Nora. "You feeling homesick?"

Reine didn't know what to do. Here he was on a boat, out at sea, where there was no telephone. What would all the old girls think tomorrow? That he was sick? Dead? Had left for good? Would Aunt Olga start phoning round all the hospitals in Stockholm asking if there was a case of twisted gut called Reine Larsson there? They'd be miserable and would start talking to each other, crying and drawing the curtains. Aunt

Olga would choose the finest ribbon, and Helena would do the lettering because she was best at it. What would they write?

There was a little twerp, who couldn't even burp . . . now, now, no burying yourself, Reine. Up and slap your own backside. Laugh . . . Reine tried tickling himself in one armpit but did not feel the slightest desire to laugh. He stared at Nora instead: what a head of hair she had! He hadn't been able to see her hair before with the scarf around her head, but now she'd taken it off. Her hair was auburn and shaped into hundreds of sausages standing out in all directions. Reine liked Nora. She seemed all right, even though she did sleep most of the time.

"Wake those pigs up," she said, nodding toward the cabin. "I simply don't know where we are. Supposing we run aground?"

Reine stuck his head down into the cabin where the two men were asleep, but they seemed reluctant to wake up. He could pull Stig's mustache, of course, but Esbjörn didn't have one. Why not wake Esbjörn the way they'd waked Nora—squirt some beer on his stomach.

"Let them sleep," said Nora in the end. "That's nicest for us."

"Are you married to Esbjörn?" said Reine.

"Esbjörn? No, we're just friends. What do you think a guy like that wants? Sex and be waited on. What do you think Stig wants? Sex and be waited on."

Were all men like that? Just screwing, then out with their slippers? If Reine ever married, it would be to a girl who was so pure and clean he would rather die than do something dirty with her. He would marry an angel with no wings. Someone he almost dared not touch. But heck, he wasn't going to get married at all. He wasn't going to go into puberty! He wasn't going to become a fat hairy old man striding around with sauce in his pants.

Nevertheless, they did wake Esbjörn up after a while, because the wind had dropped completely and they could no longer steer the boat. They were drifting broadside on toward two men fishing from a rowboat. Esbjörn came up slapping his stomach like a sealion, his face reddish-brown from beer and sun. Without warning, he threw himself head first into the water and swam once around the boat before, puffing and groaning, he was helped on board astern.

Gradually some kind of order was restored to the ship. Esbjörn got the sail down and started up the outboard engine, and the rigging rattled and sang as they shot past some small islands. There were boats everywhere, in every single bay, behind every single cliff. The Mälare was as crowded as a multilevel parking garage.

Reine hadn't had any food for over eight hours and was beginning to feel sick. Although the boat was going up and down much less now, he felt every small lurch directly in his stomach, as if he'd swallowed a well-oiled gyrocompass, a hunk of steel working away at trying to keep a balance in his stomach. As soon as he closed his eyes, it grew worse. Nora noticed that he was in a cold sweat.

"Go and lie down," she said. "It's better to lie down."

Reine clambered unsteadily down into the plastic-smelling cabin and collapsed on the bunk. Nora was right. If he lay quite still on one side, with his eyes closed, he felt better. After a while he felt so much better, he fell asleep.

"Come on up and look at the ospreys!"

Nora was standing beside him with a saucepan in one hand and a pair of binoculars in the other. How long had he been asleep? He scrambled up and tugged his life jacket back into place. His head was aching, and there was a stink of paraffin in the cabin. He grabbed the binoculars and climbed up into the seat well. They were anchored alongside a steep cliff, the boat moored to a small fir tree shooting up out of a crevice. There were a few smooth round boulders beside the boat, and Stig was squatting on one of them, brushing his teeth.

There was a shallow bay behind them, a protruding stone slope hiding it, but above the slope he could see between thirty and forty masts, black, silver, and gilt. The bay was packed with sailboats. Most of the masts were of roughly equal length, but some of them were much taller and thicker, with peculiar metal vanes on them shaped like jet fighters with pointed noses and sharply swept-back wings. Others had small red windsocks or pennants on them. A strong smell of burning charcoal was pouring out of the bay.

"The osprey! Look," said Nora, pointing with the pan of potatoes.

Reine turned right around to face the open water. A few hundred yards away was a small island with a stony beach overgrown with thin reeds. The island rose only ten feet or so above the reeds, the undergrowth a jungle of brambles and saplings, but on one point was a cluster of sturdy low pines with orange-colored trunks. A pair of flapping gray wings could be seen in one of the pines above a heap of brushwood—the bird's nest?

Suddenly another osprey came winging in from the bay like a large grayish-white gull, with the same jerky flight of gulls but more majestic and gliding. Was that a fish in its claws? The osprey appeared to be flying straight into the pine tree. Reine took the binoculars away from his eyes and formed the words in his mind: *Today we have seen sea-eagles. They live in a gigantic pine tree. They constantly fly in with dead ducks in their claws for their young.*

Stig came aboard and took over the binoculars, then directed them on to the bay.

"Nobody skinny-dipping?"

Reine was often to think about what happened next. He felt a firm grip on his life jacket and another on the seat of his pants. Someone lifted him over the railing and let him go. Then he seemed to float in the air above the water for several minutes before he finally fell in. He had time to think about a great many things: who would call up Uddevalla, whether the police launch would have one or two outboard engines, who would take his place in class at school . . . on the other hand his sojourn in the water was brief. His ears popped, water went up his nose, and he struck out once or twice before someone brutally turned him over on his back and started towing him toward the large flat stones on the other side of the boat.

Nora had jumped in and hauled him out. They sat hugging each other on one of the stones. The water stung Reine's nose, and he sneezed. Nora stroked his wet hair. Esbjörn and Stig were standing in the boat looking very angry, Stig with a silly grin on his face.

"I thought he stank of shit," said Stig, pointing vaguely at Reine.

Reine looked up at Nora. She had no hair and was as bald as a store window dummy! A moment ago she had had a great red afro-cut bush of hair. Nora giggled and pointed out over the water, where the red wig was bobbing up and down by the hull of the boat.

Esbjörn pulled out an aluminum boathook and started fishing for the wig, but it wouldn't catch on the hook and kept sliding down beneath the surface.

"Damn seaweed!" said Esbjörn.

"I'll get it myself," said Nora, wading into the water. "You find the potato saucepan instead."

Stig and Esbjörn searched for the saucepan for almost an hour, but it had sunk to the bottom somewhere. They fished up three large potatoes, but that was all. Meanwhile Reine sat watching, wrapped in a blanket and drinking hot tea with a lot of sugar in it. Esbjörn was angry with Stig and once or twice looked as if he might hit him. But alas, Reine waited in vain for Stig to be smashed to bits or keelhauled. The only punishment eventually to come his way was that he had no potatoes with his canned ham.

22 On Tuesday, Reine was once again hard at it at Olga's. His explanation that he had had to look after his sick mother had been accepted with regrets and no further questions.

In the afternoon coffee break, Reine was given the task of taking three ribbons to Skog Cemetery out in Enskede. The messenger who should have fetched the ribbons had had his moped stolen, but Reine did not listen very carefully to the explanations. He was only too eager to be off. In the long run, it was deadly boring up there under that sizzling hot roof, painting the same unimaginative farewells day in and day out. Olga gave him coupons for the subway, and he left the studio with the three ribbons, all white, hanging on an ordinary clothes-hanger. They weren't quite dry.

It was disgustingly hot and bouncy on the subway. Every time the train stopped there was a stink of hot brakes. Reine didn't especially like the ordinary suburban train, but the subway was worse, more crowded, dirtier—and bouncier. He felt seasick, the saliva pouring into his mouth and his stomach rumbling. But this time there was no cabin to go and lie down in. He held the hanger with its white and gold ribbons straight out from his body. No point in throwing up on them.

It was better when the train came out of the tunnels and he had something to fix his eye on. The view from Skanstull Bridge was stupendous: far away down there, hundreds of jostling motorboats and yachts heading for Hammarby Lock. It was like traveling through a foreign country. Reine had been in the southern suburbs only once or twice before in his life. The last time had been the previous spring when he had gone with a school friend and the friend's father to watch the dog races at Skarpnäck. Where was Skarpnäck—was it near Skog Cemetery? Did they have a special dog cemetery in Skarpnäck?

He got off at the Skog Cemetery station. Some black-clad people emerged in small groups from other cars, and people in mourning were waiting for trains going into town. The florist's store was near the subway station. Reine went in and managed to get hold of a woman in a blue smock. She took the ribbons and gave him back the clothes hanger.

"Am I to take it back?" said Reine.

"Well, it's not ours, anyhow," said the woman, moving off to see to a customer.

He stood for a moment gazing in surprise at the hanger: he hadn't reckoned on that. His working day was over now, and he wouldn't be going back to Olga's until tomorrow. Damn hanger! He thrust it under his arm and went out. It was too early to go back to Sollentuna. He might as well loaf around out here as in town; the risk of being recognized was sure to be smaller here. There was a map of the cemetery at the subway station. The Chapel of Holy Cross. The Chapel of Faith.

The Chapel of Hope. The Chapel of Resurrection—was there anything significant about which chapel you had your funeral in? In that case, the longest line in the world would be outside the Chapel of Resurrection. Then there was Skog Chapel and Skog Crematorium. He suddenly held his breath; it must smell, mustn't it?

Ah well—there was a silly twerp, who couldn't even burp. No lame ducks here . . . up and away! He grasped the crossbar of the hanger as if it were a suitcase and went into the cemetery. He didn't have his shoulder bag with him today. It was too hot. To which question was the answer DEATH?

It was beautiful and frightening inside Skog Cemetery. Grassy slopes, broad lawns, trees, shrubs. Straight in front of him was a big cross. He wanted to throw up at the very sight of it! Why? As long as he could remember, crosses had always sickened him. There was nothing special about a cross, and if you tipped it over it became an X, an utterly harmless symbol. He took a sighting from the sun before walking past the cross, since it would be the pits if he got lost in this place.

He made sure he kept at a distance from the crematorium and chose a path running in a southwesterly direction. There was a smell of flowers, earth, wet grass, hot tree trunks, and pine needles. How many dead people were there here? Was he walking on skeletons or mummies wherever he walked? About eighty thousand Swedes died every year, Lotta had told him. How many of them ended up here? Masses. Thousands. How the heck was there room for them? A thought struck him: he would open a special cosmic funeral parlor that propelled dead people on rockets out into space. That would be fun with all the wreaths and ribbons fluttering round the nose of the rocket . . . the thought entranced him so much he almost ran into a funeral procession, his hanger raised aloft. Abashed, he veered off on a smaller pathway.

How many children were there here? There was a shortage of children. Some of the tablets mentioned infants who had died the same day or week they'd been born. But they didn't really count; they'd simply paid a brief call on life. He was suddenly tired and sat down on a bench.

There, immediately opposite him, six feet down in the earth, coffins lay packed like boxes in a warehouse. But he couldn't believe it. There was no sign of it outside, or above, whichever you called it. Down there, underneath the grass, lay all those dead. How were they dressed? In suits, dresses, pyjamas? There was something called a shroud, but he didn't really know what that involved; either the corpse was shrouded in the coffin or shrouded by something else—but what, a sheet? That sounded more likely. They were lying there shrouded in sheets like a row of sloppily made mummies. What happened inside the coffin? It was dark, of course, dark as a tomb, as they say. And damp—it must be as damp as an old earth cellar, or the inside of a plastic boat. When he had slept with the others in the boat Esbjörn had rented, the roof had been covered with drops of water when he woke up. One day he would think up a suitable punishment for Stig, maybe burying him alive. In a plastic coffin.

When you die, you're put in a coffin, lowered into the ground, and covered with earth. If you were buried in winter, you were presumably deep-frozen first and lay stiff and hard, somewhat like a frozen side of salmon in the freezer. But when spring came, you started fermenting. And when summer came, you started drying out. And when autumn came—no, to hell with maggots. That probably wasn't true. Most of what you heard about bodies in the ground was probably not true, just bluff. Had anyone ever seen them decay with their own eyes? Had they once buried someone in a large aquarium so you could look into the grave from the side? He'd never heard of that. All that talk about what happened to the dead had no scientific basis. It might be just as true that bodies lay there in their sheets like the cocoons of butterflies—and when spring came, they gradually developed wings, and the bodies were transformed into huge butterflies with angel faces.

Evolution and devolution of a human being. The former, evolution, how the fetus grew out of the seed, was beautiful and captivating—something people wrote big books about and gave them away as presents. At school they had a copy of a big book full of pictures of fetuses; some photographer or other had become world famous from it. Why couldn't the same photographer dig a hole in Skog Cemetery, bore into a coffin, stick his lights and lens inside, and record the other process? That would be quite something.

Supposing evolution went backward? That would be great. Then the dead person would begin to shrink, getting younger, becoming a teenager, losing its hair, and becoming a child. And when the really great thing happened, the body would turn bluish-red and become a fetus. Something would have to be the umbilical cord and something the afterbirth. How long would it take to live all your life backward down there in the soil? A year couldn't correspond to a year, because then old people would go on being transformed down there for seventy or eighty years. And it wasn't like that. Dog years? Seven dog years for every ordinary year. In ten or twelve years, a human being would be transformed into nothing—that sounded reasonable.

The fetus twisted and landed with its head against the end of the coffin, then quickly became smaller and smaller. Its eyes slid out onto its cheeks and its nose grew flat, and gradually a tail appeared, and the fetus looked like a toy crocodile . . . no, like a whale on all fours. Finally it was just a little lump of mucus that had been an egg. A sperm backed out of the lump of mucus; then the whole person was transformed into an egg the size of a grain of sand, and a sperm so small you couldn't see it at all.

But in that case, where did all the skeletons come from? For there were skeletons. The ones they had at school were plastic, but there were real skeletons made of bone in the Historical Museum in town. But were they the remains of human beings? Or were they just some kind of toys or ornaments our forefathers had made from seal bone or the jawbones of wolves?

Reine started up from the bench; there was no point in frightening himself. He was good at that, sending cold shivers down his own spine. But one fine day he would be powerful and send cold shivers down other people's spines. That'd be great. Everyone would be forced to do as he wished. Reine the Terrible.

He started walking in a wide circle toward the exit. There was a newly made grave to the left of the path, the wreaths, flowers, and ribbons still there. He stopped. Perhaps he should check whether he had done any of those ribbons? He went over to the grave. The flowers and leaves had withered, and wires were sticking out of the carnations. There was a smell of compost. He dared not touch the ribbons, but he poked at them with the hanger. The ribbons were no longer multi-colored; they looked as if rain had poured onto a watercolor painting, all faded and run together. But it couldn't have been rain. It wasn't raining this summer. He noticed a plastic hose wriggling its way between the trees: a sprinkler, of course. He couldn't identify the ribbons. Some had fringes like Olga's; others had fringes he'd never seen before; some had none at all. Stupid—they should put one's initials on the ribbons, down in the righthand corner, very small: RL '75.

He didn't want to go straight back and be forced to pass that horrible cross. They could keep their old Golgotha. He went into an area that had not yet been brought into use. It felt good. At last he could put his feet down on the ground in the usual way. He slapped his thigh with the clothes hanger and sang: "Once a crazy melon loaded his cannon, with a lovely lemon and shot down a Mormon . . ." to the tune of an old nursery rhyme, but it didn't really work. So he reverted to the original and sang: "Mother's Little Olle through the forest did flit, lifted his shirttail and let out some shit."

Reine went through a gap in a tall hedge and came out on to a large plowed-up area. The ground was rough and scored with the tracks of a bulldozer, now resting with its scoop against a huge pile of garbage. They seemed to be building grave mounds of withered wreaths, bouquets, tissue paper, stripped twigs, and other garbage. Who rested in peace here? The old king—Gustaf III—who had died a few years back? No, heck, Helene had told him he was out at Haga.

So this was where all the wreaths ended up. The garbage heap seemed to have been dug out along one edge, where there was a dumper. Could it mean this was an intermediate station, where garbage trucks shuttled back and forth, fetching garbage during working hours? For a moment he was tempted to climb up on the heaps in search of his own ribbons, but he was scared of getting stuck, drowning, sinking to the bottom of the garbage and eventually being dug out by the bulldozer, tipped into a garbage truck, and driven away.

He followed the garbage trucks' route out, and went back to the subway station. Before he went through the turnstile he paid a visit to the men's toilet to check the situation of the day. He had not matured today, either.

23 He felt happier that morning than he had for a long time. He had awakened a whole hour earlier than usual and lain in bed admiring the money order, turning and twisting it, letting Jocke and Snoopy read it and fight over it and pretend to hide it from each other. On the money order, addressed to Harriet Larsson, it said *Reimbursement: SKr. 190.* He had found it lying on the floor in the hall when he had come back from Skog Cemetery. The sender was the Greater Stockholm Central Association for Summer Camps for Children.

Reine got up and cleared his desk before sitting down. At first he practiced Mom's signature on the back of an old *Technical World;* then he scribbled an unusually neat and flashy "Harriet Larsson," the tip of his tongue protruding between his lips like a baton as he wrote. Oddly enough, he found it more difficult to sign his own name under the heading *Signature of bearer.* He had had more practice at writing Mom's.

Before setting off for the Sollentuna station, he took out the little black notebook in which he collected The World's Most Important Questions and Answers. What had he managed to scrape up? With some effort, he translated from his own code language:

1. Chuck thinking about who Dad is.
2. Is there anyone else besides me?
3. You'll be an angel.
4. Find ten answers. Fix Stig.

5. Blow up the whole pile of shit.

That was all, after four whole weeks. Soon the whole summer would have gone. If he went on at this rate, he would have no more than about ten or twelve questions or answers. Answers? He had decided on answers. What was wrong with the answers he'd come up with so far? They were negative. That was it. Boring, negative, miserable answers. That's what was wrong. He should look ahead instead. How far ahead could he see? To the year two thousand? That seemed reasonable. He wrote:

6. Look ahead. (2000 A.D.)

Satisfied, he packed his bag with the usual things, buttoned up the top button of his newly laundered and far too tight jeans, grabbed the wooden hanger in his left hand, and left the apartment. As he jogged off toward Sollentuna station, the envelope kept tickling and prickling his stomach, the envelope he had put the money order into and then stuffed inside his T-shirt.

That day was not like the others at Olga's. They had practically nothing to do. By ten o'clock they had already finished the day's orders. They did some rather listlessly for stock, but the stock was almost full.

"Don't people die in July?" said Reine.

"Oh, yes," said Olga. "Indeed people die in July. Especially when it's as insufferably hot as it's been this year."

"Don't they bury people in July then?"

"Yes, of course."

"I mean do they leave them in the mortuary?"

"Reine!" said Kristina with horror. She hardly ever spoke, but now she was overwrought and tugging at her braids.

"Sorry."

"Of course, sometimes there are complications with holidays," said Olga.

"My mother-in-law died on the twenty-first of July last year," said Lotta, sniffling slightly. "It was extremely troublesome."

Why was Lotta always snuffling and sniveling? Was she really miserable? Reine had noticed that her eyes were nearly always watery and her cheeks red, as if she'd been crying into her pillow all morning. Or did she just have a chronic cold? Or was she allergic? Allergic to wreaths, or words? Could you be allergic to words? Get eczema in your ear? If anyone said "death," Lotta's ears started to itch, and her eyes and nose ran.

"Yes," Olga said in reply to Lotta. "One shouldn't fall ill or die in July when practically the whole country is closed for the holidays. Everyone closes, as we do."

"How's business actually?" said Reine, for no particular reason.

There was complete silence. No one appeared to have heard what he said, though he'd said it very loudly and clearly. Reine felt as if he had thrown up on the floor and no one wanted to clean it up. But he did not take the question back, just let it evaporate. Now he understood one thing: discussing the state of business at Studio Olga was not popular. What could that mean? Did Olga make millions out of her ribbons but pay her staff peanuts? Well, maybe not. The truth was more likely that Olga made peanuts out of her ribbons.

"I thought of something," said Reine. "You don't have to letter ribbons just for wreaths."

"We don't, either," said Helene in injured tones, pointing her unnaturally long arm at the banner with the golden cross and a thousand rays on it.

"You see, Reine," said Olga, looking up from her worn account books. "Sometimes we get very distinguished orders. Table banners for the Odd Fellows, ribbons for victory garlands for the Swedish Orienteering Association and . . . well."

"We ought to get much more lettering for parties and that kind of thing," said Reine. "So that we'd have something to do when funerals are put on ice . . . I mean . . . postponed."

"But how?"

"You could put a color advertisement in the *Daily News.*"

Aunt Olga laughed, and Reine realized his suggestion might cost quite a lot.

"We could go around putting leaflets in people's mailboxes."

"Who would do that?" said Helene sharply. "Us?"

"Me," said Reine. "I could go around delivering them in the afternoons."

"Parties and suchlike? What do you mean by that?" said Helene.

"This whole business is based on cooperation with florists," said Aunt Olga.

Reine scratched his head with the end of his brush. What had he been thinking of? Fiftieth birthdays? Did they have silk ribbons then? For Christmas, maybe, to decorate the tree? Never heard of that. The maypole, possibly.

"Have you considered that in twenty-five years the world will be having its two thousandth birthday?" he said finally.

Silence fell again, and then Kristina whispered in her brittle voice:

"We'll all be dead by then."

"No, now . . ." said Aunt Olga sternly.

"But if we're all dead . . ." Reine began, but swiftly swallowed the rest. He had thought of saying that if mankind dies out before the year two thousand, then there would be . . . what do they call it . . . great competition in the trade. Instead he said, "When the world is two thousand years old, there'll be the biggest party there's ever been."

"But twenty-five years!" said Helene.

"That's not far off, is it? Twenty-five years to prepare for something having a two thousandth birthday. It's a matter of doing things in time. What if we started thinking about how many ribbons and streamers or whatever would be needed. Not only here in Sweden. All over the world!"

Silence fell again. Kristina sniveled, but no one took much notice. Kristina often sniveled for no apparent reason. Sometimes she laughed, or looked up at the ceiling and got the giggles.

"What would we write on the streamers?" said Lotta, looking appreciatively at Reine.

"Simple. Two thousand. We could letter masses of ribbons with two thousand on them. In numbers. Numbers look the same abroad, too."

"Shall we do lettering for export!" laughed Lotta.

The discussion died out again. Those who should have had something to add, Aunt Olga and Helene, did not seem interested.

"Ordinary birthday greetings . . ." Reine tried rather lamely, but it was far too late now. Olga had already picked up the telephone receiver.

He was disappointed that no one had risen to the occasion. Maybe he was wrong about the two thousandth jubilee, but they could well have talked about it awhile. The year two thousand should not pass unnoticed. Not even on Children's Island. What if it was the year two thousand now: how easy it would be to write letters from Children's Island. About all the festivities, fireworks, royal visits, hamburgers every single day . . . only an idiot would play truant from Children's Island during the festive and eventful summer of the year two thousand.

Since there was so little to do, Reine got the afternoon off. At first he was dismayed, because the days were far too long when he had time off, but then he remembered the money order inside his shirt. He quickly said goodbye and leaped down the stairs. Between the third and fourth floor, he stopped by one of the windows and felt his left shoulder blade: he was so happy, wings might be growing. But all he could feel was the usual slightly tender edge of bone. He left the window; it was safest to use the stairs.

It looked as if there might be trouble getting the money at the post office. When he handed over the order with his railway rebate card as identification, he was told that was not good enough. In the end, however, the woman at the counter had given in and said, "Well, you look honest," and counted out the notes, a hundred and some tens.

Then Reine went and had a meal at the Great American Disaster, an extravagant hamburger restaurant opposite McDonald's. At the Great American Disaster he was served at the table, and the hamburgers cost almost three times as much as at McDonald's. But they also gave you almost enough to eat.

24 Reine was in a telephone booth calling Sonesson and Rilke, the sports store.

"My name is Mrs. Hammarskjöld," he said into the receiver, hoping his boy's voice would pass for a female's. "It's like this. We're having a little party and wanted to have some fireworks. If it's all right to order them over the phone, then I can send my son to fetch them. Before five, maybe?"

It was perfectly all right to order by phone and Reine chose from a price list he had picked up at the store five minutes earlier. He ordered pieces sold only to people over eighteen.

"How much does that come to?"

"A hundred and thirty-six exactly."

"Then we'll have three more Big Berthas."

Reine hung up with satisfaction and looked at his watch: twelve minutes past one, so he could take it easy for a few hours. Take it easy where? The nearest park was Humle Gardens, so he went there. The traffic in and out of the Royal Library was not nearly so lively as it had been three weeks earlier. He bought an ice cream cone and sat down on the steps, where he found himself almost alone.

Why hadn't he gone to Children's Island? Nothing would really have stopped him from thinking about life on Children's Island—or would it? It certainly would. No one could think straight with a whole lot of other kids around the place. You couldn't concentrate in a room full of other people. Even if they were actually asleep, it would still be impossible. You wouldn't be able to think freely. If, for instance, you wanted to continue along the line that you were alone in the world and other people were nothing but specks of dust in your eyes—that idea would be impossible to follow through with ten sweating, farting, moaning buddies sleeping in the same room. And if you had a room of your own? Imagine having a room of your own at Children's Island! A room with a lock and a blind you could retreat to whenever there was something important to be sorted out.

Even if they all had a room of their own at Children's Island, it wouldn't work. It would be regarded as suspicious if you retreated, if you didn't want to get in on the football or fishing. If you refused to get up one morning because you wanted to be left in peace to think—then they would call a doctor. Urine specimens would be demanded. When they'd checked your piss, you'd be forced to get up. Provided they didn't find a fatal disease! Sometimes he longed to be very seriously sick. So sick he would be given a private room in a comfortable modern hospital—no, they would have to remodel at home. He would be incurably sick with some very protracted illness. Mom would have to move out of the lounge, and they would make a complete sickroom for Reine with a hospital bed, a special drawing board, a bell, a Japanese mini-television at the end of his bed, and brown-toned glass in the window to the balcony.

In between his sufferings, he would lie in a happy semi-torpor and think about what was really important. Naturally, if you were mortally sick, you thought only about essentials, about death. When he was thinking, he would press a special button so that a red light would go on outside the lounge door. When he had finished thinking, the green light would go on. Then Mom would come in and give him something thirst-quenching, iced tea and toast. He would also get letters from far and wide. Everyone would be terribly sorry for him; they would never say so directly, but he would be able to read between the lines.

Channels 1 and 2 would both come and do a program about the little eleven-year-old cancer victim who spent his last weeks of life solving major problems. Wise old men would come trembling into the room asking what it felt like to die. We're so scared. And when he grew worse, a crowd of people would gather in the yard outside. Mom and a couple of doctors would put him in a gilded chair and carry him carefully out onto the balcony so he could wave to them down there . . . Reine sniffed and swallowed a tear. Aw, heck, he couldn't sit here drowning himself in his own sorrows.

Anyhow, living together with a whole lot of other kids at summer camp must be sheer hell. Being pushed, pinched, questioned. Being forced to laugh when others laughed, to dive into the water head first because the others did. To have to swallow air and burp because that was part of it all. To be given a new name: if you were baptized Reine, you had to reckon on that. Rain, Reindeer—Silly Soll because he came from Sollentuna? If you had to adopt a new name, you felt yourself different; you weren't "me" any longer. That's what all those demon kids were after—to stick a hole in his ego. One of Mom's friends had kept calling him Heine. Hi, Sonja Heine! Sonja Heine was some woman who was once world skating champion in Norway. Reine had felt Norwegian himself. It was horrible!

Reine leaped up from the steps and raced full tilt to the other side of the Royal Library, sprinting so his knees almost hit his chin and the strap of his bag nearly strangled him. If you really poured on the speed, you could sometimes disperse unpleasant thoughts. The sprint made him want to take a leak, so he went on up to the toilet by the small sports stadium. You probably couldn't even take a leak in private on Children's Island. Concentration camps for children.

When he came out into the sunlight again, he saw some people putting up an open-air theater on the great grass slope below the swings. He went across. It looked like the same stage he had seen half built in Vasa Park some time ago. The stage itself was ready, and they were putting up the sides and fixing the lighting. A notice said TONIGHT AT 8 O'CLOCK THE BUSKER THEATER COMPANY WILL PERFORM *THE THREE WISE MEN*.

They were rehearsing on the grass below the stage. A girl dressed as a bride was sitting with a doll in her lap, and beside her were three men in long robes. One of them had a long bamboo pole with a gold star on top of it. Not far away some young people were lying in a circle, passing round a corncob pipe. Reine went cautiously across and squatted on the edge of the circle of spectators.

"Let's do it again!" said the girl in white, who must be the Virgin Mary, of course.

The man with a star on his pole stretched out his hand to the Virgin Mary and declaimed:

"For twelve years we have wandered, we three Holy Kings from the East. We have followed the radiant star. The star that has roamed from the Levant in the East to California in the West, from Svalbard in the North to Eldsland in the South. Over the high steppes we have wandered. We have poled our way on rafts of reeds over the bottomless marsh. We have crossed the Euphrates. We have swum the Tigris. We have wriggled along the ground in the storms of the deserts. The star showed us no mercy. But now it has stopped: here!"

The man thumped the ground with the pole with the star on it, and the Virgin Mary looked at the star and threw up her eyes.

"Greetings to you, O Wise Men! Welcome, O Lords from afar! Joseph . . ."

A bent little old man in a ragged costume came running in from behind the stage, clearly late.

"Where are the gifts?" cried Joseph to the Three Wise Men.

The second Wise Man in line, an actor in a blue mantle, stepped forward and placed himself in front of the Wise Man with the star. He held up his fingers and declaimed:

"Madagascar, Kenya, Tanzania, Ruanda-Burundi! Gabon, Cameroons, Liberia! Ghana, Sierra Leone, Guinea! Gambia, Senegal, Uganda!"

The Virgin Mary picked up the doll and lifted it up before the Three Wise Men. Reine could see that the doll's face was as black as a Negro's, and he was profoundly shocked—the infant Jesus a Negro? That was too damn much, wasn't it? Since the Virgin Mary was white, that must mean God the Father, father to Jesus, was a black. He just couldn't imagine it.

"Break!" said one of the men lying on the grass smoking the communal corncob pipe. "Joseph can't come rushing in like a damn guard dog. He must be more servile, cringing, his knees bent and wringing his hands like an old Jew, a usurer. Let's do it again."

Joseph went back and crouched down behind the stage. The man with the bamboo pole thumped the ground so the gold star shook, and Mary looked up and threw up her eyes again.

"Greetings to you, O Wise Men! Welcome, O Lords from afar! Joseph!"

Joseph was already on his way across to the men, crouching and sagging at the knees. Lisping, he said:

"Vair ees da geefts?"

"Madagascar, Kenya, Tanzania, Ruanda-Burundi! Gabon, Cameroons, Liberia! Guinea! Gambia, Senegal, Uganda!"

Reine averted his eyes as Mary held up the black Baby Jesus and said:

"Look, little king. The whole world lies at thy feet! All the lands of the earth bring thee thy kingdom! Look!"

Reine covered his eyes with his hand and peeked through his fingers. He did not want to look until Mary jerked Jesus back onto her lap. Then something fantastic happened. The Baby Jesus started speaking! In a peculiar, half-suppressed voice the Baby Jesus piped:

"I am the Son of God. My kingdom is not of this world. Get thee gone, materialists!"

How the heck did that hang together? Oh, one of them must be a ventriloquist. Simple—the same trick you were always seeing on television. Some guy sat there with a silly doll on his lap and asked silly questions—and then the doll gave a whole lot of inappropriate replies, and the guy looked embarrassed. That's how it worked, and Joseph was the ventriloquist. The man, directing from the grass said:

"Joseph, you must stand right behind Mary. Stand right up close as if you were going to pinch her bottom, then lean over her shoulder and say: I am the son of God etcetera etcetera."

"I am the Son of God. My kingdom is not of this world. Get thee gone, materialists!" piped Jesus.

The Three Wise Men turned away in terror and fell to their knees, the leader having some trouble keeping the star constantly hovering above Mary and the infant Jesus. The Three Wise Men chorused:

"Before your visage all houses crumble, before your visage all steel melts, before your visage all maps burn, before your visage all boundaries burst!"

Then they gestured with their hands as if something had blown up in the air and one after another cried:

"America! Bang! Soviet Union! Bang! France! Bang! Great Britain! Bang! Canada! Bang! . . ."

"That's enough, that's enough." The producer got up off the grass, went over to Mary, and kissed her on the cheek; then the rehearsal was clearly over, because they all sat down on the grass and smoked the corncob pipe.

Reine waited. He really wanted to see the rest of the play. What would happen? Would the Jesus doll grow up to be twelve years old and drive the moneylenders out of the temple? When his teacher had told them all that about the usurers in his first year at school, nearly all the class had thought Jesus had driven the juices out of the temple. But no one had objected—why shouldn't he?

But getting back to the Jesus play, would the company have time to get right through his whole life? What would they do about the donkey he rode? And what about the water he had to walk on—how would they solve that? How would they get the audience to believe Jesus was stomping around on the surface of the water? The end would be bloodthirsty—Reine pushed himself up with his hands, but he could not see three big crosses anywhere. Perhaps they'd cut out the robbers? Being an actor looked like fun. If he hadn't been so shy, he would have liked to be Jesus as a twelve-year-old. People were smaller in those days, so being only eleven wouldn't be a catastrophe.

But there was no more rehearsing, although Reine waited for the rest of the afternoon. One after the other, the theater crowd disappeared until only the producer and an older man in blue coveralls were left, testing loudspeakers and lights.

On the stroke of five, Reine went into Sonesson and Rilke's sporting goods store. The fireworks department was in the basement. It was pretty creepy going down the stairs because there were warning notices everywhere: Danger! Explosives!

An old man in a gray coat came up, kind of sneering, apparently talking with a coughdrop in his mouth all the time, sucking in his cheeks and pouting out his top lip, then lisping:

"Can I help you?"

Reine stated his errand, thinking: well, here goes, the worst that can happen is that they turn me out. But the old man went on smacking his lips and brought a couple of large brown bags out of an inner room with steel doors marked DANGER! EXPLOSIVES!

"Hammarskjöld. That's a familiar name," he mumbled, his nose halfway inside the bag.

Reine had to go to a special cashier's desk and pay an ancient dame with brilliant blond hair. One hundred and sixty-eight, ninety, it all came to. The man with the nonexistent coughdrop stood behind him with the bags. At first not everything would go into Reine's bag, but when Reine agreed that the sticks on the rockets could stick out, it was all right. The old man brought some brown paper and wrapped it around the sticks. Reine checked the result in the steel mirror hanging by the exit—it looked no worse than if his bag had been full of tennis gear. What was sticking out could easily be the handle of a racket.

Although Reine took his time at McDonald's, he still arrived at Sollentuna far too early. To keep from having to lug all those explosives around, he decided to go down into his own basement. The key for it was not the same as the one Stig had taken, and every family had a small compartment covered with chicken wire down there. In the Larsson family compartment was an old crib, and inside that was Reine's tricycle. In the other corner were a couple of old suitcases filled with pillows and blankets. Reine's nearly new bicycle was down there, too. He dared not use it for fear it would be stolen.

He went inside and pulled the chicken wire door shut behind him.

What would be the safest place for the fireworks? The answer was obvious: in the suitcases with the pillows and blankets. If, contrary to expectations, the whole bunch should go up, there was no better damper than blankets and pillows. He had seen with his own eyes how they had used old quilts when they were dynamiting down on the site of the new Sollentuna shopping center last spring. After he had packed the rockets, bombs, and Bengal Lights among the bedclothes, he sat down with his back to his crib and took a brief nap until dusk. What was happening to Jesus in Humle Gardens? Was he facing Pontius Pilate yet?

25 Why didn't the viper viper nose? Because the adder adder 'ankerchief? A for ism, B for mutton, C for Highlanders, T for two, O for the wings of a dove. First absent-minded professor: "Do you know Lundberg?" Second A.M.P.: "What's his name?" First A.M.P.: "Who?"

Reine was in the john. He closed the joke book and felt his loose tooth. It seemed to be growing firm again. Great! If he was going to be an actor, he couldn't go on stage with a great gap in his teeth.

Reine thought jokes were the best thing in the world. He could read the same wornout old joke books over and over again. Some of the jokes were pretty long, but some weren't at all bad. Jokes should be short. Short, and what adults called really bad jokes. Real jokes shouldn't be dirty, either. Dirty jokes might be amusing sometimes, but they were in a special category. Sublime jokes were never dirty.

Reine let go his tooth and wiped his backside for the fourth time. If Mom had been at home, there would have been a hell of a row about the amount of paper used. She would have gone on about the risk of clogging the drains, too. Mom was nuts. One moment you had to brush your teeth after every meal, and the next you weren't allowed to wipe your ass. He got up, spat into the heap of paper, and pulled the handle. It did seem to be kind of a strain; the toilet filled almost to the top with water before the paper slowly started rotating and then more and more quickly swirled down into the hole, to disappear around the bend with a sharp smack.

Reine put the joke book between his teeth and washed his hands. When he had done that, he pulled up his trousers, took off his socks and dropped them into the already full tub. He padded out to the kitchen, took a box of oatmeal cookies out of the cupboard, and went into the hall to make sure the door chain was securely fastened before going into his room and switching on the television. He turned the brightness control knob until the screen became a sharp pale gray with no picture, leaving the sound on. It was company to hear someone talking out of a television set. You could half listen to talk, but the pictures were dangerous. You never knew what horrors would suddenly leap onto the screen. He would never forget that night several years ago when Mom was working nights and he was alone at home, lying face down on the lounge carpet. Suddenly, the police chief of Saigon had shot a Viet Cong officer in the temple with a short-barreled revolver, right in front of the camera. No one wanted to see such things if he was sleeping alone.

He turned out the ceiling light, then checked the television screen. It was like flying: the screen was the same shape as an airplane window. He looked to the left: no wing, no engines. He looked to the right with his nose pressed to the screen: no tail. That was how bad your field of vision was when you flew through clouds.

At that moment the late weather report started. Reine sat down on the edge of his bed and heard, but did not see, the meteorologist talking and pointing. At last the weather was going to be bad. At last there would be an end to this cursed sunshine that made it so impossible to think. Everything was going to be gray and opaque.

Poor old Aunt Olga. Imagine having to flee from your own native country, just because those bastard Russians and Germans couldn't agree. Aunt Olga had had to escape helter-skelter with her old dad. Aunt Olga's dad had been Lithuania's foremost submarine captain. But he hadn't been killed in any of all those wars. He had died in the Rosenlund nursing home in 1962. That must have been rotten for him.

Reine would have liked to do something for Aunt Olga, but what could he do that would really please her? The only thing that would make her really happy would be the end of the Bolshevik regime in Lithuania. Aunt Olga put all her hopes in the Americans. Now that the Indochina business was over, now that it looked like the U.S.A. and China were becoming friends—Aunt Olga had said as they had gone down the stairs together—the U.S.A. had time to deal with the Baltic States. The U.S.A. had the largest number of landing craft in the world.

But if America jumped on Russia, then there would be a nuclear war. You could count on that. Blow the whole damn mess up—that would be the result if Olga's dreams came true. Anyhow, he didn't think many of her friends from the old days were still alive over in Lithuania; Aunt Olga herself was over seventy.

But! . . . that was it! He could please Aunt Olga with a great display of fireworks. When he had bought all those rockets and bombs, he hadn't been quite sure what use he would put them to. He had been fulfilling an old dream: one day when I'm really rich, I'll buy a whole lot of the best fireworks in the whole world. That reimbursement money had come at a fantastically opportune moment. But how to use the stuff . . . maybe he had bought them just to show off. Maybe he'd get a buddy, or someone he wanted to be buddies with, down into the basement and show him—there couldn't be many eleven-year-olds with such an arsenal in the basement storeroom. But why not please Aunt Olga with his fabulous firework display?

Where? He could invite her back home, of course. No. Aunt Olga would never be able to crawl along the roof and then get down onto the balcony. Stupid! He could get in by the roof himself and then open up from indoors to let Olga in. They could have something good to eat—shrimp? Then, when it was dark, they could go out onto the balcony and let the whole shitload off.

But there was another but. Wasn't that too tough on all the others at the studio? Helene didn't have much fun, either, even though she wasn't from Lithuania. And the touchy Kristina, who was a little nuts—or mentally retarded, as the others said. What was life like for her? What had she escaped from? Where did she long to go? What invisible wheelchair did she sit in? And then there was Lotta, who was always so weepy. She had a husband, of course, but she always seemed depressed all the same. Maybe he was no support to her. The only one he didn't have to feel sorry for was Mrs. Bergman-Ritz, but she hadn't been there for a few weeks. Had she left?

They would never get Helene up the stairs, even if Reine got up onto the roof to let her in. The fireworks would have to be held somewhere else. At Helene's place, maybe? But she seemed so finicky, so scared about her things. And would he be allowed to let off Big Berthas in a small ground-floor apartment in the middle of town? What about out at the hospital where Kristina was, then? At the day department, or whatever they called it. Night department? She only slept there. Reine had never been to Beckomberga Hospital, but it did not sound particularly suitable. They might disturb the other sick people. At Lotta's place? No, her husband would interfere. He was sure to be one of those mean bastards who knew all about fireworks and would keep organizing and calculating—and at the last moment push Reine aside because it was "dangerous," just to be able to light them himself.

Of course! The party should be held in the studio, which already stank of paint and paint remover, so it wouldn't matter if they polluted it with a little gunpowder. They'd have to open the windows, of course, and make sure the thinner bottles weren't too near. Or what about arranging the whole thing up on the roof? What kind of roof did they have on the Palladium building? At least it looked flat from the street. They'd be able to get Helene up on some hoist or other. Kristina could bring flowers with her from Beckomberga; she'd told them several times there were lots of tulips there. That was just about the only thing she talked about, flowers. Well, then there were the eats. Lotta could fix them. Lotta was a good cook, you could see that from a long way off; she always seemed to have been at the stove all day long. And Aunt Olga herself? Olga wouldn't have to do anything at all; everything would be organized by the time she arrived. Everything fixed up. All she would have to do would be to climb up on the roof to an already laid table illuminated by nearby neon signs. By opening a few hatches in the roof, they would be sure to have some music, too—a Viennese waltz from the hundred-man orchestra of the Oscar Theater.

When they'd eaten, Reine would call for silence and go across to his firework display. The women would clap their hands at the roman candles and catherine wheels. Kristina might be slightly scared of the Big Berthas, but someone could hold her hand. As a finale, Reine would let off all the tracer lights and golden rain rockets over the center of Stockholm, so people all over Stockholm would think the city was celebrating the opening of the greatest hamburger bar in the whole world.

26 It was Friday the eighteenth of July, and Reine was lettering MOURNED AND MISSED THE ZIOLEK FAMILY. Adults have to work all day, he thought, so never have time to think anything out. That applied to him, too! The harder he worked, the fewer his thoughts. Lettering such a fierce name as ZIOLEK, for instance, meant you had to hold your tongue in the right place in your mouth. You fucking well couldn't sit thinking about what happened after death then, could you?

Reine had brought sandwiches with him for lunch that day. He had discovered that everything important happened when the women were having their lunch. But hitherto he had not been able to bring himself to resist the hamburgers. Autumn was coming, and that meant school food again—why couldn't McDonald's or Carrol's be allowed to take over school kitchens? Guaranteed success. However, today it was sandwiches, after considerable struggle with himself; two hardbread with cheese and one French roll with marmalade. Plus fizzy pear juice.

They hadn't much to do, so Reine drew a sheriff's star in gold on his T-shirt. He had been given permission and found it much more fun decorating his own T-shirts than going into a store and getting his star stamped on for twenty *kronor*. He had decorated two others as well, one with KAWASAKI on it, and another with JAP, the speedway make. The other day he had thought he would do something forbidden and had lettered FROM A GRIEVING MOTHER on a T-shirt; but he'd done that in secret out in the storeroom.

"I can't promise you it won't run in the wash," said Aunt Olga, patting him on the head. "But you've got artistic aptitude, I can see that."

Possible risks of that did not trouble Reine, since there was no need to wash the whole T-shirt. He could just put in on and smooth it out. Then he could rub detergent under his arms, and perhaps a little at the bottom of his stomach, scrub it in a bit, rinse off the suds with the hand spray, take the shirt off, and hang it out to dry on the balcony. Nothing to it.

Reine drew in a deep breath over the paint pot. If you did that, you felt like throwing up for several minutes, and when you felt like throwing up, you forgot you were hungry. As a finale to his voluntarily chosen labors, Reine gilded an old copper coin. He could always cheat some dumb twit with it.

"What are you doing during your vacation, Reine?" said Lotta from her corner. Lotta had no orders to do, either, but she didn't spend the time on herself—gilding her shoes, for instance. She just sat there like a fat pig in a flowery dress.

"I'm not having a vacation this year," said Reine.

"I think we'll have lunch now," said Aunt Olga.

They started the preparations. Olga spread a white oilcloth over one of the long tables. Kristina had brought flowers she'd picked in the hospital grounds, and Lotta had brought a large box of chocolates. Reine was impressed. He'd been missing something. Did they always go to all this trouble?

"I've actually made a little cake," said Helene, wheeling up with a cake pan on her lap. There was a foil lid over the pan.

"Oh, but, Helene, how sweet of you!" said Lotta. It sounded a bit overdone, and Kristina looked questioningly at Lotta.

"You're sweet, too," said Lotta, trying to touch Kristina's shoulder, but Kristina evaded her.

"Isn't the hospital arranging a trip this year?" said Helene.

Kristina giggled and looked around from one to the other. Then she said to Reine:

"I've been abroad."

"So've I," said Reine.

"I haven't," said Helene.

They all looked guilty, but what would Helene do abroad? thought Reine. She can't go swimming or get around to the shops, nor can she join roast suckling pig parties in the vineyards. Anyhow, she'd get sunstroke too easily if she had to sit in the sun somewhere. It was decidedly cooler in Riddarholm Church. What would the Spaniards think if a whole crowd of Swedes in wheelchairs came along? They'd think we were a country of cripples you could vanquish with one hand tied behind your back.

"I've brought a jar of meatballs with me," said Olga, putting an earthenware jar on the table. "But we'll have to have them cold, of course."

"You make such wonderful meatballs," said Helene. "What's the name of that sour cream you usually put in them? Smetana?"

"You can get it at the Haymarket food hall nowadays."

Reine felt rather foolish not having brought anything with him. He hadn't realized their lunches were a kind of party. He retreated into the john and changed into his new sheriff T-shirt. At least he could dress up a little bit, if nothing else. But tomorrow—no, Monday—he would fix something really good and bring it with him. Make a pizza perhaps? He was a master at that. How many packs of pizza mix would he need? Three or four? Heck! Lucky it was payday today.

Then pilsner glasses were put on the table and Reine wondered whether the women were going to have a chaser with lunch. But no more than two bottles appeared, so he decided the risk was slight. They ate and talked. The time went by and became half-past twelve, then one o'clock. Lunch breaks didn't usually last that long, but it was Friday, and the slack season.

"Where are you going for your vacation, Reine?" said Olga.

"I don't think I'll take any time off this year," said Reine.

The ladies looked at each other in surprise, then back at him.

"But we're closing today. You must have noticed, Reine?"

Aw, shit! Now he understood! There'd been some loose talk about vacations recently, but he'd thought they each took their time off when they wanted it. But closing? That was catastrophic!

"Who's going to take things to Skog Cemetery?" he said.

"Reine, you don't seem to have taken it in that it's *today* we're closing," said Olga, grasping his arm.

"Oh, yes, I have. I'm going to Children's Island."

"Children's Island?" said Helene. "That sounds like the thirties."

"I'm sure it's not the same as it was then!" said Lotta.

"Oh, no," said Reine. "You get a room to yourself nowadays. It's more like a children's hotel than a camp. You have your own sailboat, too. You might even call it a sailing camp. It's only the name that's old."

"But doesn't the city council run it now?" said Helene.

"Not at all," said Reine. "McDonald's does."

"The hamburger chain?"

"That's right. They've got a foundation, or whatever, and they run a lottery for the places among their customers."

"Congratulations!" cried Lotta. "And our Reine's won one!"

Reine turned red, not knowing what to do with the praise. Even if he had told the truth and earned the praise, he wouldn't have known what to do with it.

"Lotta, you're embarrassing him," said Olga.

"Well, it's nothing special," said Reine. "They have numbers on those paper placemats on the trays. You keep them and look in the papers to see who's won."

"Congratulations! I'll say it all the same," said Lotta.

"But what if an adult wins it?" said Kristina.

Heck, he hadn't thought of that! A whole lot of ancient old men and women on Children's Island; they wouldn't take that.

"Adults get a trip to Majorca," said Reine. "If they're over fifteen."

He immediately regretted saying it, because now Kristina, and maybe the others too, would start eating at McDonald's. It was mean of him to lie to them, but he had actually had no choice.

The afternoon was deadly. All his plans had collapsed, and what would he live off now? How could he have been such a dumb shit as to spend nearly all his money on fireworks? There would be no party at Olga's. There would be nothing whatsoever at Olga's.

"It's always miserable parting," said Olga. "But we'll meet again on the eleventh of August. If you haven't started school by then, Reine."

"No."

"Here you are, then, Reine. Here's what you're owed."

He wearily accepted the money: just about what he owed Mom's savings bank. When he'd settled that, virtually all he'd have left was the gilded copper coin.

Reine slipped off home almost without saying goodbye, unable to bear the sight of their delight at the prospect of a vacation. Were they really pleased? What would happen to Helene, and what about Kristina? It struck him they were all trying to look pleased about their vacation—time they might have to spend all by themselves. The fact that other people might be having a bad time put him in a better mood. No lame ducks here! But he couldn't bring himself to go so far as to celebrate at a real hamburger bar. Instead, he had a hotdog at a stand. He deserved some punishment.

Sollentuna was as empty as an evacuated town. Reine imagined there had just been a nuclear attack, a raid with soft bombs that didn't destroy buildings but just killed every living thing. He kicked at the gravel and imagined it as drifts of deadly white snowlike ash. It was not just a game. By imagining Sollentuna empty of people, he found the courage to do his roof climb despite the fact that it was no later than five o'clock and the sun so blazing hot his heels left marks in the asphalt.

As he lay on his stomach and slid backward over the edge of the roof, he couldn't feel the stepladder with his feet. He made several attempts before turning round and with tingling testicles thrust his head over the edge to see what had happened. The stepladder had fallen over on the balcony; it was impossible to get into the apartment by the balcony any longer.

There was nothing else to do except go back down the stairs via the roof hatch, then down into the basement, unlock the chicken run, and sit down and think. But however much he thought, he could find no solution. He would have to live down here for the time being. He took the tricycle out of the crib he'd had as a baby and made up a bed with some pillows. He made the suitcases into a kind of screen so that no one would see him. He decided that if they came from Children's Island to fetch him, he would light the fireworks. After a while he started sniffing and sniveling. That wouldn't work, either. He had the largest arsenal of explosives in the world to defend himself with—but he hadn't any matches.

27

"Hunger Artists. The longest time a human being has lived without intake of solid food is 382 days. The record is held by the Scot, Angus Barbieri, who voluntarily abstained from solid foods and lived exclusively on tea, coffee, and ordinary water while in the hospital. Over a period of a year, he lost 266 lbs in weight."

Hell! Now it was pitch dark again. The lighting in the basement was fixed so that it went on for four minutes after the button had been pressed, then went off automatically. With his thumb on page thirty-two of the *Mammoth Book of World Records,* Reine left his chicken run and walked the few steps to the orange-colored light indicating the light switch. He slapped the button with his palm and rushed back to the crib.

"Hunger strikes. The world record is 94 days and is held by no fewer than nine people: John and Peter Crowley, Thomas Donavan, Michael Burke, Michael O'Reilly, Christopher Upton, John Power, Joseph Kenny, and Sean Hennessy, in prison in Cork. The nine men survived only because they were under constant qualified supervision."

Up and switch on again. Before returning, he took the opportunity to take a leak in the drain in the floor at the end of the basement corridor.

"Isolation. The world record is 98 hours and is held by a volunteer, Thomas Murphy, who according to an English scientific report beat the record enclosed in a totally dark laboratory cell. Most people have visual and aural hallucinations after only a few hours of total isolation. Sojourn under water. No one has succeeded in remaining under water for more than 13 minutes and . . ."

He let the Book of World Records slide out of his hand and fall between two bars of the crib. Was it night or day? Up there, he meant. It was never light in the basement for more than four minutes at a time—or four minutes, twelve seconds, to be exact. He tried fixing his eye on the luminous green figures of his watch, but they seemed to be crawling very slowly around in a circle. However hard he stared, they refused to stay still.

Ugh, he couldn't go on sitting down here going stark staring nuts. They would come and cart him off to the nuthouse, and you could bet your bottom dollar Stig would be driving. He lay down with his hands under one cheek and tried to go to sleep. But he couldn't. Even when he closed his eyes as tight as possible, he saw small green worms crawling around in a circle. He sat up and breathed deeply for a minute or so. That was silly; the air down here couldn't run out. They built so badly nowadays, the walls were like sieves.

Why didn't he go up? Nothing was stopping him, no locked doors, nothing. He had been just about to go up at least once an hour ever since he had come down, but he couldn't bring himself to. He was not in the right state of mind to show himself in public. Not that he would be shot down on the spot or have handcuffs clapped on him. But someone would see him. Not exactly see him, and say there's that Reine who's escaped from Children's Island—no, not exactly *see*. But he would be registered in someone's mind. If other people had any minds, of course, but unfortunately there was quite a lot of evidence that that was so.

He quite simply did not want to go up. The greatest obstacle in the world is not wanting to. Instead, he wanted to stay down there in his crib with all those pillows and his monkey Jocke, who had been extracted from his bag. He and Jocke would stay together down here in total darkness and shrivel away. When Mom came back in August and went down there with her suitcase—what would she find? Well, two gray shriveled, dusty, cobwebbed potted plants, one larger than the other.

Naturally, he should never have been separated from Mom. Not this summer. Nor any summer, ever. But the fault lay much too far back in time. The fault was that they had severed the umbilical cord. He had seen a film of a delivery at school. What had upset Reine most was when the umbilical cord had been cut with a pair of scissors and tied up like any old sausage. That must be where the twisted development of mankind had started. The original human beings had neither scissors nor thread. What had they done with the umbilical cord and afterbirth? Had they done what cats do, eaten the mess up? No, they were human, and human beings don't eat parts of their own issue.

From the start, when people still lived in stunted trees on the savannas of Africa, they must have had some use for the umbilical cord. What that use was was obvious: you can't live in trees with infants without tying them up in some way. The moms took the umbilical cord with its suspended lump and threw it over a handy branch, around which the cord wound itself. Simple. The baby hung there and was rocked by the wind.

When the children grew bigger, they ran around below the trees with the umbilical cord slung over their shoulders so as not to trip over it. By that time, the afterbirth would have hardened and flattened out into something like a hand with no fingers. When you had to move really quickly, you clamped the afterbirth under your arm. You could fight with it, too, like a kind of pillow fight. If you wanted to be nasty to someone, you didn't trip them up but just jerked the umbilical cord in an unguarded moment. When you were miserable or hungry, you could stuff the afterbirth-hand-skin-bun into your mouth. It was better than a thumb. A special limb for nothing but tenderness.

What had happened when man had one day slid down from the trees, straightened his back and lumbered off into the woods? Presumably they should never have done that, but . . . well, it was too late to go back now. When treeless Stone Age man crawled into his rocky crevice at night, then all the umbilical cords got tangled up with one another, and they put each other's skin-buns in their mouths. When the sun rose and the perkiest woke up, it was enough to give a gentle jerk for the whole tribe to rise to their feet as one man . . . Reine yawned, put Jocke's tiny little cloth hand between his teeth, and fell asleep.

28 One of his great troubles was that his underpants had begun to feel like old cardboard that had been soaked and then dried. He had rinsed his only pair under the basement tap and wrung them out, but when they had dried, they rubbed even worse than before. He waddled away from the Central Station ticket office. Half fare to Gran in Gävle cost exactly double what he had.

Should he go and find Stig? Stig, who just flung a whole fifty away for such a silly thing as saying "I'm a lousy little skunk"? Then of course he had had to go through that Urho Kekkonen business, but Reine didn't mind that. He would happily stand in the middle of the Central Station saying, "Urho Kekkonen is a horrible great skunk" at fifty *öre* a time. But there was no market for that. And Stig? No, not Stig, not after he'd chucked him into the water like that. Next time it might be from a balloon.

Could he telephone Gran? Call and pretend he was in a telephone booth on Children's Island? No, he couldn't do that, because Gran had no telephone. Mom had nagged on and on forever about Gran getting a phone, but Reine thought it was something to do with the Maranatas. They couldn't have telephones, or something. They certainly couldn't have television. When Gran had been to stay with Mom, she'd watched nothing but the weather forecast.

He went and stood in the shade of the bus shelter outside the station. The sun had been switched full on for the whole of this summer. Half-naked people were trudging along in the heat, and more and more young people were going barefoot. But Reine didn't dare, because the asphalt looked far too soft, like dusty spreading lava. One careless step away from the shade, and you'd vanish with a schlurp. What should he do now? He started thinking: first he would go and take a look at the Palladium building, perhaps even go upstairs and touch the door to Olga's, just to feel slightly at home. Then he'd go down to the northern station for a bite to eat, no, perhaps he'd go to the Corner House, no, it would have to be a Wimpey Bar . . . no, he mustn't think ahead like that.

If he began every day by thinking in detail what he was going to do, it would be intolerable. Then he would have experienced the day before it had even begun. If you thought carefully every New Year's Eve about what was going to happen—when school started, then sports breaks, Easter holidays, when it was marbles time—you'd choke on the future! Or if you started thinking beforehand about what your life was going to be like, leaving school, doing military service, working, marrying, having children, and now—hadn't they lowered the age limit for a pension? You would have to pretend a new day had dawned every day. A new day with new possibilities. How long would you be able to keep up such self-deception?

Think this way instead, for Christ's sake: when you get to that intersection, a truck will have driven into a column of circus elephants, holding each other's tails with their trunks, that had gone against the red light. Bloodthirsty Swedes with assegais will come rushing out of every building to hack themselves off a good meal. The insufferable, gray, unassailable reality was always having to be translated into something else. Not surprising two thousand Swedes went and hanged themselves every year. Or swallowed pills. Or jumped into the river. Or blew themselves to bits with a bundle of dynamite. The last was one definite way of refusing, anyhow.

There was no slaughter of elephants at the intersection but what was stopping the traffic over there? A cart. Reine shaded his eyes like an Indian. A bright green cart with two high wheels. Someone holding a bright red umbrella sitting on the cart. The cart had long shafts and was being drawn by two figures in peculiar clown costumes, sort of coveralls in large-checked material that went over their heads like a hood. Two long cloth horns, each with a bell on the end, stuck out of the hood. Almost as good as elephants, and the only thing lacking was a truck charging along at tremendous speed.

But no truck ran into the cart. It stopped at the red light instead, then turned up King Street, which was empty of cars. As the cart passed, Reine could read the notice on its side: THE BUSKER THEATER COMPANY PRESENTS *THE THREE WISE MEN*, HUMLE GARDENS, 3 o'clock. Then he recognized the woman on a chair in the cart holding a red umbrella against the sun. It was the Virgin Mary! But the Baby Jesus was absent, and the two men in clown costumes pulling the cart didn't seem to belong to the play at all.

Reine followed the cart about twenty yards behind so that no one would think he belonged to the company. The clowns slogged up toward Haymarket and into the square, which was empty of stands, since it was Sunday. Some half-naked individuals were lying, sitting, or squatting on the steps of the Concert House. The cart drove over and stopped by the Orpheus fountain. The moment it stopped, a black and white police van came along the main street and stopped opposite the fountain. There were six or eight policemen inside.

Harlequins? That was it. That's what they were called when they were dressed in checked pyjamas and cloth horns. The harlequins took a flute and a high drum out of the cart and started playing. Then one exchanged his flute for a jew's harp, and that sounded even worse. The harlequin with the drum started shouting across the square.

"Boom-boom, Ladies and Gentlemen, Citizens and Peasants! Boom-boom, of our beautiful proud city. Boom-boom, hark now and listen! Boom-boom, on this day the world-famous Busker Theater Company is to perform! Boom-boom, in Humle Gardens at three o'clock! Boom-boom, entry free to all, babes in arms and ancients! Boom-boom, the world-famous Busker Theater Company presents 'The Three Wise Men'! Boom-boom, a play about the life and ways of our beloved Savior. Boomedy-boomedy-boom! Boom-boom, come and watch and wonder! Boom-boom, three o'clock in Humle Gardens. Boom-pappa-boom-pappa-boom! The fantastic amazing renowned superformidable Busker Theater Company! Boom-boom, in 'The Three Wise Men.'"

The harlequin with the drum fell silent; then the Virgin Mary got up onto the chair in the cart. You could see now that she had stuffed a big cushion underneath her dress. The Virgin Mary patted her stomach and sang:

> *Here within me lies*
> *God's only begotten son.*
> *Beneath my heart here growing,*
> *Jesus Christ himself.*
> *Here in my white body maturing,*
> *The Lord and Savior of the world.*

Suddenly the Virgin Mary swayed as if she were about to faint and fall off the chair onto the stony square. But she swayed back, regained her balance, then squealed like a stuck pig. The two harlequins rushed forward and started rummaging beneath her skirts, all three yelling like lunatics, and the Virgin Mary leaned down and suddenly held her arms up toward the sky with the newborn Baby Jesus in her hands, the same shoe-polish-blackened brat Reine had seen in the park. Each harlequin took a firm grip on one of the Virgin's legs and lifted her even higher. Radiant with joy, she showed the black Jesus to the scattered audience on the steps of the Concert Hall.

Reine found that he was clapping his hands, but stopped at once when he saw two policemen get out of the van. What would happen now? Would there be batons and tear gas? But the policemen went over to the Orpheus fountain, scooped up a handful of water, and moistened their hair, foreheads, necks, and elbows.

The theater troupe packed up and set off once more with their cart, Reine following at a distance. He had to see the birth of Jesus again. That had been fantastic. When the cart passed the corner of the steps to swing back into King Street, a man with a bare torso got up and yelled at the Virgin Mary:

"Better get to the Maternity Hospital before they close the damn thing down."

The Virgin Mary wasn't at all angry and simply threw a kiss at the disturber of the peace. What would happen now? Reine slipped along behind the cart without daring to look back. Would eight policemen hurl themselves on the man who had shouted?

The cart had to stop for traffic lights, so Reine moved right up and saw the Virgin Mary stuffing the infant Jesus between her legs and straightening out the cushion. Her time would clearly soon be nigh again. But a long time went by before anything happened; they went all the way down King Street, past the Great American Disaster as well as McDonald's, before Reine realized they were on their way to Stureplan. He was no longer the only follower. Three or four girls younger than Reine, a bus driver in uniform, and a drunk with a puncture in his bicycle tire had joined him.

As the harlequins stopped on Stureplan and started pulling out their instruments, the police van drove up and stopped a little farther on, its wheels up on the island. For a second it looked as if it might tip over, but the cops inside kept still, so nothing happened.

They went through exactly the same procedure as they had in the Haymarket square, but it wasn't nearly so good the second time, Reine thought. The Virgin Mary didn't look particularly faint, and she swayed artificially, then almost dropped the infant Jesus between her legs before the harlequins had time to get there and start groveling about under her skirts. But it was always like that: a surprise only worked the first time. Reine couldn't understand how the actors could bear going around town repeating the same thing over and over again. Being an actor must be like being a scratched gramophone record, with the needle sticking and always slipping back into the same old track.

Stureplan was clearly the last stop. The Virgin Mary got out of the cart, rolled her long skirts up over her hips, dropped both Jesus and the pillow in among the instruments in the cart, and helped push. When they crossed the street and up over the curb on the other side, the red umbrella jumped out and rolled around. Reine leaped forward and stopped it.

"Carry it if you like," said the Virgin Mary to Reine, and he did as he was told.

It was a very peculiar feeling, walking behind the green cart, lugging that red umbrella. He tried to walk as close to Mary as possible, so that it would look as if the parasol was to protect her, not him; he was only a servant or a page helping out. He looked anxiously around for familiar faces. If anyone from school had seen him and it had not been summertime, he would certainly have been beaten up at school the next day.

"That was a good play," he said to Mary, as they swung by the Royal Library. "I saw you rehearsing the other day."

"Come and see the performance. It's settling down now. The opening day before yesterday was terrible. Nothing went right. Old Clod went and got a cold and couldn't throw his voice. I had to say Jesus' lines behind a fan."

"Old Clod?"

"Claud. The guy playing Joseph."

As soon as they came to the open-air theater, Mary and the harlequins vanished into a caravan behind the stage to change. Mary soon emerged again wearing denim shorts and a blue tank top. She had big breasts that hung out at the sides, and she had a can of beer in her hand. Tuborg. Did all old women drink Tuborg? Reine was horribly thirsty but dared not ask.

"What did you do with the umbrella?"

Reine had stuck the handle of the umbrella in the prompter's box, and he went to fetch it.

"Thanks. Come back again at three o'clock. No, half-past two, if you want a good seat," said Mary, closing the umbrella, hooking it over her arm, and going back into the caravan.

Reine felt deserted. For some stupid reason he'd thought he belonged with Mary and the harlequins. But he was obviously wrong: see you, then, and that was that. There was an hour and a half before the performance, so he went and sat in the shade of the closed caravan. The curtains in the windows were drawn, and pop music was pouring out of the ventilator in the roof. Once or twice he heard sharp bursts of laughter, and the caravan rocked.

Of course, he fell asleep. In the shade behind the caravan, he fell asleep just like that. He was awakened by his teeth hitting one knee, so he lay down instead. How sleepy the sun made you. Hadn't he slept enough down in that dark basement? There oughtn't to be any sleeping-sap left in his head any longer. But there were lakes of it. Sleep started in his jaws, then the sap rose to his head, over his ears, and up into the top of his skull. Then you were right under the surface . . . he woke for the last time with a jerk . . . if the sleep-sap rose when he was lying down, it finally made its way out through the ear that was uppermost.

29 When Reine woke up with a revolting stuffed feeling in his stomach, people were already streaming in, and all the best places had been taken. Stiff and uncomfortable inside, Reine went and sat on the far left end of the front bench. At least he would hear well there—but see crookedly. The audience consisted mostly of older people and a few foreigners, all looking expectant. There was a dwarf in the audience, a tiny little man who couldn't have been more than three feet tall, wearing a light summer suit with a pale blue tie and a small straw hat. The dwarf bounced up onto the bench and then stared rigidly ahead, his minute little sandals at least a foot from the ground. Reine was embarrassed and turned away, but he couldn't get the dwarf out of his mind.

Before the actual play about the three wise men started, Mary and the harlequins performed the same scene they had done in Haymarket and Stureplan, the only difference being that they didn't use the cart. The audience applauded enthusiastically, but two women behind Reine got up and left immediately after the birth of Jesus.

The play was no good at all. It had seemed imaginative and stimulating when he saw part of it in rehearsal, but now the whole story seemed very long-winded, with a fearful fuss before Mary became with child—long dialogues between Joseph and the Angel of God who kept heralding. Joseph was angry because he was not allowed to be the father: an amusing idea but never followed through. Instead, there was a long and mostly unintelligible song about taxation in the Roman Empire.

The family did at last arrive in Bethlehem, and they were spurned at every hotel and boarding house—that was pretty good fun—and finally ended up not in a stable but in something called a bachelor refuge, where a whole lot of drunks were living. But as soon as Mary came in, the drunks turned into little lambs, stopped swearing and drinking, and started attending to her. The actual delivery was a disappointment because you saw it from the wrong direction. Mary lay on her back with her head to the audience and her legs toward the drunks and Joseph. Jesus was at once wrapped up in an old sack.

At last it was time for the Three Wise Men. They came trotting in from the park and pushed their way eagerly through the audience toward the stage. People laughed and thought it fun when the actors pushed and shoved. Reine didn't want to turn round because then he would have to look at the dwarf again, but he couldn't avoid a glimpse of the little man wriggling in his seat, trying to see over those behind him. His neck seemed stiff, and he had to turn his whole body. Not so odd, really, because the dwarf had no neck.

Reine had already seen the arrival of the Three Wise Men at the bachelor stable, so he felt in his pockets instead to see if he might have a hard-on. But he hadn't. He just needed to take a leak. Sometimes it was difficult to know which.

"America! Bang! Soviet Union! Bang! France! Bang! Great Britain! Bang! Canada! Bang! Japan! Bang! Israel! Bang! Norway! Bang!" cried the Three Wise Men, then started throwing handfuls of chocolate money into the audience.

Reine managed to acquire one coin and eased off the gold foil. What a rip-off! There was clay inside instead of chocolate. But perhaps there was some point in that.

Money? How the heck was he going to get hold of any money now that Olga had closed? If he didn't get another job, he would have to start selling things. What things? There were clothes in the apartment, anyhow, Mom's fur, a few books and comics, some record albums, and the potted plants. It would be a good deed to sell off the plants before they died. Plants? Why not start growing something—hash, for instance? Some of the older boys at school had grown hash in the boiler room last spring. This year, with its record summer, it should be just as easy in the windowbox on the balcony. Then he could hawk it in King's Gardens and be rich in next to no time. All he had to do was to get hold of some seeds. What an idea! He couldn't get at the other things in the apartment right now, but if he lay down on the roof and dropped the seeds into the windowbox, all he would have to do was to wait for a while. Hash plants grew as tall as corn, didn't they? Given time, they would grow so high up, he would be able to pick the tops off from the roof. Sheer genius!

Unfortunately, that would take too long; he would starve to death while the hash was growing up to the roof. And then you had to take the resin . . . or, yes, the leaves were enough. He could sell hash leaves as "grass" for cigarettes. That was what a man they called a drug consultant had told them in a lecture at school.

The hash would have to wait until the winter and be cultivated in the boiler room. It would probably be quicker now to drop corn seeds into the windowbox and then live off corn for the rest of the summer. What if he sold something from the basement—the crib, or his nearly new bike! Of course. How much was it worth? In a fine hot summer like this, there must be a terrible shortage of bicycles in Stockholm, with everyone wanting to go bike-riding. He might get twice the price? It had three speeds, anyhow. A bike should really have ten speeds these days, or at worst five. But if you were the son of a single parent, you had to adjust. He would never forget that. It was the politicians' fault: children of single parents should have three-speed bikes. That shouldn't be forgotten. When he was older, he would seek out some of those politicians, who by that time would be feeble and in wheelchairs. Then he would do with them exactly what Richard Widmark had done with that old woman on television. G'bye, down the stairs, and thanks for all the three-speed bikes.

It would be lunacy to sell his bike. Sheer lunacy. Those politicians were thinking of increasing the fares on commuter trains. Selling his bike right now would be lunacy. Even if prices of bikes shot up because of the heat and increased fares, it would still be lunacy. Much better to use the bike himself. Here comes nice Mike on his lovely three-speed bike.

From the first of August, he would bicycle instead of taking trains. The risk of theft was still there, but hardly in Sollentuna, since he slept every night with the bike beside him. It would be trickier in the autumn. Colder and wetter. But if he dressed right. By then Aunt Olga would be open again, and people would probably be being buried like flies. Unfortunately, there would eventually be snow and ice. Snow was all right, but ice was much worse, especially when it started to thaw and had a layer of water on it. Studded tires? Too expensive. But what if he bought some sheets of coarse sandpaper, then cut it up into suitably sized pieces, and stuck them on the tires with the sand outward? Brilliant. Like riding around on a pair of grindstones, as safe as the train. Glue? He could use the same as he used when he had to fix a flat. That was *that* problem solved.

"King Herod the Great has this day declared that all male children under two years of age in Galilee, Judea, and Samaria, on his esteemed orders, shall immediately and without exception, in the interest of the state, be *killed*!"

The two soldiers clumped round the stage rattling and rustling their wooden swords as if trying to hack their way through the jungle's lianas and undergrowth. Reine looked up into the nearest tree to see if Tarzan and Cheeta weren't sitting there laughing, but they had sensibly left a long time ago. So had Jesus, too, it turned out: he was already safely in the land of the Egyptians. Was that where he had floated in a basket on the Nile and been found by the Pharaoh's daughter? No, heck, that was Moses.

The pressure caught him unawares. Intestinal flu? It must be intestinal flu, because he'd eaten only the usual things: hamburgers, French fries, Coca-Cola, and chocolate milkshakes. Maybe he should risk a fart? He didn't dare. This wasn't the usual blown-up feeling; this was the shits. He might start throwing up any minute now, too. Reine slid off the bench, his knees tight together. He gave the dwarf a last glance, then went up behind the theater troupe's caravan. They would have a john there. But there was none to be seen. He did not dare knock on the caravan door. All the actors seemed to be on the stage now, anyhow. From the side it looked as if they were all gathering for a huge living Christmas scene, Mary with Jesus in the middle, Joseph in the wings, the Three Wise Men, shepherds, and beasts; one actor put on a donkey's head and another a lion's head. Reine sneaked away to Flora's Mound.

Flora's Mound was covered with thousands of tulips in bloom and low bushes, quite thick in some places. Reine bent down and slipped inside the bushes. There were turds and used paper lying here and there.

He pulled down his jeans and hardly had time to squat before it spurted out. His stomach was rumbling and painful, too. Was this appendicitis for real? The park keeper would find him there tomorrow morning, dead from a perforated appendix . . . no, appendicitis made you constipated, not the opposite. More came. He squatted there, sighing. Would it never end? The pain in his stomach returned, and even more came, finally nothing but water, though it felt like crapping acid, his whole ass stinging.

At last his intestines appeared to have settled down inside him. Reine imagined his innards as a snake pit in which his intestines slid and wriggled round each other like boa constrictors, grass snakes, anacondas and green mambas. Well, the snakes had now declared peace and stopped. Time to think about wiping. The leaves on the bushes were far too small. Suspiciously, he picked up an ice cream paper but immediately dropped it again. What did he have in his bag? Yes! He had a straw from Carrol's and that straw was wrapped in a paper napkin. That was it. He who saves, has.

Reine dressed and made his way out of the bushes, not daring to go farther than the nearest trash basket. There he sat on the low iron railing round the flowerbeds and carefully rummaged in the basket. Beer cans and rubbish mostly, but fortunately a whole rolled-up evening newspaper and the tissue paper wrapper from an orange. He laughed. A long time ago he had collected orange papers.

After about an hour, his stomach felt steady enough that he could slowly make his way down to the little playground with swings and a jungle gym. A kid of about three was sitting on a bench staring sullenly while his parents were swinging away to their heart's content. Reine found an empty bench, sat on the very edge of it, and started collecting small stones, which he then tried throwing at sparrows. But they were too quick, and he tried throwing at a trash basket. Not the same basket he had searched but another one. He couldn't be bothered to look in this one, though. If you had a whole evening paper, then you could cope with any old paratyphoid.

After a while he began to feel stiff and weak, the pain in his stomach returning and nausea creeping up his throat. All he could do was to try to get himself slowly up to Flora's Mound again. He had several attacks that afternoon and evening and did not dare leave the mound. When his stomach at last seemed to settle down a little, he lay down on the grass by the bushes. It was warm. Earlier that afternoon it had been ninety-five degrees in the inner city, he had heard some people say as they passed the bushes where he was sitting like Moses in the bulrushes.

30 A bird woke him up by flying so close to his face he felt the wing brush his cheek. Or had he dreamed it? He sat up; his watch said ten past four. What a morning! The birds were singing in trees and bushes, and the sun was frying the grass, making the dew steam. Strangely enough, it wasn't at all cold but felt like an ordinary summer day.

Reine cautiously felt his stomach. It was tender, horribly tender, but otherwise he felt perfectly well. But he was thirsty, horribly thirsty. And hungry. Enormously hungry. He could have eaten a whole ox. The snag was they probably didn't make hamburger rolls big enough to put a whole roast ox plus melted cheese and dressing between the two halves. He didn't mind forgoing the lettuce and tomato and onion and pickle.

He got up and peed in the flowerbed; the place was as empty as paradise. There was a drinking fountain down to his left, so he went and took a drink and rinsed his hands and face. He dried his hands on his pants and put his fingers to his nose. Did he smell of shit? Hard to make out but, of course, there might well still be bacteria there. He picked up a handful of gravel from the path and washed his hands again, then combed all his hair down over his face and wet that. He felt marvelous. It wasn't often that it felt marvelous to wash. He even felt the need for a toothbrush. He picked some leaves from a bush, wet the leaves, and rubbed his front teeth. They tasted bitter and acid. He filled his whole mouth with water, took a few strides out on to the grass, and quickly slapped both cheeks hard so the water spurted out all over him and the grass. It was marvelous to be alive! It would go on being marvelous for ever and ever.

Although it was only half-past four in the morning, they were working over at the Busker Theater. What was that all about? Reine walked across the glittering, steaming grass slope to the green wooden theater. Four men were unbolting planks. Reine thought he recognized Joseph, but he wasn't sure.

"Hi!" he called. "Are you taking it down?"

At first they did not reply, but then one of the men, surely Herod's herald, turned around and looked sleepily at Reine.

"Hi, there. Yeah, we're off. Down with the whole damn thing. The fuzz say we've got to be away by seven-oh-oh hours. Come on up and help, for Christ's sake."

Reine put his bag down and climbed up onto the stage. Might as well work and forget his other troubles. Hunger would soon strike with renewed force. His stomach would not be satisfied with nothing but happiness, not even if it went on for ever and ever. And then, if you did live off happiness, what would come out the other end when you had a crap? Unhappiness?

The planks were heavy. The men were up on the half-demolished stage, throwing the planks down onto the grass. The crashing and banging was like a continuous thunderstorm. It was marvelous working, marvelous really laying into it, feeling your muscles, stretching your sinews, taking deep breaths, sticking out your chest, planting your feet and heaving a plank over the edge.

"Steady, boy, don't go killing yourself," said Joseph—Joseph, whose real name was Claud, or Clod.

"Nah, goddam it!" said Reine, spitting into the prompter's box and increasing the tempo even more. It was a matter of working away, getting it done, tearing down resistance in an obstinate nature. Work. Work. Work. He suddenly felt giddy, but that passed when he pushed his head down between his knees and clamped them over his ears.

Working hard was happiness, feeling you were capable. The effort meant you forgot, forgot the most important questions and the silliest answers in the world. Forgot who had lived the longest, who had swum the fastest, who had jumped the highest. Get right into it, and you didn't have to run around anxiously asking if you would do. But the greatest thing about physical labor was that you forgot you were hungry. When he was getting his breath back for a moment and his stomach was allowed to speak for itself, it gave off only a slight nausea. That darned sack of mucus wasn't going to rule him.

An hour or so later a truck came crunching along the narrow gravel path, a winch behind the driver's cab for lifting the planks and wall sections. Not everything fit in the first load. The truck drove away, and they took a rest. There was nothing to eat or drink, but one of the men called Sören passed his snuffbox around. Reine put a normal layer under his lip; in his first year at school he and his friends had practiced with fine-ground coffee, so there was nothing wrong with his technique.

"What's your name, Snuff-Sam?" Clod said when Reine handed him the snuffbox.

"Reine."

"Sounds familiar," said Clod.

"Snuff-Sam," said Sören, grinning. "The guy who works piece rates."

Nothing much more was said until they had loaded the rest of the theater. No one could see now that it had ever been a theater; in fact, it looked more like a huge irregular jungle gym. Reine was feeling fit and strong from the snuff. No letting down your buddies here. He had soon got their message. If he worked like hell and didn't mind being called Snuff-Sam, he could stay. Otherwise not.

Reine was eventually allowed to help one of them called Leif, a fat man with a curly reddish beard, to roll up the lighting cables. They marched from trees to poles, Leif climbing onto a wobbly kitchen chair and unscrewing, while Reine gathered up the cable and wound it around his elbow and hand. It soon grew too heavy, so he had to unload by slinging the cable over his left shoulder—as long as it didn't injure his wing root! It really was a fantastic morning. He felt as light as an angel, an angel who liked being on the ground and didn't need wings to fly away to find happiness above the clouds or wherever the heck it was.

"So, Snuff-Sam, you saw me yesterday, did you? Did you recognize me? I was the herald angel."

"You were well masked," said Reine.

"Costumes and masks are important. You've realized that. Theater should be festive, theater should be dressing up. Doll yourself up and paint yourself up. But not many groups have figured that out. They act as if they were working in an office."

"Have you been an actor for long?" said Reine.

"All my life. All my life."

"Aren't you ever scared? When you're on stage. Afraid you'll forget or make a fool of yourself."

"Never. It's the audience that's afraid. Of course. I stand there in my purple cloak, my gold crown on my head and a long pole in my hand. I stand there with all the drama of the world in my luggage. What can I sling out? Shakespeare. Molière. Aristophanes. Strindberg. Hans Christian Andersen. Chekov. Eh? What has the audience got to set against that? What have they thought? What have they articulated? Not a jot. They're without prospects, totally. I'm the one with the power. I stand up there like the emperor in his war chariot. With the prompter as my slave. I stand there and can tug the reins and get them to turn to the left or swing to the right. I stand there with my long whip. I rule them. If I want them to laugh, they laugh. If I want them to cry, they cry. Cast a line to the swine. Fetch it! They hurl themselves on to the first best Hamlet quote like a pack of horny dogs. Briefly, theater is power."

Reine felt slightly bemused and almost dropped the cable. In that case, theater was something for him, something for King Reine the First. Unfortunately, he turned shy and tormented if he ever had to say anything in front of the class. But you weren't disguised then. Or made up. You just stood there, gray and small, like any other darned school kid. But wait until he climbed onto the platform in a Roman toga, with angel wings and a leather cat-o'-nine-tails!

"Snuff-Sam! Watch what you're doing!" yelled Leif from his chair.

Reine pulled himself together. At least twice a day he used to think about what he would do when he was grown up. Motorbike designer wouldn't be bad. Or research, of course, since he was on the track of that business of the cancer-causing properties of radio waves. Inventor. Airline flight controller. Ambulance driver—no, that plan had been swiftly abandoned when Mom had taken up with Stig. But here was a profession that combined all dreams into one: acting. One evening you could be a Roman emperor, the next an inventor in New York, and then during matinées one of the best helicopter pilots in the Murder Squad.

"Leif, do you think there's a little part in the Busker Company I could take a crack at?"

"You, Snuff-Sam?"

"Yes."

"You, Snuff-Sam, with no drama training? You, who've hardly ever been to a theater? You know piss-all about the art of acting. You've read nothing—you know nothing—you look like nothing on earth. You've got an impossible name. What do you think would have happened to Henry Irving if his name had been Snuff-Sam?"

"I'm sorry. But you have to start somewhere."

"Drama school, for instance. Or private pupil with some famous clever actor. You have to study, Snuff-Sam. To put it briefly, work."

"Maybe I could be a private pupil with you?"

"You don't make such important suggestions just like that, Snuff-Sam. You prepare the ground first. Reconnoitre. Feel your way. Wait for signs. Do you see?"

"Yes," said Reine. Leif talked to him in just the same way as any other adult. That was exactly what children always had to do: wait, find out when it was the right moment, be prepared to retreat swiftly, and most of all not interrupt or disturb the thought processes of a grownup. How old did you have to be before finally learning you were worth no more than a dog? Two? Three? When you'd learned that injustice from above was natural. Not understandable, but natural. Someone could suddenly lift you up off the floor without your being able to defend yourself. Someone could lower you into a hot bath willy-nilly. Someone could shove a spoonful of porridge into your mouth after first locking your arms. Mom was always talking about the feminist movement. Maybe women had a bad time, but they didn't run the risk of having their ears boxed if they dirtied their pants.

Leif made his way in among the trestles the seats had been on, Reine lumbering behind him, weighed down by his lengthy lasso. If you kept your mouth shut, if you obeyed every whim, and especially if you looked pleased, then maybe . . . Leif jerked at his end of the cable and hauled Reine in.

"That's done now. Take the cable and put the whole thing on the floor of the caravan."

Reine staggered up the steps of the caravan and managed to get the door open. The Virgin Mary was asleep on a bunk. It was hot and close, like being in a tent. Mary was lying face down in her blue sleeveless shirt. She had kicked off the sheet, and her bottom was bare. Reine stopped and gazed in wonder at her spine as it swung upward in a sharp bow and became a tail. A smooth white tail. Fantastically beautiful. The next moment, he flung the heavy coil of cable on to the floor, opened the door, and rushed out. He couldn't be bothered with Leif or the practically demolished theater. He ran up to the playground and squeezed in between two low sheds. Gasping, he flipped open his fly and plopped out his sexual organ. He couldn't have, could he?

31 He had to write to Mom or she would be suspicious, and then everything would fall to pieces. How long was it since he had actually managed to send off a letter? Weeks! He had composed letters in his head but never written them down. And how many letters with tens inside from Mom were lying on the hall floor?

Reine got into the jeep with Clod, and another man hooked on the trailer. They had put the big-wheeled cart on the trailer, where it looked ridiculous, a cart on a cart, as if the carts were screwing. Reine tried to concentrate: *Dear Mom. No, Dear Mom Harriet,* as it was ages ago. *One of the leaders has an old jeep. We're allowed to ride in the back sometimes. It's a real American jeep and ancient. Not a Land Rover.* Was that too much about jeeps? It wouldn't hurt Mom to learn a little about automobiles. But supposing there weren't any roads on Children's Island? Supposing the island was nothing but rocks, clumps of pines, moss, and bulrushes? Calm down; jeeps have a four-wheel drive and are meant for rough ground. *It's bright green. If you're lucky, you're allowed to steer, though only in low gear. But I must tell you we've got a theater here.*

Clod jumped in and started the engine.

"Keep an eye on the trailer," he said over his shoulder to Reine.

That was necessary. The paths were far too narrow, and the two carts several times got caught in bushes and branches hanging over the iron fencing. But Clod paid no attention and just went faster. By the time they turned into the wide road running due north from the library, the trailer looked like a carelessly decorated wagon.

They drove around half of Humle Gardens and then down past Stureplan and on around Norrmalm Square. Reine recognized King's Gardens and the Royal Palace on the other side of the water, but then he lost all sense of direction. Yes, the Parliament building, he'd seen that on a poster. They came out onto a straight main road running alongside the water. Clod accelerated, leaves and twigs swirling behind them. It was great! Roaring through Stockholm in a green jeep on an early summer morning.

Clod braked quite suddenly and slid over into the left lane. A yellow cab hooted angrily behind them, then overtook the jeep on the wrong side and slowed down level with Reine. The cab driver leaned out and yelled:

"Fucking peasants! Get the hell out of here with your old load of hay!"

Reine was extremely angry but dared not show it. The cab vanished, and Clod turned left up a narrow blacktop street. Naturally, Reine should have shouted back! He could have spat in that bastard's face. He could have put out his hand and twisted his nose. Or taken the sledgehammer in the jeep and thumped it on the cab roof. The cab driver couldn't have got at him. To do that, he would have had to stop the cab and get out—and then the jeep would already have been miles away. Reine sat there trembling: there was nothing worse than being exposed to other people's anger, justified or not.

They drove through a park, a broad grass slope on the right, water with jetties and boats on the left. *We've got a children's theater of our own. It's doing Jesus Christ Superstar. I've been given the part of* . . . no, Mom knew he couldn't sing. *I'm the prompter.* That's it. The prompter was the person who whispered when the actors got stuck. The prompter had other people's fates in his hands. He might whisper wrong. He could whisper what he liked, and they would say it. *I have introduced sign language.* Reine Larsson, the famous prompter introducing the deaf-and-dumb language into the theater. Simple and brilliant. For centuries, actors had stood on stage sweating and glancing down at the prompter, who whispered back. It must have been especially difficult for older actors. That Henry Irving, for instance. He was sure to be ancient and stone deaf. But now Henry Irving would be able to face a revival, together with the eleven-year-old star prompter, Reine Larsson. Irving need only make a little sign—with his little finger, perhaps—and Reine would at once tell him pages and pages of the forgotten play in sign language. Silently, swiftly, unnoticeably. The audience would never have time to notice anything. And in the future the deaf-and-dumb could become prompters. The poor devils probably found it hard to get jobs.

"Stop dreaming, Snuff-Sam."

The jeep had stopped on a narrow patch of gravel behind something like an outdoor theater, a complete theater with benches on a steep slope.

"Where are we?"

"Rålambshov."

They got out and took a leak. Reine found it pretty hard to get going with someone else standing so close. He glanced at Clod. Clod was gazing straight up into the sky as he splashed. He did not look down until he'd done a couple of pulls and shaken off the drops.

"Thank goodness the theater doesn't have to be put up again," said Reine.

"Think so, Snuff-Sam? You may well be right."

They went and sat on one of the benches halfway up the grass slope. It was warm and peaceful all around, but they could hear the steady roar of heavy traffic in the distance. Clod took a pipe out of his carpenter's overalls and lit it, puffed once or twice, then stuck the pipe back in his pocket without emptying it or putting it out.

"Maybe I could have private lessons from Leif?" said Reine.

"Leif?"

"Yes."

"Why?"

"If I can. If he's got time. I can't ask him direct."

"Leif? He's a stagehand."

"Stagehand?"

"Stagehand."

Reine couldn't make it out. Leif was into theater and acting in a big way, and knew that Henry Irving he'd talked about. Leif had played the Heralding Angel; that was true, too.

"Some people are profoundly interested in theater without ever going on stage," said Clod. "Maybe Leif's good to take lessons from. Who knows?"

"Are you playing Joseph tonight?"

"Joseph? No. We're not performing tonight. Not until Wednesday. We've got to rehearse *Björn Ball,* our new play for children and young people."

The truck with some of the wooden scenery came gliding onto the gravel. It was strange; trucks going really slow could be almost completely soundless. Leif and one of the other men were in the truck.

Reine didn't want to talk to Leif again. Not that there was anything wrong with stagehands, but Reine felt cheated. But maybe Leif was really pretty much like Reine, living in his fantasies to get everything to go together. But adults shouldn't live in their fantasies. What the hell would happen then? Children couldn't help it. This business of adults not being perfect was one of the most difficult things to understand. It went against nature in some way. An adult had to be clever, take responsibility, and first and foremost know how everything should work out.

32 "Look straight ahead. Smile!" said the director. "Listen now. Rune Ball, Björn Ball's dad, has just won a Ping-Pong tournament. As first prize, Rune Ball can choose between a fishing rod and a tennis racket. He gives the racket to his young son, Björn. Björn Ball at once starts practicing against the garage door at home. He persists. But he's so darned small he has to hold the handle with both hands. Hit a forehand with a two-handed grip!"

Reine stared at his hands and twisted his body and the racket to the right. Smash!

"You have to look at the ball. You have to feel the ball, although it isn't there!"

Reine twisted his body to the right again, clenched his teeth, and hit out. Smash!!

"Relax! Don't bunch your shoulders like that. The audience'll think you're the Hunchback of Notre Dame doing exercises."

Reine breathed deeply, closed his eyes and twisted to the right, and . . . smash!!!

"Uh-huh. Maybe closing your eyes is a good idea. You look more like him with your eyes closed, too. The bastard's eyes are so close together, he looks cross-eyed. Do it again. Close your eyes and stick out your chin. Yes, hell, that's right. Put the chewing gum in, then smile after the smash hit and sing: 'You'll wonder where the yellow went when you brush your teeth with Pepsodent.' It's gotta sound damn dumb, real dumb. He sings dumb."

Reine chewed, twisted to the right, closed his eyes, smashed with both hands, and sang:

"You'll wonder where the yellow went when you brush your teeth with Pepsodent."

"Too low. I didn't say whisper. You were dumb all right. But too low. How the hell d'you think people are going to hear that?"

"I'm a little hoarse today," said Reine.

"I wonder whether we should get your hair cut? He's sure to have had short hair when he started."

"Get my hair cut?"

"You'd be more like him then. Since your eyes aren't right."

"The yellow teeth aren't right, either. He darned well didn't sing commercials when he was ten!"

"Quite likely. But you'll have to talk to the author about that. Hold your hair back. No, with both hands. Let's have a look."

"Cut my hair?"

"Let's see. Do it again. You can see from miles away you come from Södertälje."

"Can't I wear a wig?"

"When you've done that double-handed forehand, then go on to backhand, still with both hands. Then you sing the same thing in backhand."

Reine concentrated, twisted to the left and hit out. But when he was supposed to sing, he had completely forgotten the jingle.

"Wait, wait . . . don't sing. I'll go and get a ball. You have to feel that you're hitting a ball. You look as if you had a snowshoe in your hand."

The director went into the caravan. Reine squatted down. He'd never get the hang of this. It looked so simple. All he had to do was a few tennis strokes and sing a jingle. No more than that. He was not going to be in the actual play. They had a real actor for that. His task was to go round with them on the green cart to publicize the performance. It should be perfectly simple, but it wasn't. The director came out again with a yellow tennis ball in his hand.

"I've talked to Laijla. She'll cut your hair later. Stand over there, and I'll throw the ball."

"But the guy who's playing Björn on the stage. Is he having his hair cut, too?"

"He's older by then. He had a headband by then. Here. Ready?"

Reine put everything he had into it and hit the ball a tremendous blow. By a stroke of luck, he connected in the middle of the racket. The yellow tennis ball soared off in a long high arc far beyond the bushes and trees.

"What was the point of that? Go and fetch it!"

Reine shouldered the racket and trudged off with it into the trees as if carrying a rifle. A hissing? He put the rounded end of the racket under his arm and pressed down the barrel with his left hand: a black panther? In that case it must have escaped from a circus. But there were lynxes. Lynxes had recently become common in developed areas. Their tracks were seen every winter. Where did they go in the summer? Into parks and open spaces, of course, lying along some branch waiting for cats or runaway dachshunds. What would he do if a lynx landed on his back? He'd be knocked to the ground for sure. Then he would have to get to his feet like lightning and protect his throat so that the lynx couldn't tear at it. He stopped and pressed the nylon strings of the racket against his throat. Good protection.

He came out on the far side of the clump of trees without having spotted the tennis ball. The wide grass slope spread down toward the water. People were lying around on blankets or on the grass, some eating, some reading or sleeping. A girl was lying on top of a boy, kissing him, the boy as rigid as a log, apparently not even breathing. Down by the jetty were several sailing dinghies, their colorful striped sails up. Three of them were bobbing up and down on the water, trying to sail round a pink plastic buoy. *Today we had the finals with the dinghies. I won and a kid called Max came second. The first prize is a new dinghy. Can we keep it on the balcony in the winter?* But how would they get it to the water? They had no car. Mom didn't even have a driver's license; it was pitiful. When friends asked why they had no car, he never said anything about the driver's license. Mom was phobic about cars, he said instead. She hadn't been able to stand them since being in a crash with her brother when they'd wrecked his handcrafted Sbarro BMW Replica. That went down well with the younger kids: with older ones the result might be a sock on the nose.

Reine did another dutiful turn in the grass, poking about for the ball. Then he rushed back through lynx territory to the open-air theater.

"The ball's lost," he said to the director.

"What ball?"

"The ball."

"Heck, I thought you meant the guy playing Björn Ball. There's some eats over there. I'll be directing on the stage from now on."

Eats! There on the steps of the caravan was a tray covered with plastic wrap. Underneath the wrap he could just see open-faced sandwiches with shrimps, mayonnaise, cheese, egg and anchovies, liver sausage with gherkins, cold ham with sections of mandarin orange. God, he was hungry. He was dripping with sweat—where? His stomach was dripping with sweat. Could you say that? Sure. His glowing hot stomach was pouring sweat. Reine took a pile of sandwiches and a beer, and sat down on the bench nearest the stage.

The older Björn Ball was on the stage. He was being played by a real actor of about seventeen or eighteen called Ellert Tidblad. Ellert—what a name! But he was going to be famous, of course. Ellert Tidblad had been borrowed from another company called the Fortune Theater. Reine gathered that the Fortune company was just very slightly better than the Busker Theater, because the Fortune had its own permanent stage in the Old City.

Ellert Tidblad was dressed entirely in white and had an Indian headband around his forehead to keep his hair out of his eyes. His white clothes were covered with badges: SAS on the sleeves, Custer Custer on the headband, Volvo on his chest, Saab on his stomach, *Daily News* on the outside of his pants, and Trojan right in front of his prick. There were trademarks on his socks and shoes, too; Björn Ball was mortgaged from top to toe. It was only a matter of time before they started tattooing him as well.

Ellert was practicing a special movement, the director standing watching a foot or so away from him. Björn Ball was tossing his racket from one hand to the other, but between hand changes he brought his free hand up to his mouth and blew on the tips of his fingers.

"Good! Great!" said the director. "Test the strings of the racket a bit, too. Bounce it against your hand."

Ellert enlarged on the gestures to order. The director was very pleased and pulled Ellert's ear appreciatively. But Reine thought it was bad. Rotten. Scandalous. Ellert Tidblad wasn't in the slightest like Björn Ball. Well, the only likeness was the fair hair. Otherwise his eyes were far apart, his nose broad and quite short, and he had freckles. Looked like hell, quite simply. Shouldn't be allowed out.

"We should really have a net across the stage, but it hasn't come," said the director. "You stand to the right and play against a South American on the left. It'll be a little short—you'll have to practice when he comes, so you don't hit the ball too far. You have to hit three balls into the audience. Three. Not four. That'd be too expensive. You can practice for a while with Snuff-Sam here, since he's around. Just volley for a while."

Reine was up on the stage and in the serve position before the director had even finished speaking.

"I refuse," said Ellert sourly. "I refuse until I get a decent opponent."

Ellert walked off the stage and disappeared into the caravan. The director sat on the edge of the stage with the manuscript on his knees, crossing out lines with a red pen.

"What's the play really about?" said Reine, standing behind the director.

"About? It's about sports and politics."

"How do you mean?"

"How do I mean? It's about the little Björn Ball who's given a racket by his dad and then goes out into the big bad world in search of gold. At any price. It's really about capitalism embodied in the sports movement. The sports movement as a system of elimination and élitism. Sports as a prototype of exploitation. Sport as a reinforcement of competitiveness. Sport as practical fascism. If you know what fascism is?"

"Yes, they burn Jews."

"Fascism means you do not admit to equality of worth and rights of the individual. Burning Jews is only a result of it. We shall see more results."

"Is everyone equally good then?"

"Every person has the same human value."

"But are they equally good? Equally—well—smart? Nice? Sharp? Bright?"

"I didn't say that. Every person should have the right to develop according to his or her abilities," said the director, crossing out another half-page of the manuscript.

Reine sat beside him, trying to understand. This was a mighty leap. From one day he, Reine, thinking he is alone in the world and everyone else nothing but specks of dust on the lens of his eye—to believing that everyone, without exception, was just as important, of equal worth.

"Should everyone be paid the same, then?"

"What? Yes, in principle."

"And everyone should be allowed to do what he wants to? Work at what they want?"

"Of course."

"But what if they can't do what they want to do?"

"Then everyone should help so that it works out all right. That's exactly what we're trying to say in *Björn Ball*. D'you see? We should have solidarity instead of competitiveness. Instead of competing, we should have cooperation. It doesn't matter much if you're not perfect. It's not only results that matter. You have to count things like job satisfaction, things you get out of being together and doing something together."

"Like acting, for instance?"

"Exactly. That's an excellent example. This isn't an élite theater company. This isn't the Royal Dramatic Theater. We all work together here. No one is a star at someone else's expense."

It all sounded great. Reine felt as if his chest had been filled with clear cool air. It didn't matter much that he tensed when he had to sing that stupid jingle about getting yellow teeth from Pepsodent. The others would help him, stand behind him and back him up.

"Listen, Snuff-Sam," said the director. "By the way, do you mind being called Snuff-Sam? Your real name is a little too sporty, you might say, just like the name Björn."

"Snuff-Sam's okay."

"Exactly. I think Laijla's ready now."

"Laijla?"

"She's going to cut your hair. Check in the caravan to see if she's there. And send Ellert out here, would you?"

"Get it cut now?"

"And listen, tell Ellert to bring the balls with him. There's a pack of six on the hat shelf."

Get his hair cut? Should he really agree to that? Didn't the director realize what it meant for a boy like him to have his hair cut? When everyone else had it long or semilong. Beaten up, laughed at, interrogated, teased, frozen out, slaughtered. And what would he say to Mom? *Today they've cut everyone's hair. Someone had lice. They didn't have time to become infectious. I look like a scrubbing brush. But it's pretty nice in this hot weather, I have to admit.*

Reine went reluctantly across to the caravan. He couldn't very well refuse. If the part demanded short hair, then that was that. Nothing peculiar about that. In other plays they had wigs or fake beards. But you could take those off. Short-hairedness couldn't be taken off, that was the great difference. But he couldn't let them down, not his friends in the Busker Theater Company. If they were going to back him up, then he would have to back them up in return.

Ellert was not available, because he was in the john; the caravan had a very cramped chemical toilet. But Laijla was waiting for him. She was a small round girl, and she must have used two shoehorns to get the two halves of her bottom into her jeans. But she looked nice. She sounded nice, too, although she spoke some kind of semi-Finnish. She was putting dark blue polish on her nails when Reine came in.

"They said I was to have my hair cut," said Reine.

"That's right, yes. I've got some photographs here."

She had laid out some old photographs of Björn from the middle sixties. He looked crazy. But at that time everyone had looked crazy; that was the difference.

"I've got some pictures from *Buster* here, too," said Laijla. "You can almost see better on the drawings."

Reine had already seen the *Buster* series long ago. He didn't want to look now. He pushed the photographs away as well. If you kept away from mirrors for four or five months, then maybe you wouldn't have to see how awful you looked. Four or five months? That was sometime in November or December. Then his hair would have grown out again. By then he would have long ago stuck sandpaper on his bike tires.

Laijla took a couple of photographs and drawings of Björn and stuck them on the mirror with tape. Then Reine had to sit with a sheet wrapped around his body. He closed his eyes and held his hair away from the back of his neck. What was it like when the guillotine blade came rattling down? What did you have time to feel? What did you have time to see as your head plumped into the basket?

He kept his eyes closed for about fifteen minutes, but then his eyes started hurting. Laijla blew a few hairs out of his ears. He shuddered.

"Look now," said Laijla. "Quite a likeness, isn't it? Can't do any better. You haven't got the same kind of hair. Maybe it would've been better with a wig after all."

"Wig!"

"Forget it. We couldn't afford it. You have to stuff your long hair into something first and then press the shorter haircut on top of it. Horribly difficult if you haven't got the right gear."

"But a wig would have worked?"

"At the Opera maybe. But this is the Busker Theater."

"I could have paid for the wig myself."

She grasped his head and pressed it against her stomach. She laughed and seemed to be saying something comforting. But he couldn't hear it. One ear was against her stomach, the other against her lower arm.

". . . not bad, eh? Look. In a year all boys'll have short haircuts."

Reine peered into the mirror, made a face, and whimpered:

"You'll wonder where the yellow went when you brush your teeth with Pepsodent."

33 "Watch out, for Christ's sake, here comes the world-famous racing cyclist Snuff-Sam."

No one heard him as he cycled across St. Erik's bridge, boasting right and left. There was nothing but cars around him. He stood up on the pedals, put his head back, and spat straight up into the air.

It was great riding a bike, and it didn't take long, either. Twenty-eight minutes from Sollentuna to St. Erik's Bridge. Add two more minutes and he'd be there. He had no aerial on the back, but he did have a fiberglass fishing rod sticking nearly six feet up into the air, a small triangular red pennant at the top. Motorists had once or twice honked at him, and he'd rung his bell angrily back at them, but on the whole the drivers seemed scared and gave him a wide berth. Except buses. The buses were so wide they couldn't get out of the way without changing lanes.

Reine was not quite sure of the way and rode up onto the sidewalk at the intersection. It was just past midday, and the sun ought to be due south. The park also lay almost due south. He'd checked on the map in the telephone booth in St. Erik's Square. He didn't really need to bicycle into town, not until the first of August, anyhow, but it was fun. You felt almost like a cowboy.

Why didn't he see any crashes? A hell of a lot of people were killed in automobile accidents, twenty-five million people since the car was invented. You just couldn't believe that, bicycling around here. Or was it all bluff? No, probably a way of trying to hide the fact. Sort of like how they made it impossible for the handicapped to get around town—so they stayed at home and then no one need see them. Clever old Reine knew how to organize good traffic propaganda: Listen now, all you nits and nuts! Don't clean up after traffic accidents. During the month of July, all tow trucks will be banned instead, so all wrecks will have to stay where they are. Simple! Within a week it would be difficult to get around Stockholm. Sales of motorcycles would soar. By the second week, for instance, the whole of Fridhemsplan would be totally jammed up. There would be even more smash-ups than usual, of course, because people would drive into the already wrecked cars. But the bad would have to be taken with the good.

What about people inside the cars? Leave the corpses there! Very effective in July. Maybe there would be an invasion of vultures. Something should also be done for bird life. Very effective. People would begin to think. Slow down or a vulture will get caught in your windshield wipers.

And the injured? What if people like Stig were sent to an uninhabited island? Ambulance drivers could be retrained there and learn to behave. They could have the evenings off to go swimming. Why was there only Children's Island? Well, there was Devil's Island, of course, but that was abroad. Leave the injured lying in the street . . . no, heck, there must be some moderation.

Reine navigated according to the sun and managed to make his way past Fridhemsplan, and right on—there was Rålambshov Park. The dinghies were bobbing out there on the water. No, there was no wind at all; the dinghies were bobbing and drifting around in the wash from all the motorboats crisscrossing the Mälare.

When he arrived, they were only halfway through the play. One o'clock was the time Reine had been told to come to rehearsal, and if they began by three, he could start congratulating himself. He locked his bike and sat and watched. They were working on Scene 8, in which Ball and his tennis friend Filas were in a locked hotel room, reading Donald Duck comics.

"Now read and chew," said the director. "At the dress rehearsal you'll have Cokes, too, but we can get along without now. Put your thumb in your mouth occasionally and pretend it's the straw. The girls? Where are the girls?"

The Virgin Mary, Laijla, and a girl Reine hadn't seen before went to the edge of the stage and started trying to climb up onto it, the idea being to make it look as if they were trying to climb in through the hotel window.

"Björn-Björn-Björn-Björn-Björn-Björn . . ." yelled the girls, leaping up and down, their arms outstretched.

"Björn, shall we let in a couple of chicks and have some fun?" said Filas.

"No chicks for me," said Ball.

"I'm feeling a bit horny," said Filas. "It's several hours ago, now."

"I've got a match this afternoon," said Ball. "I'm playing Filliol."

"That redhead on the far left of the balcony. Doesn't she turn you on?" said Filas, going over to the "window."

"Björn-Björn-Björn-Björn-Björn-Björn . . ." the girls started yelling again.

"Break! On a higher note," said the director. "Remember, they're kids. Twelve or thirteen. Maybe only eleven. Not mature women in heat."

"Björn-Björn-Björn-Björn-Björn-Björn . . ." squealed the girls, jumping up and down, but tiring rapidly now.

Reine thought it boring, too. He took his bike and went for a ride to the Marieberg swimming area and back again. He didn't dare be away more than half an hour. You never knew. He parked his bike, locked it, and sat down in the same place as before.

Björn Ball was now in the center of the stage talking to Clod, who was wearing a pinstriped suit.

"If there's TOY in the middle of my racket, the tension will be wrong," said Ball.

"Twenty thousand," said the man in the dark suit.

"I might hit too far," said Ball.

"Twenty-five thousand."

"I might serve double faults."

"Thirty thousand," said the man in the dark suit.

"I might lose the match!"

"Lose the match?"

"I might lose the match," said Ball, "if you hang so damn many ads on me that I can't stand straight!"

"If you lose the match, I lose my money," said the man. "Then we won't sponsor you any longer. We only sponsor winners, understand? We've got our match, too, called international competition. Think of Sweden!"

The actors left the stage after a wave from the director. The time had come to fix a net across the stage.

"Get a move on!" cried the director, a stopwatch in his hand. "Scene change must be quicker. The tempo sags there. We'll have to change in the middle of the game instead."

A small elderly man Reine hadn't noticed before went across to the director and spoke to him. The man was wearing a large straw coolie hat. The coolie guy and the director did not appear to be in agreement.

"D'you think I haven't thought this out?" said the coolie guy. "D'you think this is the first time I've ever written a play? If you've got lead in your heels, of course the tempo sags."

"What about a little music during the scene change, then? Some pop song the audience associates with the Davis Cup?"

"D'you think this is the first play I've ever written? How many directors d'you think I've worked with? You're the eighteenth. D'you think I haven't thought out the scene change between 11 and 12?"

"I'm sure you have. Like hell you have. At home at your desk. But this is a stage, not a desk."

The coolie guy was very angry now, thrashing his arms so his straw hat almost fell off.

"Yesterday you cut sixteen lines. I come here today without the slightest idea what you've done. There's a balance in the play you don't seem to have grasped."

The director suddenly dropped the manuscript and walked off the stage. The coolie guy bent down and picked it up. He blew on the pages as if they were dusty.

Reine's turn did not come until a quarter past four. They had lugged the green cart in front of the stage and put some beer crates inside it as a platform for him. Reine stood on his own up on the cart, looking down at the others, over ten of them now: the director, the coolie guy, Björn Ball as a teenager, his friend Filas, the girls, Leif, Clod in his pin-striped suit, King Karl Gustaf XVI of Sweden, and General Pinochet.

"Okay. Start!"

Reine launched with gusto into a double backhand, then swung around for a forehand, then back to a backhand half-lob.

"You'll wonder where the yellow went when you brush your teeth with Pepsodent."

Reine stopped with the racket far down to the right among the beer crates. Nothing happened. The people standing in a circle around the high-wheeled cart showed no sign whatsoever of what they were thinking or feeling. Had he done it quickly enough? He took a deep breath, shut his eyes tight—since they were too far apart—and went through the motions at top speed.

"You'll wonder where the yellow went when you brush your teeth with Pepsodent!" he sang.

Still no reaction. Should he do it a third time, even more quickly?

"You can come down now," said the director.

The audience dispersed and Reine clambered down from the green cart. He did some strokes in the air and a few knee bends so as not to stiffen up. You had to keep in shape to stand steadily up on that cart, almost as hard work as playing a match. Though he'd never actually played tennis, only table tennis. The difference was probably not all that . . .

"Reine, come over here for a moment, will you?" said the director.

The director was standing in the shade, knocking back a beer.

"It's like this. We've decided to do some realignment."

"Yes?"

"Realignment means you're not going to do what you'd thought you'd do in the first place. It's this prelude on the cart you've been working on. You've done your best, I know that, but now we've decided we ought to take out your section. There'd be too many Björn Balls for the audience to keep track of. We thought we'd use the same Björn Ball on the cart as on the stage. Björn as a teenager. He's the one the audience knows from the commercials."

"As far as I'm concerned . . ." said Reine.

"As far as you're concerned, you needn't look on this as failure. This often happens in theater, trying out things and then using only part of them."

"I've had my hair cut," said Reine.

"No one has commented on your hair."

Reine raised his hands to his ears, but there was no hair to tug to demonstrate his dismay. He'd been turned down. Turned down! It was incomprehensible. Hadn't he stood down there in the basement in the crib singing, "You'll wonder where the yellow went when you brush your teeth with Pepsodent" half the night? As soon as the light had gone out, he had bolted out of the cage and smacked the switch, over and over again.

"Well, as I was saying," said the director. "I must go and make a phone call. You can go with the cart all the same, of course. We always need help pulling it."

The director went off, and Reine was left silently staring straight ahead. The tears just came, simply came, as if they had nothing whatsoever to do with him, as if a cloud had suddenly drifted in over the park and started letting its drops fall. He grew angry. Not with the director of the Busker Theater Company. He was angry with the tears, like having an attack of intestinal flu at the most inappropriate moment. He started walking, his legs moving but his head not really knowing where his legs were going. He clambered back onto the cart, which was not easy, with a huge effort, hauling himself up. But not until he was up there, his feet astride the beer crates, did he realize where he was.

Leif, the theater-crazy stagehand, came along with an armful of black cables.

"Have the warhorses abandoned the emperor's chariot?" he said. "I've been waiting for seventeen years now, and still haven't even gotten onto the cart."

Reine didn't really understand. Though, of course, Leif meant he was still waiting for a chance. Seventeen years? Reine had had to wait for two days.

"Get down before the cart tips over and the shafts upend!"

It was dangerous to stand on a two-wheeled cart. Reine got down. Heck, all those training pains.

"Tears, tears are your heritage," said Leif, sitting down on one shaft.

Reine sat down opposite him, wiping his face with the backs of his hands. Turned down. Weighed up and found to be worth a rotten apple. And that in a play about being turned down, about the curse of competition. It made your head spin to think about it.

"If Björn Ball had been in the theater . . ." Reine started, but he didn't really know what he'd been thinking, so he swallowed the rest.

"Theater is a working team, don't forget that," said Leif. "Björn Ball acts mostly alone. Singles. Professional tennis is one-man theater. This is not one-man theater."

"What the others don't like gets thrown out, anyhow," said Reine hoarsely.

"What the others think is not good enough."

"People always have to be good. People always have to be better than anyone else."

"You'll never get away from that. You're better at some things than others."

"What, may I ask?"

"Something. You know that best yourself."

Best at being dumb. Best at not coping with yourself. Best at not having any money. Best at losing your job. Best at not being best.

"Some people always have to sacrifice themselves more than others. It's nasty, but that's how it is. Some people have too large a distance between their dreams and their abilities."

"One can't know that! Next year maybe I'll be better than him. Maybe he was turned down last winter!"

"Ellert?"

"It must differ. Sometimes one's better, sometimes one's worse."

"Maybe. After seventeen years, one begins to wonder whether it's definitive."

Definitive? What did that mean? Realignments. What did that mean? One day maybe he'd know all the difficult words, then hell!

"There are probably some people who aren't good at anything. Who don't know anything. Don't want anything. Have no charm and what's worse, don't realize they have no charm. Haven't you noticed there are certain people no one wants to be with? Not even the nice people. Nice people maybe try, but then they give up, too. There are some people who seem to have been carelessly made. They're like a mistake. Everyone shakes them off."

"Am I like that?"

"No, Snuff-Sam, you're not. I wouldn't have sat here talking like this if you were."

"I'd like to be like that," said Reine.

"What?"

"Be someone everyone shook off."

"I don't believe you."

"Yes, I'd rather be like that than what I am now, an in-between."

Reine started crying again. He didn't really know what he was crying about this time. But if you were worthless, you should cry. You should always cry, just as some people always go around with a cold. He would go around crying all the time. Everyone would go crazy. Insane, distraught, unable to bear seeing him. What power: crying other people into insanity.

"The noble victim. That's what the group demands of its members. Anyhow, of some people."

"How?"

"Someone has to sacrifice himself so it'll be good theater. Otherwise it'll be bad theater."

"And does it *have* to be that? Good theater?"

"That's the actual aim, you know."

Aim? What did aim mean? What are you aiming at—the aim? Did the aim mean the consequence? Or did it mean the reason? Question: the aim? Answer: the aim! Brilliant. The aim was both the question and the answer. What would the aim sound like translated into numbers: 11, 22, 5, 14, 19, 24. Eleven billion two hundred and twenty-five million, one hundred and forty-one thousand, nine hundred and twenty-four: 11,225,141,924. Millions? Billions? Bingo!

"The expedition of my violent love outrun the pauser reason," said Leif. "Macbeth, Act Two, Scene Three."

Macbeth, McDonald—where the hell was his bag with his black notebook? On his bike. What is the aim of the aim? The aim! Of course. Acting? What was that? A job for dolls, a job for word balloons in pants and shoes. Nothing for someone going to solve the real nitty-gritty of things. Reine went over to his bike. His bag was still on the carrier. He didn't even say goodbye to Leif. Theater, what was that? A speck of dirt on my cuff. He started laughing. Hell, how comical! Theater—so dumb it probably wasn't even mentioned in the *Mammoth Book of World Records.*

34 Much later that evening, Reine was lying on the roof of Bagarby Road 44C, holding a white plastic clothesline he had stolen from a nearby garden. He had made a large noose and fastened a stick to it as a sinker. He was trying to lower the noose to the balcony and get it to catch on the fallen stepladder. He *had* to get into the apartment. He was tired of sleeping in the crib in the basement, and he had to have some money. There was nothing sellable in the basement except his bike and the fireworks, and he had no intention of disposing of either. Not until his death. No, not even then. If he died, he wanted to be cremated on a pyre like the ancient Vikings, at the very top of a gigantic bonfire, tied to his bicycle. With the fireworks on the rack.

But there were sellable things in the apartment: to be more precise, Mom's contact lenses. A few years ago, Mom had spent a fortune on a pair of contact lenses, which were now in a case in the bathroom cabinet. She had never been able to get used to them, but had simply cried and said they itched. He probably wouldn't get what she'd paid for them, but they were only insignificantly secondhand. There must be a demand for contact lenses in this heat. It couldn't be much fun going around with great big glasses on your nose, like living behind a picture frame.

He should have had a flashlight. The balcony was inset under the roof and it was hard to see objects on the floor. He pulled up the line again and widened the noose, which had flopped. Would he dare tie the rope round his body and descend like a mountain climber? The line was long enough, and all he would have to do would be to wind it around one of the ventilators. He could put a piece of clothing—his T-shirt—

over the sharp metal edge where the roof ended to keep the line from fraying. The line was certainly strong enough, but it was thin, thinner than an ordinary electric cord, and it'd be very hard to get a grip on it walking down along the wall and then swinging onto the balcony.

He decided to have one more try with the noose. It caught almost at once. Talk about luck! He stretched the line and started to pull. Then came the hard part: pulling the stepladder into position so that it stood firmly. Suddenly the line went dead and he couldn't move it at all. Was the stepladder that heavy? He leaned as far as he could over the edge of the roof and looked in over the balcony. The noose had caught on the handle of the balcony door.

At first he gave up, dropping the line and feeling his ears beginning to glow. Cry, cry, cry. Heck, not likely. Every failure is a challenge; every fault a chance. It was good, actually. The line was as steady as a rock on the door. It would be much simpler making his way down a taut line fixed far inside the balcony, much easier than dangling in from a free hanging line. He got up and went over to the metal chimney which wasn't a real chimney but part of the ventilation system. The line was long enough, long enough for four times around the chimney. He knotted it firmly with three double reef knots and twelve granny knots. The line ran from the chimney across the roof and down the wall as rigidly as a lightning rod. Lucky he was agile. Lucky he had some Johnny Weissmuller in him without being so fat.

He should have had some gloves, but he didn't. So he took off his socks and put them on his hands. They did not smell particularly recommendable. Reine crawled toward the edge of the roof, then stood up to see what it was like wearing sneakers without socks. It was not pleasant, sticky and squelchy. Then he turned and put his feet against the wall . . .

"Einar, there *is* someone on the roof."

The voice came from the balcony alongside Reine's. Old Ma Enquist, who worked in the school kitchens. Reine went rigid.

"Probably only a magpie hopping around."

That was Einar, old Ma Enquist's son. He was thirty and as fat as she was, as fat as Johnny Weissmuller but without his sharp eyes. Einar had bulging eyes with layers of fat around them, so he always seemed to have several pairs of eyelids.

Should he lean over and call: "It's only me, Reine. I'm on leave from Children's Island?" No, they'd never be taken in by that. Old Ma Enquist was the nosiest, most inquisitive, nastiest, most gossipy magpie all up and down Bagarby Road.

He could hear Einar's voice out on the balcony now.

"What is it?"

"Someone's got a line down to Larsson's," said old Ma Enquist.

"Maybe it's for a climbing vine," said Einar.

"Don't be an idiot. Fetch the flashlight."

Reine got down on all fours, holding his breath, and crawled over to the hatch, dragging on his T-shirt before sliding down. It went on backward. He had to be quick now. Old Ma Enquist was always calling the police. When there was an empty beer can on the stairs, she called the police. When some kids had shot peas at Einar, she'd called the police. When someone parked illegally on the rented parking lots, she called the police. Even if the police didn't exactly come rushing, you couldn't be sure. Maybe they were down at the station, buying hotdogs, with the door of the patrol car open. They could be here in three minutes.

Reine made first for the basement, but then he turned back. If they started searching the building, they would include the basement. How would he be able to explain why he was down there in an old crib surrounded by rockets and bombs? He might as well take the bull by the horns and leap onto his bicycle. Luckily he had no lights, which would make him visible for miles. With his bag banging against the bar, Reine raced away from Bagarby Road. No police sirens so far.

He had to stop and get his breath back when he got to Häggvik. Although it was half-past twelve at night, it was horribly warm, and the sweat was pouring into his eyes. He needed a drink, too. How far was it to Gävle? Gran was the only person he could go to. True, Gran was a nut, but as long as he agreed with her, he could get almost anything he wanted: ice cream, hotdogs, new soccer gear. It was about a hundred miles to Gävle, or slightly less, especially if you took the expressway. Reine had no speedometer on his bike, but he had biked alongside someone who had, and he knew he could do about thirty miles an hour if he rode like a bat out of hell. He couldn't keep up that speed all the way to Gävle, but he ought to be able to manage an average of twenty-five. If the wind was behind him. At that particular moment there was no wind at all. Reine had never known such calm. Or heat.

He found the on-ramp for the E4 and cycled up onto the expressway, feeling pretty grandiose. The E4 ran from Lisbon to Helsinki. Now he was part of greater things. A hundred divided by twenty-five. Four. In four hours he could be in Gävle. In other words, at half-past four. Gran wouldn't have gone to work yet, so she would in fact have time to fix breakfast for him first. Then he would sleep, sleep until she came home for lunch. People in Gävle went home for lunch. Or dinner, as Gran said. On the first day it would be pork chops, as sure as eggs is eggs.

There was not much traffic on the freeway. Tractor-trailer rigs passed with illuminated Michelin men on their cab roofs, decorated along the sides like dancehalls. Reine kept well out to the right. The sky was yellowish-gray to the north, the same watery color as the yolks of baked eggs—slightly greenish, too, in fact, just like a really disgusting baked egg. Well, all right, if anyone had offered him a baked egg at that moment, he would not have refused. He was out in the sticks and couldn't expect a McDonald's at every turn.

He plodded on, keeping up a good speed down toward Rotebro, where there was a large co-op at the end of the bridge, a low building at least a hundred yards long, but unfortunately closed. N.B.—the largest hotdog stand in Sweden.

There was a thin layer of white mist about three feet above the ground where the highway dipped on the other side of the bridge. Reine held his breath and rode straight through it. Fabulous! Like having a cool swim on a hot stuffy day. Norrviken lay to the right, with its jetty for small boats. On a night like this he should be out fishing. The sun would soon be up, and it would be great to lie face down on the thwart with your arms and legs spread out, drifting across the sea, pretending you were a water spider.

He didn't hear the police car coming up behind him. It slid past him and stopped fifty yards farther up the hill. Turn back? But he hadn't the strength to change his plans, even if he'd wanted to. He rode on up the hill and drew level with the police car. They didn't even get out to stop him. He stopped level with the driver, who was sitting smoking a pipe with the window down.

35 It was a station wagon police car, a Volvo 145. They took his bicycle and put it on the roof. Reine was told to get in the back. The luggage compartment behind Reine's back was lined with fine-meshed metal netting and divided down the middle. In one of the cages was a German shepherd, glaring. It had nice light spots above its eyes.

The police said a few words into the radio before driving off. Reine wondered how fast a police car could go: it didn't have to stick to the speed limit, of course, but could belt along like hell with its blue lights flashing. What time would they get to Gävle, in that case? About two in the morning. Poor old Gran would be scared stiff to find two policemen on her doorstep at that hour.

"The staff quarters at Löwenström Hospital?" said the policeman who wasn't driving.

"That's correct," said Reine.

The car slowed down and turned off at the Upplands Väsby turn. But instead of going along the old Uppsala road northward toward the hospital, the car swung to the left at a Gulf service station. Behind it was Mamma's, a hotdog and hamburger stand built like a big red mushroom.

"You want a hotdog?" the driver said.

"Yes, please," said Reine, who would have preferred a hamburger but didn't think it worth mentioning.

The policemen got out, but Reine sat tight, regarding himself as a prisoner and not daring to leave the car.

"Got water on the knees, have you?"

Reine was out of the car in a flash and walked with the policemen over to the stand. There was lots to choose from: the menu was several yards long. Not at all like Carrol's, for instance, where they only had four or five kinds. The police ordered a grilled hotdog each, with bun and pickle. Reine thanked them politely. The hotdog was already grilled, so all he had to do was stuff it into the bun. They went back and sat in the car. The dog got up behind Reine's back and sniffed at his hotdog.

"Down!" said one of the policemen, and the dog lay down immediately.

When Reine had finished and the inside of his mouth was as dry as dust because he'd had nothing to drink, he said:

"I forgot you're not allowed to ride a bike on the expressway."

"Stig Utter—is he your dad, or what?"

"He's Mom's friend."

"Friend?"

"Yes, he's got the key of our apartment."

"And you've lost yours?"

"Down a drain."

"How come you're alone at home?"

"Well, it wasn't supposed to happen. Mom's working in Uddevalla, and Stig was to look after me for a few days and . . ."

"Do we have to contact the duty officer at the children's department?" one policeman said to the other.

"Let's ask the station."

"We could leave the kid at this Utter's. That'd be simplest for everyone."

"Stig Utter, staff quarters at Löwenström Hospital? Is that what you said?"

Without waiting for a reply, they started up the car and drove out onto the old Uppsala road. The car was an automatic and lurched gently when the gears were shifting. He had to make the most of the journey and enjoy it while the going was good. Then everything would end in the horrors. Stig would start arguing with the police, Mom would come at top speed back from Uddevala, Gran would come at top speed from Gävle, some inspector or other would come at top speed from the children's department, and someone else would come tearing in from Children's Island. But first and foremost, old Ma Enquist would come steaming over to ask him where he'd stolen the clothesline.

And yet he wasn't really frightened. If he had to be picked up by the police, it could have been somewhat more dramatic. He could have been picked up by the Chilean police and had a ride in the back of a military jeep. He could have been picked up by the American fuzz and been made to lean with his hands on the hood. He could have been picked up by the Spanish police and put in an old wooden chair, a wooden block round his neck and a corkscrew in the back of his neck.

"Stig Utter. Which stairway?"

Reine didn't know, so one of the policemen had to go and look. Stig lived on Stairway F, and all three of them went up and rang the doorbell. No one came to the door. What would Reine say when Stig eventually woke up and came to the door? No problem—the police would do the talking. If Stig didn't seem to be in the best of moods, Reine would bring up that sailing trip and who had thrown whom into the water. Was it worth it? Then it would be the children's department instead. Wouldn't it be better to cope with a sullen, unruly Stig than to have some inspector on your neck? If he stuck to Stig, there was still a minute chance of staying free and having the rest of the summer to himself instead of being deported to Children's Island, or whatever the heck they would do with him. He wouldn't be free, anyhow.

The police rang the doorbell again.

"He's usually hard to wake," said Reine. "I can wait on my own."

But the police were not going to let him wait on his own. They peered through the mail slot and rang again. If God is good, then Stig is out driving his old ambulance, Reine thought. If God is good, the police will leave me here with a warning. If God is good, I'll hop on my bike and go on to Gran's. On the ordinary road, not the expressway.

Stig snatched open the door and stared open-mouthed at the policeman.

"Utter?" said the policeman.

"Utt-*ler*."

"We've only come for the key," said Reine.

Stig got the message immediately and went in for his key ring. He took off the key and pressed it into Reine's hand.

"We're assuming you'll take care of the kid now," said the policeman.

"There's no need now I've got the key," said Reine.

"Come on in, Reine," said Stig.

"There appears to be no adult back home in his apartment," said the policeman.

"Thanks for your help," said Stig.

"Well, we'll let things stand as they are this time," the policeman said to Reine. "We'll put your bike in the bike rack. Keep off the expressway."

"Thanks," said Stig. "He's a bit adventuresome, this kid."

"The heat, I expect," said the policeman. " 'Night, then."

Stig stretched out his hand and yanked Reine in over the threshold. Just as he was about to close the door, the driver of the police car turned around and swiftly ran his hand over Reine's head.

"Nice to see a kid with a decent haircut," he said.

"Thanks again," said Stig, closing the door. As soon as he had locked it, he said curtly: "The key!"

Reine handed back the key. Stig put it into his bathrobe pocket without comment. In the righthand pocket. Just you wait. The bastard must sleep sometimes. . . .

"Who was it?" said a woman's voice from the room that must be the bedroom.

"An acquaintance of yours."

"Of mine?"

Stig grabbed Reine's arm and pulled him on into the apartment.

"Are you crazy, kid? Biking on the expressway?" he said.

"Stig?"

There was a rustle of sheets in the bedroom. The half-open door into the hall opened and a naked woman came out from behind the door and looked at the front door. Stig and Reine, now inside the living room, saw the woman quite unprotected, from behind.

"Stig?"

It was Mom. My own damn mom, Reine thought, lying here screwing the biggest pig in the world. Mom turned swiftly around, saw them, and whisked back into the bedroom, pulling the door behind her.

"That time I chucked you in the sea . . ." said Stig.

"Yes?"

"You don't seem to have taken a bath since."

"Stig, call a cab," said Mom through the crack in the door.

"Just a minute," said Stig, going over to the telephone.

Hell, one's own fucking mom.

"Coming!" yelled Stig toward the bedroom.

Mom came out eventually, and stood in front of the mirror in the hall, fixing her face.

"Harriet, aren't you going to say hullo?" said Stig.

But Mom couldn't answer at that moment. She had formed her mouth into a rigid circle and was very close to the mirror, so close there was hardly room for the lipstick between the mirror and her mouth. Then at last she went into the living room, sat down on a chair some way away from Reine, and started searching through the contents of her handbag: keys, wallet, a bundle of letters.

"When'll I see you again?" said Stig.

"Reine, will you look out the kitchen window to see if the cab's come," said Mom.

Reine went into the kitchenette and stared out over the purple asphalt of the yard. The night was definitely on its way out now. One's own fucking mom lying here like a sow. When Stig had visited them at home, he had always had to keep to the guest room at night. It was no secret that Mom went in there and saw to her guest. But this was something else. This was piggishness. Sheer swinishness. There was no sign of a cab.

"It's come," said Reine.

"When do I see you again?" said Stig.

Stig went over to kiss Mom on the cheek, but she veered quickly away. Mom had a red suitcase in the hall. Had she come straight here from Uddevalla?

"Reine," said Mom. "Don't stand there dawdling!"

They went out, and Mom closed the apartment door. Reine ran down the stairs and out into the cool. It had at last grown slightly cold now that the sun was rising. Mom backed out through the front door with her bag. No cab had come, but Mom said nothing. She stood outside the entrance of Stig's building, her arms folded, her suitcase between her feet; she was staring at it as if checking whether it was crooked or something. Reine flung small stones at a streetlight post and missed.

He saw the cab a long way off as it came crawling along the old Uppsala road; it stopped, about to turn right down toward the hospital itself, then suddenly turned in the middle of the intersection and came charging toward them. A diesel Opel. Mom handed her suitcase to the driver and got in the back. Reine got into the front.

"My bike!"

The cab braked abruptly. Reine jumped out and ran over to the bicycle rack where the police had left his bike. Someone had swiped the fiberglass rod and pennant, but miraculously—since it was not locked—no one had ripped off the whole bike. The cab driver was not amused at having to get out again, open the trunk, take out the suitcase, get out the bicycle rack, put it together, fix it on the back of the cab, put the suitcase back in the trunk, and hook on the bicycle. Reine timed the journey home. Fourteen minutes, thirty-five seconds. Mom kept blowing her nose all the way.

36 Reine seemed to have been waiting an awfully long time. He wasn't sleepy; on the contrary, his heart was racing at top speed. At four, Mom had got up and poured herself a brandy. At twenty past four, the sun had come around the corner and blazed into Reine's room. He had gotten out of bed and opened the venetian blind as quietly as possible. It was good lying there with it open, not having to hide. He had waited for another quarter of an hour before dressing and going to listen at Mom's door. At last, she was asleep. But of course, she'd been at it half the night, and then a brandy on top of that.

Mom's red suitcase was in the hall on top of a heap of scattered mail. He shifted the suitcase and went through the mail. Two letters from Mom. His first impulse was to flush them down the toilet, but he changed his mind, partly because he might wake Mom, partly because there might be some money in them. He crammed the letters into his back pocket.

Otherwise, the apartment was much as usual, the garbage bag stinking of old sardine cans, the kitchen table with so many crumbs on it it appeared to be covered with sawdust. Beside the toaster, a loaf of bread glimmered green, white, and blue with mold. Trousers and underpants lay in the bathtub in a minimal amount of water, dry on top and slimy underneath. But strung above the bathtub were two pairs of underpants, as stiff and brittle as stale thin toast.

Cap! He had to have a cap for Christ's sake. He took a kitchen chair and investigated the hall closet shelf: fur cap, skiing cap, woolly caps, stacks of woolly caps. Well, here was something, anyhow: a pale blue sunhat with a silly turned-down brim, *O.K. Co-op Owned* printed on it. Reine jammed it on his head and checked in the bathroom mirror. It'd have to do. They could see he'd had a short haircut, since nothing hung down the sides, but if they only knew . . .

Now it was a question of packing quickly. His irregular life had taught him what he needed most: clean underpants, clean socks, a clean T-shirt, maybe—and some spare shoelaces. The secret notebook? Jocke? Yes, he'd better take Jocke. But not the *Mammoth Book of World*

Records? Yes, he'd better take it in case he urgently had to find out some fact: what is the longest time an eleven-year-old has managed to stay away from home, for instance?

Naturally, he couldn't leave the key of his code in the toilet tank. He extracted the folded paper and put it in his bag. He would check as soon as possible whether he still knew the code and then swallow the paper. Nothing was to be left to chance. Things were serious now. The summer had been mostly fun until then, like a rehearsal. What was the time? Nineteen minutes past five.

The most important matter remained. Money. And a warm sweater. He jerked his thick sweater out of the hall closet, bringing down half his skiing gear with it. The sweater took up too much room in his bag, so he tied the sleeves round his waist. Where did Mom keep her cash? Her shoulder bag was on the kitchen counter. He extracted his own letters before clearing the wallet of three hundred and sixty-five *kronor* ten, of which he ought to reimburse Children's Island with a hundred and ninety. But it could hardly cost that much if he went now.

Before he left the apartment, he listened at Mom's door once more, and then went to the bathroom and peed into the wash basin. He found it difficult to reach, so couldn't really empty his bladder. With great suspicion, he examined his dick and balls. It would be the last straw if anything happened now. That would finish everything. Luck was with him. Great! Not a whisker! With the hat down over his eyes and bag slung around his neck, he opened the front door, pushed up the latch so that the lock wouldn't click, and closed the door quietly behind him.

Now for the basement. His bike was in the basement. The only time Mom had spoken to him last night was when he had wanted to take his bike down into the basement and she had considered it too late. But he had persisted. He had already decided to shove off as soon as he could, and he might have found himself standing there like an idiot, staring at an empty bicycle rack and searching for a stolen bike. There were the fireworks in the basement, too, but there was no room for them in his bag. One had to sacrifice something sometimes. He pulled four rockets off their long sticks and shoved the sticks back into the drawer. You could always replace sticks; a few twigs would do if worst came to worst. The bag was bulging like a seaman's kitbag. Rainwear? He hadn't any rainwear at all. But they'd stopped having rain in the weather forecasts this summer, no doubt something to do with the pollution of the countryside. He could always buy an umbrella if the rain came back.

He lugged up his bike and eased it through the entrance door. The sun was blazing, and balcony doors were open in several apartments, the blinds down in others whose occupants were on vacation. When he'd been up on the roof, he'd seen several people sleeping out on balconies this unusual summer. He clipped his bag onto the rack, seated himself carefully so that the sweater he'd tied round his waist came under his backside, and set off. The moment he turned into Malm Road, he remembered: the contact lenses! Mom's contact lenses were worth a thousand *kronor*. He couldn't leave that. He could keep afloat with a thousand until February at the very least. Without looking behind, Reine did a U-turn and biked back home. He parked the bike, locked it, and went upstairs. Luckily he'd left the front door open, otherwise it would have meant the roof and fishing for the stepladder again. He put his baggage down outside the door and crept in. Everything was as he'd left it, Mom's snoring audible through the door.

Quickly out to the bathroom medicine chest, crammed with hundreds of little boxes and bottles. A flat black box. No, that was her false eyelashes. The round one? No, that contained stinking pink flour—powder? That little case in plastic crocodile-skin? Nail scissors. A small bottle of nail polish with a top like a white quill fell into the basin, making a hell of a racket. Maybe he should take a bottle of scent and sell it duty-free somewhere? There it was! Now he remembered exactly what the box looked like: square, flat, and white as if it contained something nasty. He pried open the lid and looked inside. Yes, there was the whole shebang—lenses, suction cups to insert them, a little bottle of water-colored oil . . .

"Reine?"

Hell and damnation, Mom was awake! He closed the box and stuffed it inside his T-shirt. Mom was up, too, coming through the lounge. Keep cool, lock the bathroom door, sit on the lid and groan.

"Reine?"

The door handle moved.

"Soon finished."

"Aren't you well?"

"A little loose."

Mom let go the handle and retreated through the hall. Very slowly, he drew back the bolt, opened the door a fraction, and listened. She was turning restlessly in bed, no doubt wanting to take a leak herself. He pushed open the door, prepared to run, then pulled the handle. Like lightning, he was in his own room, the door shut and himself under the covers.

Mom got up and went to the john, flushed it, came back and stopped outside his door.

"Reine?"

He tried snoring lightly as naturally as possible.

"Reine?"

She gave up and went back to her room. Now he had to keep awake. He lay there going through his multiplication tables, but the yawns kept coming. So he started systematically pinching himself instead: little toe, next toe, middle toe, second toe, big toe. Calves, kneecap, back of the knee. Front of thigh, back of thigh. Right testicle—ow! Left testicle. Base of prick, foreskin. God, that was good, if only . . . no, might bring it on, of course. He quickly got out of bed and crept out into the hall, ready to rush back into bed or rush out to the john and lock the door should Mom seem restless. But she wasn't. She just damn well went on sleeping. Three minutes later, he was on his bike, pedaling like nobody's business—whose business?—which direction was this darned Children's Island?

37 He had lunch at ten o'clock at a lunch counter: sirloin steak, French fries, and Zingo. Super! Up on the bike again, into first gear, down with your head so air resistance didn't reduce your speed. Honda? Kawasaki? Suzuki? Yamaha? No, what about being Italian and slightly original today? Moto-Gussi? Montesa? No, Ducati. On the next stretch he accelerated on his Italian long-distance Ducati 860 racer. Get a move on, Larsson.

Children's Island was out in the archipelago. But where exactly? Would he have to ride up round Norrtälje, or was it one of the islands in the south? He'd face that when he came to it. Now he had to get himself to the coast, to the Baltic shores. He could always ask whether he should turn left or right when he got there. Sweden was beautiful, damn beautiful.

He had been cycling for no more than half an hour after his lunch break when he felt a cold coming on. His throat felt thick. However much he swallowed, it did not improve; if anything, it got slightly thicker. He felt as if a ring had been put around his throat, the ring off a beer can. His nose was warm and dry. That was how colds usually started: first a sore throat but no cold, then running nose and his body hot and dry all over. After a week or two, the cold left his nose and attacked his throat again before finally swelling and vanishing.

He stopped, pulled a gym sock out of his bag, and tied it around his neck. That was what Gran recommended: not a scarf, but a stocking around your neck. What was the difference? Reine didn't know but assumed it was something to do with Jesus. If anyone remarked on his silly cap, he could cough and refer to his cold.

He rode on and eventually came to a signpost that said North Ljuster Island. That sounded familiar in some way. Maybe Children's Island wasn't there, but if he headed in that direction, he would come to the sea. No sooner said than done. The road narrowed, nothing for a long-distance Ducati 860. Might as well change to something more robust. Naturally, it would have been great to come roaring into Children's Island on the great heavy Ducati, but a good motocross bike would do. Reine resaddled to a Kawasaki 250, the machine Thorleif Hansen rode. Light but strong. Scrambler bike, but fast all the same.

How many times a year did he get a cold? Or get sick? When he was well, he said never. You forget nothing so easily as the fact that you are often sick. It was natural to be well; that's as it should be. But when he thought about it, he could count up how many times, starting from the last school skiing week: three definite colds, two definite diarrheas during one of which he had thrown up at least ten times, earache once, stomachache once that Mom thought was glands. And two nosebleeds.

The traffic was pretty heavy by spells, but he scarcely noticed. It was up to the cars to keep away from him. But on one hill, when he had to stand on the pedals and his bike lurched violently from side to side, a Volkswagen raced past, honking so loud his ears started popping. Junk! Damn two-door, rear-drive heap of junk. He closed his eyes and imagined the Volkswagen running off the road down into a deep ravine, beyond the hill, bouncing against jagged rocks and finally hitting bottom and exploding into an orange ball of fire with black edges. Pure Saturday detective thriller. There would be nothing but a handful of soot left of the driver. Serve him right—he should have his driver's license taken away, too.

After he had struggled up the hill and—to his disappointment—found no ravine with oily blue smoke billowing out of it, he got off and rested his forehead on the handlebars. He was sleepy, he had a cold, he was incredibly thirsty and tired. Everything had gone by in one fell swoop this last twenty-four hours. Only twelve hours ago he had been biking north to Gran's. What a day! First rejected as Björn Ball, then discovered on the roof and hunted like a thief, then that slimy toad Stig Utter (Uttler?), then that slimy—no, he hadn't the energy to think about Mom. He felt like throwing up.

Off to his right was a small gravel road with a grass strip down the middle and head-high hedgerows down the sides, delicate rust-colored wild chervil mostly. Reine wheeled his bike onto the road, sat on the seat, stuck his legs out, and free-wheeled down the hill. He was in luck—the dip ended in a short slope up to a little hill on which was a red barn surrounded by about twenty-five aspen trees. The hill made a little island in an endless field of wheat. My island, the only child's own island. Reine boosted the bike forward the last bit; the bike stopped and fell to one side. Reine got off and pulled it into the barn. The barn had no walls, only a few posts and rafters holding up the roof, and there were some scattered bales of straw, a bundle of fenceposts, and several rolls of barbed wire inside. He locked his bike and climbed up among the straw bales, sitting with his back against one of them. The view was fantastic. The sea must be beyond the edge of the forest. He closed his eyes and let the wheat sway behind his eyelids.

When he awoke, almost five hours had gone by. A faint wind was blowing through the aspens, like a running tap. It wasn't at all cold, even though he wasn't sheltered from the wind. Must have been eighty-five to ninety degrees. Or a hundred and ninety? Maybe not, but this really was a crazy summer. He couldn't understand the hot summers starting so soon. The real heat wave wasn't supposed to begin until that nuclear power station got going and hot water drained out everywhere so all Sweden would be steaming.

He extricated Mom's letters from his pocket. One of them contained a ten, the other a photograph of Mom in a bikini, smiling and waving. Who had taken it? Goddamn slut! Resentfully, he tore the photograph into tiny shreds and flung them like confetti in the wind. It was no longer forbidden to fling your relatives' ashes to the wind. There was a special glade for the purpose at Skog Cemetery. Should he read the letters? Curiosity won the day, but the letters weren't worth reading. Mom thanked him for all his messages from Children's Island and was pleased he was enjoying himself and had so many nice friends. She herself was working most of the time but sometimes had a day off for swimming. What did the bitch do at night? Get it on with Danish junior doctors? He'd heard Mom telling a friend about someone who was getting it on with Danish junior doctors. But now Reine knew what it was all about. He wouldn't allow himself to be cheated in the future. He really ought to cut his testicles off with the pruning shears—once and for all.

Hunger should be making itself felt now, shouldn't it? He looked at his watch. He had been awake for fourteen minutes. He was seldom hungry when he first woke up, his stomach still full of dreams and mists. But then the mists would lift and his stomach start rumbling: meat! hamburgers! bread! pickles! ketchup!

A buzzard was hovering above the wide field of wheat. If only he were an angel and could keep the buzzard company, flying with that enormous bird and soaring in the warm rising air currents. An angel with long narrow wings like a glider's. As soon as his all-seeing eye caught sight of a steak or a hotdog among the wheat, he would quickly fold his wings like a gull and hurtle downward . . . no, it would be more practical to be a swift hawk and nest in a chandelier in some gigantic restaurant. A white falcon that wasn't scared of linen. As soon as he was hungry, he would swoop down on the laden table at five hundred miles an hour. One blow with his claws, an elegant loop-the-loop followed by a top-roll, and he would be back up there in the chandelier with half a broiled chicken in his beak. With a dab of mustard on one wingtip.

Reine peered out across the countryside and grew sentimental: maybe he would be still sitting here in November staring out into the yellow fog or the smoke of stubble fires. About Lucia Day the snow would start coming, the landscape grayish-white like a photograph. The table would have been cleared.

No, he couldn't stay here until ice formed in his pants and he froze to the ground. Children's Island was waiting, floating like a great bundle of foliage out there in the idle sea. He would soon be there—too soon? What would he do when he arrived that evening? Seek out a leader and explain that Reine Larsson had now been discharged from the hospital after his appendicitis? Maybe he'd better wait until early tomorrow morning? No, leaders were usually nicer toward evening.

Not at the evening meal, when they were fagged out and exhausted, but later on—between nine and ten, when they began to feel free and had had a beer or two, or some wine. Maybe he would be allowed to sleep in the leaders' quarters for the first night so as not to wake the others. As long as he didn't let them see he had a cold.

What would happen next? He would be bullied. He knew that. His contemporaries would descend on him, shoving and pushing. He wouldn't stand a chance. Why should he have a chance? He'd never been a leader, had he? And coming now, several weeks late, when everything had been done, the cabins assigned, most people given new names, everyone already knowing everyone else, and no one questioning who decided things—or never being allowed to decide and supposed to be pleased if he didn't get beaten or have his gym shorts pulled down so the girls could see. That was what was awaiting him; as soon as they were alone with him, they would undress him and force him to show everything he had in his bag: the fireworks, his black notebook, the contact lenses, and Jocke. They would probably set fire to Jocke. When that was all done, some wit would stick out his rat nose and give Reine a new name, a name that would be just as difficult to get rid of as chewing gum in your hair.

He would have to arrive like a conqueror or not at all. Best would be to come zooming in in a cloud of dust on a yellow Kawasaki and roar around a little so that leaders and silly females ran in all directions. But that entailed two things: a bridge over to Children's Island, and a Kawasaki at his disposal.

Another method would be to arrive in disguise. If he could have borrowed Helene's wheelchair, he might have wheeled slowly in toward the flagpole and made everyone feel ashamed. Add a few awkward movements and some foaming at the mouth: they wouldn't stand a chance. They would all have guilty consciences, the leaders paralyzed at first, and then they would make a hell of a fuss over him. On the first day, that is; on the second day they would start backing down. But there would be no second day. That evening Reine would sprinkle gasoline around the kitchen quarters and put a match to it. Then he would sit behind a bush in his wheelchair, ready with the fattest water hose. When they had all crowded around in panic and emptied those silly powder extinguishers on the fire, he would charge out of the bushes like a tank, raise the hose, and wash out the fire in a few minutes. The fire would give him such a violent shock he would get out of the wheelchair, and stiffly—a lot like Frankenstein's monster—he would climb out of the ruins, to be greeted as chieftain by the hysterical crowd.

After he'd cycled a mile or so along the asphalted road to North Ljuster Island, he came to a grocery store. It was past eight o'clock, and the store was closed. The placards for the evening paper were still on the door, but there were no headlines about a runaway boy. Good. Mom was lying low. Presumably, she didn't want that painful business about Stig publicized. "Mother's lover," it would have said about Stig. Hell's kitchen, serve them damn well right. "Earlier this summer, the mother's lover had brutally tried to drown the boy." Mom and Stig would be forced to lie low for a while.

The store was closed, but there was a large vending machine beside the door with its narrow white blind saying: "Closed." But the machine was out of order, most of the glass panes smashed, the coin slot broken. There was a dried-up baby bird in one of the smashed compartments. The whole shambles must have been smashed for a long time. Reine sat sulking on the concrete step. He would have to eat grain. The wheat in the field was ripening, and he could thresh out the ears and eat the seed. As long as it didn't swell like popcorn in his stomach.

There was a noisemaker lying just by the step. Reine got up and picked up the brightly colored paper spiral. He put it to his mouth and blew. The tube filled and rolled itself out with a characteristic squeak. He took it away from his mouth, and it rolled back with a snap. Fantastic! A whole squeaker. Not even crumpled. He blew out the squeaker several times and felt better. Hell's bells, no lame ducks here. There was a silly squeaker, who couldn't even leakher . . . sneaker? tweaker? greeker? peeker? speaker?

He gave up rhyming and got back on his bike with the noisemaker in his mouth. Foot on the pedal, air in the squeaker—"eeeek"—and off and away. When he had got up speed, he took the noisemaker out of his mouth and put it in his pocket; otherwise, the paper tube might have gotten bent in the wind. He hadn't been going for more than a few minutes when he saw a small camping site on a slope to his left, a whole lot of cars parked around the few tents. Nearly all the cars were big American makes painted in bright gaudy colors: metallic green, fiery red, steel blue and purple. Some had black and white grids or flames painted on them. Reine turned onto the bumpy road leading to the cars and tents. The first car he came to, an acid-green Dodge, had a sticker on the back window. It said YOUNG DRAGSTER SWEDEN.

38 The leader of the dragsters was a man called Hester. He was big and fat, and wore blue jeans, cowboy boots, and a black leather vest. He wore nothing under the vest, and his chest and swelling stomach protruded. He had broad leather straps around his wrists and a strap around his neck weighed down with a shiny ball bearing. He had a crew cut—scalped—and grinned all the time. The rest obeyed him as they would a president.

Hester had a kind of subchieftain called Edsel at his side. He was tall and had one front tooth missing. He looked like an Indian with his long, greasy, blue-black hair and brown shiny face, his long tattooed arms protruding from a fringed blue vest. Round shouldered, watchful eyes, seeing everything, hearing everything, arranging everything. There were girls there, too, like the boys, most of them fat and dressed in the same way: boots, pants, and vest, with numerous metal objects dangling everywhere—bells around wrists, broad leather belts with sparkplugs like bullets all around. The dragsters called themselves the Power Gliders.

When Reine had come gliding in on his bike, at first they had taken no notice of him whatsoever. Most of them had been inside the tent, and two were under a car. A few were rocking and jerking in front of an almost extinguished fire to music from a tape recorder perched on the hood of the nearest car. Reine had stopped and was standing astride his bike, watching.

He had stayed like that for a long time, not knowing whether he dared stay or whether they would hurl themselves on him if he turned his back to leave. After an eternity, Edsel had appeared from nowhere and walked round Reine a few times, tossing his head jerkily like a spastic; then suddenly taking a few dance steps, he handed a stick of chewing gum to Reine and disappeared. How was he to interpret that? It seemed to him that the chieftain had sent the cook out to check on the stranger they were going to have for dinner.

Reine had cheered himself up with the gum and then got off his bike to approach the two lying underneath the engine of a rebuilt American Ford with broad wheel rims and raised rear section. The whole vehicle was silver-gray with black flames painted from the front wheel along the sides.

"Hi!" Reine had said.

One of the dragsters had looked out, black in the face from grease and oil, then nodded at a heap of rags lying in the grass.

"Rag!"

Reine had grabbed a chunk and thrown it over. The man had immediately vanished under the engine. It was one of the classiest cars Reine had seen for a long time. The hood was painted matt black and remodeled with a low oval extra air intake. The broad squat tires were mounted on light metal rims with wrought hourglass-shaped spokes. The double exhaust pipes glistened like new silver coins. Beneath the high rear section, the universal joint shone red like a bull's testicle.

A moment later, Reine had become brave enough to walk around among the tents and cars and take a look. The dragsters were unmoved, paying no more attention to him than they would have paid to a puppy sniffing round, loose but harmless, free but at the same time completely under control. Then they had offered him some food, and that was when he got to know Hester and the others. They had squatted around the fire and stuffed themselves with corned beef straight out of the can. Hester had flung a half empty can at him with a grin. The others around the fire had grinned in response. Reine was now sitting slightly apart from them, digging out the fatty meat with his fingers. He hadn't tasted anything so delicious for centuries.

What would happen now? It was half-past ten on a Saturday night toward the end of July. The fire flared in the dark, the dragsters had gone from corned beef to vodka, and something was bound to happen. The cars shone in the moonlight. Elvis Presley was still rocking away on the tape recorder, although they had lowered the volume now. They were clearly all waiting for some kind of statement from Hester. But Hester was not the one to speak. He appeared totally uninterested and was sitting slashing at his boottop with a sharp penknife. Edsel rose to his feet instead—he really did look like an Indian now—shook his forearms, stretching them up toward the stars, and cried:

"Roslagskulla!"

It was as if an air raid warning had sounded over the camp. They all raced off, flung themselves into the cars, and started up the engines. Only Hester stayed behind, whittling dreamily at his boot, a fat girl in black at his side. Then he got to his feet and walked across to his car, a red Thunderbird, the girl and Edsel behind him. In passing, Edsel stretched down his long, naked, clawlike arm and grabbed Reine's neck. Reine stumbled with him across to Hester's car. The others had already started their cars and were revving up the engines so that blue smoke was pouring out like witch's brooms. Reine and the girl squashed into the back of the Thunderbird; Edsel took the wheel, and Hester sat beside him clutching the vodka bottle. Edsel waited until Hester had taken a gulp, then started up the engine, and they bumped off toward the road. The rest of the dragsters followed in a roaring, lurching caravan, the light from their headlamps swirling over the countryside.

The girl beside Reine was called Ebon. She didn't seem particularly happy. She was occasionally allowed to borrow the vodka bottle from

Hester, and extracting her chewing gum, she took a drink, then put back the gum. Edsel drank nothing. He drove fast. The glittering white line on the asphalt appeared out of the dark and was rapidly gobbled up by the car. Reine was afraid the car would soon be so gorged with white glitter it would swell up and burst like a star rocket.

Hester switched off the car stereo, turned his profile toward Ebon, and said:

"Lack?"

What did lack mean? Black meant you were broke, but lack? Ebon made a face, then sank back with her chin against the window ledge, preferring to stare out into the total darkness at the side of the road rather than talk to her fellow passengers. So lack meant "angry."

Reine turned and looked back through the low rear window. An endless snake of headlights was wriggling like a dragon's tail behind them. They were at the head of the dragon, inside the dragon's eyes, steering the whole huge monster. Why had they taken Reine with them? I'm to be sacrificed, he thought, enjoying the idea; that would be a worthy end. The dragon would twist and turn up a vast mountain and stop at the top so that the dragon's glittering scales would be visible over half of Sweden. Then Hester and Edsel would take Reine out, lift the hood, and throw him down the dragon's fiery throat. Simultaneously, all the cars would honk like maniacs. Reine would be sizzled to ashes in the red-hot eight-cylinder engine and then ejected as blue smoke from the silver exhaust pipes. That would be better than having a stroke in the year 2059 or thereabouts.

They came to Roslagskulla and roared through the main street until they reached the amusement park. It was not a big one. About fifty cars were parked on the grass slope outside, not real cars—only Volvos, Saabs, VWs, Opels, German Fords and Fiats. As the dragon slowed down by the entrance, Reine counted thirty-seven dragster cars, practically all of them American except the last one, an Opel Kapitän from the sixties.

The dragsters all stayed in their cars while Edsel got out and crossed over to the ticket office. People turned away in fear, only a few boys of Reine's age following at a distance. At first the cashier and the guard at the entrance seemed to be on the verge of closing the park, but then Edsel leaned forward and whispered something to the man in charge of the cash register. The ticket window was opened, and the colored lights above the entrance went on again.

Edsel came back at full speed, leaned into the car, and said to Hester: "He's brought it down from fifteen to five."

Hester laughed. He had a surprisingly light, tinkling laugh, almost like a girl's.

"No more negotiations?" said Edsel.

"No, for Christ's sake, can't sit around here doin' nothin'," said Hester into the neck of the bottle as if into a microphone; then he took a gulp and got out.

Ebon and Reine also got out. Hester stayed where he was beside the car, stretching and yawning. Edsel lounged against the hood, chewing. The other dragsters did not get out until Hester hitched up his pants and started walking with twisting heels toward the entrance. In silence, they formed up into a dark-clad column behind, metal plates, buckles, and nickel-plated bearings glittering in the summer darkness.

Hester ignored the man in the ticket office as well as the guard and walked straight through, followed closely behind by Ebon. They looked very much alike from behind, two plump people with sticklike legs, Hester head and shoulders taller. Reine kept close to Edsel. When Edsel reached the entrance, the man in the ticket office held out four tickets, but Edsel made no move to pay, either; he just walked in. Reine followed—there was nothing else he could do. He looked around quickly—all the dragsters were coming behind. The man in the ticket office had already pulled down his window.

It wasn't much of an amusement park. A square dance floor, which a few middle-aged people rapidly deserted; two girls went on twirling around together. A shooting gallery, a chocolate wheel with huge Snoopy dolls, a closed merry-go-round, a hotdog stand, a cotton candy booth, a couple of trailers, a shooting gallery for bear hunting (not real rifles, just points of light that wobbled about when you fired), a poker table, a tent with one side rolled up. The tent was full of one-armed bandits.

Hester started by taking a hotdog and mashed potatoes. There was no question of paying. Several of his retinue lined up at the hotdog stand. The man in charge tried to close it down, but a couple of dragsters put their shoulders to the stand and bounced it a little. The orchestra stopped playing, and there was almost complete silence. Reine couldn't believe that several hundred people crowded into an amusement park could be so silent. All he could hear was one car after another starting up in the parking lot. But they got nowhere; the dragsters' cars were blocking the way.

Hester finished the hotdog and dropped the mashed potato on the ground before walking across toward the one-armed bandit tent. But he didn't work the machines himself, only stood watching Ebon pushing coins into the slot of one of them and then jerking at the arm so that the whole base rocked. More dragsters came in, girls and boys, and started playing.

Reine never really grasped what happened next. He was standing behind Hester, on tiptoe, puffing out his chest, trying to be like Hester, when someone over by the dance floor suddenly turned a big firehose on the amusement park. Reine didn't see who started it—whether a guard or even the proprietor of the fair tried to squirt water at the dragsters, or the other way around. But when he came out of the gambling tent, two dragsters had taken over the hose and were washing down the dance floor like the deck of a ship. The remaining members of the orchestra evaporated into the darkness. Then the dragsters turned the powerful jet of water onto the cotton candy booth. The woman inside ducked down behind the counter as the water came and panes of glass shattered, sticks and pink cotton candy rushing and leaping out the door of the booth as it was forced open by the pressure.

Then they turned the jet onto the chocolate wheel to get it to go round, but that was unsuccessful because the wheel was locked. Instead, they hosed the shelves clean; Snoopy dolls, boxes of chocolates, china girls, ashtrays, combs, minipacks of cards and bookmarkers were all swept away into one great mess. Just as they turned the jet on the shooting gallery's small bears in glass cupboards, the water stopped. Someone must have turned it off or cut the hose.

That was the signal for a general assault. The dragsters, hitherto almost unnaturally silent, now started yelling and laughing. They tore up the dance floor railings and started slashing at anything in their way. The guard made one last effort to restore order by turning a spotlight from the dance floor onto Hester and Ebon, but two girls at once flew at the guard and kicked him to the ground. Reine saw Ebon put her hand inside her black shirt and pull out a rolled-up bicycle chain, not oily and black but shiny as a necklace.

Reine had only one thought in his head—to get to the hotdog stand. At last he would be able to eat his fill! He had to run a long way around behind the trailers and latrines to reach the stand, and when he got there, there was almost nothing left. The noise was deafening now, increased by all the cars outside honking for all they were worth. The hotdog stand, a large truck on low wheels, had been overturned, and a dragster in a yellow vest was standing in the middle of the wreckage eating pickles straight out of a big jar. He jumped out of the hotdog stand and flung the jar of pickles up onto the roof of the gambling tent.

With the hotdog stand empty now, Reine found the courage to go inside. There didn't seem to be any whole hotdogs left. Those lying around in the grass had been squashed to pieces, and the buns were all gone, too. There was some mustard, but someone had squirted the ketchup into the cash register drawer, already cleared of money. Reine was near to tears—wasn't he going to get anything out of this feast? He rummaged in the mess for a while. There were hotdog wrappers and paper plates, plastic forks, salt, pepper, an unopened can of mustard, and . . . yes, a bag of instant potatoes, a ten-pound bag, but it was almost empty—maybe two pounds left at the most. He snatched the bag and leaped out of the hotdog stand.

He ran outside the amusement park, where it was now calm and still. All the cars except the dragsters' had gone—someone had driven straight through the fencing between the parking lot and the road, and the others must have followed. Gone into the night, they had. The kids had gone, too. The guard and the ticket man had also gone. But soon the fuzz would be arriving—or perhaps the army. Society would react severely to this. The air would be full of helicopters and night fighters, tanks would roar across fields . . . Reine found Hester's Thunderbird and slipped inside behind the wheel. He filled his mouth with powdered potato and tried chewing, the red steering wheel smooth under his hands as he hunched up, pretending to drive. The next moment a tremendous blow over the ear flung him to the floor, and the automatic gearshift opened a long scratch on his arm as he fell.

39 Reine was curled up in the back of Hester's car, the sun just rising above the tents outside. The glittering caravan had returned to base in the middle of the night. It was cold, and Reine's arm ached. The scratch hadn't bled much, but it ached to the bone, a numb persistent ache. He had slept for a while, and his mouth was as dry as dust. He would never have thought instant potatoes could taste so disgusting.

A lot of things were disgusting, hotdogs with strawberry jam, for instance. Or chocolate pudding with mustard. Or pickled herring and ice cream. Or black pudding. Or boiled cod with snot sauce. Or meatballs with sawdust. Or peas with plastic padding. Or spaghetti with diarrhea. But powdered potato was the worst: thanks for the eats, they were fine; sixteen sickened and seventeen died . . . pity died didn't quite rhyme.

What had happened? He had committed the unforgivable crime. Under his own steam, he had gone and sat in the leader's car, and he hadn't sat in the back but *behind the wheel*. Real dumb of him, of course. He hadn't seen who hit him, but to judge by the smell, it was Ebon, whose hands smelled of some disgusting cream. As he lay on the floor of the car, he could smell it very distinctly.

Now, he was simply awaiting his punishment, for Hester to wake up from his drunken stupor and give the signal for what was to be done with Reine. He hoped with all his heart it would be quick. If they were going to run over him, he hoped it would be the Mexican method, the one he'd seen in *Film Chronicle*. Prisoners were buried standing up, with only their heads protruding aboveground. Then the riders rode their horses back and forth across the prisoner's heads until they were mush. Naturally, they could use cars instead.

He fell asleep, slept for a couple of hours, opened the car door slightly, took a leak and fell asleep again. When he woke, it was horribly hot in the car, the seats stank of plastic, and the air above the red hood was wobbling about like jelly. The dragsters were waking up now and coming out of the tents, making coffee, drinking beer, or just lying around sunning themselves like seals. That was when he realized how old the dragsters were—they could have been Stig and Mom. But Mom would never have worn cowboy boots. Stig didn't have to dress up. Whether he was in his Sunday best or naked, he looked like a fat pig-pink North American cop. The only thing needed was maybe to do something about Stig's hairstyle; that could be a little more Elvis-like, fixed lightly with hair spray.

The car was standing so that the sun was shining through the back window. Reine pondered for a long time before daring to crawl over into the front seat, keeping at a respectful distance from the steering wheel, that magic wheel. But he couldn't resist the glove compartment; he clicked it open. What he found was not at all what he expected—no instruction manual, no spare bulbs, maps, or tools, but instead, a case containing a hypodermic syringe. He eased out the syringe. It was broken, the glass cracked so the needle went in and out with no resistance. Apart from the case, there were also a few small glass bottles in white cartons, all empty, except one with a little watery milk in the bottom. The bottles all had a kind of rubber capsule on the top. He spelt his way through the labels. "Inj. in-su-lin." There was a name on the labels, too: Staffan Rosén. Was that Hester?

Something was happening outside. Reine ducked his head down a little further, hurriedly stuffed the things back into the compartment, and closed it with his foot. Edsel had come out of the leader's tent. He stopped, bent down, and picked something up from the ground. It was an empty beer can, which he flung up into the air and sent flying about sixty or seventy feet away with a fine place kick. A small fair girl in panties and a black bra came up to him and gave him a paper mug of— coffee? Edsel said something to whoever was making the coffee. Several of them immediately left what they were doing and went over to the cars on the steep grass slope to the right of the camp. The cars were driven away and parked on the other side of the camp, leaving the slope free. They were making preparations for something.

The worst of the thirty-seven hot rods, the old Opel Kapitän with its panorama windshield, was driven up to the top of the slope and parked nose downward. More and more dragster cars now lined the two sides so that a wide sloping street was formed down the middle. They're going to put me in the car and roll it down the hill, thought Reine. Two dragsters in golf caps came from the other side of the camp boosting something along. He could only catch glimpses of them between the tents and cars. Staggering, they appeared with their burden. What the hell? They had Reine's bicycle above their heads.

The dragsters carried the bike to the slope and placed it in front of the blue and gray spotted Opel. They were doing something with the front wheel, something with a piece of wood. Now he could see; they were tying a board between the front wheel and the frame so that it couldn't be steered. They put the bike upright again and placed it right in front of the car, facing in the same direction. Then they seemed to stop. Edsel disappeared. Instead, Ebon came out and walked unsteadily across to the edge of the woods, apparently drunk. What was Hester doing? Was he dead drunk or just sleeping? Very slowly, Reine wound the window down about six inches or so. It was quiet outside, the only sound a ship's whistle far away and music from one of the tents. The amazing thing about the dragsters was that they were nearly always silent. They had made an incredible noise smashing up the amusement park, but otherwise they were quiet. It was their machines that were noisy: their radios, stereo tape recorders, and cars.

Hester came out of the woods with Ebon. When had he slipped out there? Reine felt cheated. Hester and Ebon went over to the slope, where Hester kicked once or twice at the back wheel of Reine's bike. But Ebon restrained him. So he went and sat on the hood of the old cream-colored Buick and started pulling off his boots. Suddenly someone tapped on the window behind Reine, and he ducked. Edsel was lying flattened like a great black spider over the rear window of the Thunderbird, almost as if he were about to crawl up onto the roof of the car. But he didn't. He just pressed his long Indian nose against the glass so that it turned white instead of brown. Then he suddenly let go and went away.

Edsel was to drive the old Opel. He got in and started the engine, revving it up so the whole neighborhood rattled. It was a miracle the gearbox didn't come out of the exhaust. The two holding the bicycle walked slightly in front and then suddenly started running down the slope. When they had got up speed, they released the bike, which rushed straight on ahead in its splint. Edsel let out the clutch pedal, and the old Opel took a leap forward and accelerated down the hillside.

The whole process was over in a few seconds. The Opel drove at an insane speed across the stubble in its chase after the bicycle. The bicycle came to level ground and started to slow down. Just as it began to fall, Edsel caught up with it and drove over it at top speed. A front wheel and a board flew up and circled in the air, and the rest of the bicycle was flung to one side out of Reine's sight. He could only guess at what happened next. The Opel drove around in narrower and narrower circles for several minutes, dust and exhaust fumes rising higher and higher. The smell of old rubber penetrated right through to Reine.

He waited until the Opel had driven away and the dragsters had returned to their usual occupations, cars, improvised dancing, and beer drinking. He figured he had nothing else to lose now, so he got out of the Thunderbird, feeling very unsafe. Despite everything, he had felt a certain sense of security as long as he was inside the car. Now the fish was leaving the aquarium and making its way onto dry land.

No one took any notice of him. He pressed his cap down on to his head and carried his bag in front of his stomach. He might as well go down and look at the remains of the bike, anyhow, to see if there was anything he could salvage and try to sell. But he never got as far as the place where he thought the corpse of his bicycle was. Ebon came running across to him, her knock-knees knocking, her booted feet spraddling outward.

"Beat it!" she gasped.

Reine stopped, holding up his bag for protection.

"Beat it, you rotten little jerk!"

She shoved him in the side so that he fell flat. He looked at her. Was she going to kick him? But Ebon didn't kick him. She just stood there panting, not even looking at him, keeping her eyes leveled above his head. She was slightly popeyed, and her lips were brownish-blue, but that was probably makeup. He crawled out of the way and got up. He wasn't scared now and tried spitting at her but could find no ammunition, his jaws still gummed up with powdered potato. He walked toward the road instead, backward first, then with long strides: forward march!

40 He had gotten a lift with a middle-aged couple in a reddish-brown Peugeot. The old man was driving, and Reine was allowed to sit beside him. The woman sat alone in the back with a miniature white poodle on her lap. They had an enormous sloping carrier on the roof.

"Children's Island? Is that in this direction?" said the man. He came from the south.

He sat leaning forward all the time while he was driving, his chest pressed against the wheel, the seat belt loosely hanging over his shoulder but not fastened.

"Near Norrtälje?" said the woman.

"We're going to Åland," said the man.

When they got to Roslagskulla, Reine asked to get out. For a while he had been tempted to go to Åland with them and buy some of those green goodies. But that wouldn't do; the couple might get suspicious. You just didn't ask for a lift to Children's Island and then ten minutes later change your mind to Åland.

"Are you sure you'll be all right now?" said the woman, putting her pale hand on Reine's shoulder before he got out.

He leaned away. The dog stank of fish.

"Sure, I'll be fine," he said. "They pick up the milk and mail in Roslagskulla. I know the driver."

"Nice to have met you," said the man, holding out his hand.

"Hope your mother will be better soon," said the woman.

He slammed the car door shut, bent down, and waved. The old man creaked off with his old woman, his little dog, and his oversized carrier. Reine went straight back to the bus stop they had just passed, carefully not looking in the direction of the amusement park. Or what had been one.

No Children's Island for him, he decided. The brief time he'd spent in the Peugeot had convinced him of that, quite calmly, quietly, and self-evidently. You just didn't put in an appearance six or seven weeks overdue. His place had presumably gone to someone else on the waiting list long ago, and whatever story he thought up to tell the camp leader, he wouldn't swallow it. And even if he did, there were still the others. He knew them; they weren't much better than adults. He would have to expect to be crucified.

It was a dreadful afternoon. His cold had held back out of sheer terror during his stay with the Power Gliders, but now it opened its taps, and his nose ran and ran. He hadn't packed any handkerchiefs in his bag. He tried blowing his nose with his fingers but failed, leaving him with his hand full. He tried using large leaves as handkerchiefs, but they were too hard and slipped in the slime. There was nothing left for it but to use his reserve socks of pale blue terry cloth. It was wonderful to be able to bury your nose and blast away.

It also turned out to be Sunday, and the one bus had gone. But worst of all was that he stole a bicycle. Who would replace the bike the dragsters had destroyed? Hardly they themselves. The police, for instance, would never dare suggest such a thing to the Power Gliders. The police had taken no action against the dragsters' camp all Sunday morning, although it must have been perfectly clear to everyone just who had wrecked the amusement park and where they were. Would the insurance company replace it? Reine didn't even know whether his bike was insured. If it was, Mom would be sure to be the beneficiary.

Was there anyone else? Some rich person who might manage without money or bike? There was. Next to the bus stop was a miniature golf course. As Reine was struggling through the bus timetable, a large powerful man in sweat pants and red cap but bare torso came cycling along on a brand-new ten-speed DBS Winner, a gold watch on his left wrist. He parked and went onto the miniature golf course without locking his bicycle. Not until Reine was riding along the road some miles southwest had those thoughts on compensation occurred to him. The actual theft had taken place quite automatically, as if Reine had been standing to one side and watching someone else carry it out.

Would he be put in a foster home now? The fuzz would never let him live with Mom; she had been guilty of immoral actions, hadn't she? Throwing an underage son to the winds, sneaking back to Stockholm to meet her lover, and then not even going to look for him. Where was Mom tonight, for instance? No, it would be a foster home. Who took in foster children? Older people who couldn't hatch them out themselves. People who had spent half their lives longing for children. They'd probably be pretty terrible to deal with, but he'd probably be able to fix a few advantages. If he got to someone fairly rich. If he showed from the start who made the decisions. There were quite a few blackmailing methods if, for instance, you wanted a new ten-speed bike. If you wet the bed a little every morning before you got up, that was good. As soon as you got what you wanted, then you stopped wetting the bed. A week or two later, you started doing it again. When you'd got your one-c.c. glow-plug engine, you stopped for a while. You could cry for your real mother, too, at night, and keep them awake. Good method. You could hint to the school nurse that your foster father came in and showed his prick every evening before you went to sleep. He would be allowed to buy himself free with a film projector.

Crying for Mom Harriet. The picture of Mom struck him right in the chest, so that it started making everything rattle and shake inside. Damned old Mom, how he longed for her. You had to be forgiving. She was the only mom he had. His longing for her was so intense he forgot his cold and hunger; he calmed his stomach by swallowing what he hadn't been able to blow out of his nose. All that Sunday he pedaled on like a maniac, floundering along on the oversized bicycle until he arrived at Sollentuna just before ten in the evening.

He flung the bike down on the walk and rushed to the entrance. Keys? Yes, he still had the outside door key. Up the stairs and over to the apartment. The door was locked. He pressed his fist against the doorbell. He stood there ringing at his own front door for as long as a quarter of an hour without anything happening. He couldn't see Mom through the mail slot, either. None of the neighbors came out to ask what was going on. He didn't want to see any of the neighbors. He wanted to throw himself into Mom's arms.

He got the roof hatch open with an effort; it had stuck since he had last been there. He crawled across and leaned over the edge of the roof: no stepladder, the balcony door shut, the apartment dark, the white clothesline gone. He crawled back and went down into the basement. But there was a new lock on their compartment: Mom couldn't know. She must have thought there'd been a break-in.

He at once realized Mom must be with Stig. Either she had gone back to Uddevalla—or she was with Stig. And Reine was not going to Stig's this time. Mom didn't mean so much that he could bring himself to go and seek out Stig. Reine went and rummaged in the garbage room. It smelled foul, but he found a nearly whole loaf of bread that wasn't too moldy and a plastic bag containing five bones of half-eaten pork chops. The bones weren't old, because they still felt lukewarm when he put them against his cheek.

The bike lay where he had thrown it. He fastened the loaf and bag of pork bones to the slim shiny rack and set off. There was an open area by the lake where they had an old cottage for tools and notices. He could get in there by the fire escape and a roof hatch. Reine and two boys in his class, Benne and Lukas, had climbed in last spring and crouched up there for half a field day.

It was midnight by the time he found the cottage in the darkness. Amazing that it could be so dark and yet so warm, like biking through an endless dark sauna. Any moment someone would pour water onto the hot stones, and his throat would immediately constrict so that it would be impossible to stay. Stay? There was no door to dash out of. He flung the bicycle down in the grass, grabbed the food, and rushed for the fire escape as if the Deluge were after him. Just as well it was so dark. He couldn't see the ground behind him and get dizzy. The roof hatch was open, and he climbed down into the loft. The smell was not good. Someone must have crapped up here. He stood still for a moment, trying to locate the smell more exactly. Then he crept cautiously away and lay down in the opposite corner, his crotch smarting from the bicycle frame. He managed to gnaw only two of the pork bones clean before falling asleep.

When he awoke in the stuffy heat the next morning, everything had changed. He felt happy. And free! A strong, self-sufficient person who had something important to carry out. The first thing he carried out was an inspection of his penis and scrotum. Clean slate. Then he lay down and stared at a fly on the ceiling, a big green enameled fly. Thank God he wasn't a damn fly. Thank God he was a clever intelligent being with two legs and didn't have to buzz around banging his head on ceilings and walls. Well, maybe that wasn't much to be pleased about. But he was pleased. Happy! For no reason at all, he occasionally experienced this feeling the moment he woke up: a calm, self-evident, and utterly irresistible happiness.

What should he do today, Monday the twenty-eighth of July? Not that there was any hurry, but maybe the time had come to resume his researches into what life was about? Was it important? No. The important thing was he was happy, and then it didn't really matter what life was about. Look after yourself and to hell with others; stop moaning and groaning, we're off to the gloaming . . . he should be someone who wrote verse and was carried around on a golden throne by a crowd of cheering admirers. Once there was a fly that simply wouldn't die . . . but that was a lie . . .

He gathered up his paraphernalia and climbed out onto the roof. What a day! The sun was a pale blue hole whirling like a yo-yo. The earth was a merry-go-round, the grandest and largest merry-go-round in the world, whirling around all day and night. Come along. Ting-a-ling. Everything free. Choose from horses, gondolas, or racing cars. He sat astride the roof and held onto the chimney. Christ, what speed! The wind tore at his cap.

His joy stayed with him as he rode into town on his shining new ten-speed machine. At Norrtull his cold came back, but he wiped it off his upper lip with a gesture of superiority. A little snot was not going to hinder Reine Larsson! When he reached the Stockholm City Library, some of the air had begun to go out of him, but he breathed deeply several times to get the pressure up again. He parked the bike and locked it. It had only a very ordinary lock. But what did that matter? This was a free country.

He half ran up the wide steps to the library. There were sixteen trillion books in there. At least eighty thousand of them were sure to be about Dag Hammarskjöld. That must be so, because he had once read that there were only four famous Swedes: Selma Lagerlöf, Dag Hammarskjöld, Ingemar Johansson and Ingmar Bergman. One of them was his dad. Guess who? Not Selma.

His spirits sank considerably as he went into the temple of books. There was a funny smell. People were behaving in a funny way, creeping about more or less on tiptoe. No one appeared to be terribly happy about there being so many books and about all the knowledge of the world being collected in one place; all you had to do was to help yourself. Chew through shelf after shelf, swallow a book-cart or two and knock back the circulation desk for dessert. The question was just where should he start? He felt uncertainty and apathy overwhelming him. No, for Christ's sake—don't give up now, just when you're so close to your goal!

An elderly man was seated behind a table labeled Information. Reine looked round, furtively took off his O.K. Co-op cap, combed his hair as best he could with his fingers, and stepped forward.

"Er, I'd like to see a book on Hammarskjöld."

"Which Hammarskjöld?" said the old gent.

"Er, what's his name? Dag, if that's right."

"Dag Hammarskjöld?"

The old man got up and took Reine into a neighboring room and pulled a stack of books off a shelf. He went through the stack and took out one with a picture of Dag Hammarskjöld on the front.

"Perhaps you'd like to start with this one?"

Reine took the book with the portrait on it. My mouth exactly, he thought. And my eyebrows. Cheeks and hair . . . He quickly whipped on his cap and pulled it down over his forehead. He went over to a vacant table and stood leaning over it with his backside in the air, smiling at the portrait. Then he opened the book. "Dag Hammarskjöld, 1905–1961. A Memoir." There must be some mistake . . . he hadn't been born until September, the ninth of September 1964! How the hell did all this fit together? Was he a testtube baby? Silly. There was nothing more to argue about. Dag Hjalmar Agne Carl Hammarskjöld had been cleared, and no court would sentence him to being Dad. No court would have dared to, anyhow. Those damned Hammarskjölds were far too powerful. They didn't care a shit about Reine Agne Larsson.

He closed the book, left it lying there, and started to leave the library's enormous circular hall. It was like walking in a gasometer. As he hurried toward the exit, he felt the ceiling lowering itself more and more quickly, as if he were in a gigantic piston engine. Out, out, before it crashes!

41 They had opened a new hamburger bar called Bronto Burger Inc. behind the parliament building. It wasn't very full, and Reine went in. The interior decoration was all in light metal, like an aircraft factory. Bronto Burger Inc.? Ink? Bronto Burger Ink. But their hamburgers didn't taste particularly peculiar. In fact, blindfolded, he would have found it impossible to distinguish a Brontoburger from a Big Mac. But perhaps that was because he had a cold.

If he wasn't going to be a professor, maybe he would be a gourmet writer, going around checking on all the hamburger restaurants in Stockholm. Free, of course. He would soon be very well known. The proprietors would meet him at the door and pilot him to a table laid with a cloth in honor of the occasion. Naturally, they would serve only their very best. But . . . what the proprietors didn't know was that the hamburger expert, Reine Larsson, also appeared in disguise every day. As a little old woman on crutches, as a dragster, as a drunk, as Batman . . . no, maybe not Batman. But they would never feel safe! When they threw the last warmed-up hamburger of the evening, with scrappy dry bread and French fries like stringy mice, at a windblown Polish seaman, it would be in fact at R.L., also known as the Famous Foodspy.

He was going to eat as much as he could get down today, for two reasons. He had just lost his father, and he had no less than three hundred and twenty-two *kronor* plus two contact lenses at five hundred each. He stumped over to the aluminum counter and ordered a Brontosaurus, the largest in town. Those giant burgers were difficult—too big to get between your jaws. But people must have bigger jaws in America. Everything was bigger there, wasn't it? For dessert, he took something called Cheese-Cake that tasted like muck, and a quarter of a grilled chicken.

Time to write letters: *Dear Mother. I have now returned to Stockholm. On a stolen bicycle. Realized I was not welcome at Children's Island. I was home too. Now that I know Hammarskjöld died in 1961 I have to think. I suppose Stig told you he tried to drown me . . .* Was it unfair trying to put Stig down? Why did one have to pity adults? It wasn't true that people grew wiser with age. Anyhow, it wasn't true that all adults were wiser than children. He should really put that in the black book: Discovery One—adults are not always sensible. But always stronger.

That idiotic business of Dag Hammarskjöld. He'd never really believed it, anyhow. It had been more of a game. But the more he had played with the thought, the more real it had become. A week ago he had actually believed in Hammarskjöld. But that was over now. What did it matter who his father was in the end? Maybe he didn't have one at all? Jesus didn't have a dad in the ordinary sense. Why then should Reine Larsson have one? Because with Reine Larsson, the situation was that he was the only person in the world, well, the only thinking creature in the universe. Jesus was only someone who dealt with people on Earth. If God existed and if there was life on the other planets, then it was likely that Jesus had lots of siblings, brothers and sisters with the most fantastic names—Josas, Jecke, Jusus, Knesus—whom God sent to the other planets to be the Savior there. Think of that.

He went into the metal-colored john and tried to crap before finishing off the Bronto Pronto, the quickest in town. Then he blew his nose on the stiff terry sock and thought: who cares about me? Stig cares not a fig! Now, now, no more idiotic rhymes. Limes? Aunt Olga from Volga cares about me. Was Lithuania by the Volga? Helene with no legs cares about me. But she did have legs—a couple of thin sticks in dark brown woollen stockings. Aunt Lott cares about me; Great Aunt Lott takes home the jackpot. Aw, hell, Lotta never got the jackpot. Mom cares about me. Probably.

The aim. That's it—he mustn't forget the most important word of all: the aim. Funny word. It sounded like a mumbling and mouthing of a whole lot of mmmmmms. The aim, the aim, the aim . . . He'd forgotten one person, and that was Nora. Nora, whom he'd met out sailing with Stig and that Esbjörn. Once there was a whora who called herself Nora. Now, what was it? Didn't she work in the NK store's perfume department? Not that they had had much contact, but Nora had fished him out of the water. Nora had been great. She wasn't nearly so old as Mom, and neither did she seem so neurotic.

Reine left Bronto Burger Inc., taking with him his bulging bag and a stomach like a sack of potatoes. All this roving about was constipating. And yet his backside seemed to have been flayed as if he'd had the worst diarrhea in the world these last weeks. That was because of the stolen bike; he might as well leave it outside the city library. The owner could pick it up if he happened to be passing. If he came into town from Roslagskulla, it would be natural for him to come along this road.

Reine trudged on down to the NK store, his undershorts a hard saddle inside his pants. People were sweating in the heat and had all kinds of silly sunhats on. Except a six-foot black man who was wearing a thick blue knitted hood. An ancient old crone was sitting outside NK tootling on a clarinet. He should have thought of that. Too bad he'd never learned to play. But what if he bought a plastic flute and some music and sat outside NK? Wouldn't it be more heartrending with a little child than that ancient old thing, who must have a pension, anyhow?

He went in through the outer doors of the main entrance, and it was as cold as a root cellar inside. He walked straight on through the inner doors and came to a barrier, behind which twenty or thirty women with bags and carriers were sitting, all of them looking straight ahead, not speaking, just looking down at the people coming in through the doors.

They didn't have clarinets in their hands, either, or black cases between their legs with a few coins in them. Pity. They would have made a whole promenade orchestra if wind instruments had been dealt out to them. Why was it called a promenade orchestra? They didn't walk around playing, did they?

The information booth was to the left of the women not playing clarinets. What about singing, then? They could form a choir if instruments were too expensive. Reine concentrated on the information booth. An immensely cool-looking and freshly showered woman was inside it. She was wearing quite a lot of jewelry.

"Looking for someone who works here," said Reine. "By the name of Nora."

"Which department?"

"It's my mom."

"What's her other name? Her surname, I mean?"

"She works in Perfume."

"Mm-hmm . . ." said the dame, looking in a red book, "Nora what?"

"She wears a wig."

"You must tell me what her surname is; otherwise, I can't look her up in this."

"I'll go and look myself. Where's Perfume?"

"Just behind you."

Reine turned quickly and started walking between the counters. He heard the information dame saying behind him:

"Wait a minute! I'm not sure she's allowed visitors."

He crouched down and dived to the right behind one of the counters. A quick glance across the counter. No, the old girl wasn't following him. She was probably locked in that glass cupboard all day, except when she was let out for a shower. No, heck. No good crouching down between the counters. They'd think he was trying to swipe things. Don't think I'm swiping things! So don't stare like that.

He calmed down, stood on tiptoe, and peered around. The worst of it was that all the women looked exactly alike. They were sure to be wearing wigs, the whole bunch of them! They were all wearing pink smocks, had bushy curly hair and fantastically lovely nails. Nora must be one of them, but which? He stopped by an older woman who looked nice. She was drawing lines on the back of her hand with different lipsticks. It looked like fun. Reine loved drawing on his arms and hands when he was bored at school. He used to mark the parts of his body so that he wouldn't forget what they were called: back of hand, palm, thumb, forefinger, kneecap, stomach, navel. He had to write navel in a balloon and then put an arrow pointing to the real thing. It was hard work doing it crouched down behind his desk, and his stomach kept wrinkling, so the lines were wobbly.

The woman drawing with lipstick held up her hand to another woman in gold slacks. Fantastic—as if they'd dipped the whole of her lower half in some of Aunt Olga's paint. No, there wasn't room for her in them. Reine moved very close and put on an inquiring expression. The gold woman suddenly shrugged her shoulders—clad in a black blouse with a leather collar—and moved away.

"Do you want something?"

The assistant wiped the lipstick off her hand with a rag, then blew on the hand as if to cool it down.

"Nora? Can I speak to her?"

The assistant scanned the large perfume department.

"Nora? Nora Nikkola?"

"She wears a wig."

"She's probably at lunch. I think she's gone for lunch, but otherwise she's in Aftershave."

The woman pointed her newly polished hand over to the left. Reine thanked her and went off in that direction. There were a whole lot of classy ads hanging down from the ceiling and a couple of cartons: White Horse, Old Spice, Braun, Brut, Safari. An assistant was standing behind the counter and she wasn't Nora. She was opening a shaver with a minute little screwdriver.

"Nora Nikkola? Could I speak to her?"

The woman looked at her watch and then at the shaver. She sounded as if she had a cold when she spoke—all her words seemed to stick in her nose.

"She should be here by now. Wonder where the hell she is."

Reine sat down on his bag and waited. His legs were so unbelievably tired that he took the risk. But the fireworks would probably hold. As long as it didn't get too hot. If a hen could hatch out a chicken from an egg, you never knew what might happen if a person with a sore behind sat on a plastic bag of dynamite.

There was no explosion, because Nora appeared within two or three minutes. He wouldn't have recognized her, but he realized it must be her. He could see it from her figure and height. Reine leaped up like a jack-in-the-box and said:

"Can I come and live with you?"

Nora flickered her long blue eyelashes and leaned over the counter— she smelled marvelous!

"Not until I've finished work. Come back at five to five," she said.

42 Reine was standing with his cap off, looking into a mirror. Short fair hair, protruding ears, guinea-pig cheeks, brown and freckled. Heck, he looked like a cross between Dag Hammarskjöld and Alfred E. Neumann. Nora lived on Norrland Street, scarcely five minutes on foot from NK. It was no ordinary apartment, but an abandoned office in a building that would be demolished in six months, or perhaps never at all. The office was in the shape of a large L, the entrance at the top of the L. Nora lived at the other end of the L. She had two rooms there, with a door in between. Both rooms had doors into the corridor outside. You could see right across to Stockholm Hotel from the window. Why did he always end up in attic apartments? Was it the desire to be an angel that attracted him?

Nora had an enormous bed in the larger room, almost like a small stage. Her clothes were hanging on a metal stand in the smaller room, but there was also plenty of room for the mattress on the floor. A forgotten office lamp was screwed to the windowsill and drooped down over the mattress. The mirror into which Reine E. Neumann was now blinking hung on the door into Nora's room.

Reine knocked on the mirror and opened the door. She was still lying stretched out on the gigantic low square bed. Four loudspeakers in the four corners of the room were playing flute music. Nora was still wearing the pink smock, but she had taken off her wig and had hung it up on a wig stand protruding out into the room from the wall above the bed. There were six wig stands, all holding wigs of various shapes and colors: long white hair, red curly hair, tight brown curly hair, long brown hair, and yellow hair in braids. Nora herself was totally bald and shiny. She looked like someone from Mars.

"Be a good boy and open the window, will you?"

Reine walked across the thick carpeting, which did not quite cover the floor and left a large area of old linoleum bare along one long wall. The window was stiff to open, but he managed. Outside was gray metal roofing covered with pigeon shit and oily dust. The heat from the metal came up at him; it did not smell good.

"Don't think it'd be any cooler."

"Shut it, then."

He closed the dusty window again and latched it. Nora had sat up in bed and was pulling off her thin smock.

"Give me a hand, will you? I've wrenched my neck."

Reine went over to her and pulled at one sleeve so that the smock slid off her shoulder. She had nothing on underneath. Her nipples were covered with pink scotch tape, two crossed strips with a wobbly edge above each nipple. Nora started picking at the tape and whimpered again.

"Pull it, will you? Quickly."

Reine bent down and took hold of a loose corner of the tape. Nora squeezed her eyes shut. He pulled swiftly, like pulling off a band-aid.

"The other one, too, please."

Nora leaned her other breast over, and he did the same with it. He didn't know what to do with the loose tape but finally put it under the bed, as if disposing of a piece of chewing gum.

"God, how lovely!"

Nora slid out of the rest of the smock. Underneath, she was wearing a pair of white panties no wider than a bandage. Two large velvet-covered cushions were hanging in leather straps on the wall behind the bed. Nora sat down with her back to them, her arms folded across her bald head. There was not a hair under her armpits, either.

"We're supposed to wear bras at work. Otherwise our titties can be seen. Then the supervisor goes nuts. So I tape them."

"Doesn't it feel awful?" said Reine.

"No, they go all numb after a while. Sort of go to sleep. Sit yourself down here."

She patted the vacant cushion with the back of her hand. Reine sat down with one buttock on the bed and his outer foot still on the floor. She smelled fantastic, not like Mom's rotten old night cream.

"Why shouldn't titties show?"

"It's not classy to show your titties."

Reine didn't really know what she meant. But that didn't matter. He didn't give a shit for the rules at NK, though they did seem to be pretty strict, making the female staff shave off all their hair and then wear wigs. But perhaps they got a bonus for that, like when Mom worked nights. Wig bonus. He leaned back and looked up at the wigs. He wondered if he should ask—that white one, for instance? He and Nora probably took about the same size in hats. No, the white one was too long-haired. The tight curly one, then? That might be practical when you're on the run.

"Isn't it hot wearing a wig?"

"Yes, sometimes it's like going around in a fur coat. But I'm used to it. I've worn a wig since I was eight."

"Eight?"

"I got some kind of rare virus disease just before I started school.

Every single hair on my body fell out. It's never grown again."

Reine shuddered. Just imagine losing every single hair just before starting in school. What hell you'd get! Baldie! Celluloid doll! Billiard ball! Scalpie. He looked at Nora. She was beautiful. He had never seen such a beautiful person. Fine-limbed, soft, and no hair. There was something divine about her. Perhaps she had no intestines? He pressed his cheek against the velvet cushion and tried to see her shoulder blades. A human being with no hair—would she be an angel with no feathers? An angel with pink bat wings?

"How can I amuse you?" said Nora, turning over and sliding down, lying on one side with her hand under her cheek.

"Don't know . . . got any comic books?"

"We could paint."

"Paint?"

"Each other."

Nora swung her long, slim legs over the edge of the bed and got up. She had a nightstand by the bed with a cupboard in it. She opened it up and started taking out small sticks of lipstick, rouge, brushes, eye makeup, and a spray can of body paint.

Fun. If they opened the door to Reine's room, they would be able to sit in bed beside each other and paint the reflection on a big block, for instance. All you had to remember was that all letters were backward; on his T-shirt there would be LAEMTAO EROM TAE.

"Get undressed," said Nora.

Hesitantly, he started rolling up his T-shirt from his stomach; his navel was dirty. He had thought it was his belt buckle that itched.

"That's it."

She pulled his T-shirt off and unbuckled his wide belt.

"I can do it myself," he said furiously, swiftly tearing off the rest of his clothes.

Nora stepped out of her white panties. She had no hair down there, either, only a silky cushion of skin. It looked as smooth as a cheek.

He took a scarlet lipstick and looked at Nora's body. Should he put a big wound right across her scalp? Or should he let her be an Indian and draw broad lines across her nose and cheeks? After some hesitation, he exchanged the red lipstick for a purple one and drew a big black eye round her right eye. Nora opened the door to Reine's room so that she could see herself in the mirror.

"Wife-beating," she said. "Use your imagination instead."

He asked her to sit on the edge of the bed with her back to him, and he painted a pair of stunted wings coming out of her shoulder blades. They looked crazy, like a cartoon. Those stumps would never hold her up in the air. Yes, possibly, if her wingbeats were as rapid as a hummingbird's.

He grew bolder and made her nipples into eyes, huge doll's eyes with long crooked eyelashes. Then he put a black Hitler mustache on her short curved upper lip. There wasn't even any down inside her nostrils—though he hadn't looked far enough in. No, what about turning her into a motorcycle? He was best at that, anyhow. Except for the art of lettering funeral texts. Of course, he could write A LAST GREETING FROM REINE on her backside, but that would be a waste; with a bit of luck her buttocks would make good cylinder heads. He drew lots of cooling fins in silver on her backside. No, not very successful. It looked as if she had sat on a hot grill. He turned her over again. If he hadn't been so stupid as to use up her breasts, they would have been ideal cylinder heads with the titties as spark plugs.

"What'm I supposed to be?" said Nora.

"Angel with a two-stroke engine."

Now it was Nora's turn. Reine had to lie face down on the bed. Nora sat astride him and painted his back all over with letters.

"What am I writing now?"

"H . . . I . . . Hi?"

"Right. But now?"

He concentrated intensely. K . . . no, R. RA. RE. Heck, it was difficult. Were the letters backward? He tried to see over his shoulder, but she at once pressed his face down into the bedspread.

"Cheat. It says REINE IS DUMB."

He struggled up, scooted over to the mirror, and tried to inspect his own back. What the hell had she written besides? I AM A TURD? WHO IS TALKING BEHIND MY BACK? No, it looked mostly like Egyptian letters, birds, curly peel, snakes—hieroglyphics?

"Hi, Tutankhamen!"

She was sitting on her big bed, laughing so the bed rocked. He rushed over and grabbed the scarlet lipstick to rub into her, but she evaded him.

"Careful I don't scalp you!"

They stood on each side of the bed, panting and glaring at each other, Reine holding the lipstick like a dagger. Nora put her hands on the bed and leaning forward, said:

"Are you hungry?"

For a moment he was disarmed, his stomach churning and rumbling. Wasn't there a smell of roast meat in the room? It must be seven hours since he last had anything to eat. He had gone around half the afternoon feeling constipated right up to his neck, and now suddenly it all let go and rushed down his insides. The empty space was enormous.

"Let's shower first."

The shower was on the other side of the corridor. Nora put on her NK smock, and Reine was allowed to borrow her bathrobe. He felt like an emperor in an ermine mantle as he shuffled out into the passage. The shower was in what had been a doctor's examining room, and there was a peculiar tubular steel chair still in one corner. An instrument of torture? You obviously had to put your feet on two plates so that you lay back with your feet aloft. He could just glimpse the sky through a skylight.

"Was that to get me to shower?" he said, poking the filth out of his navel.

"Sure. You don't tell a gentleman he smells like a skunk!"

She gripped his arms and pressed him to her.

"Don't believe it," she said. "It was because I like you."

When they had dried themselves, they went back to the bed. Reine crept down between the cool sheets while Nora began to paint in eyebrows, fix on eyelashes, and paint around the contours of her lips in brown. It was fascinating to watch her creating a face for herself. That's it. She looked Egyptian. Like one of the sculptures in the horror show, Treasures of Tutankhamen. She finished off by clipping a little pearl to one nostril.

"Theo has promised to invite us out to dinner," she said, pulling on a thin white dress, or something, over her head; she looked more Indian now, perhaps. No, she wasn't that dark: Egyptian.

Theo Andrén was the name of the old man who lived in another part of the office. He was waiting for them by one of his doors as Reine and Nora strode down the corridor, both barefoot. Theo was thin and brown, his hair thick and white. He had a huge beaky nose and was wearing white trousers and a dark blue jacket, a red and white bandanna knotted around his neck. He had gold rings on nearly every finger.

"My beauty," said the old man, stepping forward in his white shoes, taking Nora's hand and apparently nibbling at it.

"This is Reine. He lives with me."

"Another rival," said Theo, smelling Reine's hair. "Nothing smells so good as a small boy's hair."

Reine felt flattered. He was not used to compliments. He was usually told he smelled unwashed, that his face would grow a yellow film or his hair would become caked solid if he never showered. Theo looked like someone from a film of the forties shown on television. Or thirties? Or fifties? No matter. Theo used a cigarette holder, into which he poked his flat spicy-smelling cigarettes. As he walked down the hall, he almost danced, or was he practicing tennis? Then Reine realized what was missing for Theo to be in a forties film: a sailing cap.

They went to a Chinese restaurant called the Long March, just down the same street, Norrland Street. The old man who received them and showed them to a table, snatching a red card out of the glass, could have been Chinese, but the rest weren't. Their waitress had an accent that sounded Finnish, and the chef they glimpsed behind the pearl curtains was an Indian: And the matchboxes had the Konsum trademark on them.

Theo screwed a monocle into his right eye to read the menu. But he seemed to have difficulty keeping it there, because he could only speak with the left corner of his mouth as long as the monocle was in place. He was probably a villain, anyhow, thought Reine. Not a Swedish sailor but a German ambassador, the kind that tried to kill Greta Garbo with a poisoned arrow. Well, maybe that was in another film, but there was something fishy about him, because Theo spent ages with the menu, as if it were a betting form or a crossword puzzle.

"Theo's a sculptor," said Nora loudly into Reine's clean ear.

"I try, I *try*," simpered Theo, turning his monocled eye directly at Reine: it looked horrible, like lying on your back and staring straight into a gigantic microscope at the All-Seeing Eye, as if the whole of Theo's head were a melon-sized eye with a white wig and marzipan ears.

"But before that he was a managing director, an engineer," said Nora.

"Forgotten and forgiven, forgotten and forgiven," said Theo out of the corner of his mouth.

"He was head of Child's."

Child's! Reine clutched the arm of the chair so hard his knuckles whitened. So Theo *was* a fishy type, the spider in the web, the ambassador with the poisoned arrow.

"Child Technical Manufacturers," Theo added in an aside.

What did they manufacture there? Technical Manufacturers? Children?

"They make soap and that sort of thing," said Nora.

Reine burst out laughing, laughing so much that he had to wipe his mouth afterward. Child Technical Manufacturers on Children's Island making child-soap. That was going too far, the kind of thing you dreamed about at night when the room was too hot, or you wanted to take a leak, or you'd eaten too many doughnuts before going to sleep. But in reality—

hardly. There were too many surveillance cameras in Sweden for anyone to succeed for any length of time at boiling child-soap in Stockholm's archipelago.

"Spring rolls?" said Theo, staring with his giant eye at Nora.

"But it's late summer. Soup of Chinese king prawns. Sounds good, doesn't it?"

Theo frowned and thrust his cyclops eye at the menu. Didn't king prawns fit into the crossword? Reine gazed absently at the menu. All the dishes had numbers. The last number was 285. At McDonald's, just down the street, they had six kinds. Not one of them was soup. What idiot would order hamburger soup?

"We had Peking duck for Theo's seventy-fifth birthday last April," said Nora.

Peking duck? Why not. There was Donald Duck juice. But it didn't taste as bad as one might think, pressed duck. In fact, it tasted of orange.

After they had waited for ever and ever, at last the food was brought to the table. Oblong iron dishes standing on bowls with candles in them. Really festive. But by that stage Reine was horribly tired, feeling the boards in his back, the bare boards in the cottage last night. Theo and Nora were eating away like mad at all the oddities, Theo using chopsticks as if probing in a corpse with long tweezers. Reine liked the pieces of banana in the sweet-sour sauce. The rest was just monkey food.

43 Reine and Nora had had a cup of tea in Nora's big bed before Nora went off to work. As soon as she had gone, he had locked all the doors and curled up on the bed. At first he'd thought of trying on all the wigs, except the long white one Nora had taken with her to NK. But then he changed his mind. There was no need for wigs up here. Up here, in this white room, the sun blazing and glittering into it, he was above all earthly things. He closed his eyes and tried to imagine himself lying naked on a cloud.

Reine was not going to leave this room, or anyhow the apartment, until about the year two thousand. How old would he be then? Thirty-six. No, thirty-five, in his thirty-sixth year. That would be almost as old as Theo was now. How old would Theo be in the year two thousand? Seventy-five plus twenty-five years. Smack-dab on a hundred! No, ninety-nine, since his birthday wasn't until May. Which month was Nora born in? Not a frigging clue. How old would Nora be at the turn of the century? He couldn't imagine Nora a day older than she was now, twenty, thirty, forty? No, she must be younger than Mom, for sure. But the year two thousand? Then Nora and Reine would be the same age.

Reine had often thought it would be interesting if you could in some way be in communication with yourself in the future. If, for instance, there was a supersecret telephone number you could dial—and then you yourself answered at the other end, and you were fifty years older. Or twenty-five years older: "Hi—it's me. Hi, you. How are things there? Ahead there? Great. Am I earning a pile? How much dough do I have? How's Mom—she must be dead by now, if that's how you put it?"

Supposing he was dead himself in twenty-five years? Hell's bells. You called the secret number—and no one answered. Or you got a busy signal. Or maybe a recording: "Reine Larsson is dead." What did you do then? Throw up, or faint? But maybe it would help if you changed your name. Anyone called Larsson may change his name. Maybe you could dupe the future that way? Good morning, this is Reine Larshagen. Reine McLaren. Hi, there, this is Reine Hammarskjöld—aw, heck, that's old hat. Morning, this is Reine McDonald speaking.

But Nora had no telephone. However much he snooped around the two rooms, there was no telephone to be found. There were telephone outlets in both rooms, just under the windowsills. Their desks must have been there when it had been an office. What kind of office? The shower room had been a doctor's examining room. But these rooms? Pinch and Slack Inc., Brokers. Or a rope firm, Jerk and Twist Inc., selling materials for people who wanted to hang themselves. Not too bad: maybe he could send that one in to *Mad*, signed Alfred E. Larsson.

If you had no phone, then you had to write. Wasn't there something like that on the post office posters? Remember with a Letter? Remember with a Flower. Remember with a Parcel Bomb. Do Not Fold. There was no ordinary ballpoint in the room, but there was an eyeliner that looked like a pen, except the writing came out brown. There were paper and envelopes in a little drawer. Pink paper with a wavy edge, long pink envelopes smelling of—what? Mum for Men.

To Professor Reine A. Larsson. Congratulations on your epoch-making discovery that TV programs cause cancer. That is fantastic. So simple. Amazing that no one has hit on it before. Congratulations on your Nobel Prize, too. It is a pity the money cannot be sent back in time. I could use a few thousand. You have your salary. And commis . . . was that what it was called? *And commission on the discovery. I am very well. But in future I am going to wear lead underpants and bulletproof vests. Death to Swedish Radio; Greetings from Yourself.*

But it was not absolutely dead certain he would become a professor. Some other jerk might get there before him, so in other words, one should try to cover oneself.

Dear Nora Nikkola and Reine A. Larsson. Congratulations on your fantastic discovery of the Secret of the Pyramids. Thought the slumbering mummies had stoned you. Now the newspapers say you have found gold. That under every pyramid far below the sand there is an upside-down pyramid. Just as large and of solid gold. Greetings from Yourself.

Impossible! What was he thinking about! If he sat there trying to get himself a little gold from the future—then the whole system would be disturbed! Moving a grain of sand one millimeter would probably be enough to change the whole future. The whole damned Earth might fly into the air or be turned into glass! Or take Children's Island. If in one's ignorance one messed up one tiny detail, if one was unable to leave things alone, then maybe the whole damn Children's Island would suddenly turn out to be a Mefa, a hovercraft that started flapping its rubber skirts, getting up speed, traveling over the waves, and with a hell of a racket hissing its way out into the Baltic Sea, then a bit later leaving the

Earth like a great saucer and floating out into space on course for the Outer Galaxies. Best to stick to the carpet.

There was a knock on the door. Discovered! The Avenging God was now coming with Gran in tow, holding him accountable for blasphemy. Thou Shalt Not Abuse Thy Lord God's Future. Balls. If there was a God, He didn't have to stand there knocking on the door. He could just swish through the window like Karlson on the Roof. Up and open up! It was Theo.

"Am I disturbing you?" said Theo.

"Nora isn't here," said Reine.

Theo was not wearing a jacket today, but he had on the same white pants as yesterday, the same light net shirt and the same bandanna around his neck. Was he afraid of showing his flabby chicken neck? You could see it anyhow. Theo was so old he had started shriveling and rotting. His eyes would no doubt start shriveling up soon, leaving only the monocle. But he wasn't wearing a monocle now. Theo smiled with an incredibly perfect row of blinding white teeth. How was that possible?

"Dear Nora is toiling away," said Theo.

"She works at NK's perfume department," said Reine.

"May I ask what the young gentleman is thinking of doing today?"

Reine was stumped. Should he reply—lie here in the sun awaiting the year two thousand. No, Theo might be miserable because he couldn't partake. By that time, Theo would have turned into dust and bonemeal. At best.

"If I'm not disturbing you, I'd like to put this question to you: is the young gentleman aware of Miss Nora's imminent birthday?"

"How old will she be?"

"No one knows. But I would chance a guess of twenty-two."

Nora was twice as old as Reine! What a coincidence. It must mean something—that she was twice as tall . . . no. That she weighed twice as much, knew twice as much, ran twice as fast, knew far more about what she wanted to do about life.

"Is it today?"

"This coming Thursday. Nora is said to have been born at eleven o'clock in the morning."

"You mean we ought to fix up some kind of present?" said Reine.

"Couldn't you come over to my place when it is convenient, so we can discuss the subject?"

Theo swiftly put his bony old man's hand on Reine's shoulder and shook it, massaging his collarbone with his thumb. One of the teachers at school used to do the same thing when he was talking to him. The thumb only had to slip off the collarbone for it to hurt like hell. Lots of teachers were up to that kind of trick, since they weren't allowed to beat their pupils openly. One old bitch at school always talked with her mouth about half an inch away from whoever she was nagging at. She had the world's worst stinking bad breath, sheer gas warfare. And the woodwork teacher was masterful at practically invisible fouling in ice hockey.

Theo smiled and closed the door infinitely slowly, as if someone were fast asleep in the room. Reine crawled down into Nora's bed and pulled the sheet over his head so that it became a tent. He lowered his chin and peered down at his own chest. It didn't belong to him. The whole of the lower part of his body was nothing but a silencer and exhaust purifier. Only the head was the real Reine. And the hands—only the hands, not the arms. His hands were two pugnacious crabs defending his head against octopuses, tiger sharks, emperor vultures, and anything else in the bed. He let out a test fart. Wonderful scents for sure!

So Nora Nikkola was going to be twenty-two, was she? Then she was younger than Mom, because Mom was thirty—if she hadn't gone and got older since the last time. No, Mom's birthday wasn't until December. She was Capricorn. When did adults lose the ability to understand a child? Mom had done so long ago, not to mention Stig. Nora hadn't lost it—where was the boundary? Somewhere between twenty-two and thirty, apparently. Consequently, something happened to people after twenty-two. What? They must go through some kind of transformation, a violent change, like when a fetus starts breathing, like when you die,

or when the corpse chrysalis becomes an angel? Or . . . exactly . . .
when you got hair down there! Nora had no hair down there, so she was
not lost. He lifted the sheet above his loins, put his other hand inside
his underpants and felt around. No stubble.

He leaped up with an Indian whoop and hurled himself at his bag.
The zipper stuck, and he had to stretch the bag to get it open. Marvelous times for sure! There was his arsenal of rockets just waiting for
Nora's birthday. What luck, now he came to think of it, they'd never
have that party on Aunt Olga's roof! He who saves has. Pity about the
mugs, who keep their brains in jugs . . . for sure. Nora's birthday would
be celebrated with the world's greatest fireworks. They would thunder
and roar until the roof plates started glowing and air raid warnings
started howling in one part of the city after another.

He dressed, brushed his teeth with Nora's toothbrush, stuffed the
case with Mom's contact lenses into his back pocket, and went across
to Theo. Theo had six rooms at his disposal, all in a row along the corridor. There were no doors between the rooms, which meant you had to
knock at random before finding the room Theo happened to be in at the
time. All the doors had the same nameplate on them: Theofil Andrén,
ex-Managing Director (Eng.)

For the time being, Theo was in the first room, the one nearest the
outside door and the elevator.

"Please come in."

Reine pressed down the door handle and stepped in, feet first and
head last.

"Welcome, welcome!"

It was a peculiar room. The walls, floor, and ceiling were all painted a
strange dark purple color. In the room itself—totally devoid of furni-
ture—were a whole lot of mobiles put together from thin glass rods and
electric light bulbs. Reine closed his eyes and thought: that's it, he was
in the Universe. Theo himself was sitting on a cushion. He was not
wearing his monocle but instead had a short black telescope fastened to
his right eye. The kind called eyepiece? Isis? Spices?

"Please wait on the cushion by the door," said Theo.

Reine sat down cross-legged on a black cushion just inside the door. He had not taken another step voluntarily. He felt like a fly on the edge of an enormous web, the glass rods shining like spider's saliva. Touch a thread and you'll never get free. Theo is spinning a cocoon around you and will kill you by pressing his thumb under your collarbone.

The blind was half up so that part of the room lay in a cube of light, the colors of the rainbow glittering in the glass rods and light bulbs. Millions of flecks of dust were hovering in weighlessness. Reine covered his eyes with his hand and tried to look into the dark part of the room. No dust in the air there. Gradually he managed to distinguish myriads of small yellow dots like fly specks on the almost black walls.

Seated on the cushion, his head down, Theo shuffled himself over to the window and pulled the blind all the way down.

"Shut the door."

Reine pushed the door shut with his back. Slowly the universe took on character as his eyes adjusted. The few small light bulbs sent their thin rays around between the reflecting glass rods, the fly specks on the walls glowing. They were painted in luminous paint. The blue blind was perforated with fine holes in the pattern of a galaxy. Suddenly he heard a very high whirring note. Maybe he had been hearing it for a long time but hadn't taken it in. The note rose and rose. Reine tried to fix his gaze on the slowly rotating stellar system, but it was almost impossible; it slipped away. After a while he wasn't even sure whether he was still sitting on the floor, the cushion apparently slowly gliding round the room with him, as if there were neither Up nor Down, North nor East . . .

The blind flew up with a snap, and the sun rushed into the room as if someone had opened a floodgate. Reine's eyes smarted, and he thrust his head down between his knees.

"This is the world before God came," said Theo, shuffling across the floor with the cushion under his behind.

"Is this a sort of museum?"

Theo reached Reine and opened the door. They got up and went out.

"Have you seen this?" said Theo, pointing at a little peephole in the door.

"No. Are you supposed to stand outside and look in?"

"That's right. The room has to be closed if the forces are to be able to develop in peace. I haven't finished it yet. Among other things, the windows have to be better sealed."

"Why?"

"Because I have to extract the air out of the room so it becomes a vacuum. Everything has to be as it was before God came. Otherwise God won't come."

How crazy! Did Theo believe God would be created in that old black room just because you extracted the air out of it? That was childish. The universe was a trillion billion times larger.

"How's God going to have room?"

"Since everything is on a reduced scale, God will also be on a reduced scale. Not only in scope but also in power. The new God's power will be in direct proportion to the space."

"What'll he look like?"

"No one knows. No one's seen God under laboratory conditions. But I have a camera with a flash mounted in the ceiling. It's exposed automatically."

"What are you going to do with him then? Is he going to stay in there?"

Theo laughed, took the collarbone grip, and shook Reine.

"One thing at a time. One thing at a time, young man. At the moment I hardly dare hope God will come at all. The light bulbs keep conking out. Wretched quality."

Conking—it sounded crazy when Theo said it. Old men should stick to their own language and not try taking young people's words away from them.

"I'd thought of suggesting," Theo went on, "that you come with me to find a present for Nora. Her birthday is on Thursday at eleven o'clock."

Reine pulled out the case with the contact lenses.

"This is what I'd thought of giving her. Do you think they're suitable?"

Theo took the box, fished up his monocle, and started peering at the contact lenses with his long nose like a beak against the velvet of the case.

"Very becoming. Miss Nora loves trinkets. May I congratulate you on your choice of present. Must have cost a bundle."

"A thousand."

"Indeed, indeed," said Theo, handing back the case with a brief bow. "My wife of blessed memory used half-moon glasses with mother-of-pearl frames. Very decorative but a trifle obtrusive, you might say."

Reine went into town with Theo. It was one of the hottest days of the year. They decided on a coral-red swimming cap for Nora. The swimming cap was thickly covered with small rubber horns, so the whole creation looked like a freshly boiled hedgehog. Were hedgehogs shellfish? Theo was supremely satisfied with the choice and afterward took Reine out for tea and sandwiches in King's Gardens.

44 Nora was lying face down, her hands under one cheek. Reine was squatting on her bottom, his feet on each side of her waist, and he was embracing his own knees, on which he was also resting his chin. The night was black and sizzling hot.

"You've got so many ideas," said Nora. "Why d'you say so little?"

"Dunno. I suppose I want to keep it to myself."

"You must talk!"

"Why?"

"Well, Reine, otherwise you'll become an old man going around grousing to yourself, going around talking to yourself. With egg on your tie. I've never met a ten-year-old as old as you are. Sometimes you'd think you were seventy. Or older than Theo."

"I'll be eleven in one month and three days."

"I don't care how old you are on paper," said Nora. "To me, you keep changing. Sometimes you're no more than five. Whiny and impossible. I can't leave you for a minute. I don't know what's happened to you. You can't possess another person. You can't live inside another person like a tapeworm."

"What's that?"

"A parasite in your intestines. I think you could talk for ten hours at a stretch if only you dared. If you weren't so scared of getting going."

"Twenty hours."

"Reine, dear, lift your ass, will you. We'll stick together."

Reine rolled aside and lay curled up in the fetal position beside Nora.

"What are you afraid of?"

"That I won't be me any longer if I start talking too much. About what's important."

"What's important?"

"That I know who I am. But that no one else knows. No one else can be really sure. Suddenly Reine can turn out to be someone they don't believe. The Werewolf, or someone. Yes."

"What would you do if you were the Werewolf? Bite people's throats?"

"Dunno."

"Yes, you do."

"I'd bite the throats of everyone I didn't like. If they didn't . . ."

"Yes?"

"I'd defend myself."

"If they didn't realize you were the best and greatest and mightiest person in the world."

"No!"

"Yes."

"I'm only ten."

"Admit you'd like to be the best in the world. I would. So would everyone."

"I used to think maybe there's only one person in the whole universe

and that's me. Everything in sight is just bluff! A dream, or . . . well. I'm
sitting in a traffic tower with glass windows all around. And looking.
And deciding which can go up and which can go down. Which are going
to be allowed in. If I want to, I can shut the whole thing off, the mikes,
the loudspeakers, and . . . you can close the venetian blinds, too, and
close your eyelids."

"You see! You can talk!"

"Sometimes I don't want to do anything but sleep. Not exactly die.
But sleep and not have to wake up again if I don't want to. Sometimes
everything's such hard going. I feel like saying to hell with everything,
but that's so hard to arrange."

Nora freed one of Reine's feet, turned over, and pressed his foot
against her navel.

"God, how lovely. You've got such cold feet."

"But the hardest thing probably isn't thinking like that, imagining
you're the only person in the universe. That's pretty nice. You feel lazy
and tired. Or when you've had a beer. The hardest thing is going in or
out."

"What do you mean?"

"Going in and out. Out or into yourself, or whatever it's called. You
can't just sit there staring. At school. When you're with someone.
When you're never left alone. The worst is when you're never left
alone."

"Like now?"

"No, not like now. I don't want to be left alone now. I'd mind a lot if
you went away."

"Although I disturb you?"

"You don't disturb me."

"I'm trying to get you to talk. Although you don't really want to."

"Yes, I do."

"Why?"

"It feels nice."

"Because you can trust me?"

"Yes."

"How do you know that?"

"I can feel it."

"Where?"

"All over."

"Where most?"

"In my prick, if you want to know."

"That's nothing to be ashamed of. Would it have been grander if you'd said your heart? Or your brain? Or in your chest? Or in your gouty toe?"

"It would've felt cleaner."

"What do you mean, cleaner?"

"People are pigs. I think there's something else that's . . . well, clean. Good, clean. That doesn't smell or look disgusting."

"Do people look disgusting, then?"

"Inside."

"Me, too?"

"No. Not you. And not me. We're the only ones who don't look disgusting inside. We haven't got a whole lot of slimy things in our stomachs. Or in our heads. Not us."

"What've we got in our stomachs?"

"Nothing! We're too clean."

"Where's the food gone then?"

"It's incinerated to white ash. We're so hot inside that all the shit's incinerated."

"Reine," Nora laughed, pressing his forehead to her breast. "You're crazy."

"So are you."

"We're the only people in the world that're crazy."

"I want to stay here."

"Sure."

"How long can I stay?"

"Seven billion years. Then you must go."

"So you know why I don't talk to people? Why I never talk to people?"

"Because they wouldn't understand."

"Yes, that, too. But they'd take my strength away if they knew what I thought."

"What strength?"

"What makes me into me. What makes me know, because I do, know that in the end I'm the only person in the whole universe."

"What about me?"

"You're part of me. But you're not me. And not you."

"Are there other people who're also part of you?"

"Not any longer."

"But there have been?"

"Mom. When I was small."

"No one else? No girl?"

"Girls don't understand anything! Yes, one other who almost was: Dag Hammarskjöld."

"Why?"

"I felt we were alike in some way. I think he was full of hot air, too."

"Have you read a lot about him?"

"Teacher told us. No, otherwise I've only seen pictures of him. You can get a lot from a picture. You can see what people are like, just by looking at them. Most of them, anyhow. You see it at once. You can see if they understand, or if they don't. Understand what we've been talking about."

"And you saw that I understood."

"At once. When you were sitting there steering Esbjörn's boat."

"It wasn't his. He'd only rented it."

"Esbjörn would never understand."

"Nor would that Stig."

"Stig's never understood a damn thing."

"What about Theo, then?"

Reine had to think. Theo was difficult. Maybe Nora liked Theo a lot.

"Don't think. Talk! Say just what you've just thought."

"Maybe you'd mind."

"I promise."

"No, I thought Theo was difficult. I don't know. Some people are in fact difficult. And then I thought perhaps you liked him so much that you'd mind if I said he didn't understand."

"No, I wouldn't. He's not that close to me. We're just friends, that's all."

"Are you and I only friends, too?"

"No, we're parts of each other. You just said so."

"Like lovers?"

"No, Reine. That's not the same at all. Sex is something quite different. Then you only risk moving away from each other."

"Why do people do it then?"

"I don't know. It just becomes like that. Lots of men can't talk if they don't have sex first. It's almost like food. You have to eat before you can relax. Well . . . what about Theo?"

"I think he's a little bit crazy."

"But so are you and I. We just said so."

"He's nuts, I mean. Building a universe in one room."

"He's an artist. He's exhibited whole rooms in an art gallery. One wall was taken away. He exhibited a room called Paradise. It was like looking into a little greenhouse."

"Does he believe that business about God? That God will come down if he extracts all the air?"

"I don't know. I don't care, either. We weren't talking about that. We were talking about whether Theo was a person who understood."

"No, I don't know," said Reine. "He's difficult."

"I think he knows. But he talks so much, you never really find out what he's thinking."

"Haven't you ever slept with him? I mean like we are now. Just talking."

"No. I suggested it once when I was feeling attracted to him. That we should have sex. But he didn't want to. Just as well, perhaps. Maybe we would have found it hard to stay friends afterward."

"It's probably better to leave things like that alone," said Reine.

"You never know beforehand, that's what's so hellish. Whether you'll think the same afterward. Seriously understand each other, not just pretend to."

"I'm cool at last," said Reine, pulling the sheet over him. "Are you?"

"Are you going to sleep?"

"Maybe."

"Then be a nice boy and go into your room, will you? I can't sleep in the same bed as another person. Never have been able to. I must sleep alone. You don't mind, do you?"

"Oh, no."

"Yes, you do. Come in here when you wake up in the morning and lie here until I wake up. But off you go now!"

45 Theo's second room, counting from the elevator, was anything but dark. On the contrary, there were lamps everywhere. Reine counted eight office lamps screwed either to tables, walls, or the backs of chairs, and there were strip lights in the ceiling as well. Despite the bright sunlight, all the lamps were on. Theo himself was wearing a white coat and the inevitable bandanna around his throat. Did he suffer from some terrible disease that meant his Adam's apple or vertebrae were exposed?

"My dear young friend, it's not at all dangerous. You can leave whenever you like. It only hurts a little."

Reine hesitated before sitting on the peculiar slanting tubular steel chair, the same chair that had been in the abandoned doctor's office. Yesterday, Nora and Reine had helped Theo drag it into this room. Theo must have worked all night attaching all the electrical wires and plugs to the old gynecological chair. From the socket in the wall the current came from the mains and was then reduced in a transformer used for model trains. It had Märklin on it and was their largest model; Reine had a much smaller one for his own train set.

Six thin wires in different colors ran from the transformer to the chair—a red wire to the right armrest, a yellow one to the left, a blue one to the seat, a brown one to the back, a white one to the right footplate, a green one to the left—and finally, a purple wire to an iron rod sticking up in front of the seat. There was measuring equipment on a wooden chair to the right, including an ammeter. The various tubular parts of the chair were separated from each other with sticky white insulating tape.

"Do I have to be naked?" said Reine, shivering when he saw the tubular steel; it was sure to be icy cold.

"We needn't take the whole body at once," said Theo. "If you keep your shorts on, we can take your back and feet first."

"What if I burn to the seat?"

"You don't burn with a six-volt system, my dear Reine. And there's a switch on the right armrest. Look here. On—off. If you want to switch it off, you just do that."

Theo switched on the current, and the amp needle trembled.

"There you are—you check it."

Reine quickly turned off the switch on the armrest, scared of getting a shock from the switch itself. The amp needle sank and wearily came to rest on the far left of the meter.

"So you'll give me ten for five minutes? Can I have it beforehand?"

"Five now and five later," said Theo, taking his crocodile-skin wallet out of his back pocket.

"You haven't got any silver fives by any chance, have you? I save them, you see."

Theo had no fives in coins. Reine took the five note and put it into his jeans pocket before taking them off. He took off everything except his shorts with little elephants on them, then stiffly climbed up onto the chair. Aw, heck, it was like getting into a dentist's chair. He almost scratched himself on the upright iron rod between his legs.

"Take this pushbutton switch in your left hand," said Theo. "The more you feel of the current, the harder you press. Your reaction will be registered on this cylinder here."

On an old typing table in front of the chair was a thick cylinder, about the size of a large can of coffee, covered with squared paper; a marker pen filled with blue ink rested against the paper. The cylinder could be wound up like a watch and revolved very slowly when a catch was released.

"Can we try?"

Reine lay back all hunched up, convulsively holding the switch in his right hand and the pushbutton in his left.

"I must ask you to relax and lie back against the seat. Otherwise there won't be any contact."

Reine slowly lowered his back. But the tubes weren't icy; in fact, they felt warm and sticky.

"We'll calibrate first," said Theo, starting up the cylinder and the marker. The marker drew a thin blue line that was absolutely horizontal. "Now may I ask you to close your eyes. There's no point in your seeing what I do."

Reine closed his eyes and waited for the pain. But nothing happened. Yes, possibly he felt a faint whirring in his back. He pressed the button lightly. Suddenly he felt an unpleasant jab in his feet, so sharp he jerked them off the footplate.

"Stop, stop!" said Theo. "Keep your feet there. Otherwise there won't be any contact."

Reine switched off and put his feet back. He looked at the cylinder. In the blue line there was first a little hump; then the marker had taken a leap up toward the ceiling, slipping off the cylinder, and was now lying there dripping ink above the cylinder.

"Can I get down for a while?"

"No, no, I'm only going to put a catch for the marker."

Theo put a rubber band round the marker to stop it from going too high.

"Let's start from the beginning again."

"Well, I dunno . . ." said Reine. "It's really pretty awful. Can't you use a cat or something instead?"

"But we agreed it was human suffering we should investigate. Cats aren't interesting to us. Researchers are sure to have tested a million cats in a variety of electric chairs. But you're human, Reine. That's the difference."

"I think this is all a little nutty in some way. Trying to grade people's capacity for suffering . . ."

"Then I'll start again," said Theo, smiling kindly. "Supposing we presume all people are of equal worth, all people shall have equal opportunities, and no one person shall have priority over another. That's the premise. But . . . we must also start, so to speak, at the other end and try to measure how much suffering different people are exposed to. We know that some people suffer a great deal, and others less so. But how can we make such comparisons if we have no measurements? How can we say that Pettersson suffers more than Lundström, when we haven't bothered to measure? We have to create a unit of measurement for human suffering. For instance, slight toothache, one to two units. Gallstone attack, sixteen to twenty-two units. Molar tooth extraction with no anesthetic, twenty-five units. Do you see? You understood all that just now."

"I think you get lots of illnesses from all the radio and television rays everywhere," said Reine, sitting up.

"Hardly likely. Radio waves are non-ionizable, so not active. You probably mean radioactive radiation; that is ionizable."

"I mean radio stations—Radio One, Radio Two, and Radio Three."

"There's nothing wrong with your imagination, anyhow. May we go on?"

"No, I think I'll stop now . . ."

"Stop?"

"Well, this'll sort of go on forever, won't it? If you're to find that kind of unit of measurement. Pulling people's teeth out. Or giving them electric shocks in their feet."

"My work is only a foundation, my dear Reine. Others will continue with it. I aim to do nothing more than try to create an objective unit of measurement for pain, not to draw up long tables on how much different things hurt. Those were only examples. Don't you see? If we have an objective measure, we have opened the sluice gates to a whole new world, to a wholly new, factual, and objective thought process."

"What does objective mean?"

"Something that's constant, something that isn't changed by chance circumstances. Something one doesn't only think, but one *knows*."

"That sounds good. One knows too little about people. About death and all that, I think."

Theo rubbed his brownish-purple hands with their fat wriggling veins.

"Precisely! Precisely! One fine day we'll be able to measure what it's like to die. And when we know that, we'll have created a basis for a new justice. Human beings will be able to choose how they can die. When, how. We'll have laid the foundations for an objective judgment!"

That was an idea. True, Theo was nuts, but at the same time he was a person who had caught on, who understood. Nora was right. Theo was one of those people who understood. You could trust Theo. Theo had also been eleven years old, or almost eleven, a hell of a long time ago. He hadn't retired on a pension from that soap factory until now, when he had time to do what really interested him. That sounded hopeful. Maybe it wasn't true that all meaningful life stopped forever at puberty. Maybe you got another chance when you were really old?

"I'm probably not a very good subject for experiment," said Reine. "Couldn't we hunt up someone else? Someone who needs the money and isn't so . . . so sensitive."

"I tried when I lived out in Äppelviken," said Theo, gloomily. "I hired an old alcoholic. But he just kept falling asleep. Nothing affected him at all. I must have someone young and fresh. Like you. Or like . . ."

Nora! Reine hadn't heard her coming into the corridor. Suddenly she was standing there in the doorway.

"Whatever have you been making today? A sewing machine?"

"Mankind is the measure of all things," said Theo, bowing slightly. "Young Reine and I have been devoting ourselves to weak current techniques. But I realize I must do without him now."

"He'll have to decide that for himself, won't he?" said Nora.

"I'll come with you," said Reine, gathering up his clothes. "Can't we go and shower?"

46 They celebrated Nora's birthday early on Thursday morning. The birthday girl sat up in bed and drank tea Reine had made. She had her red hedgehog swimming cap on her head, and the case with the contact lenses in it lay open on the nightstand, the fragments of glass glimmering like diamonds. Theo sat upright on a chair a long way away from the bed, making conversation. Reine was sitting on a corner of the bed with one leg tucked under him and the other foot on the floor, like a page, a guard. The ceremony was not to take longer than fifteen minutes, because Nora had to be off to NK, or rather, she first had to shower, do her face, and tape her titties. But they had time to decide they would go to Åland on Saturday, a late birthday cruise. It was just plain too hot to stay ashore.

After Nora had gone, Reine crept out into the corridor and waited around the corner for Theo to go and buy his newspaper. Reine had decided after all to be out for some of the time when Nora was working; it was pretty boring sitting up there for days on end, awaiting the year two thousand. And neither did he want to be dragged any further into Theo's calculations.

Theo left his bedroom, room number six, and walked down the corridor, feeling each handle as he passed to make sure the room was locked: the room supposed to be Paradise, with all the ferns; the room with every square inch covered with pink velvet, the use of which Reine did not know; the room where Theo had all his tropical fish; the laboratory with the electric gynecological chair; and finally, the Universe before God.

The front door opened and slammed shut again. Reine quickly followed in Theo's tracks. It was a question of not giving him too long a start so they might meet again on Theo's return trip. Reine also felt all the door handles, especially the pink velvet room. But they were all locked. Before slipping out into the hall, he glanced into the Universe. It was as dark as a wardrobe, no God flapping around in there like a captive gull.

Ten minutes later he was gasping for breath by the bicycle stand outside the City Library. The stolen bicycle was still there, but the seat and lights were gone and both tires were flat. Someone had swiped the valves. Pity it wasn't a cold wet summer. Now there was a risk of his fingerprints still being all over the bicycle. A good hailstorm would have done the job. If he'd had a handkerchief, he could have cleaned up the bike, shined it up some—but he hadn't. Now his cold had gone, there was no reason to get one, either. His sock? He sat down on the steps and unlaced his shoe, the sole of which was beginning to come apart in front, and pulled off his sock, which was just right as a glove. He was just about to start on the bell when he saw an acquaintance of his coming down the steps of the library. It was his ex-teacher.

Reine quickly got down on his knees, pulled his cap down with his free hand, and started rubbing the transparent plastic shield at the back. Would the bitch recognize him? He dared not even peep or breathe. The teacher's name was Berit Skruf, and she had been called the Gimlet, but later when she proudly announced to the class that she had come in second in the Teetotal Motorists' Association, the class had changed it to the Ginlet.

Reine fervently wished he could become transparent, as transparent as a jellyfish. Would you notice if you suddenly became as transparent as a jellyfish? Of course. You'd see it on your hands and feet, for instance. Reine glanced down at his grayish-brown ankle. The idea-experiment hadn't worked then. A dumb idea anyhow. Even if he had become transparent as a jellyfish or as jelly, his clothes would show. Almost everything you could see of other people was their clothes. Everything except faces. But it was clear the Ginlet would have the shock of her life if she'd put her hand on Reine's shoulder and said, "Why, hello," and then he'd turned up a face that wasn't there, like a plastic bag of water with dentures floating around in it. Teeth could never be invisible—they were too hard.

Reine had actually seen a transparent human being in an exhibition. A model of course, but full size. You could switch on certain lights to see the blood vessels or nerves or whatever the heck they were. Something for Theo. It'd be fun to be a person like that. Then you would attract attention. You could earn a fortune going into any old restaurant and eating. People standing around would each have to pay to see the masticated food going down into your stomach. You could race around like a living X-ray and scare the shit out of all the women teachers.

Reine sat down cross-legged and looked around for Berit Skruf. She had disappeared. He quickly hauled the bicycle away. Supposing the owner had come driving along the road in from Roslagen and had seen his own bike? Reine might be charged with stealing both the seat and the lights. He limped away with his flapping foot, past McDonald's, and into the park with the pool, where he sat down and pulled on his sock. Originally he had been going to have lunch at the McDonald's by the library, which he'd tried out before. But now the whole morning had been ruined, so he might as well go on into the center of town again.

What was it Nora had said last night? You shouldn't be so concerned with yourself. Not think about yourself, worry about yourself all the time. Because you're not that important. Yes. That was where Nora was wrong, and he'd said so. What is most important to me is me. Yes, Nora had agreed that was true. But in the long run it got dull thinking about yourself all the time. There was no risk of forgetting yourself if you also thought a little bit about other people. Well, I like thinking about other people—if they think back about me in exchange. I'm not the only one who has to be nice. I think about you, Nora had said. Your mother thinks about you. Reine had categorically denied the latter. That was just what Mom didn't do. Mom thought of no one but Stig, that old shit.

But Gran, maybe. Gran worried a lot about what would happen to Reine after death if he wasn't saved. Well, he'd face that when he came to it.

After Reine had had an early lunch at Daily's, he couldn't resist going to NK's perfume department. He was careful not to get too near the counter with toilet articles for men. She mustn't see him. He wanted to watch Nora working, to see how delighted customers were and how appreciatively her colleagues treated her. For over an hour, he fooled around in Nora's proximity, going up and down the escalators, scanning the magazine stand, checking on the cameras, or hovering by the candy counter pretending to choose chewing gum. She was so clean—and inhuman in some way. It was a miracle a person like Nora existed. Someone who was so nice you hardly dared speak her name. I love Nora, Reine thought. No, I mustn't love her. I'm not worthy of that, for one, because I'm a shit, a big shit who thinks about nothing but myself. And second, it would be insane to love her. Supposing she disappears! Supposing some damned adult rides into NK on a white horse, sweeps Nora up onto the saddle, and gallops away.

47 Early Saturday morning, they took a cab to the Åland boat. Reine had hardly been able to sleep all night. What a day it was going to be! He wanted to forget he'd ever been on the Åland ferry before. This was something quite different. It was called Åland—but in actual fact he was on his way to America. Or the West Indies via Hawaii.

Just as on the previous occasion when they had gone sailing, Nora was wearing shorts, a man's white shirt knotted below her breasts, and a scarf tied Russian fashion low down on her forehead. She had left the wig behind because of the heat. But Theo was not worried by the heat; he was wearing a gigantic knitted white sweater with a turtleneck. So there *was* something mysterious about his neck! Reine himself hadn't much to change into, but he had washed his best T-shirt the night before, the one with EAT MORE OATMEAL on it. He was going to buy a new one now anyhow. They sold them on board. They showed off a lot about T-shirts like that at school. The Åland Line was not much to boast about really; the Tor Line or the real Swedish-American Line would have been better. But hell, who cared? He wasn't going to go back to Sollentuna school, anyhow. You only learned a load of old shit there, anyhow. And met dumb kids. Not to mention the school meals.

There was an amazing crowd on the quay, but Theo had reserved a cabin, so as long as they got on board, things would probably sort themselves out. He had also been able to book a table in the dining salon because he knew someone who worked for the shipping company. Most of the people crowding to get on board were elderly, really old, between fifty and a hundred. What would happen if a forgotten German U-boat hidden away in the Baltic ever since the Hitler war suddenly appeared and fired a couple of torpedoes into the hull of the ferryboat? There'd be a hell of a stir. Everyone would have to get into lifeboats, and whoever ended up in the water and didn't sink immediately would try to cling to the U-boat itself. Before the U-boat submerged again, the sailors would go along the deck bashing people's knuckles with their rifle butts. What the hell was that series called now? Captain Albatross?

Reine had his bulging bag with him. He hadn't given the customs a thought until he was sitting on the bed in the cabin. What would the customs say when they were coming ashore again? What if they looked in his bag and found it more or less stuffed with gunpowder? And what would Nora and Theo say? He had been very careful not to show them the contents of his bag. He had entrusted his innermost thoughts to Nora—and that had been good. But tell her about his fireworks? Nix.

"Phew!" said Nora, pulling off her scarf and revealing her shiny brown head; that head and that long slim throat—so beautiful, Reine felt a piece of ice between his testicles.

Theo fished a bottle of sherry and glasses out of his pigskin case. He had bought a triangular carton of juice for Reine, and he had some peanuts, too, as well as olives. Reine scooped up a handful of nuts, and gulped down the juice so quickly a vacuum formed in the carton, and the sides caved in like cheeks.

"Just going out to check on the boat," he said, scooping up a few more salted peanuts.

"We've got a table booked for half-past eleven," said Theo. "Can we meet up five minutes beforehand? The cabin number is two five four. Can you remember that?"

The morning was calm and hot. Yachts were drooping in the channel, the surface of the water oily and sluggish, as if the top layer had been skimmed off. They went south of Vaxholm and slid into the archipelago, Reine standing in a funnel disguised as an observation bridge. The black metal was as hot as an electric plate. The wind was hot, too, the same feeling as standing under the air vent in the main entrance of NK and turning your face up toward the current of air.

This is bound to end in catastrophe, thought Reine. It can't go on being so hot for so long. They would have to pay for it. The cold had to be stored somewhere, lying in wait for the right moment to strike back. Where was it? Over Greenland or Siberia? Quickly and unexpectedly, air raid warnings would sound, and the cold would come rushing in over Sweden in the form of hailstones the size of tennis balls. Or what if the cold came from below, creeping up from wells and holes so at dawn there were lumps of ice everywhere sizzling in the sun. More would come the next night. Then more and more. One morning the sun would not be able to melt the ice thrusting up from the interior of Earth, and ice layers would start growing until the whole country was covered. Then Sweden would start sinking under the weight, the country would be waterlogged and plunge down, the south first, the north up in the air like a ship's stern. Plop!

"Got any money?"

A boy of about twelve was standing beside Reine, holding out a dirty hand.

"Na!"

"Got a banana, then?"

"No."

"Haven't you been given a banana today?"

Reine didn't answer, but pulled his O.K. Co-op hat down so it wouldn't start swirling off in the hot air.

"Heck, ain't you been given a banana today?"

The boy vanished down the stairs, the only trace behind him some pink chewing gum he had pressed to the brim of Reine's cap as he was leaving. All Reine could do was to find a toilet, lock himself in, and remove the hat where no one could see what was underneath. He found one with a lock that functioned and sat down on the lid. He couldn't get the chewing gum off, either by poking or rubbing; it wouldn't budge. He turned the hat so the gum was in front, then put the hat back on. If he squinted upward, he could see the chewing gum like a gray spot through the brim.

The line at the souvenir stand wasn't particularly long; people seemed more interested in other kinds of goods. There were two kinds of caps: the same kind as the O.K. hat except that it had FINLANDIA in blue on it, and a baseball type with a long bill and BALLANTINE stenciled on it in black. Reine thought the second cap was the best looking, but it didn't really cover the back of his neck, and there was one thing he did not wish to be exposed to, and that was having "baldie baboon" shouted at him. He didn't buy a T-shirt. That could wait until the return journey. Ditto the green goodies. They would just get eaten if he bought them now.

The ferry was a lot like a large school in construction: long narrow corridors, sudden flights of stairs, vandalized toilets with walls covered with graffiti, a garage in the shelter below. It also slanted slightly over to one side. All the schools Reine had ever been in had slanted over to one side—not much, but quite obviously to an observant person. Sometimes when he was walking along a corridor, he could feel the pressure in his knees like going up an invisible hill, and on his way home he often almost slipped on his ass on some hidden downward slope.

When he had flushed the O.K. cap down the toilet, which did indeed balk at the effort, he put on his new FINLANDIA one and set off on his first voyage of discovery. The gulls flew astern as if being towed on invisible threads by the boat; sometimes a thread snapped and the relevant gull flipped over, fell to one side and soared away as if a newspaper had been thrown overboard. Islands appeared ahead, sailing along on the shining water with a thin layer of mist between the base of the island and the surface of the water, apparently insecurely anchored. When the cold came and violent storms blew up . . . at best the islands would drift into the lee, but some of them would be sure to tip over and turn upside down, earthy, wet, all earthworms and blackened tree roots.

Before lunch, Reine managed to make a thorough survey of the upper and lower car decks and the half decks, inspecting under the tarpaulins in the lifeboats and in the playroom, catching a glimpse of the sauna and the little indoor swimming pool where the surface of the water was also aslant: two pink old men were floating in the pool—if only he'd had a herring for them. He also saw a bunch of old women playing billiards and two crewmen locking an ancient drunk into a cabin, and finally he went on a prowl through the large bar in the lounge. There he had the opportunity of surveying a portrait of Urho Kekkonen, the president of the Republic of Finland. What did lemmin makkara really mean?

Reine did not appreciate the lunch. There was a large help-yourself table, but the only edible things he could find were boiled ham and small meatballs. Every time Nora got up to fetch another helping—she had a prodigious appetite—Reine slipped into her wake to keep an eye on her, to make sure none of the drunks made approaches or tried pinching her bottom, constantly gliding along just behind her shining thighs, an empty plate in his hand, ready to use it as in karate.

When Nora slid back into her chair with a cup of coffee and a Drambuie, Reine said thank you and left the table. There was to be no dance until the return trip, so for the time being he could feel fairly safe on Nora's behalf. But what if there were a dance? Would he be able to keep close behind her all the time so that no horny bastard got at her? He remembered what it had been like on the sailboat, how both Stig and Esbjörn had always held their ground and not budged when Nora wished to pass: pressing, wheedling, rubbing the whole damn time.

There were long lines of one-armed bandits wherever there was space for them, where a corridor curved on the stairways, outside the dining salon, along the wall of the cafeteria. That was what was different from inside a school. There were no one-armed bandits in schools, only coathooks to yank at.

"Want a choc?"

Reine spun around and there was the same boy who had been begging up in the funnel, now holding out a chocolate wrapped in pink silver paper. Reine hesitated—had it been bought at Butterick's? Was the choc full of sawdust, garlic, or gunpowder?

"Here—take it. It's okay."

Reine took the chocolate and put it in his pocket. The boy was no taller than Reine but much more powerfully built. His face was pale and his hair long and lank, of no particular color. It struck him that people didn't really have definite colors. When you said someone was red-haired, that wasn't true. There were no blue-eyed, pink-cheeked, brown or black people. Most of all, there were no redskins.

"On yer own?" said the boy, as he felt in a vending machine for possible returned coins.

"No, I'm with two acquaintances."

"Too bad. Y'can have fun here. If ya look after yerself."

"I look after myself."

"Wanna try the haycutter?"

Reine gave the boy a coin. He put the coin in and carefully pulled the lever—two tens of hearts with a jack of diamonds in the middle. They pressed the stop bottom for the tens and put in another coin. With no success.

"Aw, ya don't make money on them. There's better ways."

"Are there?"

"Yeah. But let's go down to the disco for a Coke?"

Reine followed his newfound companion down into the bowels of the ship. The disco was closed, but there was a side door they could open with a skeleton key. Reine hesitated—but he still hadn't committed a real crime himself. Only joined in in good faith. They went into a poky place containing a heap of red plastic chairs and a small Hammond organ and a pile of carpeting, red and shaggy. They lay down on the carpet. There was a liter bottle more than half full of Coke under the heap of chairs. The boy put his thumb on the opening, shook the bottle and handed it to Reine.

"Here, Nisse," he said. "Have a swig."

"My name's not Nisse," said Reine.

" 'Course you're damn Nisse."

"What's your name?"

"Dick."

Reine wiped the bottle with his hand and took a big gulp. It was good, a little sweeter than usual, maybe. But Coke was perhaps sweeter in Finland. A real connoisseur could tell which country the Coca-Cola came from.

"Are you on your own on board?" said Reine, handing back the bottle.

"Yeah."

They lay there relaxing for a while. The thump of the engine was clearer down here. The heap of chairs shook, but the heap of carpeting meant they didn't feel anything. It was great: you put your hand on the floor—thump, thump, thump. You lifted your hand, and it was like lying on a cloud, a shaggy scarlet cloud.

"Ya been to Åland?" said Dick.

"Yeah," said Reine. It sounded dumb. You shouldn't imitate others, but it was hard to resist sometimes. Walking around town recently, he'd noticed he was swaying his butt just like Nora.

"Nisse?"

"My name's not Nisse."

Should he say his name was Reine? On second thought, that was probably riskier than going by the name of Nisse. Being called Nisse could be considered slightly disparaging and dumb. But Reine? Reine could be used for almost anything.

"What d'ya like about Mariehamn?"

"I dunno. It was raining when I was there."

"Yeah, Mariehamn's shit," said Dick. "I'm not going ashore."

"Don't you have to?"

"For Christ's sake, no. Have another."

Reine drank. This Dick guy seemed all right. Most of all, it was good not being alone. If Dick had had a buddy with him, it would never have worked. As soon as you were three, something happened. Especially if two of the three knew each other from the start.

"D'ya smoke, Nisse?"

Reine shook his head. Dick hauled out a box of cigarillos and lit one with a silver lighter. Then he shook the Coke bottle and breathed white smoke into it. Then he blew hard across the bottle top. The thick smoke swirled round in the bottle before pouring out in a thin white coil. The spirit of the bottle, fantastic! Reine burst out laughing. The boat was going up and down a bit now. They must have come out onto open sea. A sailor loves the ocean blue . . .

"Bottoms up, Nisse."

Reine drank. Unusually fantastically good Coke.

"That's that," said Dick, inhaling so deeply that the cigarillo hissed like a fuse. "D'ya like Cuba Libre?"

"What?"

"Cuba Libre. Rum and Coke. Really something, isn't it?"

48 Time passed—no, bounded on. There had been only three of them lying in the little room, but they were four now, the whole room red like the shaggy carpeting. The boys were red, too, as if red lights had been mounted behind their faces. Great! Shit, this was great! Sometimes he saw things very close, a nail, a hair, and the next moment the room seemed to be far away as if they had fallen down to the wrong end of a telescope. If he rolled his head, the figures fell around at the bottom of the telescope like . . .

"Heck, Nisse, sling it over!"

One of the newcomers grabbed the bottle—which bottle was that? Who cared? He'd never drink beer again. Beer just made you cheerfully sleepy. Rum and Coke. Rum. Jamaica Rum and Cocka-Coola.

The two newcomers knew Dick and were also about twelve. One was called Henry and the other Death. Henry, Dick, and Death. Sounded like some boy's storybook. Death had had an operation for a hairlip and had a white scar in one nostril like a frozen piece of snot. Henry had a big head.

"Stop tittering, for Christ's sake, Nisse," said Dick, who drank the least and had not changed in the slightest.

Titter, pitter, titty, nitty, Nisse—they could call him what they liked, because he was *content.* He'd never felt so good. A little clumsy, maybe, but suddenly the whole world seemed absolutely crystal clear. He was in control of the situation. All his past life had been a mistake, a mistake that had been put right by Rum and Cocka-Coolie.

"So go tell 'em!"

That was Dick again. Was it? Sometimes sounds and pictures didn't quite match, like lousy television reporting when someone talked and the sound came years later. Yes, it was Dick. Reine had said he had to go up and tell them he wasn't going ashore in Mariehamn. Were they there already? He looked at his watch—he could see the hands perfectly but couldn't tell the time. Time had been abolished. Good. Never again would he be scared of being late.

Reine got up unsteadily. Lucky he was a hardened sailor. His cheeks felt tight. Suddenly he didn't know what his expression was like, just like the watch. The wrinkles and creases were in a certain position— but what the hell did that mean?

"Tell 'em you've been eating liqueur chocs."

Death with the hairlip scar proffered that advice. Reine was just about to reply shut yer face, but that would have been nasty. Why shouldn't you be nasty? Why shouldn't you kick a hairlipped bastard in the face? And tip all the handicapped people overboard. You'd have to have two planks, of course, for the wheelchairs. The others would have to make do with one. That would be placed upright. They would have to cling to it at the top and then you bent the plank back and let go—sssscccchhhhwiiiiiish—plop!

Cabin number two five four, cabin number two five four, cabin number cabin? Cab number forty-eight. A moment later, Reine was sitting across a cabin corridor untangling his shoelaces. So much happened outside your eyes. Great big taps turning counter-clockwise, a river with pine trees. A flagpole. A damn big old boat close to. Everything living its own life. Time raced on, events falling like pictures off a wall. He only had to keep together. He tensed his back against the corridor wall, his feet pressed against the other side. He was not going to be washed away.

"Reine? Is that you?"

It was Nora. It was Nora, all right. A smiling face, a body standing close by.

"Are you feeling seasick?"

Impossible to answer; if he'd as much as parted his lips he'd have thrown up a cascade straight out like a watering can. A cascade of chocolate.

He was kneeling over the toilet. Someone was holding his forehead with a towel. He had stopped throwing up now; once more and his stomach would have ripped apart like tearing a newspaper in two.

"Can I sleep?" he said. He couldn't speak without splitting open his head.

They put him in the cabin with towels all around him.

"You go on ashore," he said.

"When you've gone to sleep," said Nora. "I've promised to buy some meat."

Then Reine fell asleep. He was awakened by someone banging loudly and urgently on the door. It was dim in the cabin, only a night light on. A note saying "We've gone ashore. Coming back soon. Nora" was lying on the round plastic white table under a glass of water. He felt as if he had fallen on his head in the street. But his thoughts were functioning pretty much as usual, which meant they more or less hung together. He grabbed his new hat and jammed it down over his forehead. That was better, the cracks in his skull clamped together.

Henry, Dick, and Death were outside the door, Death swaying a little, the other two quite steady. They said nothing. The moment he opened the door, they stepped in and looked all around, fingering everything.

"Bad, eh?"

Reine nodded. He felt bad. Dick had a flat liqueur bottle with something red in it. He unscrewed the top and handed it over. The smell of liquor exploded in Reine's nose, like pulling a spew string.

"Help yerself, Nisse," said Dick. "Help yerself."

Reine took a big gulp of the slippery liqueur. It tasted like raspberry jellybeans. He realized he was hugely hungry and took another gulp. Then he sat on the bunk for a few minutes with his head in his hands. What were the others doing—stealing everything lying around? Where was Henry? He'd been there a moment ago and the door hadn't opened . . . a drawn-out groan from the toilet solved that puzzle.

"Fucking boat's off soon," said Death. He spoke nasally, as if he had cotton in one nostril.

"Let's go down and clean up," said Dick. "No traces."

When Henry had finished, they left the cabin, Reine taking his bag with him. Before he left, he turned Nora's note over and wrote on the back: "Am with buddies. See you in Sweden. R." Suddenly he felt fine. No more cracks in his head. He'd felt fine for quite a few minutes. Calm, steady—no problems.

The others had swiped a few newspapers on their way through the salons. They went down and made their way into the littered disco.

"Gotta be out in three quarters of an hour," said Dick. "And not a trace."

"Christ Almighty!" said Dick. "Listen to this!"

BOYS RAPE THIRTEEN-YEAR-OLD GIRL. *A thirteen-year-old girl from Sollentuna was raped on Thursday in a Tensta basement in west Stockholm, by four boys of about the same age.*

The boys had locked the girl in the basement. A repair man heard crying and found the girl in a state of shock.

The boys have not been apprehended. The girl knew nothing but the first name of one of the boys.

"The name was Nisse," said Death, jabbing Reine hard.

"No," said Reine.

"Weren't you from Sollentuna?"

Death crept up behind him and locked his arms together behind his back.

"Nisse from Sollentuna. The rapist. How much d'ya think the fuzz'd pay for him?"

"Not a cent. Too young."

"How much d'ya think the children's department'd pay for him?"

"Save the Children, more likely."

"Damn good idea. We'll sell Nisse as a slave to Save the Children. But no checks. Cash only."

"Let go, you fucking asshole!" Reine managed to wriggle free. "My name's not Nisse. I've never been to Tensta."

"What's yer name then? Ya going under a false name?"

Reine tried to grab his bag and leave, but Henry was sitting on it.

"Yer name's Chimp. And ya haven't had a banana today."

"Gimme my bag."

"Don't ya want some banana liqueur?"

Dick had a yellow bottle, too, which he held out.

"Leave Nisse alone," said Dick. "Nisse's too small to screw anyone by force. He's got a long way to go to puberty. Look at his nose. It ain't long enough."

Henry and Death let Reine go. Maybe they hadn't meant it seriously. They seemed to be almost restless, as if they couldn't bear waiting until the ferry left Mariehamn.

"I think I'll go now," said Reine.

"Heck, no, you can't do that. This is where the fun starts. All the senior citizens is half-crocked by now. We're going to clean up now. We'll share out the booze, then go on up. Nisse, ya'll never forgive yerself if ya go off now."

Reine sat down again, this time on his bag so that no one could get it. They shared out the liquor. He had to figure on some trouble. Boys always carried on like this, he knew that. He was just not very used to it, since he hadn't been in school for a couple of months. Things like this happened practically every day in school. Someone was dragged into the can and had his dick dipped in paint. Another was shoved into the woodshed and handfuls of sawdust stuffed into his underpants. Testing. So many things had to be tested. How different individuals reacted to different things. The natural desire for experiment in boys. Drown a golden hamster, and you'll always learn something. But sometimes Reine felt the world was as idyllic as adults falsely described it—and then he was slightly confused when faced with reality again. Theft, petty crime, fraud, harassment, perjury, cheating, sloughing, torture, begging—that's what life was like in school. Not really any worse than being a shylock. You developed your talents.

They sat in silence as the boat started turning, the engines thumping and the light in the ceiling flickering. Dick and Death were smoking, Death's rigid upper lip gripping hard on the cigarillo. He couldn't make smoke rings. Henry let out a couple of measured farts. The atmosphere was expectant.

When the ferry was out into deep water, they left their hiding place. They spent the first hour looking around, buying candy, trying on T-shirts that they didn't buy, or hanging around the one-armed bandits and begging coins off people who won. Reine was happy. He felt like a lone dog which after years of mixing with people had suddenly found itself in a runaway pack. This was where he belonged.

They couldn't carry around everything they'd bought or "collected." Since the disco was now open, they had to find a new base. They took the simplest, a toilet in one of the cabin corridors. One of them stayed in the locked stall all the time to guard the loot. Death took the first shift, and Reine hung his bag on the coathook so Death wouldn't use it as a footstool.

They now had to find some suitable senior citizens who were getting sufficiently drunk. They ignored the dining salon—better to concentrate on the self-service bar that sold liquor in sealed plastic mugs. Passengers there really went in for drinking. Dick and Reine sat down with a reinforced Coke while Henry stood on guard by the largest urinal. They knew from experience that the old guys came waddling in there, put down their bags, and took a leak. If it was crowded, Henry reckoned with being able to slip off with a thing or two.

"Not so much liquor nowadays," said Dick.

As they sat brooding, Reine learned that things had been better before, and that new regulations had made it harder to buy liquor on day trips. But the customs men were idle, and the passengers just spending the day in Åland mingled with those who had spent several days there and were returning home. So far, it was not catastrophic, Dick said. But it had been better before, a couple of years ago. Then Dick had done this route with two older boys. They had got so much that they were able to sell some of it later on. Now they had to be satisfied with getting as much as they themselves needed.

A woman was sitting at a table, and she had downed four beers. They watched her beginning to nod off for brief moments. Dick had a white plastic bag in reserve, containing an empty bottle he'd filled with water, and some old newspapers.

"Nisse," whispered Dick. "Go and get the bag she's got down by her feet. Then I'll sneak up and nudge the old girl. And give her this instead."

Reine didn't hesitate. He got up, stood for a second or two to regain his balance; then together they went across to the sleeping woman. Reine bent down, and Dick nudged her.

"Sorry, ma'am, but is this your bag? It fell over and . . .

The woman dazedly took Dick's bag and eventually got it down between her legs in the place Reine had cleared. Dick took over her bag, and they set off in different directions to their meeting place. Reine went past cabin two hundred and fifty-four without batting an eyelid. He would go back there in good time. But now he was with the other guys. Adults would have to wait.

Dick was combing his hair when Reine went into the toilet. There was a man hunched over the square metal hopper with a handle; they had to wait for him to finish. When he'd stopped throwing up, they banged on the door of the toilet stall and sang out "P.A.L. Prolonged Active Life." Death opened up, and they all squeezed in. There was Finlandia vodka in the bag, two glasses that looked as if they'd been carved out of melting ice, three boxes of Fazer chocolates, "Wiener Nougat," and a Mesimarja. No tobacco.

Henry appeared a moment later with a half-bottle of Gordon's gin and a tin of Three Nuns tobacco. Now it was Reine's turn to guard the loot, and the others slipped out when the coast was clear. He was beginning to feel heavy-headed again, as well as terribly thirsty, but he dared not leave the toilet. He nodded off, but was awakened by the door rattling and a man shouting: "You flushed yourself down, you little pipsqueak?"

Reine groaned a few times and the man went off to another stall. One after another the others came back: champagne, Cinzano bitters, Larsen cognac, Skåne schnapps, Lakka, Underberg. Things were shaping up.

"Let's stop now," said Dick. "Otherwise we'll never get all this shit ashore."

"How do we get the shit ashore?" said Reine.

"We have to divide it up."

They divided it up. Reine was given two whole bottles of liquor, a carton of Underberg, and the Lakka as his share.

"Why've you given me the most?"

"Because, Nisse, you ain't got nothing else to carry."

"Like hell I haven't! What about my bag?"

"I'll help ya with that," said Dick.

"Nice of you, but I'll manage," said Reine.

"Yer pretty slow up top, Nisse, aren't you? Dim, even. I'll take yer bag. Ya get it back when we get the booze."

"You'll get that back right away!" said Reine. They were packed so tightly in the toilet they could only hiss at each other.

"Ya'll bring the booze to the Solna shopping center tomorrow at eleven. Ya'll hand over the booze and get yer bag back."

"What if I go get the man I'm with?"

An idiotic thing to say. They could keep him here as easily as anything, knock him down or tie him up. Or just go off with his bag as a pledge. He didn't have a chance. They didn't even bother to answer, just laughed so hard the spit flew.

"We could check yer bag if ya like," said Death, pulling back the zip a few inches. Jocke's head appeared.

"Hey, got yer brother in yer bag, huh? Little brother. He might suffocate in there, y'know."

Reine forced Jocke down and zipped up the bag. If they found the fireworks, he would probably never see the bag again. His only chance was to try to be a good buddy and keep them in a good humor.

"Only joking," he said. " 'Course I'll take my share. I'll take another bottle if you like."

"Ya got enough. Otherwise we might never see ya again, you old wino."

They opened the door and pushed Reine out. He stood in the middle of the tiled floor, a plastic bag in each hand, staring at himself in the mirror. By some miracle, the FINLANDIA hat hadn't come off in the crush.

49 He was lying pressed close to Nora. It was Sunday evening, and she had to be up early the next morning. He was awfully tired but couldn't sleep.

"Why is it worse to kill ten people? Why is that worse than killing one? If they don't know each other, I mean."

"I don't understand . . ." said Nora sleepily, detaching herself from him. The heat wave was still on.

"Well, you can only experience your own death. Not other people's. You don't suffer when other people die. Anyhow, if you've got no part in it. Or don't know them. Or know about it. You can't suffer for other people . . ."

"Maybe not, no."

"Why is it worse if a hundred die than if five die?"

"There'd be many more people grieving."

"What does that matter? They only grieve for the one they know. Not the other ninety-nine."

Nora yawned and stretched so that her joints cracked.

"Can't you talk to Theo about it? He's a specialist in precisely those things."

Reine decided to let her sleep. He stared at the alarm clock; soon time to be off. And yet he still couldn't understand this business of death and suffering. If every person was a whole world in himself, then it would be a great catastrophe if that one person died, as if the whole universe had blown to bits. The solution to all problems was just that. Imagine the joy if all the nuclear weapons simultaneously exploded by mistake. Everything would be a cloud of white dust within a second. Not a single person would have time to notice anything. The dead couldn't be unhappy. The dead couldn't be happy either, of course, since they couldn't experience anything. And since they couldn't experience anything, neither could they have regrets or miss life or yearn for anything. If all the bombs went off at the same time, there wouldn't be anyone left to grieve, either. Brilliant! The answer to all the questions at once. Someone had to take on the assignment of blowing the world up, as a service to mankind. It would be a great sacrifice. He wouldn't be praised afterward, because there would be no one left to do so. He would be wiped out himself. But what a tremendous unselfish assignment. He'd have to improve his mathematics, so he might choose science courses eventually. But he wasn't thinking of going back to school at all! Well, he would probably have to, to get an education, so that later on he could do mankind the greatest service of all: zaka-zaka-bang!

A few minutes later he was out in the corridor with his two bags of liquor. It had been a snap getting them ashore. The customs people had all appeared to be on vacation. He thought about keeping the Lakka for himself and getting drunk: he could say he'd dropped the bottle in the street. But it probably wasn't worth it. No risk was worth the loss of his own bag. Among other things, his little black code book containing his collected experiences was in it.

There was no sound from Theo. Reine tiptoed past all the doors, crouching low, the plastic bags pressed against his thighs to keep them from rattling. Neither Theo nor Nora had taken any notice of the bags. Theo had asked what Reine had done with his zipper bag, but he had said it was back at home; he'd had no bag with him on board the Åland boat. That was that.

Reine couldn't resist looking through the peephole into Theo's universe. Lucky it wasn't as easy to create a universe as to wipe it out. Then anyone could play at being God at any time. It would be a terrible muddle. Had chance laid any eggs? The small light bulbs were glimmering inside, the glass rods slowly dingling around. Wrong temperature maybe. Theo had only talked about extracting the air from the room. But had he taken the temperature into consideration? A few electric elements wouldn't have done any harm.

The plastic bags started hurting his hands by the time he got down to the street. No one would be so idiotic as to creep around here late at night with bottles of liquor in plastic bags. Reported missing as he was. Nora had warned him there was a lot of "prostitution" in the area. What did that mean? Something murky, of course. Drug peddling and that kind of thing. Mom wouldn't even let him go to Sollentuna shopping center after nine. Real dumb! What was Sollentuna shopping center to Stig?

He had figured on getting a cab. He could afford that, since he still had almost seventy *kronor* left from the money he'd taken from Mom. Taken? What about his own children's allowance? Did he ever get that? Never. Some parents put the government allowance into special bank accounts. But not his Mom. She used it for the *housekeeping*. What nerve! She got supplementary benefit for that—and rent relief. When he thought about it, he didn't owe her a darned cent! She had done nothing but exploit him since he'd existed. Got herself a whole lot of advantages just because she'd had Reine. Training, larger apartment. What had he got out of it? A miserable life with no dad. Well, that was all right if his dad turned out to be some dumb jerk. And that was a possibility, for why otherwise would his dad have gone and fallen for Mom. Only an idiot would do that.

An empty cab came along finally. Only a diesel, but Reine flagged it down all the same. You couldn't be all that particular at this hour of night. The cab stopped and the driver got out. Female. Quite young, but fat.

"Got any money?" she said.

Reine produced his entire fortune. Great—it couldn't be more than about twenty to the Solna shopping center. He got in and put the bags on the back seat. They drove off. He sat leaning forward with his head halfway past the bulletproof glass partition.

"How's business?"

The woman giggled. She drove well; she took no unnecessary risks, but neither did she let anyone pass her. Reine had often wished they had a car, like other families. But then he'd thought: Mom would have to do the driving. The nausea rose, and he closed his eyes. No way.

"Have you seen my little white rabbit?" said the driver, pointing to a box on the floor between the two front seats.

Reine looked. He couldn't see much—a lettuce leaf, a bit of newspaper. Possibly a pair of pink ears. But they could equally well have been parsnips.

"Wouldn't it have been better with a German shepherd if someone tried to rob you?"

"I took her with me so that she wouldn't get in my husband's way. He's got an artificial leg. He trampled the last one to death. He can't feel where he's walking. He was so miserable. He loves rabbits, and so do I. Her name's Minnie.

"Like Mickey Mouse's wife?"

"Maybe so."

They drove the length of Svea Road. Reine tried to see if the stolen bike was still outside the library, but the traffic light was green so there was no time to look. They went on round Sveaplan, Norrtull, Norra churchyard and up toward the Solna shopping center. On the hillside to the right, huge houses were glittering in the August darkness: advent stars or clambake lanterns?

He had the cab drive right up to the big yellow Renault billboard. He saw them from a long way away, standing around smoking by the steps down to the underground garage.

"Hi, Nisse. Ten past eleven."

He held out the bags but they did not take them. They didn't have his bag with them, either.

"Stop fooling around, Nisse. What if the fuzz turn up?"

They walked down toward a small side door into the garage. Dick had a skeleton key. It was easy, and they walked slowly down the steep asphalt slope—it smelled of new cars, a marvelous smell! They passed a workshop, some parked cars and a store. Beyond the store was a row of new cars, Renault 12 station wagons, all cocooned in some fatty white grease. Dick opened the back door of one of them. Dick, Henry, and Death squeezed into the back, and Reine had to sit alone in the front. Were they going for a drive?

Dick went carefully through the plastic carriers. Everything seemed to be in order. Reine's bag had been left lying in the luggage compartment of the station wagon. It was hauled out, opened, and every article accounted for. Jocke, the notebook, the fireworks, the *Mammoth Book of World Records* . . .

"There's a new edition out now," said Dick. "Yer lugging stale information around."

Reine took his things as they were handed to him, then the empty bag, then packed them all back in again.

"Let's have the Lakka first," said Death.

The liqueur bottle was passed around until it was half empty. Reine thought it tasted wonderful, like liquid cloudberry jam.

"Fuckin' junk," said Henry. "Only one thing's worse and that's egg flip. Tastes like shampoo."

Dick opened the Finlandia vodka and carefully topped up the liqueur bottle with it. He shook it for a long time, then let the bottle go around again. Reine drank—the taste of spirits was much fiercer this time. He could feel himself getting drunk, a confident feeling that everything would work out all right. He was invulnerable. It wasn't at all dangerous to talk.

"How did things go for you—did you get off the boat all right?" he said.

"Naw, we stayed on board, as ya see," said Henry.

Reine laughed. You might well say they were still on board, sitting in a well-greased amphibious vehicle that would soon start up, make its way down into the sewers, come up by the Åland quay, and zoom out onto the water. Absolutely festive!

"What about you, Nisse?" said Death. "You been screwing that Nora? What if you've put her in the club?"

All three of them laughed hoarsely. How did they know about Nora? Had he talked about Nora on the boat? Must have, though he couldn't remember it now.

"Belongs to your stable, does she?" smirked Henry.

"Great chick," said Reine. "I've been in on quite a bit. I'll say."

"Tell us, Nisse. D'ya all three screw each other? That old guy and you and Nora?"

"Cassanova Nisse!"

That was Dick. He was usually pretty quiet, but tonight he looked pretty blotto. What had he been on before? Thinner? Hash? Beer? Aw, heck, it was good to be among friends.

"Christ, yeah," said Reine. "We're at it all night. Not Theo, that is, the old guy. He sticks to his own room. Leaves the field free for Nora and me."

"What d'ya do, Nisse?"

"Do?"

"Yeah."

"The usual. In and out."

They burst out laughing and let the bottle go around again, this time leaving none for Reine.

"What's she look like when she comes?" said Death.

"The usual. She's just like all the other chicks."

"Hell, Nisse. Suppose ya do it with a banana, eh? Yer lunch banana? The chimp gives up his banana to bung it up his chimpchick's butt?"

Reine was angry, but stopped himself. They knew nothing. But it didn't matter that they knew nothing. They were no better than animals. Petty thieves! It would be an act of mercy to strangle the bunch of them.

"Here, Nisse," said Dick. "Let's go on to the vodka."

Someone grabbed his head—supposing his cap came off?—pulled it back, and pour liquor all over his face. He swallowed some, but most of it went down his windpipe, and he started coughing violently. They let him finish. Dick and Death lit up cigarillos.

"Any more bedtime stories, Nisse?" said Henry.

"You don't believe I've screwed that chick? You can bet your bottom dollar I have."

They weren't laughing now. Dick and Death blew smoke straight into Reine's face. Henry pretended to look at the roof. Reine was scared, but the liquor slithered around and washed away all doubts. This was Reine D'Artagnan sitting here with his friends Athos, Porthos, and Aramis, the noble defenders of Truth and Justice.

"Y'know what you are?" said Dick. "A fuckin' upper-class jerk."

"Who don't know nothing," added Henry, lowering his gaze from the roof.

Upper-class jerk? Was he, Reine Larsson, an upper-class jerk? He, who lived alone with his mom, and she living on welfare, and hadn't got a car, didn't have a house, didn't . . .

"Bourgeois prick," said Death, in fateful tones, stubbing out his cigarillo on the back of the seat just by Reine's shoulder.

"Hell, no," said Reine. "This guy here's on the run. This guy here's got no rich dad, like you seem to think. Wrong!"

"Upper-class jerk," said Dick calmly.

"What? D'ya think this guy hasn't been in trouble with the fuzz, hasn't swiped things, done break-ins . . ."

"Been in trouble with the fuzz, have ya, Nisse? What for? Parking in the wrong place?"

"Momma's little darlin's run away from home, has he?" said Death. "We should report you to the children's department, out of sheer pity. Before ya fall into bad company."

Dick and Henry howled with laughter, then the vodka went around again. Reine was not offered any this time.

"Got any money, Nisse?"

"Chickenfeed, that's all."

"Could ya be more exact?"

"Fifty-eight sixty-five."

"Put it in yer cap and hand it over."

Reine pulled out the crumpled notes and handed them over the back of the seat.

"In yer cap."

"Why do you think I'm an upper-class jerk? What evidence have you got, for Christ's sake?"

"The realities of life, Nisse. Yer cap!"

"What d'ya mean?"

"It shows."

"And y'can hear it. Yer cap!"

Suddenly Death ripped his cap off and held it out for him to put the money into it. Reine automatically ran his left hand over his head.

"New upper-class hairdo. Presented by Nisse. It'll be short this autumn. Half crewcut."

Death slashed out at Reine's hand, making the money fly all over the front seat. All three lunged forward and started picking it up. Dick got the most. No one dared swipe anything under Dick's nose.

"When are you going to Åland again?" said Reine.

"Åland?"

"Let's get going," said Dick. "Watchman'll be around soon."

They bundled out of the car. Reine got out, too. Death had pressed Reine's hat down on his own head with its shoulder-length hair.

"The booze, for Christ's sake!" shouted Henry.

Reine was ordered to fetch the bottles out of the car. In the dim light inside, he took the opportunity of smuggling a half-bottle into his bag. It was whiskey. Must be part of the stuff the boys had brought ashore themselves. He backed out and handed over the rest.

They jogged off through a culvert with bare granite walls. A firedoor blocked their way, but Dick had a key to that, too.

"Ya learn how to fix doors in reform school," said Dick, in an almost friendly tone. "But you've never been there, Nisse, have ya? And ya'll never end up there, because yer an upper-class jerk."

They ran down some rough wooden steps that wobbled beneath them. Suddenly they were standing on some railway tracks. Where the hell were they?

"So long, then, Reine Larsson," said Dick. "If ya go that way, ya'll get to the new Solna subway station. We're off into town. No point in yer hangin' around with us."

"Ya'd just shit on yerself, Nisse," said Henry.

"We're goin' on a little trip around. Y'know why he's called Death?" said Henry, nudging Death in the back. "He's gone all the way on the subway between Hammarby and Central *between* two cars. He had a buddy that fell off and bought it."

Reine stayed in the tunnel and watched the three of them disappear, their liquor bags swinging. Henry put his hand into his naked armpit and clamped down with his arm: a mighty fart, and the next moment they had vanished into the darkness.

The subway trains were not yet working. High wooden scaffolding rose here and there, and there were tools and materials everywhere. Spotlights on tubular stands cast an intense light on the whole scene. He started walking in the direction Dick had indicated. He had to get away as quickly as possible. There was no means of knowing whether the electric rail was live or not.

50 You had to die without throwing up. You had to keel over without . . . what was it like then: black or white? If you didn't experience anything, if you saw nothing with your eyes—what did you see then? Black or white? Gray? What kind of color was "nothing"? He had to rhyme without a dime. He had to stop without . . . a plop.

The Solna shopping center's almost completed subway station was as red as a gullet. Lucky he'd come in the back way. The right way was to take the escalator down into its throat and be tipped onto the platforms, endless scarlet caves, bulging walls, hanging ceilings, alleys, and pockets. When you'd been through the whole system you were shat out the other end like rabbit droppings.

He was half lying on a pile of old quilts the dynamiters must have left behind. He had soiled Nora, he thought. I took her in my mouth and turned her slimy and dirty. I sold her for three gulps of vodka. She'll never forgive me. Yes. But I'll never forgive her. Forgive her first for being so clean—not a hair on her body—and now being ruined and stamped in the slime by Dick, Henry, and Death. All three at once. He had to die without throwing up.

The rock caves weren't just red; after he had sobered up, he could see that someone had painted a mural of a forest at the bottom, an endless dark green pine forest, apparently in the autumn, since the forest looked bare and inhospitable. He closed his eyes and imagined the walls painted with pale green oaks, mad March hares, and grazing deer. He looked again at the endless pine horizon. That was Sweden: small scrubby pines and a ragged crow. There were smaller pictures in the gaps in the pine forest: a deserted road, a closed gasoline station, a country store, a little graveyard of automobiles, a bread van up by the crossroads; in the distance he could see a chemical factory spewing out shit.

He picked up the flat whiskey bottle he had swiped off the boys, opened the top and put the opening to his cheek . . . no, for Christ's sake! He got up, swaying on the soft cloth mountain, and hurled the bottle as far as he could, right across the platform and tracks toward the pine forest and abandoned red house.

"I hereby baptize you Children's Island!" he yelled, and sat down.

It didn't echo at all, no "craaaaaasssssccccch . . . . iiiiiii."

There was total silence. There must have been a large extractor fan somewhere, sucking out all echoes and unnecessary sounds, and grinding down all life to a powder. He lay down on the quilts. At last, at last, he thought, and fell asleep.

When he woke again, his watch had stopped. But his stomach told him he had slept a long time. He sat up; he was no longer alone. A man in blue coveralls was sitting on a wooden platform, painting a sign on the country store on the edge of the forest. A little farther away, two more men were sitting on a plank eating sandwiches, their feet propped up on the electric rail. So the current was not switched on. Covered with small grayish bits of cotton, Reine collected his gear. God Almighty, he simply had to find something to eat.

Without being stopped or even questioned, he climbed the long, unmoving escalator and came out into Solna shopping center. It was raining! He was totally paralyzed. It was raining right down on his head! That it could rain! That it could be *colder* than hot! People were scuttling between the puddles and laughing like children at the first fall of snow.

What luck! Right at the bottom of his bag, in one of his reserve socks, were two five-*kronor* coins. How had they got there? He had hidden them there himself at the bottom of his sock drawer last summer, before going to stay with Gran, so he would have something left when he got back. He might have been saved, just like Gran, he had thought. And when you were saved, what happened? Then you put ashes on your head and gave away all your possessions. But he who saves has; two shining five-*kronor* coins in a sock, for instance.

Life was a game again. He bought two packs of peanuts, a banana, and a Zingo. Then he found out about the bus into town. He felt fine. It had stopped raining, and the ground was steaming. Maybe he should go for a swim. It was nicest swimming in warm rain or just afterward, when everything was still. Pity he was so constipated; irregular habits weren't good for the stomach. He took the bus to St. Erik's Square, and then all he had to do was trot down Oden Street to the City Library and fetch the bike.

The stolen bike was still there, now somewhat defoliated, not only the seat and the lights missing but the rack, the chain guard, the reflector, and both rubber handles. The tires were flat and lacked valves. He unlocked the bike and tried it out. It wasn't too bad without a seat or air in the tires. Lucky he didn't weigh much. Before setting off, he counted his riches. Eighty *öre*. Not even enough for a small portion of French fries at McDonald's.

He floundered up Svea Road until he got to King Street and swung to the right into the Haymarket. It was an eternity since he had sat there on the steps of the Concert Hall and written a letter to Children's Island—and to Mom. He ought to send a picture postcard some time—to Mom, he meant. So she wouldn't grieve for him, thinking he was dead.

Now the question was whether Aunt Olga had opened up the studio again. She was scheduled to open on the eleventh of August. What was the date today? He looked up at the sky: clean and clear like September. September, probably. He hoped so, because in that case school would have started long ago—without his even noticing it or feeling it in his body. When you were sick in bed at home, you felt every single bell and every single break in your body—although it was miles from school.

Supposing it was the ninth of September today! Then it would be his eleventh birthday. Congratulations. Happy birthday! What should one give oneself for a birthday present. A moped? A trip abroad? A tent? That's it, a tent. A real mountain climber's tent, watertight and winter-lined. To withstand any old storm. He could put it up on the roof of the Palladium. Then he would only have to go down one flight of stairs to work at Aunt Olga's. What a flaming idiot he'd been—he'd recently had three hundred *kronor* and hadn't realized he should have bought a tent with it. It wasn't enough to have a good job; you had to have somewhere to live as well. But if he was really industrious at Aunt Olga's, he could soon earn enough money for a tent—meanwhile, they'd be sure to let him sleep in the store.

The building was unchanged. The Oscar Theater was unchanged. The bridge and the railway looked just the same as they had before everyone left for vacation. That was strange. Things, buildings, and bridges should change, too. People changed, didn't they? Time passed; the apples ripened. But not windows, stairs, pavements. The Palladium building was a strange dark-gray color. Now that it was practically autumn, it should be scarlet and bright yellow!

He dragged the bike into the stairwell so that no one would steal it, and took the elevator up. He remembered his thoughts about angels; only a few weeks ago he used to imagine he was a speedy angel stepping inside, taking little jumps in the air, feet together, whipping off his wings like lightning, and climbing in a swift spiral up the stairs. Lucky he'd got over such childishness. But he couldn't resist feeling one of his shoulder blades a little.

The elevator lurched to a standstill. Everything was unchanged. The stairs smelled the same; the elevator door was just as awkward as usual. Yes, there was another sign on Olga's door. A small square sign with black letters on it, just by the doorknob. He lowered his gaze and read:

INLAND REVENUE
Inspector's Office
Third Division

Inspector? Had he moved in and opened an office, or was it someone living in with Aunt Olga? He tugged at the door, but it was locked. Something wasn't quite right. The vacation had to be over, because that "closed" notice saying they would be opening again on the eleventh of August had disappeared. Now this damned old inspector had gone and moved in. And to crown everything, the bastard wasn't at home and available to answer questions. Where had Aunt Olga got to? Moved her studio nearer to Skogs Cemetery?

Reine trotted downstairs, incapable of thought, his brain simply refusing to function. Empty. Neither white, black, nor gray. Must be like that to be dead. Empty. But his body was functioning and did things, lifting his bike through the doorway, looking both ways, scooting across the street and up onto the sidewalk outside the porn shop, where he jumped on the bike, forgot himself and sat on the seat that wasn't there—ow—stood up, and set off. Then his body turned left toward the North Station Square, struggled across it and up a street on the other side, and finally parked outside Helene's door. There his body went in and rang the bell. If anyone was going to be at home, it would be Helene—so long as no one had finished her off out of sheer kindness, of course. There was no answer.

Reine pulled himself together. There was a tent store up by St. Erik's Square—he could bike up there and look at prices. Either he could find out by phone where Aunt Olga was, or he could probably get money some other way. By selling the bike? But first it would have to be furnished with a seat and a few other items. That might not be too difficult in the dead of night. You rip off things from me, then I'll rip off things from you—or someone else. It was a question of sharing the burden.

He parked outside the tent store. It was closed for lunch. Might as well go down to the snack stand in the subway and buy something with that eighty öre while he was waiting. Not enough for a banana, but anyhow a box of coughdrops. Good for his throat. He went back up again. Still closed for lunch. He had to do something, take some action. It was unbearable just standing staring into a store window, seeing practically nothing because of the reflections. He could see nothing but artificial moss, a bundle of fishing rods, and a row of red plastic anchors.

What about following someone just for fun, for a while, to pass the time? He used to amuse himself doing that now and again, choosing someone at random and creeping along behind, tailing him. It provided a little excitement in life. And practice. Reine had considered opening a private detective agency one day.

He placed himself by one of the crosswalks in St. Erik's Square. He would follow the fifth person crossing from the other side. The lights turned green, but only four people crossed, a female with twins in a stroller—how did you count them?—two old women, and an SAS captain with four gold stripes round his sleeve. The lights turned red.

His underpants itched, but he forced himself to stand still until the lights turned green again. A whole bunch of people came this time, because a bus had stopped on the other side. Number five? Number five— an old guy of about twenty, or maybe forty. Reine tagged on. The old guy, or young guy, went over to the tent store and stood very close to the glass, pouting his lips and putting in a layer of snuff. Then he started walking again—*back* the same way he'd come, across the street to the other side, the shady side of St. Erik's Square. Suddenly he vanished down some steps where a big sign said SQUASH.

Reine sidled after him, his head farther down between his shoulders than usual. The stairs opened out into a small hall. On the left was a counter full of rackets and a dispenser for iced drinks. Straight ahead was a long corridor. The young man Reine was shadowing appeared on the other side of the counter and tickled a girl who was already there. She disappeared and the man took over, sorting rackets, counting coins into a box.

It was becoming clearer; the old or young guy worked there. But there was something fishy about it all. Why had he gone right across the square, stood by the window, taken some snuff, and then gone back the same way? Reine thought he had the answer: he'd been taking his lunchtime walk. Private detectives mustn't be too suspicious. They had to realize that many people behaved in an apparently peculiar way. Anyhow, the whole place looked like a secret training camp for agents. The corridor on the left had a whole row of doors, and as Reine passed them, he read: Shower, Men, Staff Only. On the right there was no wall at all, only seven or eight squash courts in a row, like big white cake cartons without lids. You could walk up and down along the corridor and look down into them.

Two old boys in white trousers were playing in the first court, their torsos naked and hairy, typical agents. In the next one, two females in scarves were shouting like weight lifters as they smashed the ball around. Then one of them happened to tread on the other's foot. They glared angrily at each other, panting. They weren't agents but probably a cover for other activities. But where were the Chinese? The next two courts were empty, and neither were there any Chinese in the last one—only two Indians. They were part of the cover, too—Indians had never been any good at either torture or espionage.

The man from the counter was coming toward Reine! Heck . . . there was no way out! The man was carrying a gigantic bundle of crumpled towels in his arms. He stopped when he came to Reine and said:

"Hi, there!"

Then he pushed his way past and vanished down some stairs to the left.

51 When he opened his eyes, he was lying in a white room. White walls, white ceiling, and at the end of his bed, he could see a white tent like a propped-up sheet. The upper part of the tent pressing against his throat was also white. There was another color, too—stainless steel. Shiny knobs and bars. The whiteness was reflected in the steel. Scissors. He closed his eyes tightly. What had they done to him? He let his hands slide over his stomach. A bandage? Good; they'd cut the whole load of shit away. The Chinese had scraped away all that shamefulness between his legs. They didn't want him to grow up. There were already billions too many. Good, then he could go back to sleep again.

It was a nice dream. Mom was standing by his bed just as if it had been a hospital. She looked healthy and happy, pleased that it had at last been done. A child came up from behind Mom, a little girl he'd never seen before. The girl could have been three or six or thereabouts. She was holding Mom's hand.

"Reine, this is your sister," said Mom.

The little girl let go Mom's hand, climbed up onto the bed, and sat on Reine's stomach, joggling around. He yelled with pain. Then his naughty little sister said:

"The answer is, what do you want to give up?"

She went on jumping up and down, sometimes on her backside, sometimes on her knees or directly on her feet, as if his stomach were a trampoline. Each time she jumped, she sang out:

"The answer is, what do you want to give up?"

Reine woke up whimpering. He turned over on his side and felt like throwing up. Someone put a flat shiny bowl on his pillow. He raised himself laboriously and managed to bring up a few yellow threads. A hand with a paper tissue wiped his mouth. He opened his eyes: it was Mom. For real.

"Hi," he said.

"Are you awake now?"

The room came to order all around him, the window flying away and settling in the window frame, the light fixture rotating upward and settling in the ceiling. The sheet tent over the end of the bed stopped bumping up and down like a camel that had rushed into a Bedouin tent by mistake.

"I know I've had an operation," he said, taking Mom's hand.

Her stomach was only a foot or so from his face. Was she in the club? The stomach looked suspiciously round. Had that bastard Stig knocked Mom up?

"Where's Stig?"

"You mustn't upset yourself, Reine. But Stig isn't here any longer. He's in Sinai. They asked him if he'd like to do another stint in the U.N. force, so he went. He promised to send a card, a card especially addressed to you."

Mom wasn't pregnant. He could see that when she turned away to get him a glass of orange juice from the bedside table. It was the same old stomach.

As he sucked the juice through a thick bent straw, he thought: I know exactly what happened when I came here to Danderyd Hospital. He had suddenly felt very peculiar down there in that squash hall. It had turned black before his eyes, and he had collapsed on the corridor floor. Fainted? A fat old boy had picked him up; then they had carried him into a locker room and given him a glass of water. After a while, they'd put him on his feet again. Then he had passed out. So they had called an ambulance. He had been awake and felt fine while they waited. It seemed to have taken an hour or two. But it wasn't Stig driving. When he saw they were two quite unknown ambulance men, he had at last dared relax. At Danderyd, they had prodded him and asked questions, stuck in their fingers and wheeled him between different rooms on a stretcher. Then they had started phoning all over the place for Mom.

"They've taken out your appendix."

He nodded. He remembered throwing up at the hospital, and that his stomach was tender, like it was full of pebbles. Must be weeks since he'd last had a crap.

"But you needn't worry. There was nothing wrong with your appendix. It turned out to be perfectly healthy."

Reine didn't quite grasp it all. He let his hands glide down toward his crotch again; had they lied to Mom and cut off his prick after all? What did an appendix look like? Like a loose and slimy little prick?

"Reine," said Mom, sitting down on the edge of the bed, "I'm so terribly pleased we've got you back with us again."

"What was wrong with me if it wasn't appendicitis?"

"Don't worry about that now, my own clever little son. You'll soon be home again. The other children are beginning to come back. Micky. And that Harald you used to make airplanes with."

"Hasn't school started?"

"School? No. But we all knew you'd appear before school started. Even if you've been out on the roam, there's one thing you do have, Reine, and that's a sense of duty. You'd never miss school."

She stroked his forehead. That felt really wonderful. That's my mother's hand, he thought. She's only my mother—no one else's mother.

"I've just spoken to the doctor. He says it was small and pale. But it's just as well to be rid of it. Then it can't cause any trouble in the future."

"Did I say anything? When they gave me the anesthetic?"

"No."

"Not a squeak?"

"Yes, wait . . . in the recovery room, you said something. You said something about 'only twenty-five years left.' Don't worry about it. You were probably dreaming."

"Well, what about Stig? How long's he going to be in Sinai?"

He looked up at Mom's face. She was looking pleased and sad at the same time, tears running down one cheek, but her mouth was smiling. Not falsely but broadly and openly, as if she were just about to burst out laughing. But she checked herself. She worked in a hospital herself and knew you mustn't burst out laughing with someone recovering from an operation—spreading a whole lot of bacteria around.

The wide white door opened partway, and a woman in white put her head and half her body into the room and cried:

"Rounds!"

Mom leaned down and put her cheek against Reine's forehead. She smelled of garlic.

"I'll go out for a while while rounds are going on."

"Rounds? What the heck's that?"

"Just answer the doctor's questions, Reine. Clearly and sensibly. I know I can trust you."

"When are you coming back?"

"In a moment. 'Bye for now."

He had to lie alone for a long time before the round came. He couldn't be bothered with them, and they asked him nothing. They pinched and prodded, leafed through papers, mumbling about something. An old guy in white—the doctor?—he'd never seen before said:

"Ah, so this is our little astronaut, is it?"

Suddenly they left, pouring through the door like a Lucia Day procession. What had the doctor meant? Astronaut? Had he babbled when they'd anesthetized him after all? Mom came creeping in on tiptoe, carrying a bag of bananas. They weren't for Reine, but for herself. What luck! He wasn't allowed to eat just after an operation.

"You'll get a new bicycle," said Mom.

He nodded in reply. He wasn't feeling particularly keen on bike-riding, but he didn't want to upset her. She looked so tired, pale and tired like when she'd been working all night. Was it already the next day?

He closed his eyes and let his head sink deeper into the pillow—fabulous—like slowly sinking deeper down into a hot bath. Astronaut? He must have talked about flying or something. What happened to astronauts after death? Did they also become angels? He wanted to sleep, but then Mom would be upset. After struggling for a while, he finally managed to raise his eyelids and look at her. She had fallen asleep in the visitor's chair and was sitting there snoring slightly, the bag of bananas sliding down her lap. Dear old Mom. Dear awful old Mom, who had such awful taste when it came to men.

That would have to do. He didn't want to stay awake any longer. Put me in a glass jar like any old appendix, pour formaldehyde over me and . . . no, anesthetize me. Let me sleep as long as I like. But for Christ's sake, don't forget to wake me up on New Year's Eve in nineteen hundred and ninety-nine, so I've time to set up the rockets and see the year two thousand in. He fell asleep, multicolored ribbons flapping behind his eyelids, pale blue, green, wine-red, violet, blue, and yellow. Hi, Olga, see you across the Volga!

Ross Shideler

Born March 14, 1935, the youngest of three children, Per Christian Jersild grew up in a family strained by opposing literary and religious preoccupations. Jersild's mother felt her literary interests frustrated by the limitations of her life as a mother and housewife, while his father gained a sense of fulfillment as Secretary of the Swedish Evangelical Movement. Perhaps unconsciously responding to these parental differences, Jersild divided his own professional life, becoming a doctor on the one hand and a writer on the other. In his *Professionella bekännelser* (Professional confessions), 1981, where he describes his childhood and literary development, Jersild modestly denies any precociousness, though he knew by the time he finished high school that he wanted to pursue both careers.[1] As a medical student, he used to write before breakfast and even run home to write during his lunch hour, thus managing to publish two books while earning his medical degree.

Although he was first interested in psychiatry, chance led Jersild into an internship in social medicine and an eventual eight-year position with the Swedish Social Welfare Board. These years gave him unique insight into the labyrinthian world of modern bureaucracy, as well as material for future novels. He completed his medical career by working as an assistant professor of social and preventive medicine from 1974 to 1977. In 1977 he gave up medicine to devote himself entirely to writing.

Jersild was nourished on both Swedish and world literature. The dark pessimistic writers of the 1940s first influenced him, especially Stig

Dagerman, a writer whom one might describe as a Swedish existential-ist. Later, there was Lars Gyllensten, whose work still stands as a model for him and whose life happens to parallel Jersild's own: Gyllensten, too, is both physician and author, and one of the major philosophical writers of the generation prior to Jersild's. Alain Robbe-Grillet's famous pseudo-objective style, as in *Le Voyeur*, also set its stamp upon the early Jersild. Perhaps more important to him as a writer preoccupied with cultivating literary style, however, was James Joyce. Jersild admits that even now he occasionally returns to *Ulysses* because of its dazzling ar-ray of literary styles and techniques.

As influential for him as all these authors, however, was a course in creative writing, conducted by the Swedish poet and critic Reidar Ekner and attended by a number of people who later became important writers. The intellectual and creative stimulation Jersild received from discussing the work of Hemingway, Faulkner, Maupassant, and other authors with this vital young group confirmed his own intention to be-come a writer. Jersild produced his first collection of short stories within the context of this group.

This collection, *Räknelära* (Algebra), 1960, contained the seeds of much of his later work; indeed, he has used characters or ideas from these early stories in many of his novels. His first two novels *Till var-mare länder* (To warmer lands), 1961, and *Ledig lördag* (Saturday off), 1963, received minimal critical attention, although *Till varmare länder* has since become a minor Swedish classic and was performed as an op-era. His third novel, *Calvinols resa genom världen* (Calvinol's voyage around the world), 1965, brought him critical success, however. This story of a Rabelaisian doctor named Calvinol combines the picaresque and the fantastic. (In fact, the title character is named for the Italian author Italo Calvino, whose *Baron in the Trees* made a great impression upon Jersild; his fascination with the fantastic was clearly influenced by Calvino's work.) Moving blithely and randomly through various pe-riods of history, *Calvinol* ridicules the glorification of war and also sati-rizes other less deadly human foibles, including the medical profession.

One of the most striking characteristics of the book is that it parodies traditional literary narrative by giving its hero different, often contradictory, identities and even providing alternative versions of his tall tales. This balance between plot, style, and meaning has become a Jersild trademark.

Jersild's extraordinary reception by the reading public, as well as by critics and fellow writers, derives from the recognition of his skillful mixture of social satire and literary style. He has managed to ride the delicate line between popular writer and serious author, and his success in doing so has resulted in numerous literary prizes and, by Swedish standards, outstanding sales.

It is impossible to discuss all of Jersild's sixteen novels here, but summarizing a few will provide a context for *Children's Island*. For instance, *Grisjakten* (The pig hunt), 1968, draws upon the author's own experiences in the Swedish bureaucracy.[2] It tells the story of Lennart Siljeberg, a bureaucrat who accepts without question the assignment to eradicate the entire population of pigs on the Swedish island of Gotland. The bureaucratic language and lockstep efficiency that characterize Siljeberg are comic, but the novel's implications are dark: an unthinking and dehumanizing bureaucratic system and language can lead to the kinds of crimes committed by the Nazis in World War II. *Vi ses i Song My* (I'll see you in Song My), 1970, picks up the theme of bureaucracy and language, this time through psychologist Rolf Nylander, who attempts to liberalize the army by participating in it. Inevitably, of course, Nylander ends up becoming a part of the system, and his psychological techniques for democratizing the army simply sustain the military structure.

In 1973 Jersild published two novels, *Stumpen* (Shorty; *Stumpen* is a slang term for a little man) and *Djurdoktorn* (The animal doctor). *Stumpen* appeared first as a magazine serial. It tells in a delicate and at times poignant fashion the story of a Stockholm alcoholic who fails to be helped by the social and medical welfare system designed for people like him. *Djurdoktorn*, one of Jersild's major books, takes place in the near future at a gigantic medical research institute. The main character, Evy Beck, is hired there because of her minority status (she is a woman over fifty), which has enabled her to complete her veterinary education. She becomes the protector and caretaker of animals at the institute, but her concern for the animals begins to interfere with the institute's research. Eventually, however, under the pressure of this computerized and bureaucratic world, Evy's resistance crumbles, and she accepts the role defined for her. Jersild's own concern with the mistreatment of animals is one of the central themes of this novel, but this theme parallels the clash between the demands of society and the needs of the individual human being.[3]

Babels hus (The house of Babel), 1978, has become Jersild's most popular novel—indeed, one of the most popular in the history of Swedish publishing. This simple tale of Primus Svensson, retiree who has a heart attack, focuses on life within a large Swedish hospital. Jersild's medical expertise and his ability to capture the language of the doctors, nurses, and patients creates a realistic picture of a modern hospital that both fascinates and unnerves. Jersild's portrayal tended to offend the Swedish medical profession, but the Swedish reading public was obviously captivated by it.

Most of Jersild's later works have continued to focus on the dehumanization of humankind, as well as the potential for the actual destruction of humans as we know them. This destruction may occur on the individual level, as in *En levande själ* (A living soul), 1980, where a human brain is kept alive for commercial purposes in a thoughtless scientific experiment.[4] Or humanity itself may succumb, as in his almost terrifying postnuclear war novel, *Efter floden* (After the flood), 1982.

Jersild's sixteen novels, plus a number of plays and musical reviews, have more than established for Swedish literary critics and readers his consistency and brilliance as a writer. *Children's Island* (*Barnens Ö*), 1976, has a special place in this remarkable production, for it presents an intimate view of Stockholm through the eyes of a character with whom Jersild closely identifies.[5] This novel develops some of Jersild's favorite themes: the power of language to create and shape identity; the nature of identity, and the part played by human fantasy and imagination; the failure of modern society to meet the needs of the individual. Yet the book stands out among his works by presenting an exhilarating if sometimes terrifying view of Stockholm, as well as a charming and painful vision of the process of growing up. Moving lightly over the most somber and difficult of humanity's concerns, Jersild stamps the book with his own unique imprint through the central character, Reine Larsson.

The premise of a ten-year-old boy who succeeds in *not* going to a summer camp—called Children's Island—seems unusual in itself. But the boy-narrator's clever strategy to lull his unmarried mother into thinking he *has* gone away to camp, while she is spending the summer elsewhere, carries the reader into a world of often charming adventure. The adventures are hardly typical, however, and while the reader finds himself laughing constantly, the episodes themselves are not always fun for the preadolescent Reine. Quickly discovering that he cannot live for the summer on the small sum of money that he starts out with, especially at the price of the McDonald's hamburgers he so voraciously consumes, Reine confronts the task of supporting himself in a big city. At first, he succeeds, getting a job as an errand boy in a shop where elderly women letter ribbons for funeral wreaths. But the difficulties of sneaking in and out of his own apartment, and of dealing with his mother's alcoholic lover, who moves in and takes Reine's keys, finally drag the fanciful narrator into ever darker misadventures. Nevertheless, occasional glorious moments are achieved by this hero who so carefully avoids bathing and who rarely manages to wash the soiled clothes he throws into the bathtub. His stay with Nora, the hairless department store clerk, constitutes an adventure that any young male would remember joyfully for the rest of his life. But being beaten up by a gang of dragsters, or led into drunken exploits by seasoned juvenile delinquents leaves Reine alone and aware of his dependence on adults, particularly his mother, for whom he feels a mixture of love and irritation, at times even disdain and anger.

The picaresque tale of this diminuitive and lovable Don Quixote allows Jersild to focus on many different aspects of modern suburban life, but he is especially concerned with language, death, growing up, and problems that the most vulnerable members of society face.

Jersild uses language particularly to help Reine define his relationship to himself and to those he meets. Reine loves to rhyme, to pun, to read riddles and limericks—linguistic games that may not be unusual for a precocious ten-year-old boy. But underneath and through this preoccupation with words, Reine seeks a way to deal with reality. For him, language often works as a means of responding to or displacing reality, a way in which he can deal with religious problems, with what he sees on television, or with his own fluctuating emotions. Thus, we see Reine mentally caught in his own compulsive rhyming, or composing imaginary postcards to his mother from the summer camp where he is supposedly spending a typical vacation.

One Swedish reviewer has noted that the book's title is ambiguous, meaning either the geographical island outside of Stockholm where the children's camp is located, or the island on which children are isolated in their own little world.[6] Jersild's use of the term suggests both islands: the raucous one that Reine avoids by staying home, and the inner one from which he cannot escape. The island, of course, may also refer to modern urban society itself. Nevertheless, it is Reine's lonely mental island that dominates the novel. He devises a secret numerical code for his diary, and even his comic use of language reveals his bitter sense of loneliness: the funereal T-shirt he inscribes for himself reads "From a Bereaved Mother." Such a slogan reveals another of the novel's central themes: death.

Reine decides to stay away from camp so that he can solve life's major riddles before he grows pubic hair and becomes a confused adolescent. One riddle is that of death, and he intends to resolve some questions that attend it: what is hell like? what are angels like? are the pictures of them accurate? Having been told different stories by his devout grandmother and his agnostic mother, he begins with the simple and somewhat whimsical problems of the different sizes of angels' wings and how they are attached, but he soon finds himself confronted with darker questions. The studio in which he works places him directly in the context of funerals and cemeteries; at other times, he visits a famous church where the old nobility lie buried, sees a television version of an execution, and recollects school stories of the potential destructiveness of nuclear war.

Death may not preoccupy all children to the extent that it preoccupies Reine (one feels that an invisible but clownlike figure of death constantly whispers questions to the inquisitive boy), though Pär Lagerkvist provides an obvious Swedish antecedent for such a theme,[7] but Jersild has admitted that he wrote the book just after his mother's death. Dealing with his own sorrow—which was compounded by his not having been in Stockholm when she needed him—and with the sense that she had somehow deserted him, Jersild turned his personal loss into the novel's comic yet profound questioning of the relationship between life and death. Ironically, this painful questioning is in fact part of the maturation process that Reine both seeks and wishes to avoid.

To Reine, growing up means losing control. He fears becoming the helpless victim of incomprehensible sexual drives, or being distracted from life itself by the necessity to work and to compete for survival. Before these terrible biological and social problems overtake him, Reine wants to come to grips with life, to retain those characteristics of childhood that he loves—such as eating junk food, or not washing his clothes except when told. But at the same time, he must learn those qualities that will allow him to understand and perhaps control the adults whose decisions so totally shape his life. Sex becomes a focal point for Reine: he finds it either disgusting or mysterious. Personifying its negative image is his mother, whose bodily functions repulse Reine and whose greatest act of betrayal is to be caught naked in bed with the abominable Stig. But the salesgirl Nora offers Reine an extraordinarily positive sexual figure, and he embarrassedly admits the hint of this sexuality while sitting naked in bed with her. Without this positive vision of Nora, it seems unlikely that Reine could return comfortably to his mother.

Reine's search for his unknown father represents a subtle and unconscious attempt to find a positive male sexual identity for himself. At the same time, an ideal and dead father figure eliminates any possible competition for his mother's love and reflects a rather normal Freudian Oedipal phase. Thus, the contrast between the noble Dag Hammarskjöld, whom Reine wishes to have been his father, and the crass Stig, the only available father figure, may reflect Reine's conflicting desires to become a good adult male on the one hand and yet to ignore real men—who sleep with his mother—on the other. Reine's need for self-respect as the son of someone decent if not famous, and his need to find others whom he can respect and trust, run throughout the novel. Reine's attempt to balance self-knowledge against the way the world treats him may be part of the growing-up process that Jersild wants to show.

Indeed, Jersild reveals a view of growing up that is much more complex than we expect. The opening sequences entice us into believing that a child really can live alone in a big city for a few months, at least in a city as safe as Stockholm. But reality abruptly takes over, and every comic episode is matched by a more threatening one. In each one of these adventures, Reine unconsciously takes step after step toward the very maturity that he hates and fears so much, a fear symbolized by his daily self-inspection for the first appearance of a pubic hair.

What Jersild gives to the reader in this context is a new understanding of what children experience: the domination and lack of consideration that adults so casually thrust upon children, the dangers of trying to live alone, the accidental ways in which children can be caught up in activities far more complicated than they realize. Reine's visit to the hot rodders' campground is a vivid illustration, for here he gets caught up for the first time in those dark social forces that undermine modern society.

By presenting the ugly and violent sides of modern urban and suburban life, Jersild invites the reader to ponder the causes of such problems as alcoholism, juvenile delinquency, and mistreatment of the handicapped or the aged. All of these elements are woven subtly into the story of Reine's travels, so that the reader receives a vivid picture of the social problems that Sweden confronted in the 1970s. Even the Vietnam War and the threat of nuclear destruction appear here, as they almost had to in a novel of the 1970s, but Jersild presents them indirectly, through the oblique glance of Reine's ceaselessly wandering mind and eyes. The problems of latchkey children, of working mothers, of modern society's attempt to respond to the innumerable challenges that modern civilization creates all flash across the canvas of Jersild's portrait of modern Swedish life and of Stockholm.

Stockholm itself is a character in this novel, as important a personage as Reine's mother or her lover Stig. In Stockholm we see the theater group that enchants and then betrays our dreaming young hero, and here too we see the subways, the highways, and the suburban apartment communities that shape the lives of each of the bizarre characters that populate this episodic novel. Underneath it all lies not only a story of a curious and ingenious young boy in search of his identity but a story of the love and hatred that exist within any society. Reine's victimization in so many different circumstances firmly establishes both the role of violence in our societies and the lack of respect, human kindness, and generosity that such violence signifies. Fortunately, and perhaps rarely in Jersild's books, humor and love seem to triumph at least momentarily in this dark and light summer novel.

NOTES

1. I have used *Professionella bekännelser* as the primary source of information for this introduction. However, the *Swedish Book Review Supplement—P. C. Jersild* (1983) provides an excellent guide to further reading; the essay by Irene Scobbie with its survey of Jersild's books may be especially useful as a further introduction.

2. In "Dehumanization and the Bureaucracy in Novels by P. C. Jersild," *Scandinavica* 23, no. 1 (May 1984): 25–38, I discuss this theme in four Jersild novels.

3. In *Människan som djur—En studie i P C Jersilds författarskap* (Liber: Malmö, 1983), Rut Nordwall-Ehrlow discusses in depth Jersild's use of animals in his fiction.

4. For further discussion of this novel, see my article, "The Battle for the Self in P. C. Jersild's *En levande själ*," *Scandinavian Studies* 56, no. 3 (Summer 1984): 256–71.

5. In his early autobiographical novel, *Uppror bland marsvinen* (1972), Jersild sketched parts of his life that may be related to the details of the later book; there is substantial reason for identifying the narrator Reine with at least parts of Jersild's recollection of his own boyhood.

6. Gerth Ekstrand, "*Barnens Ö* okänd värld för de vuxna," *Dala Demokraten*, 15 Oct. 1976.

7. Pär Lagerkvist wrote a famous series of short stories *Onda sagor* (Evil tales), 1924, in one of these "Far och jag" (Father and I), a young boy discovers that he does not have his father's ability to believe in God.

A JERSILD BIBLIOGRAPHY

PROSE FICTION: *Räknelära* (Algebra), 1960; *Till varmare länder* (To warmer lands), 1961; *Ledig lördag* (Saturday off), 1963; *Calvinols resa genom världen* (Calvinol's voyage around the World), 1965; *Prins Valiant och Konsum* (Prince Valiant and the Cooperative), 1966; *Grisjakten* (The pig hunt), 1968; *Vi ses i Song My* (See you in Song My), 1970; *Drömpojken* (The dream boy), 1970; *Uppror bland marsvinen* (Revolution among the guinea pigs), 1972; *Stumpen* (Shorty), 1973; *Djurdoktorn* (The animal doctor), 1973; *Den elektriska kaninen* (The electric rabbit), 1973; *Barnens Ö* (Children's Island), 1976; *Babels hus* (The house of Babel), 1978; *En levande själ* (A living soul), 1980; *Professionella bekännelser* (Professional confessions), 1981; *Efter floden* (After the flood), 1982; *Den femtionde frälsaren* (The fiftieth savior), 1984.

PLAYS AND REVUES: *Pyton* (Python), coauthored with Lars Ardelius, 1966; *Obs! Sammanträde pågår* (Do not disturb! Meeting in progress), 1967; *Fänrik Duva* (Ensign Dove), 1971; *Moskvafeber* (Moscow fever), coauthored with Frej Lindqvist, 1977; *Gycklarnas Hamlet* (The clown's Hamlet), 1980; *Lit de parade* (Lying in state), 1983.

ENGLISH TRANSLATIONS: "The Great Man" (excerpted from *Calvinols resa*), trans. David Mel Paul and Margareta Paul, in *Modern Swedish Prose in Translation*, ed. Karl Erik Lagerlöf (Minneapolis: University of Minnesota Press, 1979), 155–65; *The Animal Doctor*, trans. David Mel Paul and Margareta Paul (New York: Pantheon, 1975); *After the Flood*, trans. George and Lone Blecher (New York: Morrow, 1986). Additional translations of excerpts from Jersild's work appear in the *Swedish Book Review—P. C. Jersild Supplement* (Lampeter, Wales: St. David's University College, 1983).